P9-CQJ-165

DISCARDED

Praise for
BEAUTY
and the
BESHARAM

"A clever, emotional book about being true to yourself no matter what. With a delightful rivalry you can't help but ship, whimsical settings, and so much banter, *Beauty and the Besharam* is not to be missed."

— Jennifer Dugan, author of *Hot Dog Girl* and *Some Girls Do*

"If you're a fan of rivals-to-lovers, look no further! *Beauty and the Besharam* is a novel bursting with swoony romance, humor, and the importance of going for it, even when it's scary. Vale shows us that love is about not compromising who you are, or loving someone despite their ferocity and drive, but *because* of it. Lillie Vale put it perfectly—'Rivalry is good, but kisses are better.'"
— Aiden Thomas, *New York Times* bestselling author of *Cemetery Boys*

"Hilarious, sharp, and sweep-you-off-your-feet romantic, *Beauty and the Besharam* is the kind of book that you will immediately want to reread. Prepare a spot on your forever favorite shelf."
— Nina Moreno, author of *Don't Date Rosa Santos*

BEAUTY
and the
BESHARAM

Lillie Vale

VIKING

VIKING
An imprint of Penguin Random House LLC, New York

First published in the United States of America by Viking,
an imprint of Penguin Random House LLC, 2022

Copyright © 2022 by Lillie Vale

Penguin supports copyright. Copyright fuels creativity, encourages diverse
voices, promotes free speech, and creates a vibrant culture. Thank you for buying
an authorized edition of this book and for complying with copyright laws by
not reproducing, scanning, or distributing any part of it in any form without
permission. You are supporting writers and allowing Penguin to continue to
publish books for every reader.

Viking & colophon are registered trademarks of Penguin Random House LLC.

Visit us online at penguinrandomhouse.com.

Library of Congress Cataloging-in-Publication Data is available.

Manufactured in Canada

ISBN 9780593350874

10   9   8   7   6   5   4   3   2   1

FRI

Text set in Dante Mt Std

This book is a work of fiction. Any references to historical events, real people,
or real places are used fictitiously. Other names, characters, places, and events are
products of the author's imagination, and any resemblance to actual events
or places or persons, living or dead, is entirely coincidental.

The publisher does not have any control over and does not assume any
responsibility for author or third-party websites or their content.

To anyone who has ever been told
they were Too Much. You are the perfect
amount. This one's for the besharams.

And to my parents,
who raised me to be one.

1.
They Don't Need to Like Me

RUINING THE START of Ian Jun's day is the favorite part of mine. He's the only person for whom it's worth going toe-to-toe with our AP Statistics teacher, who's currently gaping at me like he can't believe my hand is in the air first thing first period before he's even had the chance to start Friday's lesson.

Ian sits all the way in the front row, wavy black hair styled into a pompadour that I can grudgingly admit doesn't look totally terrible. He's probably freaking out and trying to correct the questions he got wrong on our just-returned homework. In that respect, we're the same.

He hasn't turned around yet. But he will.

I wiggle my fingers to get the teacher's attention, lifting my butt off the seat to be noticed. After a long, drawn-out moment of watching me flail, Mr. Gage unsuccessfully turns his grimace into a smile. Closing his eyes, he says, "Yes, Kavya? Do you have a question?"

Somehow? lingers like a stink.

A few titters break out from those awake enough to get on my bad side.

Ian stiffens, shoulders snapping extra straight.

I've got his attention now.

"You docked me points for question number three," I say. "My answer's correct."

Mr. Gage's round glasses seem to magnify his absolute displeasure. "No."

A unilateral no? Taken aback, I gawk. "But I—"

"We have a lot of material to get through today, so if I could get started?" He pauses as though he's really waiting for my go-ahead. The exaggerated politeness makes me think he's given up all pretense of not finding me the most annoying junior he's ever had the misfortune of teaching z-scores and chi-squares.

Next to me, my best friend Blaire Tyler shuffles to the back of her stats textbook, where the answers to odd-numbered questions are provided. She slides it across the table to nudge against my arm, tapping her black-and-silver constellation nail against question three.

Okay, yes, the back of the book, dubbed our beloved "BOB," has half the answers all the time, but I checked my work *twice*, and I choose to put my faith in *me*.

Without raising my hand, I say, "Mr. Gage, I showed my work. There's no way I got the question wrong. Could you please work it out on the board?"

"This is not one-on-one tutoring, Ms. Joshi," he says without looking up from his notes. "Now if everyone would please turn their attention to the linear regression on the whiteboard."

Shut down twice in as many minutes. That's a record.

No one's looking at me anymore, but my face still burns with embarrassment and the flame of indignation Mr. Gage didn't manage to extinguish.

I've never had a teacher this adamantly bullheaded in their own wrongness. They don't need to like me as long as they respect me for being right. I'm willing to bet that he hasn't even tried to solve the problem himself, relying wholly on his answer guide.

Parker Ellis, the boyfriend I'm planning to dump, sniggers from the row behind me. My spine stiffens with a flicker of foreboding. It's not the first time he's found my standoff with Mr. Gage amusing, but he usually does a better job of hiding it.

Blaire leans in to whisper, the small lavender beads at the end of her honey braids gently clinking. "Hey, fuck him. It's just one point. You can let it go."

I fix her with a look. She's known me *how* long, now?

"But you're not going to," she acknowledges with a sigh.

My pencil scratches against notepaper as I work out the answer again, joining the soft background drone of twenty-nine other pencils trying to keep up with Mr. Gage's speed.

"What answer did you put?" I mutter.

Blaire shoots a furtive look up front before saying, "I got the same answer you did, but I changed it when I checked the back."

"Why did you do that? You *had* the right answer."

"Like you did?" She chin-nods toward the red ink slash across the third question. "Kavs, it's one point. You still got an A on the assignment. Even if you're right and he's wrong, and the book's wrong, and everyone else in the thousands of classrooms using this textbook got it wrong, it's not worth the fight for one measly point."

I begrudge so much that she's right, but letting this point go means letting Ian Jun win. If I think real hard, squinting back the last five years, I can almost remember a world in which I wasn't constant and bitter rivals with the boy in the first row who has only now, finally, turned to raise one perfectly arched *What now?* eyebrow.

It's that eyebrow that does it. The smug assurance that I'm going to keep my mouth shut.

"When it comes to Ian, a point is never just a point." I forget to keep my voice low, hissing the words while keeping my eyes unblinkingly fastened on Ian the whole time.

"Ms. Joshi," says Mr. Gage without turning around. "Why don't you come up here where I can keep an eye on you?"

Another unmistakable laugh from Parker, but when I whip around to catch him in the act, he blanks me.

"Oooo, you're in trouble," one of the boys from the back row says with a snicker.

I hover expectantly in my seat, waiting for the teacher to call him out, too, but nada.

Sorry, Blaire mouths, big brown eyes full of sympathy.

I slowly rise. My neck and arms prickle with the knowledge

that the entire class is watching. Some with compassion, most with glee.

The acute humiliation of picking up all my things—the lavender *Sailor Moon* pencil pouch stuffed with cherry Jolly Rancher hard candies that I won't dare to crinkle in this class, the pink Texas Instruments scientific calculator, the battered textbook, and the spiral-bound notebook—and dragging myself to the front row all under Mr. Gage's watchful eye is bad enough. The indignity of moving to the front row with Ian watching is a new low.

He's not smirking anymore, but he hasn't taken his eyes off me, either. Like a big cat stalks its prey. It's not the first time I've thought of his dark, sooty lashes, glowing-ember brown eyes, and pointy-tipped ears as being particularly lynx-like. The arched slash of his still-raised brow as he tracks me completes the impression.

"Not there, Ms. Joshi," says the teacher when I settle into an empty seat at the end of the row. He points to a middle seat. "There."

The seat right next to Ian.

A flash of malice crosses Mr. Gage's face. "Now you can be the center of attention."

Throat closing tight, I force my feet into another walk of shame, squeezing myself between the backs of chairs and the row of desks behind. Ian's the only one who scoots his chair in for me to pass. His eyebrow lowers at the same moment as I do. My shame and I sink into the cold hard plastic.

Even after the teacher faces the whiteboard again, marker

squeaking out numbers, I can't concentrate enough to take notes. It's the last Friday before the last week of school, and as a rising senior, I should be content to take it easy and glide, ignoring trifling matters like one point, but the very thought of it settles over me like sandpaper: itchy and uncomfortable.

Why is it so commonly accepted to wind down at the end of something? Shouldn't this be the time to finish strong instead of coasting?

"Why are you so quiet, Jun?" I whisper. "Don't tell me you have the same answer as the back of the book."

"Trust me, I have the right answer," he whispers right back.

Restraining my snort is a Herculean effort. Yeah, right. If he got the same answer I did, there's no way he isn't making his case with Mr. Gage. And since most of our teachers like the school's golden boy more than they like me, he'll probably win, too. Even when he reigns number one at literally everything, he's the kind of person who nobody takes affront with.

Except for me, that is. The girl who's the defending champ.

There's a glint of amusement in his eyes. "What? I do." He flashes his paper at me and then tucks it away in his folder too fast to see anything, but I bet it's an infuriating 100 percent.

I cross my arms and swivel my torso to face the front. Each hard tick of the wall clock is a reminder that class is going to be over in thirty-five minutes, and if it's hard getting Mr. Gage to give me the time of day now, Monday will be even more futile.

The teacher turns around, marker uncapped, the move bringing a fresh assault of migraine-inducing chemicals my way. "Any que—"

My hand shoots into the air.

His entire expression says *you again?* He rubs his temples, scanning the entire room to make sure there's no one else he can call on first.

My arm starts to ache, but I keep it insistently up.

His fingers whiten around the marker. "Fine. Yes. What."

"This isn't about the exercise on the board, it's about last night's homework and I can show you if—actually, can I have that?" I strain forward to snatch the marker out of his hand, and instead of going around, I launch myself *over* the table, and go straight for the whiteboard.

I think I've actually rendered him speechless, because his hand stays gripped, frozen in midair, while I send the marker squealing, working out the problem for the fifth time.

"She's totally shameless," someone says in a scandalized nonwhisper I'm absolutely meant to hear.

I set my teeth and get on with it.

I'm not like Ian, who gets away with writing in ballpoint because he never has to go back to make corrections. I erase with far too much abandon, and Mr. Gage doesn't accept work that's been scribbled out or in any way untidy. He claims it's because of his poor eyesight, which may be true, but I think he's just trying to dock points wherever he can.

So it's with great relief that I don't need to erase anything to reach the answer, which is most definitely not the same one in the teacher's answer manual or the back of our textbook.

I half expected Mr. Gage to not even pay attention, but he's following my work, forehead lined and eyes squinted. And when he sighs, all gusty and exasperated, I know I have him.

"All right," he says, cupping his hand into a come-here gesture. "Everyone send your assignments to the front. I'll regrade and you can grab them at the start of our next class."

"Thanks a lot, Kavya," Parker calls to me, a bite in his voice. "I just lost my A."

Yeah, I'm not even sorry about that.

There's a few more grumbles, and I feel bad for a second that I cost Blaire her point, too, but when she flashes me a thumbs-up, I know she doesn't hold it against me.

My victory is only slightly dimmed by having to share my hard-won bounty. But it's offset with the knowledge that if my assignment is going up a point, Ian's so-called right answer means he's going down one. Mr. Gage isn't one of those if-it's-my-fault-you-can-keep-the-points teachers; he's equal-opportunity punitive.

"It's too bad you don't get to keep your perfect score," I gloat.

"Actually, I do." With a smirk, Ian turns to collect the papers making their way forward.

My stomach flip-flops. Oh, how nauseating. Only YA love interests and the hot cast from *The Vampire Diaries* smirk as much as he does. Ian's is more Katherine than Damon, though.

I grit my teeth. "Oh, really? Clearly math isn't your strong suit, but how do you figure?"

He pulls his own paper free to add to the top of the pile. I almost choke on air. Because there, in red, is the same damning 24/25 that's on mine. The same slash through question three.

In his neat blue ballpoint print, the same answer I wrote on my paper and on the board.

"Thanks for the point, Joshi," Ian says with a wink. "Knew I could count on you."

2.
The Poor Girl's Goat Is Easily Got

I CAN BE counted on for plenty of things: always showing up overdressed and never knowingly outlipsticked, having a tongue impervious to the most potent chili peppers and hot sauces, unfailingly having stellar book recs, and winning our local library's summer reading contest for three years in a row, except last year's, when Ian did.

And now, apparently, for waltzing that extra point straight into his GPA.

"I'm not really that predictable, am I?" I ask the girls as we walk into the locker room to change for gym, inhaling a cloud of chlorine and hair products.

Blaire's already regaled our best friends, Catey Hill and Valika Mehra, on the walk over with the exaggerated story of how I all but pole-vaulted myself over the desk two periods ago, and if I don't join her for track-and-field tryouts senior year, we're not friends anymore.

Catey, my oldest friend since preschool, and Blaire's girlfriend of three years, purses her mouth thoughtfully. "Why do you think being predictable is a bad thing?"

"Because Ian anticipated my move before I even made it." I twirl in my locker combination. "If you know what someone wants, you always know what they're going to do next. You can anticipate their next move."

"Okay, villain-in-training, you got all that from him turning around to look at you?" Blaire asks with a laugh, tying her hair back. Val stifles her giggle.

"It was the *way* he looked at me," I insist, shimmying out of my sage-green skater skirt and black high-necked ribbed tank. "Come on, girls. You've all seen it."

"Oh, yes, that beautiful boy's heart eyes whenever he looks at you positively sends chills down my spine," Blaire drawls with a shudder.

"Exac—wait, what?" I tug the camo tee over my head harder than necessary. My hair immediately billows with static that Catey smooths with a dryer sheet she just *happens* to have.

She's predictable, too, but in a useful way, like always having an extra number-two pencil for Scantron tests and Listerine strips to mask your breath when you've been drinking something you shouldn't. Just last week her emergency packet of fruit snacks preemptively warded off my got-an-eighty-nine-on-a-quiz migraine. I'm pretty sure the contents of her Betsey Johnson mini backpack could help the four of us survive both a) a zombie apocalypse and b) high school.

"You heeeeaaaarrrrd," Blaire singsongs, then proceeds to pucker her lips and pretends to smooch the air. My face scorches like a frying pan. Like that's in *any* way what I want with Ian.

"Don't tease Kavya," says Catey, winking as she shimmies out of her balloon-sleeved maxi dress that looks amazing with her height. "We all know the poor girl's goat is easily got."

This time Val doesn't even attempt to hold back the laugh, but when I turn laser eyes on her, she flashes her palms at me in a conciliatory gesture. "Are we actually doing gym or should one of us drop to the floor and pretend to be looking for a contact?" she asks, brow furrowed.

We'd all seen Coach Ricky, the PE teacher and boys' basketball coach, palming the red rubber ball on the way in. If we still had Coach Tina for gym, pulling a fast one would have been impossible. She wouldn't even let any period-havers bunk off swim week if they brought in a note from their parent saying they were on their period. She runs her classes with the same drive that takes her girls' volleyball team to state almost every year. I can respect that tenacity, but she'll forever be on my grudge list for threatening to give me a zero for participation if I didn't get in the pool.

"I 'lost' my contact last time, so if we're sitting this out, it's on one of you three," declares Blaire. She's already changed into bright white Jordans and a peach oversize tee that brings out the glow of her brown skin.

"Coach is eventually going to catch on that I don't even wear contacts," says Catey, settling on the bench separating the rows of lockers to tighten her laces. "And this may surprise you lazybones, but I actually like dodgeball."

Blaire bangs her locker shut. "Who actually *likes* balls flying at their face?"

"Spoken like a true sapphic," I quip, snapping the elastic waistband of my cotton shorts. "Sorry, B, I'm with Catey on this one. The only thing better than breaking up with Parker Ellis tonight is getting the chance to kick his ass again."

Everyone's face turns grave. It's no secret that this breakup has been a long time coming, and none of us are devastated about it—especially not me—but I wasn't planning on ending our two-month relationship until the last day of school. Accelerating the breakup schedule means I won't be able to avoid the whisper-whisper-nudge-nudge next week and the newest swirl of rumors that Kavya Joshi was Too Much for yet another boy who dared to date her.

"Well," says Blaire. "I'm not going to miss him."

"Or the pushy way he keeps trying to angle for an invite to Kavs' birthday weekend at the lake later this summer," adds Val, emerging from behind her open locker. Even though it's just us, she still changes in double-quick time, like we don't know what's under those loose capri pants and faded Hard Rock Cafe tee.

"Like, my guy, take a hint," huffs Blaire. "It's *always* been a moon girl last hurrah before school starts."

"Or that time he asked me if you two would be up for a

double date? Which I'm pretty sure he only wanted because he thought you'd make out in front of him?" I make a face.

"Why are boys," Catey says with a sigh, zipping up the matching bubblegum-pink tracksuit that covers her from wrists to ankles. "Come on. We better get out there."

We're the last stragglers. Unlike the flickering fluorescent lighting of the locker room, the adjoining gymnasium is brightly lit. Parker is chatting to the girl next to him and doesn't look toward me once.

When he says something to make her laugh, I think darkly: *He's not that funny.*

Coach Ricky raises an eyebrow at our late arrival, but says nothing, just gestures for us to sit on the polished wood floor for attendance. From experience, I know he won't mark us tardy.

Just like the hallway lockers, he has us sit in alphabetical order, which means I'm right next to Ian. He looks infernally amused, corners of his lips crooked upward into a knowing half smile. "Did one of you moon girls 'lose a contact' again?"

When we were kids, Catey and I had been obsessed with watching all two hundred episodes and three movies of the original *Sailor Moon* anime. We even decided that she was Jupiter and I was Venus, and when we became a trio, there was no doubt that Blaire was Mars. After we started calling ourselves moon girls, it caught on fast with the rest of the school, too.

"Did you ever stop to think that maybe I was avoiding you?" I ask sweetly.

He stretches his long legs out between us. "Not for a second. You're not a coward."

Taken aback, the witty comeback goes poof in my throat. He's right, but it wasn't the snappy banter I was expecting. I didn't expect him to see that about me, especially not when *he* was the whole reason I spent that summer so long ago being called a chicken.

Before my brain can reroute into response mode, Coach Ricky slaps his attendance clipboard against his upper thigh. "All right, kids! Ellis, Hill, you're captains. The rest of you, line up. You know the drill."

With a collective groan and a few squeaks of soles against wood, we get to our feet.

Throwing an apologetic look at me and Val, Catey's voice rings out with her girlfriend's name. Seeing it coming doesn't make it sting any less when Blaire jogs over to high-five Catey.

Parker takes his sweet time scanning everyone. I can see the short list forming in his mind as he discards the kids who are too afraid to get in the line of fire, the girls who hang back because they're worried about their nails, the eggheads who would rather be anywhere but here.

If he has any hope of winning, he needs me. And he knows it. I can see it in the deliberate way he doesn't settle his gaze on me longer than anybody else. He wants me to sweat, panic that maybe he's not going to choose me. And it's working. It's not like I'm dying to be on his team, but being Parker's first pick is better than being Catey's second.

In a messy way, it kinda makes sense that even our breakup

is a competition. We're over each other, but he wants the spectacle of coming out the winner. For me it's all about self-preservation: I just want to make it through the rest of the school year with my dignity intact.

"Sometime *today*, Ellis," says Coach Ricky. "It's high school, not a playoff bracket."

"Gimme a sec, Coach." Parker shifts his stance, pulling his lower lip into his mouth.

Is he trying to punish me for being distant? For blowing him off last weekend ever since he told me I wasn't a Nice Girl? Since he took me to his country club to play doubles with his blond-and-blonder cousins and then told me I embarrassed him for smashing every single set?

I didn't know that underneath that handsome, so-called feminist exterior was a boy who was deeply threatened by his girlfriend besting him at anything: tennis, *Mario Kart*, even a simple card game of snap.

He'd even crowed about his Pre-SAT score until he saw mine, at which point he ordered a giant stack of prep work-books and practice tests and sequestered himself in the library every day for two weeks until he scored higher. At first, I was proud of him, but it was pretty pathetic he couldn't celebrate my wins without bristling that they took something away from him.

How was he so good at hiding that side of himself away for so long that I didn't see it?

So with my new understanding of him, I see the exact mo-ment when Parker decides he'd rather lose on his own than win with me.

"Allegra," he says, too loud, as if he wants it to be extra clear that he's sure of his choice.

Dozens of pairs of eyes flick toward me, including Coach's, who I didn't even think cared about any of us enough to know who was dating who. Even Allegra seems surprised, because it takes her a few beats to join him, and she looks over her shoulder at me the whole way.

While some Parker acolytes watch me with open schadenfreude, Catey's cornflower-blue eyes are narrowed, and her fair cheeks are splotched with vivid color. Blaire and a few of the other girls look like they'd like to headshot the dodgeball straight for Parker.

Val's hand creeps against mine, but I quickly cross my arms across my chest before she can give me a sympathetic squeeze. Everyone's reading into this, and the last thing I need is for Parker, and everyone else, to see that I felt the sharp pointed tip of his snub find a way in.

Next to me in line, Ian stiffens. The movement draws my attention—and my ire.

Of course this happened right in front of him, as though stats wasn't bad enough. But to my surprise, he's the only person not gawking at me, not waiting for my reaction to bubble over.

He faces straight ahead, almost oblivious, if not for the muscle leaping in his jaw. There's a tension in his shoulders that makes them curve up to his ears, the kind that would probably ease if someone smoothed their palm over the back of his shirt. It's strange to see him be anything other than cool and effortless and glib, the way he was in stats this morning, letting me do the fighting for him.

The fact that the unflappable Ian Jun is pissed on my behalf makes my stomach do a giddy flip. It's weird to be on the same side for a change.

Not *bad* weird. I think. Just . . . weird.

As Catey calls my name next, I swear I hear him mutter, "Crush him, Kavya."

But when I turn around, his hands are behind his back, face impassive like he didn't say anything at all.

3.
The Evil Queen

BY THE END of PE, Parker looked like he'd been through a trash compactor. Red-faced, sweating from his forehead, neck, and pits; I hoped he felt like it, too. His stunt called open season on him and in the ensuing melee, after a few halfhearted reminders about good sportsmanship, Coach Ricky gave up and sat down on the bleachers scrolling his phone.

If Parker thinks his comeuppance is over, that he's getting any kind of latitude at Claudia Kim's party tonight, he's dead wrong. Because in choosing another girl over me—a girl he was making goo-goo eyes at, no less—he threw the gauntlet.

Now, it's just a matter of who ends it first. To the victor goes the breakup.

And I'm definitely going to want to look hot while doing it.

"You don't usually put in *this* much effort for your dates."

Simran, my sister, hovers in my open doorway. Her eyes skip over the discarded clothes on my bed before one eyebrow raises in question.

"It's not for him," I inform her. "This is a fuck-you outfit."

"That's cryptic. I'm probably going to regret asking, but who's the message for?"

I pause in my scrutiny of the clothing strewn in front of me: crop tops and miniskirts and spaghetti-strap summer dresses. I'd almost narrowed them down when Simran distracted me.

"Parker," I say. "I'm publicly dumping him tonight."

She takes a step into my room. "What? Why?"

I try not to betray my surprise that she's actually taking an interest. With a six-year age gap between us, she didn't have a lot of time for her pesty seventh-grade sister when she left for college, and I hadn't expected that to change the summer before she went to grad school, either.

"So I can win," I say simply, about to launch into everything that happened at school today, all the ways in which Parker and I were a total mismatch, when I hear her low laugh.

"Still the same old Kavya," Simran says, and it's not a compliment, not at all. "Ever think that your desperate desire to win at everything kind of makes you the biggest loser?"

Each awful word sends a volley of arrows straight to my heart.

She walks out before my brain buffers a response.

I stare at the open doorway until my vision blurs with hot tears. None of her little snipes have ever gotten this reaction from me before. She took something I'd always considered my greatest strength and mocked it like it was a weakness. Every ember of sisterly yearning is smothered.

My eyes flood with a fresh onslaught of prickly spikes. Mindful of my eye makeup, I don't swipe at my eyes. I let myself feel every humiliating second, driving the lesson home.

I was a fool to think this summer would change anything.

After dumping Parker tonight, all I have to do is see out the school year and then it'll be a moon girl summer—just me and my best friends. They're all I need.

But before Catey and the girls pick me up for battle, a girl needs her sustenance. Luckily, Mom made a trip to South Asia Mart for some Bombay bhel mix so Dad can make his famous bhel puri.

"Kavya! Dinner!" Dad shouts from downstairs just as I finish dressing.

I take the last three steps in one jump, landing like a nimble cat onto hardwood floors. The living room TV is on, playing one of Simran's shows. My dog, Buster, is gazing in fascination at the screen. I set my jaw and scrounge among the sofa pillows for the remote.

Low tones of conversation come from the kitchen, along with the monotonous drone of an NPR program. My parents love National Public Radio. Dad's car stereo is set to it, too, when it isn't playing the Beatles or Bollywood hit singles.

Unable to find the remote, I make a soft kissy noise and pat my thigh. "C'mere, Buster."

His tail swishes in the air, but the golden retriever doesn't even turn around.

"Be a good boy," I wheedle. "Come with me."

"Looking for something?" Simran emerges from the kitchen with a tall glass of lemonade, a bowl of bhel, and the remote tucked under her arm. She gives me an arch look and purses her lips. "I was here first. You know the rules."

I can't look at her without the hurt resurfacing. "You're desecrating the living room."

She laughs with an edge of meanness. "Did you just learn that SAT word?"

My jaw drops as she plops down on the sofa. Buster isn't allowed on the cushions, but she lets him cuddle up at her side, anyway. "Good boy," she croons, rubbing his head.

"Whatever," I say in a tight voice. "I hope you left me some puris."

"Keep hoping!" she calls out as I head for the kitchen.

Dad looks up with a warm smile as I enter but doesn't stop mixing the bhel ingredients: spicy sev and puffed rice, diced boiled potatoes, chopped onions, tamarind sauce, cilantro-mint chutney, and lemon juice. He's just as focused a cook as is he is a surgeon.

He nods at the table, where Mom is uncapping a bottle of chili garlic sauce. "Grab yourself a bowl."

Immediately, my spirits lift the way they usually do when I'm offered delicious food.

"I'll take that one," I say, pointing to the steel mixing bowl with a wicked grin.

His laugh booms. "That's my girl."

The bhel makes a satisfying, soft squishing sound as Dad plops it into my bowl using the rubber spatula he used to stir. The crispy rice crackles, *kurmur-kurmur*, like a low, staticky radio. There are still some puris left, and I stick four of them right at the top of my heaped bowl.

Mom spoons a dollop of bright-red chili garlic sauce and places it just so on the top of her bowl. It's piled high, glistening with the tamarind sauce and Christmas-colored condiments. She stands on the wooden chair and holds her iPhone perfectly flat and steady like I taught her. A click later and she has a bird's-eye view of the bhel. In the white bowl and the gleam of the cherrywood table, the contrast is beautiful. With her phone still poised, she snaps a close-up, then an angled photo, clucking her tongue.

"You've mastered the flat lay," I say, shoveling the bhel into my mouth. The zing of the lemon juice is tempered by the coolness of the mint and the sweet-and-tangy fruitiness of the tamarind. "You could be on Instagram."

Mom laughs. "I'm sending these to the family WhatsApp group."

I swallow. "Ew. Why?"

"Kavya," she says in a warning tone.

Dad catches my eye.

He and I are of the same mind when it comes to social media and our family. As he often says whenever the subject of WhatsApp comes up, Aa bael mujhe maar: it's like waving a red flag and expecting the bull not to gore you.

Mom taps at her screen. "Because Pinky keeps sending the group the photos of the kebabs and samosas she served at the last get-together. And Maya said because I live in America, I must not be cooking Indian food at home anymore, because I never send them pictures. What's that phrase you moon girls always say? 'Pics or it didn't happen'?"

I rip into the unopened bag of bhakarwadi on the table. "Who cares what they think? You have nothing to prove. You make great food, whether it's Indian or Mexican or Thai or whatever."

Mom points at the small spirals of crispy fried dough and spiced coconut. "Aai used to make those by hand when I was growing up."

Dad stifles a laugh. "You mean your mom had a cook do it."

"Well, I didn't say they were *her* hands, Yash!" Mom grins.

Dad leans forward to peck her cheek. "Every time I make bhel, it reminds me of our first date." He smiles at me and says, "It was at Bandstand, and it was during monsoon season, so we both got soaked, even though I picked your mom up in a rickshaw."

I've heard this story so many times that the explanation is unnecessary, but I think he likes telling it as much as I love hearing it. My parents are stinkin' adorable.

"Aai told me then and there I should marry you," says Mom.

Dad laughs. "Your mom never said that. Khotuh bolu nako."

"I'm not lying! She did!"

Dad eats his bhel slowly, savoring each bite like it's a memory. His thoughts are years and miles away in Mumbai. "I'll never forget the taste of that Elco bhel. Even after all these years," he murmurs in Marathi.

Mom squeezes his hand, and even though they both know I'm in the room, I still feel like an intruder. In the buttery-soft glow of the kitchen, radio and TV both playing faintly, I want to cocoon myself in the kind of affection and warmth that my parents display every day.

I want my own love story. Sweet, simple, everyday love. Prem, amore, ishq.

All my beatific thoughts about love fly out the window when Simran enters the kitchen with an empty bowl. Buster trails after her. Seeing me, he bounds to my side. I rub his back until he lies down and shows me his belly, tail wagging. Crouching low, I give him a belly rub that has his tongue lolling out in seconds.

Mom finally gets a good look at me. "Your makeup looks nice. Is that the miniskirt we got last weekend?"

Simran joins us at the table with her second helping, the last of the puris stuck on top in a Stonehenge circle. Her tone turns wicked as she says all gossipy, "Do you know the reason why Kavya is breaking up with Parker?"

It's not like you *stuck around to hear it*, I think vengefully. My eyes flash fire at her. How dare she try to make fun of me with Mom and Dad, too?

I seethe. "At least I *have* a boyfriend to dump. How long has it been for you, Simmy? Who's the loser now?"

Simran's face blanches. "Mom!" she squawks.

Just as I expected, she can dish it out but she can't take it.

Buster barks over Dad's horrified *"Kavya!"*

Mom scowls across the table. "Kavya, you know better than that. Someone's worth is not dependent on whether they have a romantic partner"—she floats her eyes to Simran—"or not."

"Aren't you going to apologize?" Impatience sharpens Simran's tone.

"Are *you?*" I challenge. She knows what she said.

Mom and Dad glance at each other, a wordless exchange that I know is about me.

Simran scrapes her chair back and moves to put her bowl in the sink. "You're such a bitch sometimes," she says in a low voice, turning around to say it to my face.

I gasp, skin prickling in shock. Her reactions are *never* this confrontational. I'm the one who reacts to everything, but Simran's disdain is usually punctuated with an eye roll or a weary sigh, something to convey that she's the wise older sister who's so above it all that she can't even lower herself to fight fire with fire. Nothing makes me feel smaller or more insignificant to her, even though I don't think she does it on purpose.

Mom especially hates the word *bitch*. We can get away with the occasional *fuck*, but *bitch* is really where Mom draws the line.

She narrows her eyes like she wants to reprimand Simran—I wait for the scolding—but after a pause, she lets the comment stand.

"Seriously?" My voice rises. "Do you want to know what *she* said to me—"

"Girls." Dad pinches the bridge of his nose. "Please."

Mom steeples her fingers together like a tent. "Kavya, enough. It doesn't matter who started it. You're going to be a high school senior. Simran, you're about to go to graduate school. Is this really any way to behave?"

Disappointment sweeps over me—is it mine or Mom's?

I drop my eyes. *Bitch* is better than the other B-word weaponized against me: Besharam.

Bossy. Audacious. Rude. Mouthy. Boastful. Shameless. Bold. Overly ambitious in a way that wears well on a boy, but never on a girl.

It's an amorphous cloud of a word that transmutes to fit any situation. I'm besharam when I contradict my grandmother that reading books isn't a waste of time. When I call out an "uncle"—not even a real uncle, just any Desi man who happens to be at a potluck with us—that *actually*, what he said was wildly racist.

When people take it for granted they're getting the Desi discount and go directly to Mom to ask me to do the calligraphy for their party and wedding invitations; their infuriating expectation of free labor and the sheer impertinence of cutting me out usually gets walked back when I follow up with my rates.

My parents have never used it against me, but when literally everybody else has, how could they not think it, too?

Any way you cut it, in every culture, it's universal: Kavya Joshi is Too Much.

I *am* besharam. Something Mom and Simran should be proud to be, too.

But it never takes long for the words I ache to say to melt on my tongue like a Listerine Cool Mint breath strip.

Simran is the first one to look contrite. She presses a kiss to Mom's cheek. "Sorry, Mom." More grudgingly, she adds, "Sorry, Kavya." She doesn't mean it, but we both know our parents expect it, anyway.

I know my words must have hurt her, too, but underneath the faint regret is an underpinning of resentment. Mom and Dad just *assume* it's my fault because I call things as I see them. Because I'm the rude daughter who always causes problems and Simran is the "good" one.

My heart stings. No one sees that she hurt me, too.

Mom looks at me expectantly. When I don't say anything, she adds, "I'm sure Sonal and Sunny don't behave this way."

If it isn't abundantly clear, I am not, nor will I ever be, a Perfect Indian Daughter. The comparison to the Kapoor girls is chalky in my mouth, leaving my tongue grainy and dry. This is what failure tastes like. I wish it wasn't so familiar.

I twist my mouth and cross my arms over my chest. "You're kidding, right? That's bullshit. They're sisters. Of *course* they fight."

"Kavya," Dad says in a warning tone. Speaking my mind is fine, but backchat is not.

I pin my stare on Simran, seeking solidarity, but she rubs her nose, not looking at me.

My ire flares hotter. I let my licked-clean spoon clatter in the empty bowl.

"Sure, the Perfect Kapoor Sisters never have a fight," I say. I should let it go, just like that point from math class, but I can't. "They exist in harmony and birdsong, and frolic with small woodland creatures."

My joke doesn't break the tension with the laughs I expect. Not even from Dad.

In the hush that follows, Buster's wagging tail swishes through the air, slapping my calves. Simran eyes me, face standoffish and lips pursed. Dad gets up to mix more bhel and Mom tiredly meets my gaze.

"You know, Kavya, there is a middle ground between Snow White and Evil Queen," says Mom. There's no harshness in her voice, which makes it worse. "I suggest you try and find it."

4.
The Authority on Moon Girls

AS THE MOON girls and I get out of Catey's car, borrowed from the older sister she lives with, I feel a slight twinge. Another boyfriend bites the dust. The worst of it is that when we started going out, I thought he was such a prince. Turns out he was Gaston, instead.

And I know a thing or two about princes. I work weekends and summers at Poppy's Party Playhouse, a children's entertainment company specializing in party princesses.

One thing I can say with absolute certainty is that love is *nothing* like a Disney movie.

"Smile, Kavya, it's a party!" some jerk shouts as he and his friends pass by.

Blaire flips him her middle finger. "Keep walking!"

"I'm fine," I say, shying away from Val's worried, probing gaze.

"Wishing it was less public?" Catey asks, tucking her keys away. We all stare at the street packed with cars. "You don't have to break up with Parker tonight, you know. It can wait."

"Yeah, I do. Because everyone needs to know who broke up with who, and the only way that happens is if there's no mistaking who did the dumping. Which is where the audience comes in."

"What is it like being in your brain?" asks Val. "And why do I imagine it looking like Mojo Jojo's evil lair?"

"When they cut me open for science, maybe they'll tell you," I say, slinging an arm around her shoulder.

She worries her lower lip with her front teeth. "You're cute together. Maybe there's—"

"Don't say hope," I cut her off.

I don't just want cute; I want the real deal. Someone who likes me for the ambitious goal-getter I am. Someone whose confidence can overcome their ego.

The Kims' house is on a cul-de-sac, with a circular driveway big enough to fit nine cars, but the street's still crammed bumper to bumper. Claudia's parents let her have the house for parties as long as there's no drugs, booze, or more than thirty people. But tonight it looks like everyone brought a plus-four. The cheer squad spills out of the minivan parked behind us.

"Wow," Blaire says with a low whistle. "This is definitely more than thirty."

Claudia is standing in the open doorway like she's thinking about being a human barricade, silently mouthing numbers, but her face unclenches when she says "Kavya, hi!"

"You okay?" I ask, hanging back while a passel of laughing seniors overtake us.

Fretting, she draws her lip in her mouth. "This is way too many people!" she shrills. "My neighbors are totally going to tell my parents."

"Claud!" One of the senior girls throws her arms around Claudia's shoulders. "What a cute and intimate little party," she says with a braying laugh, holding up her phone. "Don't worry, I got the word out."

Claudia's right eye twitches, but her resolve must be made of butter, because she lets all five of them cross the threshold. "I don't know what was worse," she says to me. "Being hugged by a stranger, being called *Claud*, or the backhanded compliment that this"—she spreads her arms—"is a small party. Like, *what*?"

"Should we, I don't know, call your mom or something?"

She contemplates this for a moment, then shakes her head and pulls a face. "And have the entire school know my party got busted up by my mommy?"

"Okay, fair. Just know that I am totally willing to be your bad guy and kick people out."

She gives me a genuine smile. "You're the best. Now quit bottlenecking the door. And get them to turn the music down."

When we slip inside, Blaire beelines for the theater kids, and their corner of the living room erupts into cheers like they haven't seen her in weeks.

"Must be nice," Val mutters. She's beautiful in her skinny

jeans and coral, gold-embroidered kurti that she stitched her-self. She tugs me close. "Kavya, don't forget I have to be home at eleven."

"That's still two hours away," I point out. She has a way of counting down the clock, tempering her fun with a good dose of fear.

"Yeah, but the girls always cut it so close," she whispers. "You know Papa. If I'm even five minutes late, I won't be able to go out with you guys next time. I had to *beg* for eleven."

Her curfew's usually nine, which means her mom helped her out this time. Val's dad has a pretty warped idea of what high schoolers are like. Any second Val isn't right in front of his eyes is a second that she could be getting up to something involving short skirts, boys, and tequila.

"*Kavya.*"

"Yeah, okay," I whisper back, disentangling myself from Val. "I promise we'll keep an eye on the time. But I need to find Parker."

Her face flickers with a comment she doesn't allow herself to make. "Fine."

When we split up, I scout the room for Parker.

He isn't where I thought he'd be, throwing back drinks in the kitchen and recounting to a crowd of doe-eyed freshmen his glory days as the youngest kid ever to make varsity foot-ball. He isn't even in the next place I thought he'd be, arguing with his best friend about which is the best Spider-Man when Miles Morales is literally right there. Though Tom Holland is a close second.

From the other side of the room, Claudia waves at me with both arms. "Check upstairs!" she shouts. "Some of the guys are on the PlayStation in the game room."

"Watch out," some hulking senior growls as I bump his shoulder going up the stairs. As if a girl my height could actually hurt him. Normally I'd apologize, but I don't appreciate someone getting in my face over something as trivial as grazing his fucking arm when he could have slid to the wall instead of walking right in the center like a dick.

I whirl—two steps taller than him—and spit back, "*You* watch out."

As I reach the top of the landing, an amused voice breaks through the soft background noise of the PlayStation and says, "Still making friends everywhere you go, I see."

I scowl. I'd know that voice anywhere. Because of course *he'd* be here. Even at school, escape is unavoidable. After all the Johnsons and Joneses in the locker hallway, it goes like this: Kavya Joshi, Ian Jun, then Claudia Kim.

Ian Jun is draped against the wall, hands shoved in his pockets, doing that cool-guy lean he's perfected down to an art form, and smirking at me with the full force of his annoyingly shaped mouth.

I eye him. "Why are you skulking?"

"I resent that, Joshi. I never skulk. For your information, I was patiently waiting my turn at the PlayStation when I heard your ever-so-demure voice and came out to investigate."

"Don't you ever get sick of revolving around me, Jun?"

"Never," he says cheerfully. When I just huff my annoyance at him, he groans. "Oh, come on. Don't tell me you're mad again about what happened in stats."

"*Again* implies I ever stopped," I say coolly, and if anything, his grin widens.

Up close, his new hairstyle looks even better than it did at school. Maybe it's because I'm seeing him in a new, obviously expensive light. Like everything else in the Kims' house, the recessed lighting is flattering and casts everything in soft pools of buttery glow.

"Seemed like we called a truce in gym, though," Ian suggests, pushing himself away from the wall. "You, me. Not to mention you brought your famous desk-hopping agility to the game. Admit it—we made a pretty good team."

I quirk my brow. "Us and ten other people."

He makes a low humming sound. "Something tells me you asked Catey to pick me."

He can't be serious. I drum my black slingback flats against the carpet, but they fail to make a satisfying thwack. "She was the captain. It was her call."

"And moon girls never do anything alone," he counters. "So."

"Uh-huh. And you're the authority on moon girls?"

"Maybe just one of them."

Somehow during all this he's moved nearer, closing the gap between us. I have to look up to meet his eyes, another power move that makes me feel even smaller than my height of five feet, three inches.

It's hard to imagine I used to be friends with the know-it-all boy whose dark, inky eyes I'm currently staring into like he isn't ranking number one on my grudge list.

My mom used to take me to his house, where we'd play Pokémon and Zelda on Nintendo 3DS, jump on his trampoline until we couldn't walk straight, watch *The Lightning Thief* (which I always thought was pretty terrible compared to the Percy Jackson books, despite my crush on Logan Lerman, but Ian loved it), and yell our *hi-yah!*s as we tried to outdo each other practicing our tae kwon do forms before working up huge appetites for slices of his mom's banoffee pie.

When we were ten, we both earned our black belts, and we celebrated by splitting a whole pie between us right at the counter of the Juns' Audrey Hepburn–inspired retro-fusion diner, Holly Gogogi. It's the same classic that Mom orders every time we grab carry-out, whether there's something to celebrate or not. The tradition has stuck, like bits of toffee between our teeth. But Ian and I, we don't share anything, anymore.

Except this. Whatever this is. I'd call it a game, but that would imply it's not real.

The wooden banister railing prods the small of my back. We're looking out over the foyer, I realize. Anyone could look up and see us. The energy between us has become charged, electrified. A thrilling spike of danger sends meteor showers down my spine and arms.

"You know, it really bothers me how pristine you always manage to look." I reach up and ruffle his hair, unable to stop myself from seeing him just that little bit out of place.

His lips part in shock, eyes flaring with something like warning.

"There," I declare, drawing my hand back down to my side. "Less perfect. More human."

My fingertips tingle. I wonder if his scalp does, too. I can't believe I voluntarily touched him. I guess I momentarily forgot he wasn't one of my friends who I could just reach out for whenever I wanted to. So, then, it was doubly strange that he'd *let* me.

Ian's brow furrows. "I'm not perfect."

I tick each one off on my fingers. "Right. Four-point-three GPA, boys' varsity tennis captain, junior prom king, Film Society president, French Club president, public library summer reading program winner, and you're a shoo-in for National Merit. Yeah, you're the picture of mediocrity."

"Achievements don't make me perfect," he says, shaking his head.

"What's your game? False modesty?"

Surprise shaves off a few years, turns him back into the boy I once knew. "No game. I just don't deserve the credit you're giving me."

Humility. That's his angle? After I recited the contents of his résumé?

I frown. "I wouldn't say you played fair and square for that point in stats, but I'm not *giving* you anything. Everything you've got, you've earned."

Gross, this boy's got me out here boosting his self-esteem.

I wait for him to peacock, but he doesn't, so in the lull,

I throw a glance over my shoulder to the twelve-foot drop. "You know, if you toss me off, there's a good chance you could be valedictorian next year," I say in a conversational tone.

The offhand comment makes him blanch, just as I'd known it would. But he recovers quick. "I wouldn't need to touch one hair on your gor—gargantuan head in order to win."

"Prodigious. Mammoth. Brobdingnagian."

He gives me a slow, measured blink. "What?"

"I was giving you alternate synonyms. So you can brush up on your SAT vocab."

Ian snorts. "You think I need help from you?"

I give him a saber-toothed smile. "You did before."

He leans in close, bringing with him a whiff of fresh laundry and Juicy Fruit gum. "Why exert myself when I could still get what I wanted with minimal effort?"

My eyes narrow. "I knew it."

He smirks. "You're just annoyed you didn't think of it first."

"You've got me. I'm so annoyed I'm not an underhanded point piranha like you."

"Oh, you're definitely a point piranha." He taps a finger against his lower lip. "Just not sure what adjective to give you, yet."

I scowl. "I have a few choice adjectives for you."

His eyes light up. "Isn't it a little too soon for dirty talk?"

Just as I'm about to spring into the litany, a kid I vaguely remember from gym passes by with a red SOLO cup. He eyes me for a second and then pounds on the door behind Ian. "Yo, Ellis. Kavya's out here. You're welcome," he says, raising his empty cup before heading downstairs.

"Thanks?" Just as I'm about to brush past Ian, the door opens.

Parker's tugging his head through the shirt he's wearing.

A shirt I got him, and I remember because he's struggling to get it over his ears, and he always complains the neckholes on new shirts are too tight. His pecs are hard and perked, skin red, glistening with . . . is that sweat?

I tense, breath trapped in my throat. The questions race, even as time seems to come to a standstill. Why is he half dressed? Why isn't he in the next room playing PlayStation?

I catch the briefest glimpse of a toned stomach and the light brown fuzz of a happy trail descending from his navel.

My shoulders curl inward, huddled. My mouth is dry. I can't think. Can't drag my eyes back up to his face, even though I dimly register someone saying my name.

"What were you doing in there?" I ask too loud, even though the door is still open and I could see for myself if I take another step.

There's a flash of movement beyond Parker's shoulder. Bare skin. A pretty dandelion tattoo across a narrow back. The spores are sprinkling away.

That's how I feel. Like I'm not there anymore.

Ian steps into my field of vision, drawing the door shut behind him. A hard, final click that brings sound and time rushing back like I've emerged from underwater.

"Hey, let's go downstairs," he suggests, voice impossibly gentle and unlike his usual cocksure timbre, and as I stare blankly into his eyes, that's when it hits me.

He knew.

5.
The Bitch Who Just Broke Up with You

SHAME ENGULFS ME like drowning, a black wave that plunges down my throat, stealing away my words and my breath. It dampens my anger into sluggish numbness, but I still manage to make it down the stairs despite Ian catching at my elbows, saying my name over and over.

It's not Parker's cheating that makes me flee like the coward Ian doesn't think I am, but the seething resentment that Parker thinks he's won. He didn't have to say a word. He didn't have to make a scene. He just had to be his horrible douchebag self and make me the victim. Instant victory. I'm seeing his character now in 100 percent full brightness.

This is what hurts the most—that I had been so close to winning.

"Kavya!" This time, Ian's insistent grip and even more insistent voice gets me to screech to a stop. Following so close on my heels, he teeters on the step above, about to fall forward. He grabs the banister before I can ready myself to brace him.

The nothingness ebbs away, sours into a complicated, alien tangle of embarrassment, umbrage, and defeat. The multiple little things in stats, the battle line Parker drew in gym, and now a front-row seat to this? Ian couldn't have planned the timing better if he'd tried.

"Are you okay?" he actually has the temerity—the utter *temerity*—to ask.

I wrench my arm away. He won't understand it's not heartbreak that made me run.

His lips part, about to try again, so I cut him off. "These are tears of *frustration*. You won't believe this, but I came here tonight to break up with him. Wait, why am I telling you?" I scoff. "You probably enjoyed the show."

Ian's jaw tightens, and he rolls his shoulders the way he does in school when he's got a stiff neck from too many hours spent hunched over books in the library.

"Why do you think I'd enjoy witnessing that?" he all but growls.

"Oh, I forgot. Perfect Ian. You're above all this high school drama." I wave my hand, blurred vision clearing. "You don't date; you're never the subject of any spurious rumors; none of the teachers are out to get you. Is this the game now? Pretending to care?"

He holds himself perfectly rigid, neck so taut and corded,

that I'm reminded of gym again. The fresh memory washes over me, this time not dragging me under, but pulling me out.

"It's not pretend," he says. "I never thought he deserved to be with you."

"Because how could one of the hottest, most popular guys in school want to be with the predictable point piranha, right?"

"That's *not* what I meant." He scowls. "What kind of beast do you think I am?"

"I don't think about you at all," I shoot back. "Look, why are you even—why do you care? It's not like I don't know the boys' swim team was taking bets on how long Parker would stick it out with me. So, what, you got in on it, too?" I shake my head. "Leave me alone. I don't want anyone's pity."

Ian's eyes narrow, but before he can say a word, Parker stumbles down the stairs. Almost in a hurry, except if he wanted to come after me, he should have left minutes ago.

"Do you have to be here, dude?" Parker snaps. He's still a little red-faced and sweaty, pulling at his tight collar. "I'm trying to have a conversation with my girl."

My stomach clenches tight. "Oh my god, you're disgusting. For the record, I'm not your *anything*. We're over. *Over*."

"Kavya, will you let me talk?" he snaps like *he's* the one with a reason to be mad.

I glare at him. "Speak."

"I wasn't cheating," he says in a rush. "I was going to break up with you tonight. You're cool, but this hasn't been working out. You don't know how to treat a guy nice."

It's almost funny how he thinks any of that absolves him.

"Let me get this straight. You think that *this*"—I gesture wildly—"isn't cheating because you planned to dump me *in your head*?"

He pauses, taking a moment to puzzle it out before nodding.

But I'm not done yet. "And by treat you 'nice,' I assume you mean I wouldn't put out?" I take a step toward him. Up close, I can smell cheap beer on his breath. Alcohol I know Claudia didn't provide, and for some reason, this rule breaking makes me angrier.

Ian still hasn't left. Parker looks comically confused. The way he's looking at me is like he's seeing me for the first time. My body glows with this awareness, this brilliant, splicing anger, and I'm brought to life like Pygmalion's statue.

"Kavya," says Parker, a strain in his voice. He reaches a hand out, grazing my shoulder before I flinch. "C'mon. Let's not do this here." He glares at Ian.

"I'm not going anywhere with you," I scoff, dodging Parker's second grabby attempt.

"Dude, this isn't cool." Ian steps in. "She said it's over."

"*Dude*," Parker sneers. "You can see yourself out of this conversation."

There's way too much testosterone flying around. My ex is no prince, and my rival is no knight in shining armor. I'm not in need of saving. I can look out for myself, thanks very much.

"Babe," Parker entreats again, this time skirting past Ian to stand right next to me.

Ian makes as if to say something, but I pin him in place

with a quelling look. Far be it from me to stop anyone, even a belly-crawling slug like Parker, from digging their own grave.

"What?" I snap without an ounce of grace.

Smugness blooms over Parker's face, as if he thinks I've chosen him over Ian. "Be classy," he says in the tone one might use to reprimand a child. "People are staring."

The world floods red. I've never really seen my mad face, but Catey once called me a baby dragon, so I hope Parker takes full stock of my fiery wrath when I shriek, "I wouldn't sleep with you if you were the last guy on the planet, you drunk, sexist asshole."

"You bitch!"

Everyone's eyes fly to us, the lo-fi music throbbing out of the Kim's stereo slamming to a stop way too fast to be the end of the track.

Every word I said to Val about wanting an audience mocks me now.

I look up slowly to see Allegra craning over the second-floor railing. When our eyes meet, brown on blue, she hurriedly glances away.

"Yeah," I say to Parker. "That's me. The bitch who just broke up with you."

Over the football and swim teams' whoops and hollers, I make sure to put enough sass in my sashay as I make my way down the stairs. I don't look back at Ian or Parker.

The next few seconds will decide how people remember me tonight: scorned or triumphant. Victimized or empowered.

Forcing a smirk to my face, I ask the nearest cluster of boys, "So who won?"

••••••••••••••••••••••••••••••••

The moon girls regroup in the downstairs bathroom. They gnash their teeth with anger and worry, nails pincer sharp as they pull me close and whisper words of vengeance in my ear. We emerge only when my makeup is freshened, game face and armor class leveled up.

Upstairs, boys' laughter booms. The music's started back up, money's changing hands, and Parker's huddled on the bottom step with Allegra, both of them shooting me daggers.

I tell myself I don't care.

"I don't care," I tell the moon girls. Their anger has washed over me, cleansing me brand-new. "No, don't," I say, catching Blaire's wrist as she makes to head for the stairs. "Leave it. He's not worth it."

"Of course he's not worth it," says Catey.

"But that's not the point," finishes Blaire.

I understand her urge. I love her for it. We're the same, her and me. The dark side of the moon. We need Catey and Val to balance us out. In a moment, they do. Catey's arms batwing around me, hugging me close. "Should we leave?" she whispers.

The words are a tickle of breath in my ear. "And let him win? No way."

Val rubs my back and checks her watch.

"Yeah, and why should you have to hide? You've got nothing to feel embarrassed about," says Blaire. "Leave that to Parker." She tosses a sneer in his direction.

He's still slumped on the stairs, ignored in a way he isn't used to. Even Allegra's left him. I don't know her that well, but I'm familiar with how unpleasant his bruised ego can be.

"Ian's joined the others in truth or dare," says Catey, voice lilted.

Blaire shoots me an arch smile. "If he's playing, you know Kavs will, too."

"Please. I don't do things *just* because he does," I huff.

"She's right," says Val, tapping her chin. "It's only the top nine out of ten reasons."

"Traitor," I grumble, bumping her hip with mine. "Adding you to my grudge list, FYI."

"Quelle horreur," whisper-shrieks Catey, who is too nice to flex at anything, but has a French grandmother who made sure Catey and her three older siblings could drip the language of love off their tongues by the time they could walk.

I bet dear old Grand-mère had no idea how attractive those breezy, rolling Rs would be to the femmes at our high school.

On our way to the kitchen for sodas, we're stopped by a yelp. I turn to see Parker stumble into the foyer. A red cup sails through the air, hitting him smack-dab in his forehead.

"Get out!" yells Claudia, pelting him with more empty SOLO cups. "The invite said no booze, and there are three freshmen puking in my mom's vase!"

When he doesn't move right away, she snaps her fingers at the two tall boys in varsity jackets closest to her. "Throw him out," she commands imperiously.

Val takes my arm, laughing herself silly, and Blaire presses her mouth to my shoulder, body quaking. "Oh shit," she manages to say between breathless giggles.

Parker's unceremoniously tossed on the lawn. He fumbles with his keys, dropping them twice. There's a confused, bewildered expression on his face, like he can't believe he's being kicked while he's down. A second later, Claudia slams the door.

After making sure to relate what just happened to everyone in the vicinity, we join the party game in the living room, squeezing past the ring of onlookers to sit on the thick plush carpet next to Samer Saab.

Samer, pronounced with a long *a*, was born in Lebanon, but his family naturalized in eighth grade—I remember his mom bringing in red-white-and-blue cupcakes with star sprinkles. He was already popular, but his mom's absurdly delightful baking cemented it.

We work kids' parties together as Charming and Snow White at Poppy's Party Playhouse, where we make painfully sure to use generic names for our roles instead of Disney copyrighted ones. He's perfect for the part, and he's always trying to get me to come back to play the Jasmine (Desert Princess) to his Aladdin, even though my original stint was super short. I didn't want to stay long-term in a role that was coded Middle Eastern, not Indian, so we totally lucked out when an Iranian American drama major took over.

It's impossible to know for a fact at this angle, but my neck prickles as if Ian's peering at me around Samer's thick head of boy-band-swoopy hair. So, naturally, I avoid eye contact like he's a chatty auntie desperate to introduce me to yet another nice Indian boy.

I steel my face into indifference. He's already witnessed far too much of my emotion. I'll bottle the residue until it's radio-active before I let him see me weak again.

Samer sends me a distracted, sympathetic smile and mouths *Sorry about the dick* before resuming googly eyes with the gorgeous, fat brunette girl smiling and blushing opposite.

Next to her, Claudia sighs. "Are we playing truth or dare or flirting?"

Samer blinks. "There's a choice?"

"No." Claudia turns to the boy on her other side with an air of anticipation. "Rio, you just went, so you have to pick someone."

Just like I have my moon girls, Ian has Samer, Claudia, and his best friend since first grade, Rio Moreno-Ortiz, a trans boy with a devastating tennis serve and even more devastating smile.

Rio groans and swipes the cup out of Claudia's hand, down-ing it in a gulp. "This is boring. Everyone's picking truth."

Val goes still. She hates this game. In general she spends most parties in mortal dread, but party games make her extra nervous. It's a wonder she joined in for this one, but maybe that has more to do with the boy sitting cross-legged next to her. She'd chosen a more cramped spot even though there was plenty of room where the other moon girls were.

"If you pick me, I'll do a dare," I say.

From the corner of my eye, Ian's head swivels toward me. Half my face and neck erupt in fizzy tingles. "Of course you will," I swear I hear him mutter.

I bristle but don't respond. After what happened with Parker, I have something to prove.

Rio's eyes scan the circle like he's narrowing down his choices, coming to a stop on me. Then his copper-penny eyes slide to Samer. And then to Ian. And then back to me, upper lip wickedly curling with the promise of a *really* good dare.

But before he can officially choose me, Claudia interjects in a rush. "Since Rio's taking too long, I pick myself for a dare."

"You can't do that!" Rio throws an entreating look to the circle for confirmation.

Ian grins and flashes his palms. "No way, dude. Not getting in the middle of a you-and-Claudia fight. I want to live."

Huh. So he's only combative where I'm concerned.

Claudia tosses Rio a victorious smirk. "Hostess rules! So? Am I getting a dare or not?"

Rio taps his forehead, pretending to think. "Fine. Then sing 'WAP.' The explicit lyrics. And do your best version of the dance. Full out."

Claudia, bless her, stands up with the grim-faced determination of a woman up to a challenge. "*Nobody* better film this," she warns.

No less than five iPhones shoot into the air.

"Fuck you all," she grumbles, but then she gets to it.

As the music pulses from her dad's precious stereo, nausea inches up my throat, elaborate sailor's knots looping and tightening in my stomach.

I can't shake the feeling that maybe it was supposed to be

my dare instead of hers. Wasn't Rio about to pick me? The way he'd roved over me, Samer, and Ian in equal measure . . . It was almost as though he'd intended for it to be me all along but didn't want it to look obvious.

Does Rio *know*?

My blood runs cold. Every muscle in my body springs tight.

If Rio knows, then as his best friend, Ian does, too. I can *feel* his eyes.

Which means I have every reason to be as wary of this game as Val.

6.

Kavya Joshi Is Too Much

THERE'S NOT A lot I slink away from in life or party games. But there is one thing. And now I'm positive Rio and Ian know it—I can't sing worth a damn.

It's a job requirement to be a children's entertainer at Poppy's Party Playhouse, but I get by with speak-singing in a lilt alongside the cassette in our portable stereos. The birthday girls never notice that their favorite princess isn't belting the words out with gusto.

Years before I even auditioned at Poppy's, I was enthusiastically trying out for solos in choir, and Catey, bless her heart, voice coached me through nailing all the notes even though we both knew there was no way I could beat her first soprano.

She was the only one who clapped when the song ended. The rest of the class stared with dinner-plate eyes or laughed behind their hands. The teacher let several beats pass before saying uncertainly, "Well, thank you, Kavya. We'll certainly keep you in mind. That was . . ."

She couldn't even summon an adjective. Or maybe she just didn't want to lie to my face.

And that was the moment I knew I was objectively awful. Soulless, toneless. Don't-even-sing-in-the-shower awful. Lip-sync "Happy Birthday" awful. The musical talent that flowed through the entire lineage of Bollywood-bellowing, sitar-strumming, tabla-thumping Joshis had skipped me.

I didn't take choir as an elective the next semester. Or any semester.

And I thought that since it happened in middle school, my shame was buried deep enough that it would never resurface. My heartstrings twang with a wrong note as Claudia, pink-cheeked with exertion, draws to the end of the song and dance.

If it wasn't for her interference, it would have been me in her place. There's no way I can pick dare tonight, or ever, if Rio and Ian have this embarrassing knowledge about me. I have plenty of haters who will use it against me. There's no way I'm singing in front of such an unforgiving audience. A girl has her reputation to uphold, after all: never show weakness.

Luckily, it's a nonissue. Because when Claudia's dare is over, it's someone else's turn. And so on and so on until it's Ian's turn at last, and my heart explodes in panic confetti that settles like gravel in my stomach.

Because there's no *way* he's not picking me next. Half the circle has had their turn.

"Brave enough for a dare?" a senior girl asks, blowing Ian a kiss.

Val's face pinches. She glances at her watch, then sighs with resignation.

"Sorry to disappoint." Ian swings both pointer fingers in arcs. "Y'all are sadists."

Which, fair. It's high school.

Catey already had to reveal who she'd fuck, marry, or kill (which sounds like an easy one, except she fretted over the first, didn't even have to think about naming Blaire as the second, and took so long for the third because she didn't want to hurt anyone's feelings that I advocated for her to be let off the hook).

Blaire had to read out a smutty scene from the three-hundred-thousand-word Bonnie x Damon AO3 fanfic she's been working on. And considering five people asked her for the link after the six-page vamp foreplay, I'd say it was great promo.

Rio just took his third turn, for a total of two dares and one truth, because he's such a good sport about being picked and always plays to his audience. Now he's rubbing his hands together in glee, pretending to come up with a truth so soul-baring that Ian's cool-for-the-summer ease is going to be well and truly torpedoed.

"So it's truth?" Claudia asks Ian, her softly rounded black eyebrow lifting.

Some unspoken warning passes between them.

There's a tightness in his smile and I hate that I notice.

Because Ian Jun has exactly eight smiles and this is the one he wears when he's trying hard to appear casual. Where the corners of his mouth hold a tension that makes his cheeks stiff, unlike his natural one-sided smile that tugs the right side of his mouth, drawing out a dimple.

The last time I saw this smile, we were slow dancing at the eighth-grade farewell dance.

Not by choice. Our moms were parent chaperones and while keeping an eye on the punch bowl, they put their heads together to supremely embarrass us. One minute I was awkwardly shuffling by the wall with my friends, the next Mrs. Jun was animatedly gesturing at me while my mom beamed. And Ian came over, feet dragging, cheeks bright as a tomato.

"Wanna dance?" he'd asked, biting his lip, not quite able to make eye contact, leaving no doubt in my mind that he *sooooo* did not want to be there. Which, in turn, only made me dig my heels in. Ian was going to dance with me and he was going to enjoy it, damn it. What surprised me was that it didn't take long—or much—to get him grinning.

Smile #4: face two inches from mine, singing Katy Perry's "Firework" until the song abruptly switched to a slow dance and we leapt apart so fast that Catey swears to this day she heard the screech of Velcro.

I flick wary eyes back to Rio, who's pretending to stroke a long wizard-y beard.

"Truth," Ian confirms, throwing up a middle finger.

Rio grins and steeples his fingers together. "Excellent. So I'm *dying* to know why you've been single since you broke up with Erin Hatchet sophomore year."

"No one wants to know that," Ian says, rubbing his nose.

An immediate chorus of *yes we do* flares up, scrabbling voices refusing to let him off the hook. Interest catches like a spark, and it doesn't take long for the whole room to set ablaze.

After being nemeses for as long as we've been friends, I know Ian's tells better than anyone. And despite my self-assured smugness in flying too close to the sun in stats, I know that, right in this minute, his comfort level is minus ten.

Just like mine. My stomach lurches and I shift uncomfortably, wishing we'd just taken off when we had the chance. Gone for FroYo at The Daily Scoop on the Riverwalk, or maybe a bubble tea at the Cold Brew Bros next door to Holly Gogogi.

Rio teases, "Fine, new question: Is there someone here, at this party, that you like?" His words are tinged with meaning, like he already knows the answer.

Ian groans. "If I say yes, will you drop it?"

Rio agrees, but he can't speak for everyone else. When Ian picks a girl in our grade and gives her an easy question, she turns around to put him back in the hot seat.

"Does her first name start with an A?" she asks slyly.

"Very not subtle at all, *Abby*," whispers Catey, accidentally loud enough to carry.

"No," says Ian. Unfortunately for him, his cool-guy image cracks as much as his voice, which is all it takes for everyone to pile on.

I don't feel sorry for him. For once it's not me in the crosshairs of attention.

Every successive question comes back to him, our classmates working their way through the alphabet. By C, Ian's
caught on. When we reach E his exasperation turns to a tes-
tiness he does a decent job of hiding, still trying so hard to
appear chill.

He makes eye contact with me before biting his lip.

The second I start to feel sorry for him, I harden my heart
like a Metapod. The funniest part is that he's the only friend I
had who would get the reference; while my moon girls were
all about magical girl squads, they couldn't care less about
Pokémon.

I bring my forgotten cup of soda to my mouth and gulp
down all the cherry Coke, hardly tasting my favorite flavor.
Even when it's all gone and my tongue feels fuzzy, I keep the
cup tipped back so I can pretend I'm not paying attention to
him. It has nothing to do with getting sucked into a black hole
whenever he looks at me.

Sure, I *guess* some people would be into the way he looks at
you like you're the only one in the room, but it just makes me
squirm. Like being on a rowboat going over a rough patch of
sea during a storm without sails or oars or any nautical knowledge at *all*, and lately it's been happening more than usual.

Must have something to do with the end of the school year.
He knows there's only one more week to get under my skin.

I thought people would get bored by the time H rolled
around, but our peers' masochistic drive, it seems, is even
stronger than mine. Ian's still striving for blasé, but his hands
are balled in his lap so tight that his arms are starting to vi-

brate. At one point he even gets up under the guise of grabbing a drink, but he only makes it a few feet before someone
pulls him back down so he ends up across from me.

I scratch at my wrist. I don't have a clue why he hasn't quit
playing. The game isn't fun anymore, not that it really ever
was.

What is he trying to prove?

"Singling him out is mean," Val whispers when the letter J
bites the dust, too.

"I should never have—" says Rio in a low voice. Louder, he
calls out, "Hey! Let's back off, okay?"

"He still has to pick someone," says Abby. "Unless he's
chicken."

I can't take it anymore. "Val and Rio are right. This is *beyond* ridiculous. What's next, spin the bottle?"

"Yeah, that's a good idea," says one of the senior girls.
"We'll quit playing if you"—she points at me with a smirk—
"kiss him."

I roll my eyes. "Yeah, right."

"Call it senior prerogative," she says. "Didn't he get you so
steamed that you jumped over a desk? Don't tell me there's
nothing between you."

"Yeah, there is. And it's called three years of rivalry," I shoot
back.

"Y'all aren't being serious," says Blaire with a low whistle.
"Let people keep their secrets and lips to themselves, damn."

Catey nods resolutely. "No one should have to kiss if they
don't want to."

"If they wanted to, it wouldn't be much of a dare, would it?" comes the bitchy response.

Every single person rubbernecks except for my friends and Ian's. Val's eyes are rounded with horrified sympathy. Despite Mr. Gage's accusation that I always have to be the center of attention—*not* true, by the way—I would happily vacate the limelight right now.

Both Ian and I are backed into a corner.

And there's only one way to get myself out of it: I have to pretend like kissing Ian Jun, former friend and current rival, isn't a big deal. Not even a medium deal.

Claudia's eyes harden. "You find out Ian likes someone who's here right now and you seriously want him to kiss someone else? Not cool."

Samer rises to his feet. "C'mon, man, let's just go grab a soda."

I recognize the look on the senior girl's face. She's digging her heels in.

And the one person who should be fighting this is silent. My options aren't great: If I go for it, he'll know it's because I was manipulated. If I refuse, I'm a chicken and lose face. And that's never going to happen again. Once was more than enough.

I know they all think Kavya Joshi is Too Much. And I am. I'm a lot of things, but what I'm absolutely *not* is scared and reluctant.

I close my eyes and swallow, drawing my lips into my mouth. My gums are achingly dry; I wish I'd saved a sip of soda. Then I force myself to insert a bored drawl into my voice as I say, "All right, I *suppose* we can give the peasants what they want."

Ian startles like he's been yanked out of a nightmare only to awaken in one even worse.

"Kavya, you don't have to—" he begins, but I'm already following through.

I *always* follow through.

My upper thighs are shaky as I crawl to the center of the circle, heart stress-ball-squeezing. A boy's donkey-laugh flies over my head, followed by: "Who knew Ian Jun would be the one to get Kavya Joshi on her knees?"

Lava sears up my neck. Instinct screams at me to turn around and clap back at whoever it is, but I hesitate a second too long and my moon girls are there instead, words flying out of Blaire's and Catey's mouths so fast that I can almost hear the squeal of his ineffectual backtrack.

There's no way that kid could know that was the one thing Parker always wanted me to do for him. That even though he accepted that I wasn't ready for sex, he was persistent in asking for oral whenever things were good between us. *It's not even real sex, Kavya, jeez*, he used to say.

When everyone knew that, yes, it was. We learned that in sex ed, for crying out loud.

I didn't have anything against giving head, in theory, but Parker never inspired the passion to make me even want to.

I tug my black denim miniskirt down, even though I know my army-green shirt jacket is long enough to cover my ass. Nothing can be done about my gray V-neck shirt that's dipped low enough that the people in front of me can see the baby-pink lace of my 32D cups and the fuchsia on my cheeks that no one will mistake for heavy-handed Glossier Cloud Paint in Haze.

"Gonna meet me halfway, Jun, or do I have to come to you?" I all but snarl.

To my surprise, Ian's eyebrows are already drawn together in a scowl. His mouth's tight, not concentrating-on-a-math-problem tight, but like he's actually pissed. It takes me aback for a second before I figure it out, and by the time I do, I've already forgotten the jeer.

What, was he was so confident that I wouldn't kiss him? He thought I'd let the challenge go unanswered? Let him *win*?

As he inches across the carpet to join me, the perfect punishment strikes: I am going to give him the best kiss of his entire life. The kiss that will be the measuring stick for all future girlfriends or boyfriends, and the best part?

He'll never be able to forget who gave it to him.

Ian's moving gingerly, going old-lady-in-the-fast-lane slow. It's clear he hates this.

With an impatient sound, I reach out to grab his crewneck. Crush it in my fist. My fingers have inadvertently curled into his collar, and the warmth of his skin against my knuckles is dizzyingly intimate. And we haven't even kissed yet.

I mean to make the first move, but before I pounce, he's in my personal bubble. His hand grazes past the silver crescent moon studs in my ear and slips into my hair.

I'm close enough to notice a smattering of sun freckles the color of warm honey across the bridge of his nose.

His eyes do that black hole thing again as he swallows me within his gaze. "Can I?"

It takes me a second to figure out what he's asking, but at my nod, he leans in.

I expect his mouth to mash against mine, with unyielding lips and hard teeth, the kind of kiss meant to prove how distasteful he finds kissing *me* of all people.

Instead, Ian's lips suck at my bottom lip, teasing out an invitation. The scent of his cherry ChapStick reaches me before the taste does and my lips part in surprise. That's all it takes for him to deepen the kiss.

The fleeting annoyance that he stole what was going to be *my* move dissolves along with coherent thought when one of his hands steals deeper into my hair to massage my scalp. The other circles around my neck, tugging me a breath closer.

My lips reciprocate of their own accord, moving against his, sloppy and out of sync at first, and then . . .

Tingles start in the backs of my knees and meteor shower down my calves. Oh my god, I must be losing sensation from the pressure on my knees. The only rational explanation.

The white noise of the party is forgotten. This is . . . truly, objectively awful. Repugnant, even. This slow, gentle pressure. An unhurried pace that gives the impression he could do this for hours without running out of breath. Definitely not how I imagined Ian would kiss. Which is obviously not something I imagine. Ever. At all.

There's that black hole again. No, it's just my eyelids. When did I close my eyes?

Without warning, the ambient noise returns in a *whoosh* of catcalls and giggles. Ian breaks the kiss first, coming away with a lipstick-smudged, swollen mouth. He blinks a few times, slow and sluggish, the way you do when you just wake up.

It could have been endearing on anyone other than him.

It takes a few beats for my mind to work its way out of the unruly, brambly thicket that is Ian Jun and his nearness. I take a mental hatchet to it, finding just enough space to squeeze through with what remains of my senses.

My stomach somersaults as I relive the playback like I'm watching it through a fun house mirror, distorting reality so completely that I barely recognize myself. My hand is fisting his tee so tight that even when I let go, my fingers don't quite straighten. Neither do the creases in his otherwise unrumpled shirt.

With a short, disbelieving laugh, Ian runs his hand over his face. Then he pauses to inspect the black sleeve of his Adidas track jacket, which has come away streaked with the strobe-light champagne highlighter on my cheek.

Looking him in the eyes has just gone from uncomfortable to impossible. Muscles turned to unset Jell-O, I scrabble backward.

I'm used to measuring my interactions with him in wins and losses. But this time, I have no idea who came out on top.

One thing's for sure, though: the playing field has changed.

And for the first time, I don't know the rules of engagement.

7.
Maybe It Would Have Been Different

"WAS HE A good kisser? He looks like he'd be a good kisser," is the first thing Blaire says to me the next morning as she clambers into the back of my Toyota Prius, passed down from my mom when I got my learner's permit.

My groan fills the car. "You know, your girlfriend had the decency not to badger me with odious memories the second she hopped in."

Blaire flashes me a grin in the rearview mirror before scooting to the middle seat. "Really? How remiss of her."

We are absolutely the girl gang that goes to the bathroom together, only today it's the public library. We're signing up for the summer reading program, plus Blaire and I have holds to pick up, and Catey wants to get a head start on this summer's book drive. That means hours spent in musty storage packing up donation boxes of all the retired-but-still-in-good-condition books.

Val isn't with us, stuck working at her family's Indian grocery store the way she's had to most weekends. She didn't want to complain after her dad agreed to let her stay out late last night, but in hindsight, I wish he hadn't. If we'd left earlier, I would never have kissed Ian.

"I'm going to perceive your avoidance to mean 'Yes, Ian's kiss blew my mind; thanks for taking an interest in my love life,'" Blaire says glibly.

Catey twists around to give her girlfriend a quick peck. "Blaire," she says in a tone that lets me know they probably agreed not to talk about last night's kiss in front of me.

I shoot her a grateful look. The more I tried not to think about it last night, the more firmly it lodged itself in my mind.

Blaire leans far enough forward to fiddle with Catey's plugged-in iPhone, switching from her upbeat *Get Stuff Done* playlist to *Road Trip Tunes*. "Kavs, you barely said a word on the ride home yesterday. And you totally left the group chat hanging."

As the latest Taylor Swift song rings out, I flip open the sun visor mirror and wince at the tired half-moons under my eyes. "It's called going to sleep."

"How could you just *sleep* after that?" Her voice is incredulous.

I'm saved from answering when her parents emerge from the backyard. Mr. Tyler takes off his Indiana University cap to wave us off. Mrs. Tyler's makeup sweats off her face, but she still looks gorgeous and cheerful, which is more than I can say for myself after my restless night.

Blaire's twelve-year-old sister, Kiely, barely glances at us from the front porch swing, azure goddess braids bent low as her fingers move furiously over her phone screen. It's weird to think that just a year ago, she thought we were the coolest people she knew.

"For the good of us all, *go* before Dad invites you back to look at his new raised tomato beds," says Blaire. "It's kinda adorable how proud he is of the backyard oasis, but oh my god, I know way too much about compost-to-topsoil ratios at this point."

As I pull away from the curb, Catey cranes around in her seat, straining against the seatbelt. "Oh, come on, it's sweet."

Blaire groans. "If I hear another word about soil pH, stakes, and chicken wire trellises, I'll scream. I almost wish he'd go back to grilling me about my college apps."

Catey gets a teasing glint in her eye. "Hmm, so I guess you feel the same way when I talk about gardening too, huh?"

Catey's parents run a farm-and-equestrian center in the country, just twenty miles away, but she lives with her older sister in town to go to a better school district. You can take the girl out of the country, but you can't take the country out of the girl.

"Uh . . ." Blaire sounds sheepish. "No?"

Catey laughs. "You are a terrible girlfriend," she says, but she doesn't mean it. That's how she always talks to Blaire, like she's so happy that she can't *not* have a smile in her voice.

She's got the greenest thumb I know, and with the occasional help from her veterinarian sister and Blaire, she runs the Fork & Crumb—her outdoor weekend stall at the farmer's market—selling both sweet and savory pies.

Her dream is to start her own farm-to-table bistro right here in Luna Cove, and after three successful years of making a profit and proving her mettle with the stall, her parents are springing for an affordable indoor bistro space. It's a family business: they'll own it as an investment for Catey to one day take over, but Blaire's mom—who turned her IU campus gourmet pretzel cart into a franchise that's in every Midwestern mall—will manage the day-to-day.

Blaire isn't the green-thumbed domestic goddess her girlfriend is; when it comes to anything crafty, she's all thumbs. But when it comes to class presentations or anything to do with a spreadsheet, she's your girl. She plans to do dual-credit college business courses next year, and in the meantime her mom's teaching her about finance and accounting.

When Catey faces the front again, Blaire uses the gap under the headrest to push aside Catey's short, sun-streaked blonde hair and massage her neck. "But you love me anyway?"

Catey wiggles a bit to give her better access and stretches her pink Converse sneakers in front of her. "If you keep this up for the rest of the way, yes."

I'm not jealous of my best friends, but it's hard to look at them being this cute and not crave what they have with the kind of intensity normally reserved for my grade point average.

It's far from the first time I've yearned for the quiet intimacies they share, as second nature as breathing, but this time the wanting sticks. Nestles close. Warrens straight for my heart.

As we pull into the library's parking lot, sharp and clear as a bell, I think: I know I'm not for everyone, but I deserve to fall in love with someone who accepts me—all of me—as I am.

Parker was my third strike, just another guy who showed himself the door. Even the girls I'd sparked with couldn't see themselves with me, too wary of my wildfire. I don't want to dilute myself into someone who goes down easy, palatably. Someone who holds herself back so she doesn't outshine her partner.

I want to be with somebody who wouldn't even *want* me to.

Luna Cove's library is smack-dab in the middle of downtown's busy Main Street, a white gabled two-story Victorian that used to be the home of the city's first mayor. We're just one street away from the green murk of the White River and its elevated stone-paved Riverwalk winding along the bank.

The pedestrian-only quayside is dotted with large umbrella tables for fancy waterfront dining, while still being wide enough for foot traffic, mostly joggers and dog walkers. On a Saturday, it'll be totally packed.

We're just one street away from Holly Gogogi, too. Despite the warm day, a cold lick of trepidation slinks down my back as I get out of my car. Ian's probably working at the diner, but being in his radius feels like a jinx just *waiting* to happen.

The unwelcome thought pricks at me that if we'd stayed friends, I would have known what he got up to on the weekends. Maybe it would have been different if his little sister, Grace, hadn't died. Now comes a different kind of yearning. I don't linger in if-onlys and paths-not-taken as a general rule, but today . . . this sticks, too.

"Kavs!" Catey shouts, waving her hands above her head. "Get out of the way!"

I startle, realizing I'm dawdling in the middle of the parking lot. A woman glares at me behind the wheel of her SUV, and I mouth *Sorry* at her before catching up with my friends.

The three of us enter the library together, arctic blast of AC slapping us hello. Too late, I remember I left my denim jacket in the car. Or maybe there's another reason my skin tingles cold, goosebumps shivering over every inch of me.

A six-foot-one reason with a shock of jet-black hair and a dove-gray button-down.

Blaire shakes her head. "Girl, where was your head at?"

I swallow past the tumbleweeds in my throat. "Ian," I say hoarsely.

Blaire grins. "Lost in the magic of his kiss again, were you?"

"No." I give her an unimpressed look and point to the children's room, peeking out from behind a sturdy rainbow archway of books with gold-tooled leatherbound spines.

As if on cue, Ian Jun turns. Whatever he was saying to the pretty blonde girl with him trails off as his face slackens in surprise. The girl eyes me as she pulls books from her book cart and gets to work stacking the shelves.

What is he doing here?

Okay, it's a small town with just two libraries. This one is closer to Holly Gogogi and his family's home above. Realistically, his being here shouldn't be such a coincidence. And yet.

He starts to lift one hand, but doesn't quite wave, like he doesn't know what to do, either.

Annoying. He was pretty damn confident last night.

I march right past, heading straight for the holds shelf next to the self-checkout machines. As usual, the shelf with the Js is almost entirely mine, all yellow-tagged with the NEW YA stickers. Blaire grabs two books from the Ts before joining Catey to talk to my favorite librarian, Mrs. Carnegie, about the book drive.

I slide three books into the crook of my left arm before remembering my Out of Print book tote, just like my jacket, was left behind. By book five, I'm seriously regretting the oversight. By book nine, my muscles are straining.

Kavya, you've lifted way more books than this for Instagram pictures. This is nothing.

The air shifts behind me. "Need one of these?"

Ian's hand stretches out, holding the straps of a plain black tote. It's not even as cute as mine, but it would still help lug my haul.

I half turn, not wanting to give him the satisfaction. "No thanks. I'm good."

He doesn't take the hint, following me to the self-checkout. I set my load down and purposely don't look at him as I dig my library card out of my purse.

Ian keeps to the other side of the table, but before I can stop him, he snatches the first book from the top of my pile right as I'm about to scan it. "So *you're* the one," he says.

"Hey!" I whisper-hiss, mindful of our surroundings. I make a grab for the book, but he dodges. And contrary to popular belief, I don't go leaping over every table I see. "*The One?*"

Erm. That's . . . deeply unlikely. I mean, it was just one kiss. I already regret asking.

His pale-pink lips are even rosier than they were last night, like he just applied a fresh slick of ChapStick. Or maybe it was for someone else.

My gaze darts to the pretty blonde, who's still shelving. She's around our age.

"The one who's been checking out all the new young adult books the second we get them in," Ian continues, handing the book back to me. "I put a hold on them when I see new acquisitions in our system, but I'm always second in line."

Oh. That "one."

"Since I make the requests for the library to buy them, I *should* be the first to read them. And what do you mean 'we get them in' and 'our system'? It's not like you—"

My eyes catch on the blue lanyard around his neck, then trail down to the ID holder.

LUNA COVE PUBLIC LIBRARY. VOLUNTEER. IAN JUN.

"You work here," I realize out loud.

It is incredibly unfair he gets to ambush me in my refuge, of all places.

"What, did you think I was following you or something?" His dimple winks at me.

"It wouldn't be the first time," I bite out. Quickly, I scan each of my holds. I've got to admit, it feels nice to beat him at something without trying. Even better to have him acknowledge it. It's the high I keep chasing.

"I guess you know the summer reading contest starts today," Ian says conversationally.

"Does it?" I tilt my head, feigning ignorance.

He rolls his eyes. "I saw you comment a heart-eyes emoji on LCPL's Instagram post."

Exasperated, I stab my finger at the touch screen to print out the due dates. "Then why did you ask?"

"Why did you lie?" he counters.

Catey and Blaire are both officially going on my grudge list for leaving me on my own.

They're still chatting with the librarian, so I can beeline straight there without Ian thinking I'm dodging him because I can't keep up with his verbal repartee or, worse, because I feel awkward about our kiss last night.

"Don't you need to get back to work instead of pestering tax-paying library patrons?" I stuff the receipt in my purse before grappling with my towering stack.

He sighs and holds the tote out again. "Seriously. Take it. These are brand-new books, and the last thing I need is for you to fall."

I raise my eyebrows.

"Don't want anything precious getting hurt, right?" He waves the tote at me.

"Your concern for the books is truly admirable," I say dryly, but I accept it and start piling my books inside. "Thanks. I thought the library wasn't providing bags for people after they started that eco-initiative last year."

"Um, yeah, we have some leftovers in the office."

"Oh. Okay. Cool." I heft the heavy tote to my shoulder. "Well, thanks again."

"No problem." He shoves his hands deep into his chino shorts' pockets.

I start to back up, hand half raised to wave, but change my mind last minute. I'm not going to do anything to undermine my smooth getaway.

I get to the front desk in time to catch the end of Mrs. Carnegie's sentence: ". . . I'm so glad that these books are getting to the organizations that need them."

Catey flushes with pride. Even though it was sort of all our idea to do a book drive, she's the one who launches all our projects into action. Plus, she makes all the snacks and color codes everything with her million-and-one gel pens.

Mrs. Carnegie beams at me when I sidle up to the desk. "Kavya! First day of our summer reading program," she enthuses. "I had a feeling you'd show up."

I return her grin with a broad one of my own. She's been at LCPL forever, or at least since I was a little kid, and she's one of the few adults in my life who doesn't think I'm a nuisance.

She also manages the library's social media. Whenever I Bookstagram library books, she always reposts it. At this point, about a third of their feed is my content, which has been great in building up both our follower counts, but since my art style is distinctive, I'm always worried someone from Luna

Cove will figure out who I am. It's not like it's a secret, exactly, but it's always bizarre when your online life collides with your real life.

She's hired me the last two years to design bookmarks for the library, which only paid enough to buy a couple of new releases at my local indie, but I loved that something I made was getting slipped into books all over town.

"I can't wait to get this year's bookmarks printed and sitting pretty right up here with the ones from last year," says Mrs. Carnegie, gesturing to the dwindling handful left on her desk.

"I'll email the design to you soon," I promise. "Finals week kicked my butt."

Mrs. Carnegie rummages through the shelves below her desk and emerges with a stack of white cards, counts out five for each of us, then points to the clear glass fishbowl near the edge of her desk. "Just stick 'em in there when you're done, same as last year. Three young adult or middle grade books per slip."

Middle grade books, so full of wonder and whimsy, are quick reads that'll pull me into first place. It's a change from last year, when middle grade only counted for the children's program.

"Guess what else is new this year?" She leans in conspiratorially. "One of our teen volunteers *finally* convinced them to okay graphic novels. Oh, there he is!" she says, smiling at a spot somewhere beyond my head.

My friends turn, but I already know who it is. I can hear

the squeak of his white sneakers, so clean that they have to be new, against the polished wood floor. I angle toward him anyway, so no one thinks I'm rude.

"Hey, Ian," says Catey. I envy that she doesn't sound flustered. "I didn't know you volunteered here. You wanna lend a hand sometime to help us box up the"—I dig my elbow into her side—"*Oomph.*"

"I'd love to help. It's a great cause," he replies, giving her a genuine smile. Not one of the smirky ones he always levels at me. "I'm taking off, but I wanted to grab a few of these, first."

I suck in both sides of my cheek meat. Not only had Ian squeaked by to victory as president of French Club and Film Society, he'd also logged more books than I did in last year's summer reading program and took home the grand prize: ten coveted advanced reader copies of forthcoming YA books. Catnip for a Bookstagrammer. And it's the same prize this year.

This means war. Or at least turning pages really, really quickly.

I *have* to win the grand prize this year. No way is he beating me again.

Mrs. Carnegie is oblivious to my plight. "Sure thing, Ian. How many do you want?"

"Ten's good to start," he blithely responds.

My mind comes to a screeching stop. *Ten???*

I stare at the five cards in my hand.

"Someone's confident," says Blaire, raising one perfectly arched eyebrow.

"Gotta keep up with Kavya somehow," he says, including

me in his smile like we're friends. "Last year's tally was super close. She really keeps me on my toes."

And then, as if on cue, he aims Smile #8 at us, the one that he only uses to sweep people *off* their feet. My right eyelid twitches. Now he's got all three of them smiling at his false humility and graciousness in talking me up. Ugh.

I tap my foot in agitation until we say our goodbyes, but even then, I'm not off the hook. Ian falls easily into step beside us, right next to me, close enough for our arms to brush.

I'm positive he did it on purpose.

"Nice shirt, by the way," he says.

I glance down at the HAVING FUN ISN'T HARD WHEN YOU'VE GOT A LIBRARY CARD *Arthur* meme shirt tucked into my high-waisted distressed-fringe shorts. "Oh. Um. Thanks."

The automatic doors glide apart and all of us step out into the sunshine and wet blanket of humidity. Ian slips on his Ray-Ban aviators, pushing them up his nose with a long, elegant finger. I, on the other hand, squint uglily into the sun like someone who's never seen daylight before.

There's a red Subaru pulled up to the front, blocking the book and DVD drop-offs. The blonde girl from the children's section is swinging into the front passenger seat when she pauses to call out, "Bye, Ian!"

He raises his hand while heading for the nearby bike rack. "See ya, Kori!"

I shoot him a suspicious glance as he pries the lock off his bike.

Kori with a K? He seems pretty friendly with her. They've

probably bonded after all their shifts together. She does look familiar, like someone who could have been at Claudia's party last night. And for whatever reason, he hasn't told her how he feels yet.

A slow smile spreads over my face. Maybe Ian does know my secret, but now I know one of his, too.

8.
How Do You Feel about a Seashell Bra?

MY PHONE BEEPS the second the three of us pile back into my car.

"It's Ian saying he misses you already," Blaire cackles.

Catey reaches back to flick Blaire's knee. "We should swing by South Asia Mart and see if Val's free to get boba with us," she says over her girlfriend's surprised yelp.

I buckle up and reach for my phone. "Yeah, I'll ask her. Lemme just check this first."

My phone screen lights up with the new message from Poppy's daughter Amie:

KAVYA, SHE JUST QUIT. GET HERE NOW.

My heart leaps into my throat. There's no shortage of jobs for teenagers in Luna Cove: the new FroYo place has HELP

WANTED signs in the windows, and Luna Caverns, which gained notoriety during Prohibition as a moonshine den, loves young tour guides to keep it hip.

But the best job of all, which I already have, is working as a party princess at Poppy's Party Playhouse. Two years ago, I had walked in confident for my Belle audition, but Poppy cast me as Jasmine and later Snow White.

But this year, the girl who always played Beauty—legally, we couldn't call her Belle because of the Disney copyright— must have just given notice.

I turn my screen to show both my friends. I can't hold back my smile. "Girls . . . it's time."

"Step on it," Blaire commands. There's no time for boba.

The Playhouse is painted bubblegum pink with the words POPPY'S PARTY PLAYHOUSE hand-lettered in gold paint across the frosted windows. Fake pink towers are constructed above the entrance, with a mechanical Rapunzel inside, set to appear in the window every hour, on the hour. Whimsical falls short. White, purple, and magenta petunias spill over the window boxes, almost drooping onto the ever-growing family of gnomes below.

Next door, the bakery is winding down as the last of the lunch crowd peels away from the parking lot. I can smell the bread, not gross and yeasty, but fragrant with rosemary and molasses, accompanied by the tiniest cloying sweetness of Yelp-famous blueberry scones.

"First of all, Kavya," says Catey the minute I park. She tilts up her chin, giving me her steeliest look. "You've got this."

She's absolutely confident. There's no doubt at all that I will achieve everything I want. This is the power of a best friend.

"I've got this," I repeat like a mantra.

"And be direct," adds Blaire, poking her head up front. "Make sure she knows how important it is for you to play Belle."

"Beauty," I remind her.

She waves a hand. "Girl, there's no one better to play a beautiful bookworm." She waits a moment, daring me to say anything. "And I've seen the guys you've dated. Clearly you don't mind beasts—"

Catey gasps, cutting her off. "B! That is so rude!"

My phone beeps. It's Amie again, telling me to hurry up.

As if she senses that I'm about to throw open the door, Blaire leans forward and grabs my shoulder. "Kavya, wait." She holds out her pointer finger, the black-and-silver constellations nails still perfect. "Moon girls on three."

I hope we never get old enough to be embarrassed by this tradition. Catey and I follow. I start off the count, and the others join in, exuberantly shouting, "Three!" as we pull our fingers away.

Once inside, I'm greeted by a blast of AC and CHANEL N°5.

Poppy swoops toward me with two exuberant air kisses. "Kavya!" She rattles off a stream of French that I should probably understand after taking three years of it and clasps my hands. "Amie told me you were coming."

Amie, a part-time Tinker Bell—or Fairy Princess—and

full-time receptionist and social media manager for her mother's business, winks at me from behind her desk and cloud of dark-brown curls before diving back into a pack of Welch's Fruit Snacks.

Poppy herds me to her office, which is like the woman herself. Effusive, warm, and unlike the rest of the princess-y pastel colors of the store, painted as vivid a red as a poppy flower. One of the walls is lined with pictures of the cast, and across the room, a bookshelf houses leather-bound copies of fairy tales and folklore. She has a couple of rare first editions that she let me borrow last year.

I take the seat opposite Poppy's desk.

"Soda? Water?" She pulls them out of the mini fridge and slides them both across to me.

I reach for the water, and she pops the can of grape soda back in. "I know Rosie quit, and I was wondering—I was hoping—"

"You want Belle," Poppy finishes, smiling crookedly. "Honey, everyone wants Belle."

I fidget with the water, twisting the cap off and on. "I've been Snow White for two years, and I'd really like to play another role. Give me a chance to audition for you."

"Kavya, it's not a matter of auditioning. I promise you." She taps her long, manicured nails against the desk, then sighs. "You're so good as our Snow White. The little girls love you. And don't forget you knocked it out of the park as the Desert Princess."

I'd gotten her to change that last year. Most parents

wouldn't care or even be aware, but despite the controversy about Aladdin's origin, other than the Taj Mahal–looking palace, what else about the movie implies it was set in India? It's crappy how some movie makers think of Asia as a monolith.

Poppy has a huge, diverse troupe, and she tries her best to cast the right ethnicities and hire people of color for traditionally white roles, something that her competitors still don't do. They're convinced she's losing money, but the Playhouse is fully booked every week while their businesses still have to rely on the Luna Cove yellow pages to drum up new business.

"So about Belle . . ." I purse my lips, shooting her a hopeful smile.

"Hon, Belle is such a popular character. She's in demand year-round, even on weekdays. I don't want a part-timer for this. I'd like someone who's going to stick around for a while. High school kids go to college or get 'real world' jobs." Poppy sighs. "You're, what, going to be a senior? SATs coming up? Applying to colleges soon?"

I nod, feeling a tight knot in my stomach as I sense where all of this is leading.

"Well, there you go. And you told me on day one that your parents would only let you work weekends during the school year. Rosie was full-time. There were some weeks she had a party every night," Poppy stresses. "Can you put in those kinds of hours?"

No, I can't. Though I'd gotten my parents to relent and allow me to work on weekends, there is no way they'll budge if I ask them for this.

"Kavs? You okay?" Poppy peers at me, worry etched into the fine lines of her eyes.

What she's saying makes sense. I don't blame her for doing what's best for the Playhouse. But my shoulders still slump, all hope sapping away. Not that it matters, but Rosie never even liked to read. She didn't like her job and she didn't like kids, and I *know* that I can do it so much better than she can.

Once, I'd caught her smoking outside in the parking lot. She'd ground her cigarette beneath her heel and flipped her middle finger toward the Playhouse, saying the movie was fucked up because Belle fell in love with her captor.

She was right. But I can still hold a grudge, even if my fave is problematic.

"Listen," says Poppy. "I know this isn't what you had in mind, but the reason I asked you back here was to offer you another role in addition to Snow White. You filled in for a no-show Mermaid Princess last year. How do you feel about doing it again?"

The idea of playing a princess who gave up her voice doesn't exactly appeal.

Poppy consults her planner. "We've seen an upswing in requests for her and her prince. Not enough to hire someone full time, but my current mermaid doubles up on several other roles, so she's totally swamped. I really need to fill the part ASAP, and you'd be a great fit."

Before I can get a word in, she rushes on, sounding more and more enamored with the idea. "And when the school year starts, you can decide if you want to keep playing both. I know it's not what you want, but this could be the perfect change of pace for you."

We have different definitions of perfect. But I do love working here, and Poppy's one of the few adults who thinks the world of me, even to the extent of training the other teen newbies. With that kind of faith in me, I refuse to throw it back in her face.

"And you look great in a red wig," she adds.

I give her a small smile. "You can stop selling me on the idea. I'm . . . I'm in."

She beams. "How do you feel about a seashell bra? Promise it's not revealing!"

It's no different than wearing a bikini. "I'm fine with it."

Her expression brightens. "Oh, and the best part, the guy I just hired to play your Shipwrecked Prince goes to your school."

I blink. There aren't a lot of guys who would find this place cool, not when they could lifeguard or talk about moonshine for their paycheck. "Seriously?"

She nods emphatically, pointing to the wall where my picture hangs between Amie's and Samer's. "He said the two of you were friends. And I thought, well, it's kismet."

I lean forward, curious. I get the feeling she's loving the slow reveal. "Who is he?"

Poppy pulls open her desk drawer and fishes around. With a soft exclamation, she pulls out a folder and opens it. "Here we go." She removes the paper clip attaching the headshot from the paperwork and flutters the boy's photo in front of my face. "Know him?"

I suck in a breath. Hell yes, I do.

I would know him upside down. I would know him two inches away.

This can't be happening. I'm going to star in a seashell bra in front of him?

I *wish* I hadn't already said yes.

When my eyes start to sting, I remember to blink. "Poppy . . ."

"I swear, this kid is Prince Eric—oops, *Shipwrecked Prince*, come to life," she trills, clapping her hands. "You two will look adorable together."

Adorable is *so* not the word I would use.

The only way this could be worse is if it were Parker's headshot in front of me.

"And he's perfect for the part," she continues, missing the shell-shocked look I'm sure I must be wearing. "You and Ian Jun are going to have so much fun together."

Ha. Sure. *Fun.*

If we don't drive each other bananas first.

9.
My Best Enemy

MY HALF-FINISHED HONEYDEW milk tea condenses and drips on the mango-wood desk in my bedroom. Val's dad didn't let her take off early, and her pleading-face emoji with puppy dog eyes on my Instagram post sits heavy in my gut.

Saturdays are usually when I try to get all my homework done. Today, the only thing on my to-do list is the Pocket Full of Sunshine activity for AP English. The assignment feels a little young for juniors, but it's fun—creatively decorate a brown paper bag for our classmates to drop in little notes of affirmation on the last day of school.

Late afternoon sun spears through my open second-story window, partially obscured by the maple tree that blocks most of my view of the Kapoors across the cul-de-sac. I stare at the hot-pink Post-it stuck on the edge of my Mac screen that reads: *Normalize Taking Breaks.*

I wrote that a couple of years ago, at the start of freshman year. The Post-it was green, then, and the fabric on my chair hadn't yet begun to tear from too many hours sitting with my feet tucked under me. Just the burn of my gooseneck lamp, the scrunch of my back wound tight as a new Slinky, and whatever cherry-flavored candy was fueling my self-appointed impending deadline.

Whenever I need the reminder, I take the note down and rewrite it. Different Post-it color, different marker thickness, different font. Sometimes fancy calligraphy, but usually small, rounded cursive or all-caps sharp slashes intended to make me take the affirmation more seriously.

God, I already want a break, even though I've done literally nothing. I sigh and reach for one of my many mugs of markers, running my thumb over the caps. The familiar gesture does little to ground me, so I grab my phone next.

My brain is scrambled eggs I message to the moon girls' group chat along with a picture of my sad-looking bag. Was going to draw Belle and the Beast waltzing but . . . Is it melodramatic if I don't know who I am anymore?

Catey's reply is immediate: Yes. You are more than books and brown hair.

Blaire follows up with a red heart and a strong-bicep emoji.

Rationally, I know that an animated Disney character doesn't define me. But the irrational part feels the loss so keenly that my eyes water.

Belle *is* me. I *am* Belle.

While I love Rapunzel and Elsa and Moana, growing up,

Belle spoke to me in a way no other character had. She had hobbies—*actual* hobbies—in the Disney animated film, and not because someone locked her in a tower and forced her to read, paint, and bake to entertain herself in her solitude. Belle was a *creator.*

I had no doubt in my third-grade mind that we would both have gotten in trouble for reading in class. She spoke her mind and called out Gaston and the Beast when they needed it. Because of her, I felt like it was okay to want *more,* a little less like the only one out of tune when everyone else sang a jazzy opening number about my besharamness.

"Kavya, were you raised in a barn? Put a coaster down."

I swivel around in my chair to see my sister leaning against the doorjamb. Simran *tsks* and gestures at my boba, water pooled around the base. I shuffle around the clutter of art supplies, succulents in pretty ceramic pots, and loose charging cords to unearth the pressed-flower resin coaster I bought from Etsy.

It was hidden beneath my iPad Pro I use for digital illustration. If I tap the screen, it'll light up with my latest project: this year's bookmark design for the library.

I place the plastic cup on top of the coaster and raise an eyebrow at Simran. *Happy?*

She wanders into my room with an auctioneer's eye, skimming and cataloging everything that's different from previous years. My room used to be princess-y glam, pink walls and bedding, black tufted headboard and faux sheepskin rug, and a three-tiered crystal chandelier from Pottery Barn that was so expensive Dad made me swear I would never get bored of it.

The chandelier is still here, but now it pops against a smoky black ceiling. The walls are the shade of soft sand, but the wall perpendicular to the window is smattered with colorful art prints from my favorite artists in thin black frames, vintage Disney movie posters, and clipped Polaroids of me and the moon girls strung together in a rainbow arc. Gone is the twin bed, replaced with a full that's artfully undone with muted rose-colored sheets, and ruffled duvets layered in varying shades of almond and gray.

In addition to the two IKEA Billy bookcases, a tall stack of books is shoved into the corner by the closet, preventing one of the accordion doors from opening fully. Summer dresses ripped from hangers now lie discarded on the floral-sequined purple Jaipur pouf, and this morning's makeup and jewelry is scattered all over my dresser.

Simran's so busy looking around that she doesn't see me study her in return.

I bristle at what can only be criticism in her eyes. "Did you *want* something?"

Her lips thin. "I was going to ask you if you were okay. When the girls were here earlier, you all seemed pretty, uh, wound up." Her eyes flick to my boba. "And you didn't get your usual Almond Roca. What's up?"

No, I'd wanted something sweeter to make up for the chalky taste in my mouth after leaving Poppy's. The honeydew is sickening in its sweetness, but I grab it and take an extra-long slurp to make my point—she doesn't know me as well as she thinks she does. "I just wanted a change. This flavor was a *great* choice. Ten out of ten recommend, Simmy."

Simran lifts an eyebrow. "So what was all the ruckus about?"

Ruckus. That feels like the word you'd use for loud, hyper children. I frown, but tell her.

Not about the kiss or the library reading program—things I'm sure she'd only make fun of me for—but about working with Ian this summer as a couple who's supposed to be so in love that one gave up their voice and the other killed a sea witch.

Simran's lips tremble, then she stops trying to hold back and lets the laugh ring out. I shrink, embarrassed for telling her. Annoyed I thought she'd actually sympathize and offer some kind of sisterly advice. I can't believe I fell for this again. Her interest is never genuine.

Of course she finds it hilarious that I'm going to be working fin to fin with Ian, of all people. With her complete and total lack of compassion at my misfortunes, sometimes it feels like she's my warty, wicked stepsister.

But I've seen our birth certificates. We share DNA, even if we don't share anything else.

"If you're going to laugh, get out of my room, Sim," I say, taking another aggressive slurp of too-sweet boba before uncapping one of my markers. The black Sharpie swirls and careens across the brown paper bag, the nib fresh and inky and pungent.

She wrinkles her nose at the chemical smell. "Come on. It's a *little* funny . . ."

I cap the marker and stare, waiting for her to apologize, but I should have known better. "Don't you have a boyfriend to bother?" I ask, the words tart and meant to hurt.

I don't even get the reaction of a glower. Simran's face is impassive as she walks out. With a twist in my stomach, I return to the scallop-edged bookcase I've drawn. A second later, Mom makes a sound of surprise from the hallway, and I figure the two almost collided. There's a low rumble of voices before Mom enters, arms laden with a stack of fresh laundry.

"Dad's making bhel," she says, placing the clothes at the foot of my bed.

I brighten at the mention of my favorite food. "Thanks, Mom."

She casts her kohl-rimmed eyes over the disarrayed dresses, the copious towers of books pushed against the wall, and the clothing tossed on the embroidered Jaipur pouf stool.

Then she glances out the window, attention diverted from my mess.

"Who are we spying on?" I ask, wheeling my chair closer.

She shushes me, even though there is no possible way anyone out there could hear us. "Khushi Kapoor just drove a Mercedes into her driveway."

I scoot back. They upgrade every two years. "So nothing new, basically."

Mom clicks her tongue. "Khushi didn't take it inside the garage. That means she wants everyone to see it. Why else leave a brand-new car on the driveway?"

You wouldn't even know that Dad and Mr. Kapoor graduated university together. The same framed picture of them is in both our houses. They have big dorky grins, arms slung around their pregnant wives. Our moms are wearing our dads' tasseled graduation caps and posing like they're best friends. It's hard to imagine they'd ever been that close. In some ways, Mom and Khushi auntie's lost friendship reminds me of me and Ian.

Mom sighs, then retreats from the window, but she doesn't leave. She hovers, uncertainly, and I know something awkward is about to happen from the way she's pinching the trumpet sleeve of her silky blouse.

"Kavya, my maushi said you don't like or comment on her pictures on Instagram. She's still waiting for you to follow her back."

And there it is. Mom's maternal aunt is a pro at getting people into trouble with her innocent confusion about why X person hasn't? done Y thing yet. The problem with Instagram's helpful People You May Know is that it hinges on the expectation that I want to know them back.

Frustration makes my voice gravelly and loud. "I was already guilted into getting WhatsApp," I say. "I only follow my friends and other cool creators on Instagram. Besides, I *have* commented on her pictures a few times. I can't keep up with everything everyone posts. Her expectations are unfair."

Mom's eyebrow twitches, but it's too late and I may as well see the rest of this through.

"I can't believe none of them stopped to consider whether a teenager really wants her entire extended family to know what she's up to." I exhale, then say, "I'm entitled to privacy."

My teeth hurt from clenching my jaw and I relax the muscles, sensation springing back with a vengeance. It feels like my besharam biting back. Reminding me it's there.

"Kavya." Mom's pretty face turns to gargoyle stone. "They're family."

I don't need the reminder, or the lecture I'm sure to get if I keep this up, but her answer isn't good enough. Maybe she knows it, too, because she sighs and sits down, one elbow digging into my pile of laundry so it doesn't tip over.

Ignoring or denying a friend request is only one of the many, many things on the Can't Do list of commandments for good Indian children, apparently.

It's not like I don't know what the aunties already whisper about us, the first- and second-generation Americans. Stuck up. Coconuts. Acting white. ABCD: American-Born Confused Desi. It's a ridiculous derogatory catchphrase when there's *nothing* about me that I'm confused about.

Catey had once suggested making a second, fake Instagram account, but it's the principle of the thing—I shouldn't have to.

I shift on my chair, going in half circles back and forth until Mom's eyes prickle over my skin. She's on my side, but I wish she were more like me—besharam enough to draw boundaries.

"So I never get any privacy, then?" I ask, resigned.

Mom gets up and puts an arm around me, bringing with her the scent of rose perfume and sandalwood incense. She squeezes my shoulder and says, "I respect your privacy. Don't forget to put those clothes away, little monster."

She pecks me on the forehead and leaves the room with a reminder to come down in a couple of minutes for bhel, leaving the door open despite my shout for her to close it.

I heave myself off my chair and hang my summer dresses back in the closet before tackling the fresh stack of folded laundry.

My stomach releases an involuntarily rumble. All I want right now is to eat my stress away with a bowl of Dad's bhel. I love drizzling mine with extra cilantro-mint chutney and lemon juice, making it super tart, but Simran eats hers dry as a trail mix, with as many puris as possible. My parents, on the other hand, both have a sweet tooth and dump the leftover tamarind sauce to make the snack sopping wet.

If I beat my sister down there, I could snag most of the deep-fried, savory, round puris for myself. I'm pretty sure she picked them all out of the Bombay bhel mix package last time.

Ping! I grab my phone, assuming it's one of the moon girls.

An unknown number.

I can preview part of the first sentence, and it's enough to get my right eyelid twitching.

It's not from my best friends, so it can only be one person— my best enemy.

Lookin' good, Sushi. Excited to have me all to yourself this summer? A second later the taunt is followed by a screencap from *The Little Mermaid.* Ian's photoshopped our yearbook photos over Ariel's and Eric's faces. With our dark hair and eyes, we do look freakishly like an attractive power couple, but I'm not telling him that.

My fingers fly over the screen. Sushi? Really? You can do better than that.

His response is a GIF of a red-haired mermaid wriggling and squalling on a chopping board while a knife descends.

I roll my eyes. Wow. So mature.

Ian sends back so many laughing cat emojis I actually feel dizzy. What is he *doing*? Emojis are for besties and banter—*not* the bane of your life, your enemy with exactly zero benefits. Then, because I guess he figures I'm taking too long to respond, he adds, Admit it, Kavya Joshi, it's not summer without me.

The arrogance. Without your enormous ego around there'd actually be more oxygen for the rest of us.

Next time I see you, I'll hold my breath.

You can't hold your breath for that long, loser. I scroll for the huge tongue-sticking-out emoji before it occurs to me that it could be perceived as sexy instead of snarky.

Too late, it's already sent.

I've had a lot of practice.
You moon girls excel at taking my breath away.

Whoa! Smooth!
How long did you have that one up your sleeve?

He sends back a dozen laugh-crying cat emojis. He's incorrigible.

Fingers poised over the keys, I wait for him to say something else. Strangely enough, I'm actually having fun. Eager to see what he'll say next. But with each second that ticks by without an ellipsis bubble, the anticipation dims from one hundred watts to sixty, and then fizzles out completely.

Pretty freaking anticlimactic.

"Kavya!" Dad hollers, sounding close, like he's standing at the foot of the stairs. "Snack time! Are you joining us?"

"Yeah, I'm coming!" After one final look, I toss my phone on the bed with a scoff.

I'm not mad that Ian left me hanging. I'm just mad he had the last word.

Obviously.

10.
What's Another Contest Between Rivals?

"DON'T FORGET TO take your bags with you on your way out!" our AP English teacher calls over the peal of the bell.

It's finally Wednesday, the last day of school, and after four days of toil on this silly little assignment, I'm more excited about my design than the notes inside.

I was working on it at the kitchen table while Mom was making our favorite family dinner: butter chicken, the sauce simmered for hours; homemade naans scorched just right; jeera rice fragrant with cloves, cumin, and green chilies; and a smooth and creamy vegetable korma.

When we all dug in that night while watching a movie together, Simran sat as far away from me as possible. She barely talked to me at all, not even when she recognized the paper bag activity as one she'd done a few years before with the same teacher.

By the time the end-of-class bell's shrill ring tapers off, I'm one of the first people at the door. We have big plans for tonight. Blaire's dad just built a pizza oven in their backyard, and Blaire invited us over for the first inaugural pizza party and a sleepover.

Between now and then, all we have to do is clear out our lockers.

Val's trying to dig through her notes while walking and doesn't see me waiting at the door, running into me with a muffled *"Ooof!"*

I stumble a half step sideways, jostling the person next to me. "Sorry."

"All good."

I almost jump at Ian's voice so close to my ear, so I gesture at the door. "Uh, you go first."

He gives me an amused smile. "So chivalrous."

"Well, I did read the entire *Fairy-tale Handbook*," I say, smug and superior in my knowledge of our orientation manual.

His smile doesn't drop. "I'm sure I can catch up."

Of course he can. Everything comes easy for Ian Jun. Especially things that are supposed to be mine. I grit my teeth behind my smile so he doesn't see it falter.

"You know, it was so funny how you got a job at the same place where I happen to work," I say as we pass through the door. He waits for me to precede him, and short of a back-and-forth volley of insistence, I let him win this round.

Ugh. How dare he be so civil.

"Samer works there, too," he points out once we're in the crowded hallway.

"Don't you already have a job?" I scowl at him askance, but he doesn't see it. "Don't your parents need you at Holly Gogogi?"

A flash of *something* crosses his face, but he's saved by Val grabbing my arm.

"Hey, did you look at your notes yet?" she asks.

"What?" Distracted, I glance down at the bunch of notes she's gripped tight in her fist. In the meantime, Ian hangs back to wait for Samer and Rio. "No, why?"

"It's crap." Val stuffs the notes back into her bag, prettily designed with three models on a runway, shimmery gold and silver Sharpie spotlights shining on each one.

Even though her figures don't have discernible features, it's not their faces that are important. Not when Val can sketch ball gowns that look like a frothy Teuta Matoshi creation.

"Crap why?" I ask as I reach my locker.

Val's just at the other end, M for Mehra, but she waits with me as I twirl in my locker combination. "I only got two notes that weren't totally generic, and one's from you. Pretty much everyone just wrote H.A.G.S. I can't believe the time I put into writing thoughtful notes and doodles to those ingrates."

"Have a great summer? Really?" My locker opens with a clang of metal. "Fuck them."

"I hope—" Val darts a look to Claudia, who's obliviously clearing out her locker. Still, Val lowers her voice. "I don't rec-ognize his handwriting, but I hope the other note is from"— and lower still—"*Rio.*"

I send her a hopeful smile. "Maybe it is."

"Check yours," urges Val.

"Okay." I reach into my bag and come up with three, all on lined notepaper, ripped at jagged angles like the writers waited until the last minute.

As I read the words, my heart hammers and my breath hitches. None are as short as H.A.G.S., but I pretend that they are and let them drop back into the bag and out of sight. "Pocket Full of Sunshine," my ass. At least I'm a quick thinker.

"Ugh, you're right." I make a face. " 'Had a great time with you in class' and a few 'H.A.G.S.' Why did they even bother, you know?"

Val sighs. "I better get a move on. I don't want to lose even one minute at Blaire's."

She doesn't need to elaborate—we both know it's because she hates having to leave early. Her parents are willing to pick her up at ten, but they never let her spend the night at anyone else's house.

When she moves off to her own locker, I start unscrewing the adjustable hot-pink locker shelf and remove all the moon girl Polaroids wallpapering the metal. With any luck I'll be out of here before Ian shows up.

While I strip all evidence of myself from the locker, I can barely focus. All I can think about are the words on the notes I didn't share with Val:

You'd be cuter without that big mouth LOL

FREE LIFE LESSON! YOU DON'T ALWAYS HAVE TO BE THE SMARTEST PERSON IN THE ROOM!

Argue less, smile more ☺

It's obvious that everyone in class thinks I'm besharam, too, even though they don't know the Hindi catchall word. For a second, my eyes smart, but I shove my hurt aside.

I carefully tuck my paper bag into my backpack so it won't get crumpled. At least something good came out of this assignment.

I'd illustrated a gorgeous bookshelf jam-packed with books of all different sizes and colors: some face out, some tilted at an angle, but most heaped messily one on top of the other. I'd used a fine-line marker to write out the titles of all my favorite books on the spines and thrown in a calico cat snoozing on a shelf next to a vase of lucky bamboo.

If I focus on what I'm proud of, I won't have to think about what hurts me.

"Another big party tonight?" I ask Claudia as I bend to zip up my backpack.

"Yeah, right. The neighbors told my parents the party got out of hand. I'm lucky I'm not grounded." She slams her locker shut. "Hey, guys."

The moment I turn around, Rio throws his arm around me. He's not alone; Catey, Blaire, Ian, and Samer are with him. Ian gives me an I-have-no-idea shrug before putting in his locker combination. From a distance, I can see Val hurrying over to join us.

"What's going on?" I ask my friends. "I thought we were meeting up outside?"

Catey and Samer look vaguely guilty, but Blaire's bouncing on the balls of her feet like she's dying to spill a secret. There's an undercurrent that I can't quite put my finger on, and my stomach flutters at the idea that there's something I don't know that the others obviously do.

"Get any interesting notes?" Ian asks, giving his bag an experimental shake. His bag is covered in blue stars and his name big and blocky in all caps.

"Sure. You know me, people always have nice things to say," I reply coolly.

His eyes light up. "Did you see mi—"

"What's going on?" Val interrupts, slightly out of breath. Ian slumps into silence. Val stares at me and Rio standing together, then sets her jaw like it's somehow *my* fault.

I wiggle out from under his arm. "That's literally what I just asked." I give Rio my best no-nonsense face. "And I'm still waiting, FYI."

"I thought we said we weren't going to go through with it," says Claudia. It's her turn to shut her locker, and the bang reverberates down the emptying hallway.

"Go through with what?" Ian slings his backpack over his shoulder, the move shifting his gray tee just enough to catch a glimpse of a well-defined abdomen.

Dear god. I skirt my eyes away before anyone catches me ogling.

"I don't know if you two have noticed," says Blaire, pointing to me and Ian. "But you've been at each other's throats all year." She eyes me with a silent *Mostly you, Kavs.*

"And so it occurred to us," says Rio, putting an exaggerated emphasis on *us*, "that there's only one way to put you two to bed."

"*What?*" I yelp, loud enough that a teacher actually pokes her head out the door.

Rio waves a hand. "I misspoke. What I meant is we can put *this rivalry* to bed for good with one more competition." He smiles. "After all, what's another contest between rivals?"

Claudia groans. "You do realize this will only make them both more insufferable—sorry, Kavya—right? I want it on the record that I said this wasn't a good idea."

"The six of us," says Blaire, "will pick three challenges for you two to compete over. Best of three is the undisputed winner, and then you two will *finally* know who is number one."

"And with all this extra time together, *we'll* finally know what's really between y—" Samer begins, but Catey officiously clears her throat and says, "But it's completely your choice."

Ian's been silent during this exchange, but I recognize the smile drifting across his stoic features. I'm not one to let a challenge go, but it's clear that our friends' competition appeals to him, too.

No doubt he's got his eye on stealing something else away from me, I think sourly.

The only things Ian hasn't managed to wrest away from my grasping fingers are Art Club and tennis—the former because the supervising teacher refused to go through the hassle of voting (read: she didn't want me to become more insufferable with the power), and the latter only because the sport isn't co-ed, so we can each reign without fear of the other snatching our crown.

One of Ian's black eyebrows arches like a taunt. "How about it, Joshi?"

Like I even need to think about it.

I stick my hand in front of his chest. "Deal."

"Kavs, don't you want to think about it?" Val, ever cautious, worries her lower lip. "Is this really how you want to spend your summer?"

Doesn't she see that this also gets *her* time with Rio this summer? I flick my eyes to him, trying to silently communicate this to her, but she just looks bewildered.

Ian thrusts his hand out lightning quick, as though he's afraid I'll give in to Val's doubts. "You're volunteering to spend time with me *and* giving me bragging rights when I beat you?" He gives me a lopsided grin, flashing the deep indent of his dimple. "If you say so."

I give him a switchblade smile as my fingertips graze his palm. "May the best rival win."

Ian's answering grin speaks volumes: I've said something to tickle him somehow. His fingers slide against mine. It's more intimate than the time we were kids and I was afraid to go down a waterslide alone, so he got behind me, skinny thighs on either side of mine. But unlike that day that changed everything between us, this time I'm going to prove myself.

"I'm sure he will," he replies, with no hint of that sweet, earnest boy I used to know.

The one I tell myself I don't miss, not at all.

I square up to him, squeezing his palm harder. "I am *sooooo* looking forward to wiping that smile off your face."

"You could always kiss him again," suggests Rio.

Ian blanches and slackens his grip. We both drop each other's hand at the same time.

I flip Rio the fuck-you finger. "Good one. Come on, girls." Then I flip my hair over my shoulder and walk briskly away before anyone else even *thinks* about having the last word.

"I wasn't kidding," I hear Rio complain as the moon girls stride down the hall. "Why does everyone always think I'm kidding?"

11.
Summer Finally Feels Real

THE FIRST DAY of summer never quite feels like summer, even when you sleep in until ten a.m. with your friends because you were up late re-binging the first season of *Schitt's Creek*. The second day still feels like a Sunday, and even though you know there's no school on Monday, you still feel the dawning of the coming week.

And then finally, on the third day of vacation, which in some strange stroke of fate happens to be a Saturday, summer finally feels real.

I wake up craving shrimp ramen and lychee juice, which sleep-brain says is the cure-all for falling asleep with a book on my face at dawn, but Simran's watching me like a hawk the second I enter the kitchen. I don't put it past her to tell on me. I reach for the coffee instead. She's writing poetry in her Moleskine journal, but snaps it shut when I join her at the table.

"You just smudged your ink, you know." I scoot my chair in and tear into a new packet of Parle-G glucose biscuits.

One dunk, two dunks. Before the biscuit can get soggy, it's in my mouth.

Simran delicately sips at her green tea. "Late night?"

Before deciding how honest I'm going to be, I gauge her voice for any hint of judgment. "Yeah. I was reading. I'm already on my third book."

She snorts, but it's not unkind. "I almost forgot the summer reading program started."

"You have any idea how many epic books are coming out this year? The grand prize is a stack of popular ARCs and it's going to be *mine*. I bet Ian hasn't even started yet."

"I think the world should be grateful you don't have an evil lair and a trust fund to put to questionable use."

I wipe the smirk before she can see. "That's a shitty thing to say to your kid sister."

Simran grins. "She doesn't take it personally."

The familiarity of a morning squabble after the last few days of dancing around each other is a relief. Mom's smile will be bright at the breakfast table.

"You've met me, right?" I dunk another biscuit. "I still have my list of grudges."

Her laugh tinkles around me like moonlight and silver and love that we can't express like normal sisters, because what would be the fun in that?

Buster barks. A second later, the doorbell rings.

Simran's laughter fades. She wraps her hands around her cooling tea. "Don't tell me you've ordered more books. You haven't read everything you already have."

"It's not hoarding if it's books!" I'm at the door already, nudging Buster behind my legs. It's Khushi auntie on the other side, balancing a covered plate and a too-bright smile. Her eyes rake over me and I shift on my feet, uncomfortable in my ratty sleep shorts and unbrushed hair.

"Good afternoon," she says, with a very deliberate stress on *afternoon*. I frown. It's just a little after eleven a.m., which still qualifies as morning.

"Khushi, I didn't know you were coming over," says Mom.

I turn; she's coming down the stairs wearing a fluffy robe, which means she was still in pajamas, too.

"Mona," says Khushi auntie, bustling past me.

Buster barks.

"Chup." Khushi auntie levels a no-nonsense look at the dog. He looks like he wants to bark again, but thinks better of it.

Mom fidgets with her collar. She clearly hasn't expected the drop-in, but she springs into hostess mode with grace. Nothing about her smile gives away that this is inconvenient. "Chai?"

I crouch to Buster's level and loop my arm around his neck as the two women head into the kitchen for tea. He butts his nose against my cheek for a moment before traipsing after them.

In the kitchen, Mom is making masala chai while Khushi

auntie talks to Simran about poetry. "Published?" she exclaims, leaning forward to squeeze Simran's hand. "Arey vah!"

"Thank you," my sister mumbles.

"What publisher? Macmillan? HarperCollins?"

"Um, no. It's a poetry journal."

"Yash and I are so proud of her achievements," Mom says lightly. Her back is to us as she prepares the sweet, spicy black tea. The aromatic blend of cloves, cinnamon, cardamom, and fresh-peeled ginger pleasantly tickles my nostrils.

"Tell me," urges Khushi auntie. She hasn't picked up Mom's subtle deflection. "You'll be in bookstores, won't you?"

"It's just an online journal," says Simran.

"Online? You mean a blog?"

The excitement has given way to something else. Like it's something unpleasant that's just been stepped in.

"No, it's a college literary journal. It's not circulated in print." Simran pauses, and then, miserably, "It's just online."

Just? There's that word again. The one that undermines the rest of the sentence in one stinking syllable. The one that subordinates my sister into someone hedging and tiptoeing and embarrassed.

"It's very prestigious," says Mom, squeezing Simran's shoulder after setting a cup of tea in front of Khushi auntie.

"Prestigious? They must have paid a lot of money!"

Simran looks into her mug. "No, they aren't paying me. But um, like Mom said, it's an honor just to be chosen, so . . ."

Most literary mags run on pennies—being selected is honor enough, but for most Indians we know, success is measured in coming first, going to Ivy League schools, and graduating at the top of your class. Big houses, big cars. Not in something as intangible, as abstract as being chosen. Not for something like this. To Khushi auntie, this is the equivalent of a participation ribbon or a gold star.

Weariness creeps over my skin, itching like a too-tight sweater. It feels like we've had variations of this conversation so many times before; the vividness of my anger blurs with the monotony of the past. Simran meets my eyes, and something dark lurks there, but then she blinks, and the moment is gone.

Mom comes to the table with the pot of chai; in wordless unison I slide the woven coaster underneath. Maybe she reads something in my face, because her eyes warn me not to say anything. Simran doesn't often get The Look, but I do. Little monsters tend to misbehave more than big sisters.

"So what's up, Khushi auntie?" I ask, trying to reroute the conversation.

Khushi auntie zeroes in on me with a smile, putting down the china cup. Her lipsticked mouth leaves smudges on the rim.

Khushi auntie peels back the aluminum foil on the thali she brought. She's not one for half measures; the steel plate is filled from edge to edge. It holds two dozen overlapping round vadas, each vegetarian patty fried golden-brown and embedded with kernels of corn.

It's a bit annoying that she's made enough to feed a small army, and the most impressive thing *my* family has done so far is wake up.

"Just something I made this morning for today's kitty party," she says with a bright smile. "I wanted your mom to have a taste first."

A kitty party has nothing to do with cats, like I thought when I was little, to Mom's great hilarity. Women in the kitty party each contribute a set amount of money every month to the kitty, or pool of money, which is then handed to each month's rotating host, who also arranges a get-together. It's supposed to be a fun, safe space for women, but Mom gets stressed out every time it's her turn, because Khushi auntie always interferes.

I slide one vada loose. It's still warm.

"Arey, eat, eat," says Khushi auntie.

I bite into the crispy corn masala vada. The little kick of green chili at the end hits the spot, and I smile around my bulging cheeks and start on the second one.

Khushi auntie leans back in her chair with satisfaction. "Mona, I'll WhatsApp you the recipe. You always oversoak your chana dal, that's why your vadas aren't crispy. Oh, and make sure to deep fry. I know you like to bake them, but food always tastes better when you stand there and put in the time."

Mom nods like this is brand-new information, even though it's not. "Thanks for the tip." She meets my eye and busies herself with refreshing the teacups.

I swallow the rest of the vada, wishing she hadn't agreed with Khushi auntie. So what if she oversoaks the lentils and bakes the patties instead of frying them? Mom's vadas are fantastic. Even after twenty-three years of marriage, Dad's eyes light up when he tastes Mom's cooking.

I wish Mom would stand up for herself. Why is she agreeing like Khushi auntie knows best?

I hate the deference Mom—and every other Indian woman—shows Khushi auntie. Everyone's trying so hard to keep up with the Kapoors, and for what? In that second, I hate the helpful little smile on our guest's face, the insensitive way she sits in our kitchen and criticizes my mother's cooking. I hate her for thinking she's better, and us for thinking we're worse.

A frisson of anger goes through me. "We love her cooking. And baking is healthier." I make sure to keep my face blandly pleasant as I reach for a napkin from the ceramic holder. I rub it between my fingers, smile still in full force. "Less oily."

My blatant act of bravery gives way to pure panic. Has Khushi auntie gotten my innuendo? No, she doesn't look mad . . . or is she just pretending not to get it? I wasn't that subtle.

Mom doesn't miss my dig. Her mouth tightens at first, like she doesn't want to approve, and then relaxes into an acknowledging half smile.

Simran murmurs an excuse and leaves the table, her journal strapped between her arms and chest like it's full-body armor.

Khushi auntie takes a sip of her tea, oblivious to the undercurrent of tension in the room. "You know your calligraphy hobby? Sonal really likes it. Would you like to help out with her engagement party invitations?"

Mom lets me handle it. She always respects that it's my labor, so it's my choice.

Khushi auntie made the distinction that I wasn't professional, so there's a good chance she thinks I'll do it for free. People always think art is something that should be cheap and easy, devaluing it until free becomes the best price point. But I know my worth, even if she doesn't.

"How many invites do you need, auntie?" I ask.

"Fifty, sixty," says Khushi auntie. "Maybe more."

She still hasn't mentioned payment, so I give her a blank stare. There is no way I'm going to put myself through this kind of stress for free. My hand already aches as I imagine the effort involved.

"Free nahin," Khushi auntie says quickly.

I smother a victorious smile. My lack of enthusiasm must have made it clear that I wasn't going to agree without negotiating the price. "So, like, how much are we talking?"

"Besharam," says Khushi auntie with a laugh.

She makes it sound less horrible than it is, but the slight still rankles. Why is it shameless? Part of me wants to push the issue, point out that it isn't shameless to ask to be compensated for your time and skill.

But sassing elders isn't what good Indian kids—especially girls—do. And while Mom might have appreciated my earlier loyalty, she won't be cool with outright disrespect.

Still, I'm not embarrassed to ask for what I want, so I avoid Mom's pink, embarrassed face, and say, "I'll WhatsApp you with my rates. Fair warning, auntie, I'm expensive." She can always back out.

The conversation soon turns to Sonal's wedding arrangements, and I tune out, stirring the last of my biscuits in my now lukewarm coffee. While Khushi auntie enumerates the features of her new Mercedes—the one still on her drive-way—I decide to make a break for it.

The trail of their conversation follows me, the not-so-hushed tone of Khushi auntie calling me besharam again, this time with the sting of a rebuke.

I grit my teeth against the surge of anger that makes me burn to about-face and confront her.

Still dwelling on Khushi auntie's words, I don't see Simran until I bump into her. She smells like my bodywash and is already dressed to slay the day in one of those maxi dresses that only people with her height can pull off. Her still-damp hair curls against her brown, freckled shoulders. Her longish face and golden skin tone come from Mom, while I have Dad's heart-shaped face and fair skin.

"Whoa, whoa!" She puts her hands on my shoulders, holding me at arm's distance. The way she always holds me. "What's up?"

"Nothing, just getting dressed."

"Are you going someplace?"

I must be mistaking the wistfulness in her voice. "I have a kids' party from three to five with Samer, and then I'm meeting the girls at Luna Soleil to check out the Fork and Crumb's stall space. Catey's and Blaire's parents are still setting up the kitchen."

It's such a babble of overshared information that, for a second, I'm tempted to ask if she wants to come with, but then I remember that that wouldn't be us.

Simran rolls her expressive eyes, flicked with black liner at the outer corners. "I guess everything's going okay with Ian, then. You're not whining about him as much."

I despise the archness in her voice. "That has more to do with my maturity than him," I say with a tiny snort.

I don't tell her that the summer of contests has changed the stakes between us or that I'm nervous about performing together at our first party—but then, we don't tell each other everything.

"What maturity?" She follows me into my bedroom, despite my pointing to the DO NOT ENTER sign on the door. Simran casts an unimpressed look at the heaps of books against the walls. "You're such a hoarder," she drawls.

"I *told* you it's not hoarding if it's books." I rifle through my closet, ignoring the laser-burn of her eyes on the back of my neck. "Are you still here?"

"Are you still rude?" she counters.

Oh my god, why can't I be an only child?

I pull a blue tie-dyed *Sailor Moon* graphic tee from the shelf and scowl at my sister. "Why are you hiding up here?" I ask, changing tack so swiftly that surprise slashes across Simran's face.

She masks it well, though. "What do you mean?" she asks, suddenly very interested in peering at the sparkling jewelry dish on my nightstand.

"I mean, why are you up here and not down there?" I tug my sleep shirt over my head.

Simran is silent for a long moment as she picks out some of my delicate rings and slides them on her fingers. While I change, the silence seems more conspicuous than ever.

Just when I'm sure she isn't going to answer, she mumbles,

"The aunties are always asking when I'm going to get serious about the future. Which in their mind means marriage. I know that not everyone needs love to have a good partnership, just look at most of the aunties. But love isn't something that I ever thought I—" She stops herself and scowls in my general direction, even though I know I didn't do anything. "And now that Sonal is engaged, the aunties are more persistent than ever, especially Khushi auntie. I feel sick whenever someone, however well-meaning, thinks it's appropriate to tell me how to live my life."

"But you're about to go to grad school," I say slowly. "Just tell them you're too young to get married."

This is false—girls younger than my sister get married every day. Our own parents were high school sweethearts, not that they called it that back then. They liked each other, but courting wasn't really accepted until after college.

The truth is I can't imagine my lemon-lipped older sister being anyone's wife mostly because it's weird to think of her as a grown-up at all. Our age difference, coupled with our oil-and-water personalities, means that whenever she's home we slip back into our roles of big sister and little sister. Part of me is afraid that by the time I go off to college, we won't know each other as adults at all.

To me, she's just Simmy. Annoying, impossible, manic-poltergeist-nightmare girl.

"Even if I was a 'spinster,'" Simran says with a snort and air-quotes, "why should I be interested in some 'eligible boy' just because Khushi auntie consulted her astrological charts?"

She raises her hand to her face, looking at me through her fingers. I get the impression she's not eyeing the gold glint of my rings against her skin. "I'm sick and tired of hearing about good omens for marriage."

Confused by the sudden venom, I scrutinize her. "Tell them you'll meet someone the old-fashioned way. Get them off your back."

It's easy to see that she's humoring me by the twist of her smile. "Oh yeah? You think it's just that easy?" she asks. "Wait until you leave high school. You're all Bubble Wrapped right now, thinking there's a meet-cute around every corner. There isn't."

"Simmy, there's apps that make it ten times easier. Go on Tinder. Seriously, like, one in three girls finds a partner online these days."

"Not buying that statistic. I know what grades you get in math."

"Um, I got a ninety-five in stats, I'll have you know."

"When I took that class, I had a ninety-seven." Before I can say a word, she beats me to it. "Kavya, I know you like to think you're some kind of Disney Princess or whatever, but seriously, you've been wearing a costume too long if you're buying the true love crap that the aunties are selling."

"I was just trying to help."

Everything about this conversation confuses me. We don't talk like this. My sister is never this open with me, never this frustrated. I want to keep talking, but I don't know how to keep it going. Any second now, we'll fizzle out.

My heartbeat overrides my senses until all I hear is *tick, tick, tick*.

Simran laughs, but it doesn't reach her eyes. "I know you were. Everyone wants to help. All the aunties are so full of advice. They act like being unattached is something to be pitied, for fuck's sake. It's so cringey and gross, and don't even get me started on the heteronormativity."

The wrath in her voice, that sharp dagger's edge of pain drowns out the ticking clock. I feel a teensy bit terrible for finding the silver lining, but here is proof positive: My sister is more like me than she knows.

I want to wrap my arms around Simran, but instinctively, I know it won't be wanted. Instead, I will cocoon her the best way I know how. I like to keep my anger on a low simmer so it's easily accessible, and now it burns brighter.

I am a gasoline girl before the match strikes, and I spark out with, "You should tell them where they can stick their advice."

For a wild, glorious second, I think Simran will actually agree with me.

That she'll say they are so out of line and have no business sticking their noses into her personal life. That she'll take my advice and politely—preferably not so politely—tell them to butt out the next time they bring up intrusive topics. In my head, I write out the dialogue I hope she'll say on her own.

But then . . .

There's that humoring smile again. The one that says I'm just her ignorant, Bubble Wrapped little sister. "Why is your solution always being rude and nasty?"

It's not a real question. She says it so matter-of-fact.

"What makes you think backtalk is good advice, Kavya?" she continues, voice rising, and then, just as quickly, lowering. "You want me to give people a hard time and give them *more* to gossip about?"

"If you're giving people a hard time, it's because they're *putting* you through a hard time." It's so simple. "You were so weak back there with Khushi auntie; you *let* her make you feel less than."

Her eyes flash. "She wouldn't stop—"

"Then you make her!"

Silence.

Simran's eyes are bottomless. Her face eases back into neutrality with frightening speed. She's perfected Mom's look of disappointment to an art form.

A twinge. "Simmy, I—"

She cuts me off. "Sometimes you don't even act like you're Indian at all." She gets up, leaving my silver jewelry dish on the bed. The rings make soft clinks against the metal as she slips them off, not looking at me anymore. Her voice is low as she says, "If you don't have anything useful to say, maybe just don't say it. I shouldn't have even said anything."

Shouldn't have said anything *to you* goes unsaid.

I still hear it. My throat closes up and my lips stick together. When my eyes begin to smart, I push my tongue against the back of my teeth.

What just happened?

I had hoped we could be angry together, share our fire to

keep ourselves warm, but now Simran's fire has turned on me, and I'm the one who's burned.

And what does *being Indian* even mean?

Biting back our words and tasting the blood?

She sweeps out of the room without looking back, and I can't help but feel a little broken in her wake.

12.
One Itty-Bitty Hint

"YOU'VE GOT TO be kidding," I say, gaping at my so-called friends a few hours later. We're at Luna Soleil, sitting at a wall counter outside a café whose cute, quirky charm could have been plucked from Austin or Portland. "You're *seriously* not going to give me one itty-bitty hint?"

Luna Soleil used to be an automobile factory but was transformed into an indoor art deco farmers market in the late nineties. The iconic side-by-side moon and sun, hammered silver and bronze, are above the lintel of almost every entryway in the old brick building.

"Kavs, it's not that we don't want to," protests Catey. "But we put in a *lot* of effort with Ian's friends over the last couple of days to make sure the tests were as fair as possible."

"If you're so worried about it, why didn't you just walk

away?" Val asks as she sucks on the straw of her long-finished cold coffee.

"Kavya walk away? Yeah right," Blaire says with a snort. She downs the last of her dark-chocolate-banana latte with peanut butter mousse.

"She can't weasel out of a bet." Catey gives them a severe look. "She shook on it."

"Well, if she shook on it . . ." Val messes Catey's hair.

It's uncharacteristically playful, and it takes me a second to figure out why: Her dad gave her the whole weekend off. No shifts at the store. No need to keep tabs on the time.

Blaire stirs her straw, rattling the ice. "Kavs." I look at her. "Can you beat him?"

I'm not a girl who knows how to lose. "Yes."

Blaire nods, satisfied. "Come on," she says, hopping off her barstool. "The first competition isn't until next Saturday. Let's go check out the Fork and Crumb."

My legs wobble, but my lie stands.

We recycle our empty cups and leave, our tiny wall counter scooped up by another group of friends within seconds.

"Over here!" Catey waves over the crowd, and we squeeze our way toward her.

She's standing in front of a covered storefront window. Over the door hangs a painted wood sign with an inlaid over-size steel fork spearing an equally oversize crumb. The sign reads: THE FORK & CRUMB.

The bistro is in a prime location opposite a popular Spanish gastrobar that has the best five-dollar tapas and virgin margaritas. Catey ushers us in before any lookie-loos sneak a peek.

Val and I are seeing it for the first time. We peer at the plain white space outfitted with brand-new commercial appliances. Catey's dad constructed trendy stools and tables made out of old wine barrels, and the steel accents around the table rim and footrest match the high gloss on the concrete, imbuing the room with a sleek, low-key lunar effect.

It's been Catey's dream to open a bistro here since we were kids, and now it's *actually* happening, thanks to her parents' support. She links hands with Blaire, face glowing with pride. "I know it's pretty bare right now, but what do you think?"

Val wrinkles her nose.

"Sorry about the smell," says Catey. "We had to clean the old concrete before sealing it."

Looking past the faint whiff of vinegar and the empty dining area is easy with an artist's eye. Some pattern, some color, some decor . . . that's all it needs. I glance at Val, but she isn't looking too impressed. Blaire's watching her with a small, worried tug on her bottom lip, too.

Filling the silence, I say, "I think . . . I think it's amazing. I can't believe how real it's starting to get. When you told us, you said it was such a long shot to get in here."

Blaire gives me a huge grin. "It was! But they give preference to businesses who source from local producers, and since we're using a lot of food from Catey's folks and some of their neighboring farms . . . You know, most of the stuff in here is actually upcycled by our parents or made by Indiana artists. We still can't believe we're actually here."

Val hasn't said anything yet, which isn't totally out of the ordinary for her, but something about her silence seems different. She has a look on her face I can't identify, something that's a little angry and sad at the same time.

"We're going to be working here every weekend until I can do this full-time," says Catey.

"Hmm," says Val. She picks at her fingernails. "So your parents are still bankrolling this?"

"I mean, they'd hardly change their minds after sinking in all this effort and money," Catey says with a laugh. "I have one year of waitressing at my brother's steakhouse on the Riverwalk, two years of running my outdoor stall, and multigenerational gardening and cooking knowledge. What else did my parents think I was going to do?"

Blaire's nodding along as Catey adds, "I'm so lucky they've been supportive of my dreams from day one. This would have been impossible without them. It's such a privilege to be working and learning from our parents."

Val's indecipherable countenance intensifies, but I seem to be the only one who notices.

It's not like it's a secret that Catey comes from money. Her grandparents own one of the biggest dairy farms in east-central Indiana, and her parents gave each of Catey's siblings a lump sum for their start in life. But where the older Hill girls used it for college and setting up their own practices—veterinary and law—Catey followed in her older brother's culinary footsteps. Her goal is to take night classes at the community college and take over the farm-to-table bistro when she graduates.

Both sets of parents want to keep them as involved as possible, especially with the business plan. Even though Blaire's GPA is high enough that she could go out of state on a scholarship if she wanted, IU and Notre Dame are the highest on her list. She wants to major in actuarial science or managerial finance, staying in Indiana to be with Catey and help out at the bistro.

Now that I think about it, Val seemed a little bummed even a couple of weeks ago when we sampled Catey's new menu. I chalked it up to a fight with her parents, which seems to be happening more often lately, but we all know she'll never tell us what's bugging her until she's good and ready. She's a lot like Simran that way.

Before anyone can notice Val's reticence, I say, "Girls, let's get shrimp ceviche."

As Catey locks up, the rest of us get in line. It's long, and while we wait, Blaire touches Val's arm. "Hey, maybe I'm totally off base with this, but back there, were you—"

"Ooh, a table just opened up. Val, come with?" I blurt out. Tapas are half off during happy hour and free tables are a precious commodity, but that's not the only reason I ask her.

It's easier to go up to the counter than wait to be served, so while Catey joins Blaire to place our orders, Val and I save the table. Keeping one eye on them, I hang my purse on the chair and fix Val with a look. "What's going on with you?" I ask without preamble.

Her answer is too quick, too nervous. "Nothing. Why?"

"You didn't seem happy for them."

She shook her head.

"*Val.*"

She hugs her purse in her lap, arms wrapped around it tight.

I sigh. "Whatever it is, just say it. I'm not going to jump down your throat."

Nothing.

"Valika Mehra, you tell me right now."

She cracks a smile. "You don't have the mom voice for that."

"What's so bad you can't even tell me?" I try to reason. "You barely said a word to Catey and B. And this is big. You know how much Catey wants this."

She frowns. "Are you calling me a bad friend?"

"N-no." I press my lips together. "You're acting kinda weird and I figured it might have been about them. And I think Blaire sensed it, too."

"Maybe they should notice." She crosses her legs and turns away.

I follow her gaze, finding our friends in the packed line. "Are you mad at them?"

"Not mad. Just tired. I'm sick and tired of cheering other people on."

Other people? They're not other people, they're our friends.

Then a spiky thought occurs: Does she feel the same way about me?

"They worked hard on this," I say slowly. "You know that."

"Sure. It's *so* hard asking Mommy and Daddy for a handout.

You know *my* dad said he wouldn't pay for me to do fashion design at college?" Val's cheeks flush. "He said he and Mummy didn't come here and toil to pay off loans and mortgages for me to be anything other than a doctor. Catey and Blaire have *no* idea what it's like."

I dig my teeth into the meat of my inner cheek. "That's not fair."

She keeps going like she doesn't hear me. "Papa doesn't even *pay* me for working at the store. He can pay the other employees, but not his own kid? I have to ask my parents for pocket money for *everything*. Every time we go out, it costs—" She stops, glaring at the table. "He almost made me work today."

"V, I'm so sorry. I wish I knew how to help. Your dad can be really unfair sometimes."

"Why should I just suck it up? Keep leaving sleepovers early while *you* get to stay?"

This one stings. Her rules aren't our rules, yet we always feel shitty when her parents come to take her home, and Blaire *did* ask her mom to convince them to let Val spend the night on Wednesday, but no dice. It's always been this way. Val's mom relents on curfew sometimes, but she's just as protective as her husband.

Val's mouth grows small, wobbly lips screwing up. "At least you get to work somewhere that isn't under your dad's thumb. All three of you earn your own money. You know Blaire actually gets paid for babysitting her own sister?"

"All families are different. You can't hold it against—"

"Papa won't give me a penny if I don't do what *he* wants.

If I don't study medicine, I'll have to work in the store for the *rest of my life."*

Her resentment begins to make sense, but it still rankles that she took it out on our friends.

"I didn't know that," I say. "You never—"

"Yeah, I know I never. Because you'll all give me some shitty advice about just talking to them and telling them how I feel." She rolls her eyes.

The girls are back before I can figure out what to say. Maybe I'm a bad friend to be so relieved, but the truth is, I'm not the one people go to for comfort. I can hand out actionable advice by the gallon, but Val's right. My advice won't help her.

Simran's disappointment rings in my ears, followed by Val's resigned, bitter frustration.

My advice might not be as good as I think it is.

"What'd we miss?" Blaire asks as she slides into the seat next to me with a tray of small plates. "Kavs grill you for details on the first battle of brawn?"

Interest piqued, I lean forward. "Battle of—"

Catey interrupts with, "Figure of speech." She sets the tray of ice waters down. "Remember, we aren't supposed to give away any hints—itty-bitty or otherwise—about the competitions, otherwise this is all for nothing. You're being tested on your adaptability without the benefit of being able to practice in advance."

The words are for me, but the reminder is bull's-eye-aimed at her girlfriend.

"You think *his* side is going to stick to that?" Blaire rolls her eyes. "No way."

Catey gives a little huff. "His side *came up* with the idea of keeping the challenges secret!"

"Fine, fine." Blaire shuffles the appetizer-sized plates around so we each have different items in front of us. "Dig in. You can Venmo me later."

I catch the quick pinch on Val's face, but then Catey nudges a plate toward me.

Though the portions are small, my mouth waters at the sights and smells: the zesty shrimp ceviche I love; fried calamari rings with lemon wedges; fresh, tender octopus sprinkled with sweet Spanish paprika; golden-brown ham-and-cheese croquettes; and a plate of oil-marinated olives, on the house.

I cast a quick glance at Val. "Girls, it's on me," I say, lifting my glass of ice water in toast. "To, um, celebrate the Fork and Crumb. Which is incredible, by the way."

"Kavya, that's so sweet, but you don't have to," says Catey.

"No, seriously, I insist." I'm already pulling my phone out of my purse to pay Blaire back. With the tapas half off, the damage isn't bad. Poppy pays generously per hour, depending on character and activities involved. Rounding up and covering the tip, too, I Venmo Blaire.

"Thanks, Kavya," she says, clinking her water against mine. "You're the best."

"And soon Ian will know it too," I joke, trying to defuse any residue of tension that might still hang in the air, unresolved. "Now that I've bribed you with food, are you *sure* you still can't give me any hints about the first contest?"

Blaire laughs. "I knew there was an ulterior motive!"

Yes, but it's not the one she thinks. I'm careful not to look at Val.

Their conversation fades out as we all dig in. I poke a toothpick into a piece of octopus and bring it to my mouth, looking at each of my friends in turn. Catey, animated and sparkling; Blaire, whip-smart and feisty; Val, quiet and enigmatic. The moon girls are solid. Whatever this is with Val, we can fix it.

My phone screen lights up with a new notification. It's a text from Poppy: Don't forget to come in early for a fitting before your first party with Ian! followed by both the prince and princess emojis with two pink revolving-heart emojis in between.

My stomach up-downs in rapid succession, like doing jumping jacks or skipping rope. I knew this was coming, and that our first performance together would follow soon after. I can't think of a job that pays as well as Poppy's without a degree, but I'm positive Ian's only working there to mess with me somehow.

I've never actually *seen* Ian waiting tables at Holly Gogogi, but I'm sure he helps out, same as Val at her family's small business. He doesn't *need* to work at Poppy's. His parents were always generous with his pocket money; I'm sure they must pay him the same as they would any other employee.

A whole afternoon spent together in wardrobe and then at our first party? The perfect opportunity for stealth bonding. My smile grows Cheshire as I stab a toothpick through an olive.

Fraternizing with the enemy. I quite enjoy the sound of that.

13.
Don't You Dare Be Civil to Me

THE SECOND CATEY'S car takes the gravel turnoff, tires spewing out *chunk-a-chunk-a-chunk* down the sloping drive, our destination is obvious.

"This is the first contest?" I ask incredulously, straining toward the middle seat to look out the front windshield. We inch past a weathered old board staked into the ground; the engraved sign reads: THE KAYAK GIRLS.

"Are you there yet?" Val's voice buzzes through the car from my phone, but it's the look on her face that stings the most. Her lower lip is pulled into a sulk and her eyes stare through the screen like she's trying to squeeze out every last detail. "I wish I was," she says, not for the first time.

Her dad stuck her with working the morning shift at the store, and she's been messaging me all week to grouse about the unfairness. I always feel shitty that the only thing I can offer her is sympathy.

"We do, too," says Blaire. She twists around in the front passenger seat and gestures for me to angle the phone toward her. "It was really tough to get everyone's schedule to align what with everyone's jobs." She smiles encouragingly. "Next time, yeah? We'll make sure you can make it."

"You could have done that *this* time," snipes Val.

A flash of annoyance crosses Blaire's face. "I'm sorry, V. We really tried, but it's hard to coordinate so many schedules."

Val doesn't drop it. "You got the date to work for *your* schedule. Yours and Catey's. And Kavya and Ian, and all his friends, too."

"Kavya and Ian are integral to this whole competition," says Catey, chiming in with her airy, effervescent voice, the one she uses to calm a skittish horse at her parents' farm. "And we promise to video chat the whole time so you don't miss a thing. Honestly, I'd trade places with you in a heartbeat. There's always *so* many mosquitos hanging around the river."

This seems to pacify Val, because she sighs like the fight's gone out of her.

"I've never kayaked before," I say to break the silence.

"That's the idea," says Catey as she pulls in next to Claudia's gleaming red Nissan and Rio's bright-blue Honda CR-V. "I told you we put a lot of thought into this."

"It wouldn't really be a test if one of you had an advantage," says Blaire. She smirks and does Damon's eye smolder. "As for the others, that's for us to know and for you to dot-dot-dot."

Catey laughs and releases her seat belt, leaning over to cup Blaire's chin for a sweet, swift kiss. "That may be the single most ominous phrase in the entire English language, babe."

We clamber out of the car. I hand my phone over to Blaire for safekeeping. The last time we were here was for tubing on Catey's fifteenth birthday. Afterward, her parents had taken us to Holly Gogogi's for gochujang fried chicken and waffles. Mrs. Jun had sent Ian over to refill our drinks, and Catey told him to join us even though I was widening my eyes *No* at her. He'd slipped onto the bar stool next to me, our elbows briefly knocking.

Bright plastic kayaks in every color of the rainbow are neatly stacked on outdoor racks, brought out to customers by the all-female staff sporting hot-pink polos.

I scan the waterline for Ian.

"There!" says Blaire, pointing. "See, they've already got the kayaks out."

Our sturdy shoes crunch on the gravel as we join Ian, Claudia, Samer, and Rio by the water for launch. One of the Kayak Girls employees, a pretty Korean teenager with glossy black hair held back with a bandana headband, comes over scribbling on a clipboard. I vaguely recognize her from school.

"Hey, Ian," she says when she finally looks up. "Great seeing you again so soon."

When did she see him before? Suspicious minds want to know!

He tips his face so he can look at her over the top of his sunglasses. "Hi, Khloe."

It's only when I see her nametag flash in the sun that I realize it's Khloe with a K.

That's the last letter we reached during truth or dare. Now I *really* want to know how he knows her. She's in our grade, but not in any of our honors or AP classes, and I've never seen them hang out together. The only thing I know about her is she spends all her free periods doing extra gym, conditioning for track.

The thought sprouts like weeds on a perfectly manicured lawn: Is Khloe the girl Ian likes? Or is it Kori from the library?

I glance between them, heart thumping wildly even though we haven't even started paddling yet.

Ian flicks his gaze to me, totally oblivious.

"Catey Hill and Rio Moreno-Ortiz?" asks Khloe. "Since the kayak rentals are in your names, I need both your signatures on the liability forms and a valid photo ID from everyone who's going out on the water today."

While we all fish the required documentation from our pockets and purses, a peppy "Hi Rio!" chimes from my phone in Val's voice.

Everyone looks around in confusion until I clear my throat. "It's Val. On video."

"Crap!" Blaire pulls my phone from her back pocket and shows Rio the screen. "Sorry, V." *OMG* she mouths to the rest of us, pulling her mouth to the side in a sheepish half smile.

"Hey?" Rio glances at his friends as though he's wondering why he was singled out.

Once all the paperwork is squared away, Khloe passes out

life jackets and says, "You can push off from anywhere, but we recommend beginners start here where the water is gentlest."

Ian clambers into the cockpit of the orange kayak before shrugging on his life jacket. The back of Ian's baby-blue shirt has huge red-and-white comic text with the words HOLLY GOGOGI exploding out of a retro-pop-art-style Audrey Hepburn's speech bubble.

"I *love* your shirt," says Khloe. "I'll have to buy one when I come over on Sunday."

"Can't wait," says Ian, the words delivered with a smile so wide it crinkles his eyes, which suddenly, are no longer looking at me.

Come over? Like . . . for a date?

No one else seems to think she's said anything out of the ordinary.

Samer's helping push Ian out into the water, and Catey is spraying her bare legs with mosquito repellent. Blaire is panning my phone to give Val a three-sixty view while Claudia and Rio are quietly arguing over the map of the river that came with their paperwork.

"Oh, your jacket's a little sandy," says Khloe. She reaches out to brush some off Ian's shoulder, her hand lingering on his shirtsleeve and upper arm instead of the plasticky red vinyl.

"Thanks," says Ian, ducking his head like he's embarrassed, but even with his back to me I can tell by the curve of his cheek that he's smiling. Probably another toothpaste-commercial smile. Smile #2: self-conscious and bashful.

Right on cue, she giggles. Actually *giggles*. I grit my teeth and try to control my breathing. And that's when I hear it. The way I should have heard it the first time, except that tiny spike of jealousy—so small it could hardly be called jealousy, honestly—distracted me.

Great seeing you again so soon.

Not only do Khloe and Ian know each other, but she saw him recently. As in *she saw him here kayaking because he had advance knowledge of our contest and didn't tell me?*

"Val, is it okay with you if we cut off the livestream so we can film this for posterity?" Catey calls over her shoulder. "Thanks!"

When Samer returns to climb into his tandem kayak with Catey, Claudia says, "We're going to do this one." She points with a glossy fingernail to the even glossier map.

We all crane forward to look; it's a fairly straight line with no surprises.

"I can follow along easily from the shore," says Blaire, holding up my phone. "Went tubing here once . . . *Never* again," she adds with a shudder.

Even if she wasn't filming, she's a little leery of swimming in anything that isn't a pool. The White River, on the other hand, is so murkily olive-tinted that you can't even see the bottom of the sand bed, let alone what's swimming right beneath the surface.

"Nice choice," says Khloe approvingly. "That's a good beginner route."

I bristle. I am a beginner, but so what? Paddle to the left, paddle to the right. We're moving at five miles an hour, probably. Turtle slow. Plus, it's not like kayaking is *hard*.

"Hey, what's wrong?" Blaire whispers, nudging my hip with hers.

I wonder what tell gave me away. Surreptitiously, I pass a hand over my nose, checking my nostrils for baby dragon flare. Nope, it's not that.

Blaire smiles with understanding. "It's your angry-eye-sexing glare."

I turn it on her.

She winces and throws up her palms. "Now it's a killing-the-messenger glare."

Ian laughs at something Khloe says. The sound makes my stomach twist, and not because I want him to laugh like that for me. I kinda don't want him to laugh like that for anyone.

But I'm not jealous.

Because that would imply—

"We should do this one," I say, jabbing my finger at the map hard enough to leave a dent.

Claudia peers at it, a crease forming between her brows. "But—"

I smirk. "Unless you're chicken, Ian?"

He narrows his eyes. "Claudia, show me the map."

"You are both impossible *children*," she says with a huff, but passes it over to him.

Ian scans the route, with all its winding bends and hairpin turns before it joins back up with the White River, and then pushes his sunglasses up his nose, shielding his expression. "You're on. May the best rival win," he says, throwing my own words back at me.

"I'm sure she will," I say sweetly.

Oh, she *definitely* will. It takes an unholy amount of willpower to not turn around and check exactly how far ahead I am. Ian's splashes sound like they're coming from far away, and between Rio and Claudia's bickering and lack of synchronicity with the paddles, and Samer and Catey's unhurried, lackadaisical pace, I overtook them several minutes ago.

Okay, one little peek.

I half turn to catch a glimpse of the others. As I suspected, the tandem kayaks are totally out of sight, but Ian's making his way toward me like a sleek fish. The sunlight bounces off his hideous red life jacket and dapples his skin. His paddle blades cut through the brackish water with smooth, graceful strokes.

He's so good at everything, seemingly without even trying, but I can't shake that toe-biting feeling that he's not as unpracticed at this as we were led to believe.

If I don't speed up, I'll lose my advantage.

With a vengeance, I take up the paddles again, ignoring the fresh pinch in my shoulders. It's harder to start again and build back the momentum. My muscles quiver as I strain forward, trying to make up for lost time with swift, sure strokes.

Left, right. Left, right.

Even my thighs—clenched tight since we set off and so sweaty that I stick to the hard plastic seat—hurt. I know that by tomorrow morning they'll be the kind of sore that rivals a day of trail riding at Catey's parents' farm.

I can't believe I ever thought this would be easy. I release a string of creative swear words under my breath, most aimed at me, but some at Ian, too.

Left, right. Left, right.

The questions ricochet around my brain like one of those old-fashioned pinball arcade games at Holly Gogogi: Why did Ian have to smile at Khloe's flirtation? If he knew this test in advance, why didn't he tell me? I never thought of him as a cheater, but am I wrong about his sense of fair play?

Water drips down the paddle, lands on my knee, and slides down my bare calf in a cool lick. The gritty black silt on the floor crunches when I move my feet. I hold my neck extra stiff whenever the Orpheus-like urge to turn around and seek out Ian gets too strong.

Left, right. Left, right. Left, right.

My thoughts race with the current, faster on this stretch of the route than from where we'd set off. I can't tamp down the questions coursing through my mind, even though what I should be doing is keeping an eye out for water hazards.

Always be aware of your surroundings, Dad reminds me every time I ride the trails at Catey's farm, even though I've been comfortable around horses for years. He ignores my good-natured eye roll and yeah-yeah hand wave as I beeline for the driveway when Catey comes to pick me up. *Don't get distracted and don't try to be better than anyone else. It's not a competition. Be safe and remember to have fun.*

Being the best *is* fun. But I get his point.

I glance up at the bank. It's shrouded in dense trees and I can't see Blaire anywhere.

Gnarled, hairy roots peek out of the dirt, thick as an arm. Bent and broken branches reach out into the river itself, victims of our latest summer thunderstorm.

We're so far away from our launch point that I can't hear the hollers of the families and kids tubing on the beginner route. Not even the strokes of Ian's paddles.

It's so quiet. No, not quiet. Disquieting.

Somewhere, a cicada screams.

CRASH! I startle out of my thoughts. The hull scrapes against a rock and I catch a spray of water to the face. "*Fuuuuuck*," I hiss.

Dad was right—don't get distracted.

Fuck fuck FUCK.

"Hey!" Even from a distance, Ian's voice reaches me. "Did you run into trouble?"

"I'm fine!" I shout back, but there's a tremor in my voice I can't hold at bay.

I wedge my paddle under the rock, find a bit of leverage, and push, praying that it doesn't break under the strain of dislodging the kayak.

"Are you stuck?" Ian's voice is closer now. "Do you need help?"

I grind my teeth with exertion. How is he always just *there*, ready to be chivalrous?

"Don't you dare be civil to me, Ian Jun!"

I've finally found purchase and with one last, final heave, the kayak is back on course. Even though I know better, I can't help myself—I lean over to check the hull. Khloe's warning rings in my ears: *You're responsible for any damage to the kayaks.*

Whew. Not a scratch or scuff on it. That's a relief.

I go around a bend too quickly, trying to put distance between me and Ian again, but in doing so I forget the second warning Khloe gave us before we set off: *We don't have any rapids here, but be careful around river bends and curves where the water picks up speed.*

"AHHH!" I lose my center of gravity, and even though these kayaks are supposed to be stable, I tip into the gross green river. During the spill, my paddle gets away from me.

Coming up with a mouthful of briny, unpleasant water, I spew it out, but some of it's gone down already. I'm pretty sure I've swallowed chunks of something. I gag at the taste, shrieking and splashing. My throat feels like it's coated with a filmy sour residue.

"Kavya!" There's an urgency in Ian's voice as he approaches.

I cough. "My k-kayak."

The current's swept it away, and without my weight, it's picked up speed. Dismayed, I stare after it. Sure, I'd wanted distance between our kayaks, but not like this.

"Oh my god, Kavs, are you okay?" Ian shouts, concern making his voice tight. "Are you okay to swim to the bank?"

"I'm fine!" I repeat, shrill. I already know he won't be able to stop. "Ian, the *kayak*!"

"Forget about the kayak, you're more important!" he yells back.

Our eyes meet, brown on brown, as he glides past where I'm bobbing. His cheeks are flushed, and his hair is damp against his sweaty forehead as he rakes his hand through it, brushing it away from his face. There's a frazzled energy to him now, a worry that goes beyond a lost paddle and a careening kayak.

I'm not scared, but Ian looks scared enough for the both of us.

"I—" I swallow, taken aback by the naked emotion on his face. "I can swim to shore."

I'm a strong swimmer, but he stays twisted around to make sure I reach the bank before he sets off with a new fervor.

I haul myself against the trunk of a tree, ignoring the moss crawling up the side. Finally, I have a chance to catch my breath—and collect the spill of my runaway thoughts.

He's going to win this for sure. All he has to do is reach the finish line. Like he said, I make it easy for him to win.

As I sit on the bank, sore and shivering, translucent clothing sticking to me like a second skin, I see him towing my kayak to shore. My annoyance at Ian playing my knight in shining armor returns tenfold. The kayak is rescued, but my pride is forever lost in that damn river.

My blood runs hot under my skin, itching and clawing. I wasn't in any real trouble. I bet I could have swum after it myself. It was only a little downriver. I could probably have climbed into it by now and made it the rest of the way without incident.

I could have *won*.

And by the time our friends catch up to us, I've convinced myself of it.

Catey leaps out of the kayak before Samer even reaches shore. "Oh my god, Kavya!" she shrieks. She whips a towel out of her backpack and starts vigorously rubbing my arms.

"I'm fine," I say, the words weak even to my own ears. I try to wriggle away.

"Stay still," she scolds.

"What's going on down there?" Blaire calls from an embankment above us.

Samer cups his hands around his mouth. "Don't come down!"

But she doesn't listen, crashing through the trees and tentatively making her way down the steep bank. "Did you *fall in*?" she asks, mouth dropping.

"Don't you even think about recording this," I say.

She pats her back pockets, where both our phones are safely stowed.

Ian jogs back, out of breath, by the time Rio and Claudia land on shore. He gives me a quick once-over, making sure I'm okay, before giving me a small nod. His eyes are impossibly soft and the tiny curl of his mouth is new. A not-quite smile, and yet it is one.

An indecipherable one. A smile I've never seen before. Smile #9.

Under his scrutiny, my mouth goes dry. But that could also be grit residue.

All their faces are etched with concern. It's like no one wants to speak first. After a long moment of silence, Claudia asks, "What happened?" She glances toward where Ian left my runaway kayak, safely next to his, no worse for wear despite its solo adventure.

Kavya happened, I think, hanging my head. *She was showing off*. Miserably, I wait for Ian to crow about my hubris, tell them what happened.

"She ran into a patch of rough water," says Ian. "But she handled herself."

My head shoots up. He meets my gaze steadily.

He's trying to save me again. So nobody knows what a dumbass I am.

I don't want to feel grateful. I don't want to feel relieved. I don't want to be rescued.

So I let myself fill up with the emotion that's closest at hand, and all of a sudden, I'm warm. Warmer than Catey's toweling me dry. Warmer than the twisty sensation in my tummy when Ian looked at me with *that* smile.

"This wasn't your first time kayaking, was it?" I ask in a low voice.

Ian's eyebrows draw together. "Excuse me?"

"You can tell them the truth. I didn't 'handle myself,'" I say, air quoting. "I fucked up."

He looks uncomfortable. "I wouldn't say tha—"

"I would," I tell him. "And I did. I got ahead of myself because I was trying to get ahead of you, and I was reckless and arrogant. And you . . . you were calm in a crisis. Almost like you've done this before. But you haven't, have you?"

I look to our friends. "I mean, that was the whole point of choosing this activity, right? Something neither of us had done before?"

"*Yes*," says Rio slowly, exponentially stressing the syllable.

"Wait. Let me get this straight." Ian's eyes are hard. With a pang, I realize how much I miss the way he looked at me a few seconds ago. "You think I snuck in practice before today?"

I let the silence stand.

"Wow, Kavya. Just wow," Ian scoffs.

Claudia crosses her arms across her chest. "We didn't tell him. We aren't cheaters."

"Then how come Khloe knew you?" I challenge. "She was all . . . over you."

Blaire makes a sound, but Catey digs her elbow into her ribs, and it turns into a cough.

"She was being nice," says Ian. "You know, 'nice'? The thing that you don't seem to be capa—" He stops on the precipice of what he really wants to say.

My words come out scraped raw. "Nice. Real nice."

My whole life, people who don't really know me have told me to be something I'm not. Someone a little more polite. Someone less ambitious. Someone sweet and frothy. But that's not who I am. I will never be Disney Princess perfect, and I'm okay with that, but it still hurts when I get called on it.

"Kavya, you scared the crap out of me when I saw you go in the water. I owe you an apology. I was mad at you, but I shouldn't have said you weren't nice. I crossed the line." Ian swallows. "I know Khloe from Korean church. She and her family eat at Holly Gogogi every week. They're family friends."

"So she's not the girl you like whose name starts with K?"

"You are so ridiculous," says Ian, and it's not an answer. At my expectant look, he huffs all exasperated. "The girl I liked would never have liked me back. She never even saw me—never looked at me twice. I promise it's not Khloe. And I certainly didn't sneak in extra practice. I can't believe you think I'd stoop to cheating instead of playing fair."

"Fine," I say grudgingly, not quite sure if I believe him.

"What do we do now?" asks Samer. "I mean, do we . . . keep kayaking?"

Ian shrugs. "Give the win to Kavya. She was in the lead before she capsized." With a last lingering look, he heads back to his kayak.

He's just giving it to me? That's . . . really big of him. This contest could have been declared void, but he actually acknowledged that I would have won if not for falling in. Parker would never have done that.

Even though all I can see of Ian is his back, I can't shake the feeling that I've disappointed him. It stings more than I'd like it to.

"But she didn't technically win," points out Rio.

"Why don't they just continue from here?" suggests Blaire.

The chatter turns into white noise as my focus tunnels on the only thing that's important right now.

"Wait." I stumble after Ian on jelly legs. "Ian, wait. *Please*."

He turns, a question in his eyes.

"I'm sorry. I'm *really* sorry I accused you of cheating. I should have known that you wouldn't do that. We'll share it," I decide. "One win for each of us."

He gives me that smile again: Smile #9.

I'm no closer to figuring it out.

14.
You're the One Wearing a Cummerbund

I SEE IAN the next day in wardrobe in a *very* different light. It's literally different. Bright yellow fluorescent bulbs add a warm glow to his pale skin and make the guyliner ringing his eyes even more smoky. I'm not prepared for the way my stomach leaps; it doesn't just somersault, it does a freaking Olympic Yurchenko. Somewhere between back handspring and final backflip, he looks up and sees me watching him.

Clearly, I'm still a bit nauseated from falling into the river. His eyebrow twitches.

"Hold still!" scolds Amie. She holds a small brush close to the arch of his eyebrow. "I still have to blend this."

I step through the open doorway. "Knock, knock. Your mom said you were back here."

"Kavs!" She twists her hips to look at me. The tips of her

honey curls spill out of the poufy bun at the top of her head. "You're just in time," she says with a wave of the brush. "Your wig's in front of the mirror."

The red curls have been brushed into flowing, soft Ariel waves. It's more hair than I've seen on any other wig we use at the Playhouse, rivaling even Rapunzel's.

A pang of longing for Belle's beautiful updo and sunshine-yellow dress hits me. Hard.

I watch as Amie uses light sweeps of the brush to mimic real eyebrow hair. She moves with grace, each brushstroke even and careful.

I can't help but envy her. Amie is gorgeous. If she wants, she could play any princess in her mom's company. Poppy was a Brit living in France when she met Amie's dad, a soccer player from Senegal. Between her height, fawn skin, and practically poreless complexion, Amie has inherited the best of both their features and a hint of her mother's accent.

"Do we have to do this?" Ian crosses his arms. "My eyebrows were fine before."

"Um, have you seen Prince Eric?" Amie puts a hand on her hip, jutting out the elbow. "How that boy managed to get an eyebrow game that strong in an animated movie is beyond me. You have good definition, but we need to fill in these hairs."

His eyebrows are filled in with dip brow, defining the arch with sharp, clear lines. Even underneath the foundation she'd patted on his cheeks, I can see his blush.

"I'm fine with a weak brow game," says Ian. His eyes flick to me, then away.

Is he being avoid-y because of yesterday's awkwardness? Or is he trying to be professional in our workplace? I'll show him. No one out-professionals me.

Addressing me for the first time, he asks, "Isn't this great?" in a tone that sounds like it's anything but. His fingers pluck at the deep, plunging V-neck tunic he wears.

"Are those . . ." I blink. "Women's jeggings?"

The cuffed dark-wash fabric makes his legs even slimmer, and Shipwrecked Prince's waistband is an appalling shade of red. It kind of matches the color of my wig, actually.

Ian's gaze slides down his legs. "They're jeans."

I point to the ripped jeans I'm wearing. "These are jeans. *Those* are denim jeggings." I drag my eyes to his waist. "And that cummerbund is . . . I mean, what can I say about it?" My grin is positively feral.

"It's not a—" He clamps his mouth shut. "Amie, this is a sash, right?"

"Mm-hmm." Amie takes a step away and cocks her head to the side, scrutinizing her handiwork. "Kavya, do these look even to you?"

Ian's eyebrows shoot up. "Does what look even?" he asks, voice alarmed.

"Relax your face!" Amie tugs me to her side, standing right in front of Ian.

The unfortunate part about scrutinizing his eyebrows is that they both happen to be right above his eyes. His big, brown, Bambi eyes. Ian's unfairly good-looking, which makes it all the harder to remember he's my self-professed nemesis.

Val swears up and down that if you look real close, you can see gold flecks, no matter how often I pop that bubble by reminding her that only boys in books ooze that level of sexy.

Amie looks at me expectantly. "Well?"

I kind of want to make him sweat it out, but I grudgingly admit, "They're even."

"Get started on your summer reading, yet?" he asks, smoothing his face.

I suck in my cheeks. Huh. Gauntlet thrown in the first five minutes.

I don't buy his look of innocence for a second.

"Making good headway," I say, trailing my eyes up and down appraisingly. "You?"

Amie's peridot eyes volley between us.

"Ah, you know." He shrugs, equally vague.

I don't know! That's why I'm asking! So I can divide his total number of books read by how many days of summer vacation have passed, and calculate—

My face must give me away, because Ian grins a showstopper of a grin. In an all-too-knowing way.

Infuriating boy! Of all the summer jobs, why come here?

He could tutor! Mow lawns! Lifeguard!

"I gotta grab you the right boots." Amie turns in the direction of the storage closet. She gestures to his feet. "You're a ten?"

Ian winks. "Ten out of ten. Glad *someone* here noticed."

Amie laughs. "Save the charm for your princess, bud."

His silky black bangs fall in his eyes, and he does that stupid swish with his neck to swoop them to the side.

"So . . ." I sling my thumbs in my belt loops and rock on my heels. Aiming for casual, I say, "You're actually going through with this."

"Money's good. And it's close to my house."

I can't see Mr. Perfect being comfortable with little kids. Especially cake-sticky elementary kids who want to hold your hand or glue themselves to your side during the whole party, rattling off random princess facts or showing off all their Disney stuff.

"Poppy prepped you with the dos and don'ts of the job, right?" I settle at my own dressing table. Our eyes lock in the mirror. "Do you want to go over anything in the *Fairy-tale Handbook*? If you mess up, I look bad, too."

"I don't think you could look bad if you tried."

My chest glows with warmth at the unexpected compliment. I'm the first to look away, busying myself with the red wig. There isn't a hair out of place, but I still feign smoothing down the crown as if I'm only talking to him because I'm pre-occupied with something else.

He clears his throat, suddenly looking a little queasy. "But, um, I'm good. Trust me, I studied it with the diligence of a SAT test-prep workbook."

"It's pretty chonky," I point out. "Are you sure you don't want to go over anything?"

"You don't have to worry." Ian makes a face. "Do you really have to wear that thing?"

"Wait until you see the rest of my outfit," I say with a snort.

Too late, I realize how much that sounds like an invitation.

On cue, compounding my embarrassment, Amie returns with a pair of glossy black boots, a pastel-purple seashell bra, and a green mermaid tail. "Ta-da!"

Ian tries to muffle his laugh into a cough, but he can't quite pull it off.

"Yeah, yeah, laugh it up," I say. "You're the one wearing a cummerbund."

That quells his laughter pretty quick. Victory in my hands, I shoot him a smirk in the mirror. His reflection scowls back at me.

Though I'd had my doubts it would fit, the stiff plastic bra cups my boobs so that there isn't a hint of cleavage visible. Just like Poppy promised, it's not revealing at all.

As I waddle out of the changing room, Amie claps her hands. "Beautiful!" she proclaims.

Ian echoes no such sentiment. Instead, he eyes my outfit. "Can you walk?"

The sparkly green dress was sewn to look like a mermaid's tail, which means it hugs my hips and thighs, but cinches tight at the calves and ankles before flaring out in swathes of fabric resembling fins. I prove him wrong with a hobble-hop back to my dressing table. It's far from graceful, but at least it's a small victory.

. . . Until I almost trip over my own feet at the last second, falling onto the chair with a clumsy fumble.

I studiously avoid eye contact with Ian. If I don't acknowledge it, it never happened.

"Just try to take smaller steps," says Amie.

"Too bad, Joshi." Ian smirks without any trace of his earlier weirdness. "I could have kept it authentic by actually sweeping you off your feet, after all. For the kids."

I huff. "Can't I wear one of the other outfits?" I know we have recreations of the simple blue, blush-pink, and glittering teal dresses that Ariel wore in the movies.

"Sorry, babes. It's a pool party, so the parents specifically requested this outfit." Amie shoots me a sympathetic smile. "Now let's get that wig on you."

While she fusses over my hair and makeup, I watch Ian in the mirror flipping through the *Fairy-tale Handbook*. He has the disconcerting habit of licking his pointer finger before turning each page.

"He seems a little nervous," Amie whispers as she adjusts the angle of the wig. "But you're a pro at this, Kavs. And you've definitely got the chemistry to pull this off."

I laugh, startled. "What?"

She's seen us together for what, all of five minutes? How could she mistake our verbal sparring for something as patently ridiculous as chemistry?

I squint at Ian in the mirror. He's obliviously flicking through the pages.

"You two." Amie grins. "Back there. With the banter." She bumps her hip against my arm. "Don't think I didn't notice the flirting."

Me? Flirt with him? The only flirting being done was with disaster.

"That was—we weren't—" I sputter.

She quirks an eyebrow. "I might not be into guys, but even so, he's objectively *fine*."

"The only thing between us is animosity."

"Animosity or animal attraction?" She whistles.

Ian looks up, searching our faces, then ducks back into the handbook.

"Amie, seriously," I say in an undertone. "He's not my type."

Disbelief cascades over her face. "Gorgeous isn't your type? He's the Peter Kavinsky of boys. With hot Captain Hook guyliner." She nudges me. "You're blushing."

Scoffing, I say, "If I am, it's only in secondhand embarrassment for how totally you've already fallen under his spell." I wiggle my fingers for effect. "He's perfected his dark magic over the years until no one is exempt from his evil charms."

Amie laughs. "Oh, babe. He's not doing a thing. He's just being himself." But she drops it, sweeping aquamarine eyeshadow over my lids to the tune of "Part of Your World."

In the background, Ian's mumbling his lines. A pause. The ruffle of a page. Back to mumbles.

"Hey, when did you get this?" Amie touches the back of my right shoulder, just above my shoulder blade.

"A few weeks ago. Do you like it?"

It's a small black tattoo of my own design: A small *Beauty and the Beast*–inspired rose held between the pointer finger and thumb of a hand in the shape of a mudra, a Hindu and Buddhist symbolic pose. The tips of the fingers are detailed with a mehendi design.

Growing up, I'd pored over the glossy full-page illustrations in the Indian mythology books Mom got us. I loved the classic Mysore paintings, but the scroll art was my favorite. They told the stories of the ancient heroes and heroines, their quests, their triumphs, and their tragedies.

"Yeah! I love it." Amie spins me around on the makeup chair. "Where'd you go?"

I give her the name of the place, a tattoo parlor in our historic downtown I'd researched extensively before making the appointment. "If you ever want one, I can design it for you."

"Wow. *You* designed that?" Amie's mouth drops open. With an apologetic wince, she adds, "But I do have to cover it up. Handbook rule. It sort of shatters the illusion that you're the real Ariel."

"Yeah, I understand."

Amie dabs foundation on my shoulder with a sponge, covering the tattoo. "You could make some money at this."

I drop my voice so Ian can't hear. "You know my Instagram?" She nods. "Some girl saw my work and asked how much I'd charge for her to take a design to her tattoo artist."

"You've gone pro!" she crows. "What did you say?"

"I told her twenty bucks. I was shitting myself the second I pressed send. Like, what if that was too much? I had no idea what to charge, but she agreed, and the next thing I knew, she posted photos of her tat online and tagged me. Some of her followers started messaging me for price quotes, and it sort of went from there. I spoke to some other artists on Insta to figure out what my rates should be."

"Girl, what are you doing working here?" Amie lightly swats my shoulder.

"Yeah, but where else do I have the joy of wearing an outfit as uncomfortable as this?" I wiggle my bottom half for emphasis. "Women threw out tight-ass corsets decades ago."

"You two better scoot," Poppy calls out, sticking her head through the door. "I loaded up the car with all the party gear." She glances at my stiff legs. "Ian, you'd better do the driving."

"Good luck, you two! Good luck, Ian. You'll be brilliant," says Amie.

"Thanks," he says, actually sounding a little grateful. Then he ruins it by saying, "Come on, Sushi, get a wiggle on."

"Who are you calling—"

He ignores my outrage and strides out the door.

Chemistry, mouths Amie.

Sure, I think to myself, blood boiling as I mince my way out the door. We have about as much chemistry as fire and gasoline. A freaking Chernobyl level of chemistry.

By the time I reach the exit, my boobs are sweaty and the underside of my wig is sticking in damp clumps to the back of my neck. "You could help me, you know," I point out.

Ian holds the door open with his back. He, on the other hand, in his deep V-neck with the billowing white sleeves, is looking lusciously cool and chiseled. Of course.

I have to angle awkwardly to squeeze past him.

He holds out a hand to stop me, a whisper away from my midriff. "I could," he says, putting his mouth so close to my ear I can feel the warmth of his breath. "But the view is so much more amusing from where I'm standing . . ."

I hope my glare conveys intent to telekinetically murder.

He very deliberately smirks, a slow and curving seduction that he excels at, just like everything else. ". . . Sushi."

I draw myself up, mouth dropping open. I don't have a snappy comeback. I know that I'd think of the perfect retort when it was too late, and I don't want to let him have the last word.

"Cummerbund," I manage to sputter. As far as retorts go, it's weak.

"Really, Joshi?" he drawls, letting his arm drop. "You can do better than that."

He has this competitive thing about using my last name when we're sparring. I'm never sure whether I like it or not.

Ian tosses the car keys in the air, scanning the parking lot until his eyes settle on the Pepto Bismol–pink sedan. Small towers are erected on the top, along with pink ribbons. It's either a nightmare or it's adorable. "Is that our ride? Jeez. It's hideous."

It's true. It is indeed hideous. But I relish in his grimace, taking in the barely there curl on his upper lip, the way his eyes squint as if he still can't believe it. For a moment, we're united in solidarity. It's not him against me. It's him *and* me.

It's tenuous, this tiny truce. It can shatter in an instant—it does.

"I don't know," I say, drawing each word out slowly. He can make all the fishy jokes about my costume he wants, but the delicious part of it all is the look of horror on his face as we head for the car. "The view looks pretty good from where I'm standing."

The look he sends me is pure evil.

I would attempt to genuflect as I quip, "Lead on, chauffeur," but the mermaid tail straitjackets me. I can barely sit, let alone bend a knee.

Ian holds the door open for me, eyebrow raised as I wriggle onto the seat, forced to slide down a little. "Joshi, you can't tell me you wouldn't have missed this if you didn't have me all summer."

"My blood pressure skyrocketing every time you open your mouth? Nope, I wouldn't."

He laughs, a wholly delighted sound that he has no business making after I've just rebuffed him. But he laughs anyway, and damn if the way he throws his head back, exposing his throat to me, isn't incredibly sexy.

Then he actually has the temerity to lean over and buckle me up. "Well—"

"Hey!"

"—I would have missed you." He shuts the door.

I'm left gaping at him, round-eyed and slack-jawed. He stole the last word. Again.

I'm more determined than ever to win each and every single contest between us this summer. I can already taste the victory on my tongue, sweet and light and magical. It feels like the last three years of high school were leading to this moment, this gauntlet.

Game, set, match.

15.
A Special Serenade Sounds Like a Lot of Fun

I SETTLE INTO my seat, shoulders stiff. The air between us thrums with an energy I can't place. When I sneak a glance at Ian, I can't read his face. The ground beneath me isn't solid, with known boundaries and precedents like at school.

It's new and uncharted. Exhilarating. Terrifying.

I've always been competitive, a little too naked in going after what I want, a little too eager to prove myself. Traits that, in a boy, would have been encouraged. Desirable, even.

My parents are always proud of me, but I can sense a hint of their embarrassment whenever our friends and relatives make one of their backhanded comments. The ones about my relentless drive and perseverance that prickled under my skin, tensed Mom's mouth with the effort it took to be polite.

With Ian, I've met my match. My ambition is rivaled only

by his own, and he gives as good as he gets. I never feel as me as I do when we're throwing down. I never feel as real as I do when we're nose to nose, arguing a point, trying to get the upper hand.

The GPS *ding* splinters our silence when we arrive at our destination. We park a few houses down from the birthday girl's. We always make sure to get there after the party begins so no one sees us arrive. It's another one of Poppy's rules: Do nothing to break the suspension of disbelief. Seeing a princess step out of a Toyota tends to have that kind of effect.

I curl my fingers around the door handle, ready to leave, but Ian doesn't make a move. The keys are still in the ignition. He's still. Too still.

"Are you okay?"

"No."

I freeze, too. His honesty takes me aback. No one actually ever says no.

I don't know what to do with that. Oh, this is bad. What if he freaks out and can't play his part? What do I do?

"Can we just sit here for a minute?" Ian asks, still not looking at me. He doesn't release the death grip he has on the keys.

"Sure." I sink against the passenger seat.

We're a few minutes early. It'll be fine. He just needs a minute to get in a fairy-tale prince's mind-set and work up the courage to face twenty hyper, sugar-fueled children.

I glance out the window. Almost all the houses on this street are huge two-story brick or stone, with manicured lawns and immaculate flower beds. It's the kind of street where people pay other people to mow their lawns for them, to take care of the koi in the fishpond, to clean their houses. Most people who hire us for their Princess Party are well-off and these clients are no exception.

I tug at his sleeve. "Hey, you good now? We're cutting it kinda close."

No one complains if you get there early, but you never hear the end of it if you're late.

"I . . ." He clasps the keys for a second before dropping his hands into his lap. He balls them tight and doesn't finish his sentence. The only sound in the car is his heavy breathing.

"I get that you're nervous, but—"

"I'm not nervous," he says. His voice is loud.

"Okay." I study him. The tenseness of his jaw, the rigidity of his pressed lips. The way he still isn't looking at me.

Where's his trademark Ian confidence? It's just a bunch of kids, nothing to be scared of.

Ian still doesn't say anything.

We've been hired as a couple, so we have to arrive together. I *need* him.

"I know this is your first time, but you read the handbook," I say, using my most soothing voice. "You're ready. Think of this as an exam you've studied really hard for. And I'll be there the whole time, you don't have to worry about—"

"I can't do it."

Shock ripples through me. I must have misheard him. There is no way he just said—

"I'm not going in," says Ian. He keeps looking straight ahead. "I mean, what I mean is . . . I can't."

The world gets quiet, a fog rolling in and clouding my brain until I lose my ability to form words. Or understand them.

Can't?

He can't go in?

As in physically unable to move his legs? Unable to open his car door?

It isn't *can't*. It's *won't*.

My heart hammers against my rib cage, raging like the Beast's anger at his own situation, at time running out.

The confused fog lifts as I say, "You're messing around, right, Ian? This is our job, you got that? Which means you can't just decide you won't get out of the car."

His silence fans my fury even more.

"Those people"—I jab my finger toward the house—"hired us for their daughter's fifth birthday party, and goddamn it, we're going to put on the best party she's ever seen. We're in the business of making kids' dreams come true. You knew that when you took the job."

If he'd make a peep, if he'd apologize, if he'd just say something. But his face is stoic and calm, as if I haven't just ripped him a new one. He doesn't look at me. He doesn't even twitch.

I get out of the car, which isn't easy when you're wearing a mermaid tail. I right myself and try to hide behind the door as I fix a wedgie.

In my mind I count, trying to give Ian a last chance to follow me out.

I can't even reach ten. By seven my emotions bubble over, and before I can hold back, I stick my head into the car. "Ian. *Ian*. Look at me. What's going on with you? *Let's go*."

Throwing aside my pride, I inject a plea into the last sentence, but he remains immobile, face marble-smooth and statuesque. It's the kind of still that pigeons could land on.

I'd never wanted Ian as my partner. If I could go back and tell Poppy no, I would have. He's too green, too new. He may have led the boys' tennis team to state, but I see no hint of those leadership qualities right now.

If he doesn't help me, I'll be the one who has to carry all the inflatables while pulling the suitcase full of arts and crafts, waddle my way to the front door without tripping, all to finally face down a room full of kids and their parents expecting a prince on my arm, not a seahorse floatie.

I don't mind performing alone; I've done it before. But now I'll have to give some kind of explanation to the parents, assure them Poppy would give them a partial refund, and then brave my way through two hours of singing and storytelling and face painting.

It's enough to make my own anxieties swell and crescendo, crashing over me like a tidal wave. I want to howl my confusion. This isn't the Ian I know. This cowardly lion version of him is a stranger. It's an Ian who isn't giving me his best; a Magikarp rather than a Gyarados. This is an Ian I don't know what to do with.

"What is *wrong* with you?" I don't yell, but I punctuate my sentence by slamming the door.

The sound makes him jerk, and I want to take it back immediately.

But I don't.

....

I vaguely remember speaking to the parents, making an excuse for Ian without combusting, and then plunging into the
backyard with my princess-perfect smile in full force and four
inflatable seahorses hooked on each arm.

The kids emit piercing shrieks when they see me, and the
birthday girl is the first to scramble out of the pool. Dripping
wet, she picks up her jeweled tiara from a lawn chair and
places it with somber precision on her head.

I press the button at the top of my seashell bra, activating
the speaker. "Hello, boys and girls! What a wonderful pool!" I
croon, my magnified voice oozing with sweetness.

Some of the kids openly look at my feet. Satisfied that I
have a tail, their eyes shine with unbridled childish belief.

Over the cacophony of *Ariel! Ariel! Look at me, Ariel! C'mon!
Come play with us!* the birthday girl sticks out her hand. "Princess Ariel," she greets in a very serious little voice.

"Happy birthday, Kaylee," I say, princess beam in full force.
"Would the birthday princess like to help me pass out some of
my friends from the sea?"

I hold one of the inflatable seahorses in front of her. The orange creature has a seat for children to sit in, and if they pump
their legs, they can participate in a seahorse race. It's popular
with the kiddies and is stable enough that parents don't have
to worry.

Kaylee sticks close to my side through the seahorse race,
finding excuses to hold my hand as often as she can. It's normal for the birthday girl or boy to monopolize my attention,

but today my patience frays with each new question she asks me. She clings to me, keeping up an incessant stream of chatter, asking me about my dad, King Triton, and if I was scared when I lost my voice, and when is Prince Eric coming?

The first two questions I can answer with ease, but when it comes to making an excuse for my partner, the erstwhile Prince Eric, I fumble.

"Oh, sweetie," I stammer, "you know, I think he just hasn't found his way here, yet. The ocean's a pretty big place."

She opens her mouth to ask another question.

"Time for a song!" I hurry to my black roll-along suitcase. The front flap holds a tablet programmed with the theme songs from Ariel's world. "Shake a fin, kids! Join me on the grass, if you please!"

One press of a button and music pipes out, earning a new round of squeals from the children who recognize the opening of "Under the Sea." I can't afford to fumble on the lyrics, so I push all thoughts of Ian out of my mind.

While kids are forgiving of my crap singing voice, the one thing they won't tolerate is butchered lyrics. I lead them in song after song until the fidgeting begins. When that happens, I switch direction and tell everyone to get back in the water so we can play one of my favorite under-the-sea circle games, Flounder, Flounder, Sebastian!

Perched on the edge of the pool, I allow my thoughts to wander. Is Ian still sitting down the street, or has he taken off? Will I be stranded here until Amie picks me up?

The idea of standing on the sidewalk in a purple bra and

inflatable toys on my arms makes me want to cry. It wasn't like he was the only one nervous about today. It was my first time playing Ariel, *and* I had to carry the whole show on my bare shoulders.

I throw a surreptitious glance at the open garden gate as though Ian would come striding confidently through at any moment. My chest heaves as I try to calm down. My fingers curl into very unprincess-like fists, seafoam-green nails digging into my palms.

Don't cry, Kavya, don't cry.

I wipe all trace of worry from my face as I teach the kids the steps to the water waltz, followed by face painting. My muscles ache with the effort it takes to remain peppy and upbeat as I paint tropical fish on squirmy, giggly cheeks.

"How long will it last?" Kaylee asks, shoveling a frosted-and-sprinkled sugar cookie in her mouth. "Until I go to day care tomorrow?" She glances furtively at her mom.

I give her my practiced princess giggle. "Of course not! Your Mommy makes you wash your face, right? Well, good princesses always go to bed with a clean, scrubbed face."

"Oh, okay." The belief shines in Kaylee's eyes as she hangs on to my every word.

Kaylee gives me a toothy grin. "Does your color wash off when you go home?"

It takes me a moment to understand that she means my underwater kingdom. "Yes," I say. "But that's okay. I'm enjoying it so much right now."

Her friends crowd around for their turns. My little acolytes throw me rapid-fire questions. *Were you scared going to Ursula? When did you get your voice back?*

And then the most dreaded question of all: Am I *sure* Prince Eric isn't coming?

Honestly, that's something I'd like to know, too.

My jaw hurts from smiling and laughing. I love how much energy there is at children's parties, that molten ooey-gooey feeling when kids look at you like you're their hero. A princess, not a beast. Some questions are adorable, some will throw you.

But this question is one I don't know how to answer.

We have to get back on track. "Now why don't we sing 'Part of Your World' to the birthday girl before we make our swords and tiaras? A special serenade sounds like a lot of fun, doesn't it?"

The kids sit cross-legged around me on the grass. The song will only buy me a few minutes. While the soundtrack plays and everyone sings their little hearts out, my thoughts lead me back to Ian.

My harsh words haunt me. I am literally Ursula in this scenario, not Ariel. Sure, Ian let me down—and let the party down—but I'm ashamed I lost my cool.

His total lack of a reaction makes me feel guiltier. He should have gotten out of the car and yelled at me. Told me that I had crossed a line. But the way he'd frozen, gone so still and unblinking . . . it was like he hadn't even heard me.

He'd hung me out to dry and I have no idea why. I definitely deserve an apology for that, but I owe him one, too.

Only when Kaylee stares at me do I realize I've stopped singing midway through the song. I take a deep breath and rally. Enough dwelling on Ian. I still have a job to do. I just need to get through one more activity and the cake-cutting, and then I'm home free.

Just as I open my mouth to belt out the next verse, the kids all jump up and start to squeal. The song is forgotten. The *Fairy-tale Handbook* stresses the importance of not scolding or disciplining the children, so I fight past my first impulse to tell them to settle down.

Instead, I turn to see what has captured their attention.

16.
Three Magic Words

IAN STEPS THROUGH the gate like a knight in shining armor. His face belies his confident swagger as he approaches, but the kids are too excited to notice the naked terror. The party's almost over, but now here he is, sweeping in like he's saving the day.

Ian's throat bobs, and I wonder if he's swallowing past his dry mouth. Finally, he unglues his lips and manages to get out, "Is there a Princess Kaylee here?"

"Me!" The princess in question shoots past me and grabs Ian's hands, sending a new wave of emotion across his face.

He catches my eye. The regret is there, painfully obvious to see. My breath catches. What changed? What made him decide to show up, after all?

The kids all clamor for Prince Eric as Kaylee leads Ian to

our sing-along group, chattering a mile a minute about all the Little Mermaid stuff she owns. Only children can make rampant consumerism seem charming.

Ian makes all the appropriate oohing and aahing noises, compliments everyone on their beautiful face paint, and kisses a few hands. In the span of a minute, I am chopped mermaid.

Once again, he's managed to charm everyone around him.

Ian doesn't quite bask in the attention, but it doesn't take long for him to relax around the kids, who don't seem to notice he isn't as outgoing as me, or that he still has a panicky look in his eyes. By the time everyone calms down, the tablet switches to the next song in the playlist, and our singing is forgotten.

While music plays in the background, Ian and I get the cardboard swords and tiaras out, and the kids exuberantly start decorating. I take a step back so I can stand next to Ian. "You came," I say, keeping my voice low so no one can overhear us.

He doesn't acknowledge me at first, and just as I'm about to bristle and move away, he whispers, "I know it's probably too little, too late, but I'm sorry, Kavya. I . . . I couldn't move. I didn't care that it would make the company look bad, or that you'd have to do it alone. Every thought in my head was screaming *Don't go in there.*"

My eyebrows draw together. Feeling sympathy for my nemesis is somewhat unexpected, but I guess it's stemming from the residual protectiveness from the spin-the-bottle kiss. Maybe that explains my emotions, but I still can't figure out why he was so scared or why it had come on seemingly so suddenly.

As he opens his mouth to say something more, I lightly touch his wrist. It's barely a second, but the skin-on-skin contact electrifies me. From his sharp intake of breath, he feels it, too.

"Not now," I whisper. "Later."

Do not break character is another rule in the *Fairy-tale Handbook*.

He nods and crouches to help a little boy glue rhinestones to his cardboard sword.

A few of the boys want tiaras, too, and even though one parent tries to object, I calmly distribute extra tiara and sword templates to everyone, while Ian hands over the container of sparkling gems.

The face paint will wash off, but I know from the parent testimonials on our website that the kids will wear the crowns and swords until they fall apart. The mementos we leave behind are as precious to them as the party itself.

Kaylee's parents bring out the cake before the kids get hungry and cranky, and Ian and I lead everyone in singing "Happy Birthday." While the kids smear icing over themselves, we are momentarily forgotten. The timing is perfect. I sneak a quick look at the tablet, which reveals we'd gone a few minutes over the two hours we'd been paid for.

"Time to pack up," I murmur to Ian. "While the kids are distracted."

Between us, we clean up the craft area and pack the unused

materials away. My shoulders begin to ache, and I crave the silence and solitude of a nap.

Goodbyes are always the hardest. No one wants to see us leave, but it's best to slip away on a high note.

"I'm afraid it's time for us to go home," I say, dropping to my knees to give a personal farewell to Kaylee. I kiss both her cheeks. "I had a wonderful time with you today, and I hope you have a very, very happy birthday."

She grasps at my hands. "But you'll come back soon, right?" She looks up at her parents for confirmation.

"Maybe you'll invite me back for your next birthday," I say. "Or you might see me at a friend's house one day."

"You'll bring Eric?" Kaylee peers at Ian, who's waiting for me with the suitcase.

I bite back a smile when Ian waves at her. Her cheeks are flushed and her eyes are bright. I may be her favorite princess, but there's no question who stole her heart this afternoon. I half turn, sneaking a peek at him. I'm still not over his ditching me, but his surprise appearance has definitely been a step in the right direction.

I turn back to Kaylee with a smile. "If you tell your parents that's what you want, then I'm sure we can come back," I say. It may be another pair of performers in our place, but after a year's time, Kaylee won't remember.

Her beam stretches from cheek to cheek.

Once we leave the backyard, I let out the breath I've been holding, just like the girl in the latest YA romance I devoured.

Walking back to the car, I dart furtive glances at Ian. There is no trace of his earlier meltdown as he swings the seahorses from his arms, face tilted to enjoy the warmth of the sun. It doesn't escape me that he's slowed his steps so I can keep up in my straitjacket skirt.

Will we talk about what happened? Should I thank him for coming back? No, I won't thank him for doing the job he was supposed to do.

He unlocks the trunk and spreads out a sheet of plastic. "Just push the suitcase to the side," he says in his usual pompous, know-it-all voice, "so the water doesn't get on it."

I bristle. I've been doing this for two years, he doesn't have to tell me. "Do it yourself, then."

Instead of helping, I sashay to the front passenger seat and let myself in. The car is about ten degrees hotter than the outside temperature, and the hot metal buckle of the seatbelt scalds my fingertips. With a soft yelp, I latch the belt.

Ian's eyebrows furrow. "You okay?"

Our eyes meet. My momentary annoyance fades as questions reel and twist in my stomach like a pit of snakes. What happened to make him shut down? What snapped him out of it long enough to join me?

My lips part, but I stop myself, forcing the curiosity to fizzle out in my throat like the last sliver of a spicy Altoid. No, I won't ask him anything if he doesn't want to share, not even if I want to know. I'd tasted my own venom two hours ago, and have no intention of repeating the experience. There is no sign of the stranger who sat in this car before, the boy who literally couldn't speak to me. The person left in his place is cool, composed, collected Ian Jun.

"I'm fine," I say, even though I don't think I am. Something between us has shifted imperceptibly, or maybe it's a yawning divide, or maybe I'm just letting the game get to me. "But, um, are you okay?"

Color blooms across his cheeks, contrasting against his pale skin like a streak of red paint. It crosses my mind that he could pretend nothing has happened, and I wonder if he'll take the out.

"No," he says, clearing his throat. "But I will be."

His honesty again takes me by surprise. Who is Ian, really, when he isn't tennis captain Ian, or French Club president Ian, or voracious reader Ian?

Is he all of those people? Or none of them?

All I know is that the Ian in front of me now is unlike any of the faces he's shown me before. It's tough to reconcile all the Ians I've seen today with my Ian, and it's a little terrifying that there even is such a thing as *my* Ian.

My heart zings with the surprising awareness that I actually want to dissect him, want to know him and understand him. The snakes slither up, wrapping and constricting around my heart. Oh, this is painful.

"I have anxiety," Ian says at last. The fuzzy, soft moment that is cocooning us lifts. I blink away the haze as he says, "I should have probably told you, but I thought I had it under control. I thought the more I studied the *Fairy-tale Handbook*, the more okay I'd be."

"I was really anxious the first time I went to one of these parties, too—" I say, but he cuts me off.

"No." Ian shakes his head. "You were anxious. I have anxiety. There's a difference."

Shame creeps over my skin, hot and itchy. I open and shut my mouth. He's right. I stress all the time, using it as fuel to bulldoze ahead, but it's not the same. "I'm so sorry."

"It's okay. You didn't know. It looks different on everyone, and the way I go through it is different than the way someone else might. I can usually manage it, but this time it got to me."

How could I have missed the signs? I rub at my wrist, swallowing hard. "Thank you, but you don't have to minimize it. I really am sorry for yelling and walking away like that, without making sure you were okay. Please, if it happens again, just tell me what's going on? I was worried about y—" I clamp my lips shut. I hadn't meant to say that last part. It just slipped out.

The silence lingers until it becomes uncomfortable. Both of us suddenly find it difficult to look at each other, so Ian starts the engine and hits the radio. A loud, catchy song from *My Little Pony* comes on, startling us both.

"What the—" Ian swats at the buttons again, switching to the five p.m. drive-home show. One of the top forty hits of the week begins to play, and he relaxes in his seat, face an amusing shade of pink.

The giggle bubbles out of me even though I clap my hand over my mouth.

"Do you actually listen to that?" Ian asks incredulously. One of his perfect Shipwrecked Prince eyebrows rises.

"No!" My laugh turns into a cough. "It's Amie's mix CD."

"People still make those?"

"She listens to these obnoxious songs to get her in an up-beat mood. She swears by them. Calls it the 'roids of entertainment because everyone is their best Disney self," I say.

"Not me." He shudders. "I'd go bananas."

"Me too. The beat gives me a headache."

Ian glances at the rearview mirror before pulling away from the curb. "So what do the faux-Marvel entertainers listen to?"

"Imagine Dragons."

He gives me a huge, unabashed grin. "Makes sense," he says gravely.

We drive in silence until we hit a red at the intersection. He turns to me, and I can sense his hesitation.

"Yeah?" I cock my head.

"I was just going to say . . ." He pauses. "I didn't really earn my paycheck. I was unprofessional. I'll tell Poppy to make it out to you, instead."

Taken aback, I say, "No, you don't have to do that."

"No, I do," he says. "You did all the work. I just showed up at the end. I don't think she's going to keep me around after—"

I don't want to win like this. "Ian, stop. I'm not going to be the reason why you lose your job, okay? Poppy's understanding. First day jitters are normal, and I'll help you get through it the next time, if it happens again." Flustered, I give him what I hope is an encouraging smile.

He seems surprised. "Really? You'd do that?"

For a quicksilver flash of a second, I realize that there is an opportunity here to extract something from him. A beastly, besharam opportunity. Tell him not to run for president of student government next year or to nominate me for French Club president. Make him throw his support behind me. The temptation shines apple-red, snake shameless. And then I look at him.

The thoughts flee as soon as I see the gratitude in his face.

Kavya, try to be more fairy-tale Princess and less fairy-tale villain!

"Then let me at least treat you to a burger or something," says Ian. He holds up a hand when I open my mouth to argue, and says the three magic words, the words I'm aching to hear, the ones I'll dream about tonight.

"I owe you."

"You're late," Ian says as I step through the doors of Holly Gogogi.

I sniff appreciatively; the most delicious saucy, garlicky smell is wafting from their kitchen.

"I *did* tell you I needed time to get ready," I say with a small *hmph.*

Ian's smile is a thousand watts as he eyes the words on my shirt. "Because this is a date?"

"I—what—no! You do realize girls wear makeup for reasons other than boys, right?"

This is absolutely, categorically *not* a date. Yes, I did go home to shower first, but that has zip, zilch, zero to do with *him*. And sure, I scrubbed off my mermaid makeup and replaced it with something a little more me, but I'm looking good for myself, not anyone else. All he has to do is look at my white tee with the Usagi BOYS ARE THE ENEMY meme to realize this is not a date by any definition of the word.

"I know." He's still smiling. "That highlighter looks familiar. It looks nice."

An innocuous remark, if it weren't for the fact I'm wearing the same one from the night we kissed. I keep my face straight under my bright-purple MAC Heroine lipstick and NARS Orgasm blush. This is another one of his games, trying to unsettle me with what sounds like a compliment but is probably masquerading as something else. I've noticed he's quite good at quips that could go either way.

The Korean American fusion diner is located in the heart of the Riverwalk in downtown Luna Cove, next to the Cold Brew Bros where the moon girls got bubble tea the other day and the Sicilian pizza parlor that allegedly gets lax about carding on busy Friday nights.

An ode to Ian's mother's favorite movie and actress, the walls are covered in framed Audrey Hepburn photos and *Breakfast at Tiffany's* posters. The red-and-white checkerboard floor gleams underfoot, even shinier with the reflective glow of the cherry-red chrome pendant lights.

While a comeback coalesces, my eye catches on the walls. There are pictures of Ian's little sister, Grace, framed behind the cashier's counter. Her glossy black hair is styled in a bowl cut that adorably frames her face; I vividly remember my mom subjecting me to a less flattering one when I was Grace's age. But where I sulked in photos until my hair grew out, Grace is smiling, happy.

Forever a little girl: sucking her thumb going down a slide, hanging off her dad's back like a monkey, sitting next to a giggling Ian at the diner counter with two fries sticking out of her mouth like a walrus with a bulgogi pizza between them.

Ian's mom emerges from the kitchen. "Ian, you're home!" Catching sight of me, she beams, smile almost as disarming as her son's. "Kavya! It's so nice to see you."

"Hi, Mrs. Jun. Same to you."

I've seen her a hundred times at school and Holly Gogogi since Grace passed away, but I always see her the way she looked the first time my mom and I ran into her at the grocery store after the funeral. I remember my mom's hushed condolences, Mrs. Jun's drawn face and baggy, nondescript clothing. The way she folded into Mom's arms like she wanted to stay there for an eternity.

Today she's wearing a black shirt that reads SUPER MOM, SUPER TIRED in silver rhinestone letters and slim-fitting black pants. She glances between me and Ian like she's about to tell a secret. "He talks about you a lot."

Nothing good, I'm sure.

"We do enjoy a very healthy rivalry," I say with a wry, self-conscious laugh.

She looks confused, but as she opens her mouth to speak, Ian jumps in with, "Mom, I thought we'd grab dinner? To celebrate. I couldn't have gotten through today without her."

His mom hesitates, and I realize it's because she probably wants to ask Ian about his first day, but not in front of me. "I'll let your dad know you're back." She disappears into the kitchen.

"Let's grab a booth," says Ian. "If we sit at the counter, she'll grill you about your plans for the future." He grabs a menu for me and leads the way to a table in front of the window.

It's early for dinner; the only other people here are older couples and parents with young children. They look up and smile as we pass, like they think we're a cute teenage couple. My spine tingles as I sit down on cool leather. I curl my toes inside my shoes, repressing a shiver at the idea of being a *we* with my nemesis.

Swiftly, I put my menu up, creating a wall between us.

"So, um," he says, breaking my concentration in pretending to look over the menu. "I wanted to thank you again for covering for me. I appreciate it. I promise it won't happen again."

I shift, wincing at the squeak of the leather. "Yeah, it's . . . yeah. Don't mention it."

The next silence is longer. I go back to taking an inordinate amount of interest in the menu. I swallow past the dryness, a contrast to the clamminess of my palms.

"You still like the bulgogi burger?" Ian drums his long, lean fingers against the tabletop.

"It's my favorite." I pause. "You remember that?"

He scoffs. "Of course I do. I—" He breaks off, eyes shining dark as onyx. "I help my dad out in the kitchen sometimes. I recognize your order. I mean, your family's order."

"But I never see you. Ever since I started driving, I'm the one who does the pickup."

He smiles. "Kitchen, remember? I hate doing the customer-facing stuff."

"Because of your anxiety?" I lower my voice on the last word, and take the menu with it.

"You don't have to tiptoe. It's not a bad word."

"No, sorry, of course it isn't. I didn't mean to . . ." I trail off, biting my lip. "Sorry."

"It's okay. I get it. You're a Leo *and* you're Kavya. You never want to look bad."

Pinpricks dot my arms, skitter down my neck, tingle my scalp. Ian says it like he's studied me, deciphering my equation by isolating every individual variable. I flash back to stats class and the way he knew exactly what I was going to do. Like math, he can count on there being only one outcome when it comes to me.

"Am I predictable?" I ask him suddenly.

He gives me a quizzical look.

"Nothing. Never mind." I busy myself with the menu again, even though we both know I'm going to order the bulgogi burger in the bao bun with extra pickled daikon and carrot.

"Read any good books lately?" he asks conversationally.

I peek at him over the top of the menu. "I know what you're doing."

"I'm not doing anything. I'm making conversation with my co-worker." But the sparkle in his brown eyes tells a different story.

"Have *you* read any good books lately?" I counter.

He dimples before saying breezily, "Fifteen of them. All solid five-star reads."

My eyes bug out. "Fifteen—!"

"Sixteen tonight." He steeples his fingers together and lets his fingertips dance against each other. "I'm racing toward the climax of this amazing fantasy."

I swallow. Hard. He sure does have a way with words.

He's trying to psych me out. There's no way he's that much ahead. My knee-jerk reaction is to make up an astronomically high number of books that I've supposedly read, but knowing him, he'd just make it his personal mission to exceed my benchmark, and then I'll be worse off.

"I'll go tell Dad what we're having," says Ian, sliding to the edge of the bench seat with a knowing smirk. "And when I get back, maybe we could talk about last week?"

My heart lurches. He wants to talk about the kiss? Putting it into words?

Calm down, Kavya. He's goading you again.

I feel like I'm losing my grip on something, and even though I hate running from anything or anyone, the niggling thought occurs that I could probably make it out the door before he comes back. But no, I'm not going to be underhanded, and even though my go-to move would be to one-up Ian somehow, I *can't* after what he's shared with me. I don't want to imagine the wounded look on his face once he realizes I've slipped out while his back was turned.

"Anything I do to you, you'll see it coming," I mutter.

"Did you say something?" Ian's back with two cans of pear soda so cold he has to actually shake some feeling back into his hands when he sits down.

"Erm, no," I reply with a straight face.

"So I'm just going to come out and say it," he says. "I was wrestling with whether or not to even mention it, but it felt wrong—"

"—I couldn't agree more—" I interject.

"—not to give you a heads-up," Ian finishes, giving me a weird look. "Wait, what are you talking about?"

I hastily pop the tab on my soda and take a deep swig. Bubbles effervesce in my mouth, and I swallow before I have to cough. "No, sorry, you were saying?"

Ian leans in, hair falling slightly into his eyes. He brushes it back with a soft sound of annoyance. "My friends accidentally dropped a hint that the next contest is going to be a game of Scrabble. I promise they didn't mean to; it just slipped out while we were chatting." He flashes me a teasing grin. "Don't worry, I know how to spell *Brobdingnagian*."

"Scrabble?" I raise a doubtful eyebrow. "That seems pretty tame."

"What did you expect? Fisticuffs?"

No, that only happens in sexually explicit Victorian romance novels. Like the one I was reading last night before bedtime. With a guy wearing a billowy white cotton shirt. Similar to the one Ian wore today as my Shipwrecked Prince.

Correction, as *the* Shipwrecked Prince.

I take another sip of pear soda before asking, "Why are you telling me?"

Honestly, if our positions were reversed, I'm not sure I would. Unless . . . he's trying to throw me off. Get me to waste time preparing for Scrabble, when really the bet is about something else. Spreading misinformation under the guise of a truce.

I steel myself. One burger does not a friendship make. He's got another think coming if he seriously believes I'm going to accept his overture at face value.

"Why wouldn't I tell you?" Ian seems surprised. "It wouldn't be fair if you didn't have the same info as me."

"That hasn't usually been the case when I'm competing with a guy," I say tightly.

"Yeah, well, you've had pretty awful taste in boyfriends," he says with a shrug.

I flex my fingers around the icicle-chilly can. "Aw, you jealous?"

His eyes darken at my mockery and he leans closer, opening his mouth to speak, when his mom's cheerful voice chirps, "Don't you two look cozy!"

She sets down two plates loaded with bulging bulgogi burgers and BBQ-gochujang kimchi fries piled with seared flank steak, a confetti of green-and-white shredded scallions, and a generous dusting of toasted sesame seeds. "Bon appétit!"

"Thanks, Mrs. Jun," I say, ready to dig in.

I might be breaking bread with my rival today, but for our second test I'm going Old Testament on his ass.

17.
We Ride at Dawn

BY THE TIME Saturday comes around, I've suckered my family into playing enough cutthroat, no-holds-barred games of Scrabble to convince myself I have what it takes to beat Ian so soundly that the loss shadows him all the way to college. Three shouting matches between me and Simmy—that could only be solved by Dad refereeing with *Webster's*—later, Mom's forbidden us from playing this board game ever again.

Just in case Ian's telling the truth, I want to show up today prepared and ready to battle wits. But according to our friends' rules, if either one of us doesn't show up or arrives late, we forfeit the game. After all their complaints about our longtime rivalry, they've weirdly gotten into the spirit of it. I grind my teeth and eye the car clock as the minute changes.

I glance down at my phone, where Ian's most recent

message from this morning is open on my screen: the "So it begins" King Théoden GIF from *Lord of the Rings: The Two Towers*.

It's perfect. I wish I'd sent it first.

Instead, I'd sent the moon girls group chat the "We ride at dawn, bitches" Big Bird–riding-a-carriage meme. Catey, Blaire, and Val had responded with hearts, flames, and prayer hands, respectively.

I might not have Aragorn's sword or Legolas's bow, but at least I had my girls. Big moon-girl energy was all I needed to win this battle.

"Finally," I say when Mom emerges from the kitchen-garage door. Her hair is set in large, bouncy curls, and her face glows with the new products she got from Sephora. I've been waiting in her car for five minutes already, just seconds away from honking.

"Why are you so antsy to get to the library?" Simran's bare toes prod my arm. She's sprawled out in the middle of the back seat, legs propped up on the center console.

I scooch away until I'm up against the window. I unwrap a Cherry Tootsie Pop, my favorite flavor, and stick it in my mouth, careful not to smudge my lip gloss. "No reason."

"You *always* have a reason."

I can hear the archness in her tone, the surety that she knows me. Ian sounds like that sometimes, too, as though he's the only one with the cheat codes to figure me out. That brings a smile to my face, the implication that I'm a final boss that you have no hope of defeating unless you're super leveled up.

Mom scrutinizes all her shoes on the shoe rack before selecting a pair of espadrilles. I dart an aggravated look at the car clock. "Come on, come on," I mutter under my breath as she waves them at me, then slips them on.

"Right. You're in no rush at all," drawls Simran. "I completely believe you."

So I tell her about the best-of-three summer competition, wrapping it up with, "Today's the second one. Ian gave me a heads-up that it's Scrabble."

"So *that's* why we played all weekend." A beat. "Who won the first?"

"Uh . . . we tied."

Mom gets in with an apologetic smile. "I'm stopping by the Indian store after dropping you off. Any requests?"

"Mango juice and masala noodles." Before she can lift her mirror to check out her makeup, I say, "I'm going to be late! You look great, Mom. Can we go? Please?"

"You've got it." Mom puts the car into reverse.

While Simran chatters in the back seat about how her latest poem just got accepted to a paid journal, I stare at Ian's GIF as we pull out of the driveway. By the time my screen fades to black, Mom and Simran have started singing the latest Harry Styles song along with the radio.

"Kavya, why don't you join in?" Mom asks, turning the music up a notch. "Remember those cute little duets you two did when you were kids?"

"Please, for the love of god, *nooooo!*" Simran good-naturedly squeals. "I still have nightmares!"

And *that's* why I don't sing anywhere other than work. Not even in front of family. In my heart, I'm still that girl who struck out for a choir solo. It had taken every bit of bravery to stand on the auditorium stage and belt out my audition, only to be rejected.

That will never happen again.

"Come on," cajoles Mom. "I can see you tapping your feet to the rhythm."

I deflect by saying, "When I make my comeback tour, you'll be the first to know. Until then, there's no way I'm embarrassing myself in front of you two nightingales. I'm fine being left out."

Simran's toes dig into the back of my arm. "You sing Disney songs at work!"

I elbow her away from the armrest. "That's different! Kids don't laugh."

By the time Mom pulls up in front of the library, it's T minus sixteen minutes.

"Good luck! Kick some butt!" Simran calls as I dash from the car, black tote folded in fourths under my arm. I lift my other arm to wave without looking back.

On my way to the wide, winding staircase that leads to the second floor, I stop to drop my completed reading cards into the clear bowl at the front desk. Mrs. Carnegie isn't there, but her cardigan is on the back of her office chair.

I follow the fall of my cards to another entry right on top. It's easy to make out three Rick Riordan titles written in all caps and the name printed in neat blue ballpoint: Ian Jun.

I sigh. Because *of course.*

"Kavya!"

Mrs. Carnegie bustles toward me with a steaming mug of coffee from the break room. "I was hoping you'd come in; there's something new in the YA section I think you'd love." She rubs at the lipstick on the rim before gesturing for me to follow her.

I throw my eyes skyward. *Please don't let this take long.*

Luckily the YA books are right by the staircase. At the top of the new-release bookshelf is an acrylic stand with a flyer inside.

MYSTERY DATE WITH A BOOK: DON'T JUDGE US BY OUR COVER! IF YOU GIVE US A GLANCE, GIVE US A CHANCE. WE MAY SURPRISE YOU!

Corny. But cute. I can't resist smiling. I'm intrigued by the books placed face out, wrapped in brown paper. Scrawled across the front in familiar writing are clues as to what the book inside might be. The writer has a flair for pinpointing popular tropes, writing them in a quippy, juicy way, like someone might tease you with details about the mystery date they're setting you up with.

"Turned out great, right?" Mrs. Carnegie bumps my shoulder with her own.

"Yeah, this looks really fun. Who did it?"

Her mouth parts in surprise. "Oh, gosh, I'm sorry. I meant this." She reaches out to grab a brochure holder from the top of the new-release bookshelf. "Your bookmarks."

I tear my gaze away from the "Mystery Date with a Book" shelf to stare at the four bookmarks I designed and emailed over to her a week ago.

"I had them printed. High gloss," she continues. "Don't the colors really pop?"

I'm saved from answering when Ian's voice behind me says, "I see you found my latest project. What do you think, Kavya? Trust me enough to let me pick a book for you?"

I turn around with a smile plastered on for Mrs. Carnegie's benefit. Pretending to think about it, I say, "No. *I* have good taste."

His brown eyes up-down my leopard-print minidress and matching buckled platform sandals. With a lazy grin, he says, "I think we both do."

I return his interest, noting the coral dad-on-a-cruise shirt he's wearing that looks impossibly worn-in and soft, strewn all over with hibiscus flowers. The Ray-Bans tucked into his collar and the braided, tawny leather bracelet on his slim right wrist. He's . . . I don't want to say *hot*.

"Nope," I say coolly. "No discernible overlap between us whatsoever."

"Right." His eyes laugh at me.

Mrs. Carnegie looks between us with a faint crease in her forehead. Then she breaks out into an encouraging smile, as if she's come to some realization. "Kavya, why don't you take one? Like you said, it'll be really fun."

Ian freezes in the act of plucking out four of my bookmarks.

His grin widens, turns a little wicked. Smile #7. "You said that?"

Then, as if he knows I'm not going to dignify that with a response, he selects one of the wrapped books from the shelf and thrusts it at me. "I think you'll enjoy this one."

Mrs. Carnegie beams like she's successfully socialized two squalling, hissing cats. I stare at his hand. I don't want to accept the book.

But Mrs. Carnegie clearly expects me to take it, and if I don't, Ian will read into it, but taking the book feels like I'd be admitting something, and I don't quite know what that is or why my stomach is twisting. Half-formed ramblings ricochet in the space between his outstretched hand and my hesitant fingers as I—finally—accept the book.

I graze his fingers by accident. They twitch against mine, and in the shock, I drop the book, catching it seconds before it hits the floor.

"Nice reflexes, Joshi," says Ian. "I mean, it's no desk jump, but full points for effort."

I scowl and extend the black tote to him. "Thanks for the loan."

"Keep it," he says, ears turning slightly pink.

"Isn't it library property?" I glance at Mrs. Carnegie.

She sticks the bookmarks back on the shelf. "Oh, no. Ours are green. Remember? We got rid of the plastic bags when LCPL started our sustainability and clean earth program."

"So then whose—" I start to say, but Ian clears his throat.

"We have to go," he says. "We have that *thing*." He flicks his eyes to the stairs.

Mrs. Carnegie eyeballs us with interest.

Nice going, Ian. Very not suspicious at all.

"Thanks for commissioning me to do these again this year, Mrs. C.," I say, grabbing four of my bookmarks. One of each design. I wait for Ian to put his back, but he doesn't. And then, because he makes no move to recover the bag he gave me, I drop them all inside along with the wrapped book. The bag's not cute, but it's mine now, I guess.

Ian and I take the stairs two at a time, watching each other from the corners of our eyes instead of the steps beneath us. Honestly, it's a miracle neither of us trips.

Our friends have reserved one of the private study rooms on the second "silent" floor. The rooms are soundproofed, but there are still signs everywhere reminding us that there's no talking allowed. Each room is named after a famous literary character, and there's a certain irony that according to the gold placard on the door, this one is called DARCY.

We're the first ones to arrive. T minus five minutes.

Inside, DARCY is all dark cherrywood and green, stained glass Tiffany lamps. As I fling the door open, dust motes suspended in the entrance are illuminated by shafts of light from the hallway window.

Ian waves my bookmarks in the air, scattering the dust motes into a tiny tornado. "Thank god I took my allergy meds this morning." Without skipping a beat, he adds, "You've got your plotting look on."

I spare him a glance. "Excuse me? My what now?"

"You know, the attractively diabolical face you wear when

you think you're ahead. Pretty similar to your 'Any day that ends in -y' look." He smirks, slinging his arm around my shoulder like we're friends. Casual, something he doesn't think twice about doing. He does it all the time with his friends, and once upon a dream ago, with me. But that was a very, very long time ago.

"I don't have either of those." I don't shake him off.

"You do. It's a close cousin to that murderous look you're wearing now."

My whole face scrunches. "I don't, and while we're on the subject, how is that even a thing that you know? Do you just watch my face?"

He doesn't miss a beat. "Only got eyes for you, Joshi."

"Sound creepier, why don't you?" I mean it to sound less of a challenge than it does.

Ian laughs. The sound melts over me like chocolate left out in the sun.

"Ah, right. I got it. Keeping your archenemy in your sights at all times, right?" I slide away, jutting my pointer finger a hair's breadth away from his chest. Not touching. "Friends close, enemies closer type of deal?"

"People don't have enemies in real life, you know, let alone archenemies." He pauses, then waggles his eyebrows. "Do I need to watch my back? *Et tu, Kavya?*"

I scoff. "If I'm stabbing anyone, it's going to be in the front so you can see me coming."

Ian takes a step closer, shirt brushing my finger. "Good to know," he purrs.

His shirt is absolutely as soft as I thought it would be. Ugh. Horrendous.

I go still to keep myself from curling my fingers into the fabric like that one time I refuse to think about.

"Are you excited about the trip to the Grimaldi Castle Hotel?" he asks, mercifully giving me a respite from the very, very weird direction my thoughts have taken.

One of Poppy's clients is hosting their daughter's eleventh birthday party at a swanky castle venue in northern Indiana, and they hired almost the entire fairy-tale cast to make the weekend magical. Amie gave me the permission slip to take home to my parents right after a Snow White party with Samer earlier in the week, but how does *Ian* know about—

He must read the question on my face, because he arches a brow so high it could go into space. "Did you forget I'm your prince?"

"There's a couples' waltz on the agenda; Poppy's having all of us come in next week to practice. I can't play two roles at once!"

He shrugs. "Samer said he's paired with another Snow White."

"What?"

It's a good thing the room is soundproofed, otherwise everyone else on this floor would have heard my screech. My fingers scrunch into his shirt, inadvertently pulling him closer.

His eyes widen. "Don't kill the messenger!"

Unfreakingbelievable. This is what I get for not letting him quit when I had the chance. A whole weekend of Ian's hands on my waist, leading me around a ballroom, staring into my eyes like I'm the only girl in the world, leaning in with his eyes closed and his lips parted—

There's a sick tug at my navel as the room spins.

This is all because of that truth-or-dare kiss. It has to be. It's the only variable in our relationship that's changed.

"Don't worry," Ian says quickly. "It won't be a repeat of our first party. I won't let you down. It's just the first time doing anything new that makes me freeze. Everyone experiences anxiety differently, but for me, it's the not knowing exactly *what* is going to happen *when* that triggers it. Once I know what to expect, I'm ready to tackle whatever comes my way. I, um, meant to tell you earlier, at Holly Gogogi's."

I chew my lower lip. "I'm not worried about that. I'll be there with you every step of the way." It's odd offering myself as someone's source of comfort, especially when that person is Ian. "So what made you take the job at Poppy's, anyway?"

"My anxiety. I wanted to do the scary thing. I wanted to know that I could."

"Oh, are you interested in acting? Or some other job working with kids?"

"No, nothing like that, I just hoped to impress—"

"Hurry up! We're almost late!" peals from outside, followed by immediate shushing.

Ian and I spring apart. My hand flexes against my thigh, the nerves in my fingers tingling and trembling like they'd fallen asleep and just woken up.

A second later, the door is thrown open.

"Thought I heard your familiar dulcet tones," I tell Catey, who blushes.

Our friends crowd into the room, taking seats around the table. Blaire and Val each shoot me an enthusiastic thumbs-up, and when Ian isn't watching, Rio does, too.

"You ready?" asks Samer, lifting the box of Scrabble he's brought with him. "Lucky for us, I had an unopened game at home, so we know for sure that all the tiles are accounted for."

See? says Ian's eyebrow rise. *I wasn't lying.*

I dip my chin in acknowledgement. I was wrong about him.

"Surprised?" Blaire asks, unable to hold back her grin.

"Totally," I say as the others start ripping into the plastic. "No Claudia?"

Samer shakes his head and slides tiles over to Ian while Val does the same for me. "She had a family thing. Couldn't make it."

We all know the rules, so it doesn't take long to set up the game. I don't know whether I score all those early double- and triple-word scores because of all my mental preparation or because Ian gave me a heads-up, but either way, I'm in the lead.

Still, I try to pace myself. I don't rush to make the biggest words possible if adding just one letter to the end of Ian's word—and landing on a bonus square—can get me a triple-word score. With just one letter, a word can turn into a completely new one.

"Nice one," Ian says appreciatively when I turn his *host* into *ghost.*

The unexpected praise is pure serotonin. I smile back. "Thanks."

Adding just the right prefixes and suffixes to his already-played words lets me piggyback on his score, racking up a higher number of points and preventing him from moving in on them himself. I watch his face carefully when I turn his *us* into *rust* and then into *thrust*.

"Someone's a pro at Dirty Scrabble," says Ian with a grin as he takes his turn. His eyes twinkle at my furious blush. "It's almost as if you've been practicing."

"How could I?" I say smoothly, not breaking eye contact even when I desperately need to blink. "I mean, it's not like I could have known we'd be playing *regular* Scrabble, right?"

Rio and Samer flush, but Catey looks between Ian and me with a squinty expression.

"This is more boring than golf," Val whispers to Blaire, who nods in agreement.

Rio's voice turns low and gossipy. "Thank god the next one is a test of—"

"No hints!" whisper-shrieks Catey.

Ian and I exchange matching looks of disappointment. *So close.*

I'm less than thrilled when he makes his next move, using the F in my previously played horizontal *foe* to make the longer—and pointed—vertical *friend*, outscoring me. I give him a message of my own when it's my turn again, spelling out *never* with his N.

There's a familiar challenge on Ian's face. I read it clearly: Never say never.

We continue playing. A few turns later when I scan my tiles, I don't get hung up on the fact that I have a Q but no U, making my next move, cinq, the French word for *five*, with confidence and a smirk.

Ian stares at the board. "Last time I saw someone use Q that effectively was—" He stops, swallows. "When I played with Grace in the hospital. She had all the letters for QWERTY. I tried to tell her it wasn't a real word, but she found it in the dictionary and got pretty scary when she made her case."

There's a soft smile on his face as he traces the corner edges of a tile, letting it dig into the pad of his thumb. "Would have made a good lawyer."

"Grace was smart as hell," says Rio. He puts his arm around Ian's shoulders. "Plus the kindness to go with it. She was so little and probably didn't understand any of it, but she never misgendered or deadnamed me. Not even once."

Ian gives Rio a wan smile and then adds one letter to turn *come* into *comet*. "She was good at games and she loved to win. A lot like Kavya in that way, actually."

I squirm. I don't remember her the way they do even though I spent part of my childhood growing up with her at Holly Gogogi's. But that's how it was. She'd follow us around, the way I used to trail after Simran. The way Blaire's sister, Kiely, used to trail after us. And then Ian and Kavya stopped being Ian-and-Kavya, and that was the end of pies on counters and bounces on trampolines.

"It's your turn, Joshi," says Ian.

I feel like I should say something, too, but it's too late, now. The moment to say something in her memory is gone.

He must have assumed I was wrestling with the board. "I'm thinking," I say, tongue thick and wooly with the lie.

His mouth quirks. "Ladies and gentlemen, I give you Kavya Joshi, the master tactician."

"This is strategy, not tactics," I say absently, rearranging my tiles. "Strategy is the long game. Tactics are smaller steps. In Scrabble it's all about thinking ahead. You have to do a cost-benefit analysis to determine if you want to play the tiles you have right now, or if they'll be more valuable to you in a future turn."

Ian throws up his palms. "Mea culpa."

What is it with him and Latin today?

He's been such a good sport right from the first tile. It's disconcerting that between my rival and my bored friends, I'm the only one who seems to remember this is a competition.

I almost smile as I place each of my tiles down on the board, making use of the V in my *never*. "Happy?"

Everyone cranes forward to see the word I made: *rival*.

"No," he replies, frowning. Then his eyes light up with an expression I can describe only as boyish devilry. With slow, careful moves intended to heighten the tension, he places six tiles horizontally from my R to make a brand-new word: *romance*.

He leans back with a triumphant twist to his lips, a not-quite smirk that reaches his eyes.

I know what he's doing. He's trying to psych me out.

But I'm not going to fall for it. Competition is where I excel.

Keep a cool head, Kavya. Don't make a hasty decision just to distance yourself from that look in his eyes.

I scan my remaining tiles. Nothing useful. "I'll trade these in."

"Are you sure?" Ian asks as I sweep them into the bag, give it a shake, and pluck out new tiles without looking. He scoots forward, eyes impossibly earnest. "You'll be giving up a turn. Zero points."

I glance up at him from under my eyelashes as I arrange my tiles in front of me. He's worrying at his lower lip. Weird. If he thinks I'm making a horrible mistake, doesn't it make more sense to let me dig my own grave?

His concern is, well, not *touching*, because of whom it's coming from. Bared-teeth banter is far more familiar and, if I'm honest, better feeds and fortifies my own desire to win. There's no way I'm going soft just because he's taking sportspersonship a step too far.

The game moves on, and us with it. Three turns later, I'm glad I played the long game.

Time for the kiss of death . . . the bag is empty and I just have two tiles left. These two tiles will win me the game.

Now it's my turn to smirk. Romance, my ass.

One, two. I lay them both on the board, then lean back with a cat-who-ate-the-canary smile.

"R and Y make *rivalry*," I declare. "I win."

F	O	E					
R							
I		R	O	M	A	N	C	E
E		I					
N	E	V	E	R			
D		A					
		L					
		R					
		Y					

18.
Only One of Us Can Lead

"ARE YOU SURE this is, uh, strictly necessary?" I try to keep as much space between our bodies as possible as Ian spins me around to the instrumental version of "A Whole New World."

Since my Scrabble victory, getting off on the right foot with myself in the lead 2–1, there's been a wrong-footedness between me and Ian. It lingers like a stink, but I can't tell where it's coming from. It's amorphous and intangible, just a feeling that something's not quite right.

Maybe part of that wrongness stems from how hard it is not to feel clunky and ox-footed when you're in Ian's arms. For learning purposes, obviously. We're at the Playhouse rehearsing for the Grimaldi Castle party, and it couldn't be going worse.

"Hands-on practice is the best way to learn theory," Ian says with a poker face.

"Easy for you to say. You're not the one wearing *this*." I hope my speaking glance down at my Mermaid Princess costume conveys it all.

"Better than a tail," Ian says diplomatically.

Once, I thought this dress would be preferable to the tail and seashell bra, but I've come to revise my opinion on this puff of cotton candy: My pink dress, replete with frothy white tulle and intricate bodice beadwork, is a breath too tight, the bodice digging into my ribs. My breasts squeeze together and swell over the top. The shoulders are poufy, with long, skin-tight sleeves that cling to my clammy arms even with the AC on. And my feet *hurt* and I'm pretty sure I have blisters on the backs of both ankles.

"Joshi," says Ian, raising an eyebrow. "Only *one* of us can lead."

"Sorry. I didn't mean to take over. I don't know how that happened."

"Just came naturally, huh?"

I start to bristle at the dig before I realize he's teasing me.

The truth is, while he's taken to the waltz like he was born to the rhythm of "one, two, three," I'm a fish out of water, literally floundering in his arms, except for when, apparently, I accidentally try to lead. Five other couples move around us, and Ian's agility and grace are the only reason we don't blunder into them.

Samer gives me an encouraging smile as our eyes meet

across the room. It's a tight squeeze for all twelve of us, plus Poppy, who's prowling the perimeter with a watchful eye. Samer's Snow White does cotillion, so she's skilled enough to make him look like he knows what he's doing on our makeshift dance floor.

I hurl him a *Save me!* look over her shoulder, but Samer pretends not to see, whisking them both out of my eyeline.

Ian's fiendishly warm palm presses into the small of my back, bringing me closer. "Oof."

I wince. Though he tries to keep his voice low, it's obvious I've just stepped on his feet for what feels like the hundredth time. "Sorry. I was hopeless at bharatanatyam as a kid, too."

He cocks his head. "What's that?"

"Oh, it's Indian classical dance. Your family came and saw me perform once." I smile. "It's pretty strenuous. Mom would make me practice in the living room. She was convinced I would get better if I just tried harder. Simran tried to help, but . . ."

I have the grace to flush. "It was hopeless. No matter how hard I worked, my movements were never as coordinated as the other kids in the class. I don't want to do something if I can't be good at it. The payoff has to be worth the effort, you know?"

"I get that," he says, and then he ruins it by tossing me a wink. "I mean, not personally. I'm good at so many things."

"Humbleness not being one of them," I retort, making sure to step on his toes.

Annoyingly, he doesn't falter at all.

"Get a chance to read my book yet?" he asks.

"Your book?" I scoff. "You just chose one at random!"

He looks surprised for a second.

The book sits on my desk, still in its brown paper wrapping. It could be a Trojan horse that puts me in a reading slump for a week. I've been on a great five-star reading streak, and that's because nobody knows my taste better than me. I have so many other books to read, anyway, so I don't even want to open it.

I don't know how irreparably it would change things between us if it turns out he *does* know me. I hate to admit it, but I'm scared to find out.

I squeeze my eyes shut as he gently spins us around the room.

"Relax," murmurs Ian.

He laughs when he sees the expression on my face. The timbre is low and deep, like slow-grinding gears. Ian's hands have spread warmth all over my back. My skin prickles and my dress somehow squeezes extra tight.

"It's hot in here, right?" I ask, fidgeting away from his furnace-like palms. It just brings me closer to his front. And his pointed chin. And his pale-pink lips.

Don't notice his mouth. Never notice his mouth again. Do not even *think* the word.

"Your hair is slipping loose," he says, breaking our hand-hold. "Can I?"

At my slight nod, his hand brushes my temple and I feel the tug of the silver-and-pearl fork clip as he adjusts it tenderly, pushing it in place behind my ear.

"You do look pretty hot right now." Ian's biting back a smile as he says it.

I must look obviously flushed. My scalp and forehead do feel a little sweaty. This could be heatstroke. Maybe I need a water break.

No, what I *need* is space between us. "Excuse me for a moment."

"Kavya . . . ?" Poppy calls after me as I dart past her.

I try to rationalize that this is not running away and is definitely not hiding, but after skulking in front of the water cooler in the foyer for five minutes, those excuses hit the road.

Everything about Ian Jun aggravates me to the very core of my being. His smug, superior attitude. The way he gets under my skin. His ability to make me *want* to let down my defenses.

"Hey." Speak of the devil. "You okay?" asks Ian. "You ran out looking pretty flushed."

"Did you *follow* me?" I hope my glare is as hostile as my voice.

"I was thirsty, too." He leans past me to grab a cup, filling it to the top.

My eyes unwillingly glue to his neck as he swallows. I start to feel hot again. I dart my vampiric gaze away before he can catch me and get the wrong idea.

He refills his cup and gives me a curious look. "Aren't you thirsty?"

"*What*?! Oh, um . . ." Distractedly, I fill my own cup and take a sip of the chilled water.

Ian straightens and wipes his mouth with the back of his hand. A droplet glistens on his top lip. "I'd get it if *I* won our Scrabble game, but why are you acting beastly? You won."

I hate that I'm fair enough that he can see me turn red. "I just think it would be better to hold each other at an arm's distance. Per our little competition, it's not a good idea for us to fraternize."

"Fraternize," he repeats, drawing the word out so it sounds almost dirty.

"Don't say it like that."

His eyes are entirely too innocent. "Like how?"

"Like *that*," I emphasize. "How did you get so freaking *good* at the waltz, anyway?"

"You've been off all practice. Aren't you even a little excited about this away party?" he asks. "A freaking *castle*, Kavya. I'm not exactly jazzed about wearing jeggings, but it's my first trip without my parents and I don't care if you know how excited I am. Even if it's woefully 'uncool,'" he says in air quotes.

"I don't think it's uncool to be excited about things," I say with a frown. "I read books on Friday nights and weekends. And then I like to talk about them. I like to read the acknowledgments and geek out if my favorite authors are friends with each other, and then I like to recommend them to everyone I know. And if all of that isn't nerdy enough, I hand-letter my favorite quotes on Insta and tag the authors because I love their books *that* much, so please don't ever think that I think anyone is uncool, ever, because it's not true. Okay?"

It's so much. It's so many words. *I'm* too much. Too Much. Oh my god.

"Too much?"

I don't realize I've verbalized it until Ian's look of concentration breaks.

He looks a bit startled to have gotten this much of a rise out of me.

"*Never*," he says, voice solemn as a promise.

When he says it like that, it's almost like he really means it.

"Kavya? Ian?" Poppy pokes her head into the foyer. She gives a tiny not-really-a-cough cough. "I'm just going over the steps to the waltz one more time, and I thought you might, uh, benefit from seeing it again."

"That's putting it delicately," I say, and she smiles, relieved. "We're right behind you."

I swallow the rest of my water before following Ian, who holds the door open for me. I fidget with my clip to make sure it's secure.

"Now that we're all here," says Poppy the second the door swings shut behind us, "Let's go through this again. Everyone watch closely because we don't have much time before the party, and this needs to be perfect. Ian, you seem to have the hang of it. Would you mind demonstrating with Amie?" She gestures for them to join her in the center of the room.

The look in Ian's eyes is one of desperation. Of being rooted in place, superglued to the floor the same way he was superglued to the car at our first party.

"Can I do it instead?" I ask, taking the heat off him without pausing to examine why I even want to. "I could really use the extra help."

As Ian demurs, I trail behind Amie.

"Good luck, Kavs!" says a striking young trans woman in her midtwenties dressed as Rapunzel.

Amie's taking the lead, which leaves me to be the putty in Poppy's hands as she adjusts my hands and shoulders. Amie lurches into motion at a quick one-two-three beat, and I almost stumble keeping up with her. While we demonstrate, Poppy walks around the room fussing over the rest of the cast.

Forward, side, together. *C'mon feet, you can do this.*

It takes a few tries, but once Poppy grudgingly deems us competent, she starts the music again. With a wink, Amie twirls me back to Ian. "Thanks for the dance!"

"Whoa." Ian's hands shoot out to steady me. "I've got you."

I clear my throat. "So how bad did I embarrass myself out there?"

"Trust me, I couldn't look away."

Like a train wreck? My lips screw into a bitter smile. I still can't believe that I voluntarily looked a fool to spare him. I accidentally tread on his feet and decide not to apologize.

Ian's smile, on the other hand, is full of gratitude. He tucks me into him so we move as one, toes and chests almost touching. "Thank you," he says quietly.

I didn't expect that. Surprised, I manage a jerky nod of acknowledgment before promptly stepping on his toes again. "Sorry. Still getting used to this."

He tilts his head and smirks, bringing me closer. *"I could get used to this."*

After the learning curve of our first class, Poppy schedules the entire cast for weekly waltzing lessons to get us ready for the Grimaldi Castle Hotel party the second week of July. Between dance practice, kids' parties, and our iMessage book count, not a day goes by without Ian in it, which, annoyingly, isn't as annoying as I thought it would be.

This is how it starts:

Seventeen! he sends one day, apropos of nothing, followed by a GIF of Legolas.

I'll have no pointy-ear outscoring me! I send back, along with a GIF from the same scene of Gimli at the battle of Helm's Deep. I get back to my book with a vengeance.

A day later he follows up with Legolas's exuberant shout of Nineteen!

It goes from there, and a whole week passes before I realize we're chatting like friends.

All I can think is how very *fun* it had been to dance with him, even though I wasn't good at it, let alone number one. Fun in a way that I couldn't remember anything being in a long time, in a way that playing tennis at the country club with Parker certainly never was.

I'm not completely dense.

I know what this is: A wholly inconvenient crush on Ian Jun.

19.
Getting the Girl

UNLIKE ME, CATEY never has to yell. With her sweet-as-molasses voice and blue, Bambi eyes, she gets what she wants. It's only after you get to know her that you hear the commanding, no-nonsense Borg undertone beneath her fluttery laugh, and then you have to wonder just how much she's "sweet-talked" her way into.

I've got to hand it to her; she's a *great* project manager.

The Fork & Crumb is running like a well-oiled machine by the time we get there.

"Hi, girls!" Mrs. Hill waves at us without breaking her hold on the ladder she's steadying for Mr. Tyler, who's securing the copper pots behind the order counter. Blaire's mom, who will be running the restaurant full-time, is in back with Catey's dad fitting the chef's kitchen, the sounds of their conversation drifting out.

Claudia and Blaire, both great at styling, are hanging clusters of framed floral prints and oversize forks on dark navy walls. Val and Samer are painting the back wall a cheery yellow, laughing and talking quietly while Ian and Rio arrange the bistro tables and chairs.

"Catey," I hiss, yanking her to a stop. "You didn't say he'd be here."

"Didn't I?" Catey's wide eyes aren't fooling me. "I thought we could use the help."

Ian. Me. In one small, confined space. Populated with parents and all our friends.

Oh my god.

"Not moving," I say out of the side of my mouth. "Nope. Nuh uh."

"Don't be such a baby," she says. "Wouldn't it be nice to be friends again? Maybe even more than that?"

I go in with her only to prove that I'm not a baby, and I even manage to smile.

"Very convincing," Catey says dryly. "I totally buy that you don't want to kill me."

"Good," I say through bared teeth. "Then you won't see it coming." I mime a stabbing motion. "Et tu, Brute?"

She actually laughs. Ugh. If you can't strike terror in the hearts of your nearest and dearest friends, then who can you?

The laugh draws Ian's attention. He looks at me, then away, setting down his end of the table with a thump.

"Kavya," Catey says loudly, "would you mind doing the menus with . . . Ian?" She even pauses right before his name, like it's a total accident she landed on him.

"How totally not suspicious at all," I mutter.

Blaire helps Val and Samer fold up the paint-splotched plastic sheeting and wince-smiles at me, but it doesn't make up for her girlfriend's machinations.

Catey's name slides onto my grudge list.

Ian and I sit down at one of the tables and get to work inserting the paper menus into the acrylic menu stands.

He nudges the finished ones aside to give us more room. "Not that I'm not thrilled to pitch in, but uh, when I agreed, I was hoping you'd be here."

I bite my lip. I'd hoped we could get this done quickly without the need for conversation.

"I know you said no fraternizing," he says in a low voice. "I get that you don't think we're friends, but I—"

I hope I can say this without blushing. "I wouldn't say we're *not* friends."

He leans in. "Then how *do* you see me?"

I think back to Claudia's party on the last day of school, a month ago now. I'd quoted a litany of his academic and extracurricular accomplishments. He hadn't peacock-preened at the praise. If anything, he seemed resentful of it.

Achievements don't make me perfect, he'd said.

"Kavya?" he prompts. His fingers tap on the table, the only tell that gives away how eager he is for my answer.

It would be a mistake to see him only as his achievements. He's so much more than that.

"I'll let you know when I figure it out," I tell him honestly.

Smile #8 lights up his whole face. "I'll be waiting."

He makes it sound like it's a promise he's going to hold us to.

"Did you draw these?" Ian's finger traces the bright jewel-colored peacock rangoli design on the menu's edges. "They're amazing."

"Yeah, they're not bad."

He sends me a *c'mon* look. "You're a lot of things, but humble isn't one of them. These are fucking awesome, Kavya."

I shift on the chair, avoiding his gaze. His earnestness is uncomfortable, partly because a part of me craves the praise, and nauseating because I don't want to want it. "Thanks?"

"I see you draw all the time at school."

"Yeah, I always take an art class. Helps balance out the APs."

"No, I mean the doodles you do in the margins of your notes. The back of the textbooks." His laugh is molten. It sounds the way a softened caramel tastes, warm and gooey in all the right places. "I thought only the 'bad kids' defaced those."

"I don't write rude things in them or anything," I rush to point out. "And those books are ancient. Simran said she used the same book when she was in high school. If anything, I'm increasing their value until we switch to digital textbooks next year."

He folds his arms over his IN SCIENCE WE TRUST tee shirt. "I love how you justify things."

"And I love—" Just saying the word while he's looking at me makes my throat close up. I swallow.

"You were saying?" he asks archly.

I really hate Catey.

"Art," I say. "I love art."

He taps his shoulder. "And tattoos."

Oh, right. He'd been in the dressing room when Amie had covered up the rose mudra on my back. I half smile. "I love it, but when I'm thirty-seven, I hope I don't regret it."

"Or maybe when you're thirty-seven, every time you see your tattoo, you'll never forget what it was like to be seventeen."

"Maybe," I admit. "Not to get all philosophical on you or whatever, but at seventeen, everything seems like it could be a really, really bad decision, or an epically good one. Trouble is you don't know which until you do it. I, uh, struggle with that sometimes, as you probably figured out when we kayaked. And starting now we don't mention it again," I say in a rush.

He nods at my shoulder. "Was that a good decision?"

"I think so." I crack a smile. "My parents didn't."

"My parents wouldn't either." He rubs his wrist in a gesture that looks a tiny bit self-conscious. "I thought about getting something once. But my mom—"

"I get what you mean. It took a while to get my parents to give their permission," I say. I hesitate, then add, "I named my Instagram account baddecisiondesi. Sort of like my fuck you to everyone who thinks I'm"—my tongue trips over the words—"not a nice girl."

I've only shared this with my best friends. My usernames are very, very private. Anyone who's had an online life knows that it can get messy when real life blunders in.

"I know," says Ian. "Mrs. Carnegie reposts your pictures sometimes. I, um, may have followed you."

He peeks at me from under his lashes like he thinks I'll be upset somehow, but I'm not.

"How did you know it was me? I don't use my real name."

"I'd always know you," he says simply. "Your art is so distinctive that I'd know it anywhere. It's so *you*. You've got something special." He shoots me a secret smile, Smile #9, and then rattles off a string of French. "Quelque chose de magique."

Has snarky Ian left the building? He's being his *most* charming right now, and it's *so* weird. Good weird. I'm warm all over, but not from anger this time.

Magic. The last word he said is magic. He asked me how I saw him, so how did he end up telling me how he saw *me*?

"Show off," I mutter, but I punctuate it with a smile. I make a mental note to check my followers as soon as I get home, figure out which one is him.

"I'm super uninteresting, so my account is mostly hamstergram," says Ian. "In case you were thinking of following me back or anything. But you don't have to. You wouldn't be missing anything," he says with a short laugh.

I'm not sure why he's giving me an out when it seems pretty dang obvious he *wants* me to follow him. "Hamstergram?" I ask curiously.

"I run Holly Gogogi's Instagram," he explains. "So obviously, it's a lot of food photography. Doesn't exactly leave me with a lot of content to post on my own account, you know? So it's mostly my friends, my book, and my pet hamster." His cheeks pink. "She's really cute."

I unsuccessfully try to hide my smile. "Does this 'really cute' hamster have a name?"

"She does," he says with a grin. "Yeobo."

I test the word out. It's familiar in a way I can't quite place.

"It means 'honey,'" says Ian. "When I was little, I loved the word. My parents use it all the time as an endearment for each other. And Yeobo's a teddy bear hamster, so when I got my first Yeobo for my sixth birthday, I thought, 'Hey, bears like honey,' and the name stuck."

"That's a sweet story. For what it's worth, I think it's an awesome name. Like Ramona Quimby and Chevrolet."

His answering grin is pure serotonin. "Or Kavya and Buster Baxter. You named your dog after one of the weirdest, coolest best friends any kid could ever have."

"I think I remember meeting Yeobo once when I came over."

"I couldn't get you to hold her. You were afraid she would bite you."

"Oh my god, and you got so offended that I called her a rodent," I say with a laugh.

"Grace monopolized her." Ian smiles, showing that he didn't mind it. "Moved the cage into her room when she decided one day she loved Yeobo more."

"Um, don't hamsters have a really short life span?"

His smile fades. "They do. The first Yeobo died after three years, but I was too young to realize Mom replaced her with a new one. The second time it happened, Mom did it so Grace wouldn't find out. She thought Grace was too young to know about dea— And the third Yeobo died a few months after Grace did."

Ian's eyes swim with unshed tears. Without thinking, I reach my hands out to cover his.

"Mom kept swapping Yeobos for me," he continues in a lower voice. "I don't know if she realizes I know the truth, but I don't want her to know. Dad asked me at breakfast a couple of years ago if I knew how old Yeobo was. He was trying to gauge whether I knew the extent of it? Mom almost burst into tears. I just shrugged and kept eating my cornflakes, and she calmed down. I think it's better this way, if we just have this tiny hamster that never grows up or grows old. At least a part of *her* is still with us."

I have the urge to cry, but I can't, not when he's still being stoic and blinking back his tears. I can't make this about me after he's just been vulnerable and shared something I get the feeling he's never told anyone before.

His hands are warm beneath mine, so I give him a small squeeze, trying to show that even though I'll never completely understand his grief, I'm here sharing this moment with him.

One fat tear dangles on his eyelash before slowly rolling down his cheek and dripping off his chin. Ian doesn't break our hold to wipe at his face. He doesn't mind that I've seen it.

He's not alone. The sometimes-nice boy is here with the not-so-nice girl, and they're going to be okay. Ian's so still that I think he doesn't register my touch at first. But then his thumbs loop around mine and return the gentle pressure.

We stay like that for a few seconds before he draws back. His hands slip from mine, but I keep my hands where they are just in case he's not ready to be done yet. I give him a moment to collect himself.

"My parents remember her every day," he says, "but even after years of family therapy it's hard for them to talk about her. I don't want it to be that way for me."

The silence lingers. A quick glance around the room reveals that we're alone. At some point during our tête-à-tête, the others disappeared into the kitchen.

I feel a little guilty for not working when everyone else is, but it feels so good to not be tense around Ian, that for once, I kind of want to let the camaraderie linger. Easing back to familiar territory, I tease, "So now that we've ascertained that you creepily watch me doodle at school, do *you* draw?"

He cracks a smile. "I can't even draw happy little trees."

I snicker. "Sorry, I'm not laughing at you, it's just that you know Bob Ross."

"Yeah, yeah, laugh on, Joshi." But he doesn't seem mad that I'm still giggling. In fact, it's the exact opposite. He looks so contented when he's smiling like that. Not like nemesis-Ian at all. "It helps me get to sleep when I'm wrecked from studying or can't stop thinking about something that's out of my control. You've heard of ASMR, right? Bob's scratchy paintbrush sounds are so soothing when I'm feeling restless or on edge. Helps my anxiety, even if it's temporary. Sometimes staves off whatever's building up."

It just got real, so I lay off the giggles. He's soft and happy, and the way he looks right now is the way a fleece blanket makes me feel. And it troubles me how untroubling I find that. "I saw someone do an ASMR video with slime. Wet, squelchy noises are not my jam. It made me feel weird? Tingles, but not the good kind."

"I like dry sounds, too," he says. "But there's this one make-up artist who massages the model's face a ton with all the skincare products, and those videos are the *best*. Nothing puts me to sleep faster."

"Not even Mr. Gage first thing in the morning?" I tease.

Ian's grin makes my heart twirl acrobatics in my chest.

Catey pokes her head of the kitchen. "Hey, come to the back and grab something to eat, you two." Behind Ian's head, she catches my eye and holds it. *Foreplay,* she mouths.

I widen my eyes at her until she disappears into the kitchen again.

"I'm not really hungry," says Ian. "You?"

"No, I'm good here." Even though we've done more talking than working.

"Are you going to study art in college?" he asks.

"Maybe animation. It'd be cool to work on a Disney movie."

We share a smile that feels like a secret.

"Is that why you work at Poppy's?"

The truth is, I could work anywhere. My mom would love it if I also worked somewhere that would look prestigious for my college apps, but Poppy's has something the other places lack.

The unbridled, unapologetic love of magic. Of happy endings. Of suspending disbelief, if only for a few hours, and becoming someone else. Someone who is so totally different to me that my soul sometimes aches at the contrast. Someone nice.

I yearn to tell him this, but I pretend to misunderstand the question instead. "My parents get me a lot of my material, but yeah, some of my paycheck goes toward the things I need. What about you? I know you said you wanted to do the 'scary thing,' but you could have worked at the caves, done the prohibition tours. Mowed lawns. Whatever guys like you usually do."

He tilts his head. "Guys like me?"

"Guys who are good at everything without even trying. Perfect people."

"I'm not perfect," he says stubbornly.

"I try and I try, and sometimes I'm still not first. But you? It all comes so easy."

"That can be a curse of its own, you know." His voice is taut.

Before I can ask him what he means by that, he adds, "You'll laugh if I bare my soul to you about what made me pick Poppy's besides the obvious reason."

"Probably, but tell me anyway."

The earlier darkness fades from his voice as he says, "I just really love Disney. Pursuing impossible dreams. Getting the girl." And there he goes again with his damn twinkling eyes.

"I pity whoever it is you like, pal," I say with a snort. "Your persistence makes me think you're more of a Gaston than an Eric."

The word *pal* just slips out, breezy and kidding around. But it feels right, *unlike* Gaston.

I want to take it back as soon as the words escape. Gaston does not exist only on a screen. Guys like him, like Parker, they're the poster children of toxic masculinity and misogyny.

Ian gasps, clutching at his heart like he's mortally wounded.

A rose blooms in my chest, petals unfurling to meet the dawn, and for a girl who loves words so much, I can't find *one* for how amazing it is to make a dig in fun rather than rivalry.

"All jokes aside," says Ian, "unlike Gaston, I can take no for an answer."

"So why are you so convinced that she doesn't like you back?" I ask, curious despite myself. "You said she wouldn't look at you twice. That's pretty hard to believe, and I'm looking."

"Yeah," says Ian, voice a little strangled. "Yeah, you are. Now."

"Don't you two look cozy," drawls Rio's voice.

"Hardly," I scoff, retreating out of the moment with Ian. "We're being put to work here."

"Oh yeah, sure," says Rio. He cocks his head at the box of menu holders we still haven't finished. "There is a *lot* of hard work happening here. You know, some of us actually came here to help and not flirt. Now move over," he instructs, grabbing a third chair to join us. "You up for some pool time and pozole after this? My dads were up early to simmer it for *hours*, so you know it's going to be amazing."

"I . . ." I glance at Ian, who's busied himself with the menu inserts with renewed diligence.

"Oh, you wanna know who else is going, huh?" Rio winks. "Well, how about it, Ian?"

"I'll be there," Ian mutters from the corner of his mouth. He keeps his head bowed over the inserts like they really need his full attention.

I let myself peek at him when I'm sure he can't see. And I look at him. Really look at him. I think about the question he asked me earlier: *How do you see me?*

I didn't know how to answer him then, but now I think maybe I'm starting to.

"Yeah, okay," I find myself agreeing. "I do really like . . ."

Ian looks up at me.

Maybe I'll text him tonight. Something casual that he can't read anything into.

Maybe.

". . . pozole."

20.
I Dare You

MEXICAN AND INDIAN cooking have a lot in common, so the minute we step into Rio's house—a pretty two-story with white trim and an abundance of potted geraniums around the welcome mat—it feels like coming home.

The unmistakable scent of tomato, onion, and garlic (several bulbs, not the one tiny clove most recipes seem to call for) permeates the air. Rio grins when he sees me sniff appreciatively, and waves us through the entrance and into the kitchen. Through the sliding glass doors leading to the backyard, I can see the kidney-bean-shaped pool and Ian floating on his back.

Though the kitchen's small, it's a hub of activity as Rio's dads move from counter to counter. A huge pot boils on the burner, delicious steam escaping through a vent in the lid.

"Hi, kids!" one of them says, waving a huge chef's knife hello before making a confetti of the cilantro on the chopping board, sprinkling it into a bowl of diced tomatoes and red onions.

"Can we help with anything?" Catey asks politely.

Both Mr. Moreno-Ortizes shake their heads and wave us out to the backyard, where Claudia and Samer are sprawled on lawn chairs with cold lemonades in their hands.

Blaire throws a longing look at the pool, but Catey tugs her down to share a lawn chair, whispering something in her ear that makes Blaire grin.

Val immediately snags the seat next to Rio. All she could talk about on the drive over was how relieved she was that her parents were both working at the store, which meant she didn't have to ask for permission when we all went home to change.

I head to the pool, the late-afternoon sun roasting my fair upper arms. I'm more golden now than I was at the start of summer, thanks to outdoor kiddie parties—enough to buy a new shade of BB cream.

Ian doesn't hear me approach. I take a moment to pause and watch him. How serene he looks. Untroubled, carefree. Boyish.

"Hey," I say, hovering at the edge.

Ian smiles, eyes still closed. "Hey, you."

With a devilish smile, I kick off my flip-flops. The water looks cool and tempting, and I don't kid myself that my urge to jump in has nothing to do with the boy floating in the center of it.

I've moved on to my shorts and pelican print cover-up when he asks, "Care to join me?"

No sooner does he get the words out that I cannonball in, splashing water all over him. He sputters, flailing in the water for one gloriously ungainly second, then rights himself. I'm going to pay for the amusement in a minute, but it was well worth it.

Ian looks like a shaggy dog with his bangs falling over his eyes, and he even shakes his head side to side, spraying me with a fine shower. Then he looks at me, a promise in his eyes that I know he's going to deliver on.

I'm totally prepared for the wave he sends my way, but the water still gets up my nose and into my eyes. I recover fast, reaching backward to splash him again.

It starts as slow, teasing fun. The fun I remember having with him when we were kids, before he started getting good at everything and I was left scrambling to keep up.

For Catey's eleventh birthday our whole class was invited to a water park. The boys all thought it was hilarious that I, Kavya Joshi, was too scared to go down the slide.

It wasn't like I was going to win a prize for most brave or number-one cool girl, but I couldn't bear anyone thinking I was a coward. While the boys made annoying clucking sounds from below, I went up the ladder and stared down into what was sure to be my doom, ready to pee myself. I was gearing up to slide when Ian clambered up behind me and said we'd go down the tight, dark tubing together.

Then, his pale, skinny thighs around me, my back to his

front and his arms around my waist, we descended into the unknown. I screamed the whole way, but not in fear.

I was *furious* I hadn't been able to prove myself by going down alone. Humiliated that everyone thought I'd only been able to do it with his help.

He was one of my best friends. He knew me. He should have *known* how much I'd hate being helped if I hadn't asked for it.

Afterward, I'd told him why he hadn't really "helped" me.

But I don't think he really got it, because a week later at another pool party, when the clucking started again, he jumped to my defense. And that was the end of Kavya-and-Ian.

I realize now what I didn't at age ten. He was being a good friend by helping me. I also realize that ten-year-old Ian didn't understand, but he understands now. He didn't jump out of his kayak to try and save me; he asked me if I needed help, and then he let me save myself.

Another splash of water gets me in the face.

"What are you waiting for?" asks Ian.

"Trust me, I have every intention of getting you." I circle the perimeter of the pool, keeping my eyes on him. It doesn't sound as threatening as I intend.

He laughs, utterly unthreatened, and mimics my stance, prowling around the edge in tandem with me.

"I mean it."

"I know you do, Joshi." He has the effrontery to twinkle at me.

Twinkle.

With his big ol' Bambi eyes. Like that's going to do any-thing.

His next splash catches me in the face. I *knew* he was doing that flirty eye thing just to—

"Hey!" I sputter as he gets me again. "I wasn't ready!"

He cocks his head to the side. "Isn't that sort of the point?"

Just as I rear back to send a flying wave his way, he catches me by the wrist. He's in my bubble, just a few inches away from me.

I'm suddenly all too aware of how little we're both wearing, how droplets cling to his eyelashes and gather in his clavicle and how my breasts are rising and falling from breathing too rapidly, how his pupils are blown wide.

I flick a self-conscious glance backward, but our friends are completely oblivious to what's playing out in the pool: Catey and Blaire are animatedly talking with Samer and Claudia; a preoccupied Rio's grinning down at his phone, thumbs mov-ing rapid-fire over the screen; and Val's gazing at them all, looking a little forlorn.

"I'm kinda surprised you came," Ian murmurs, voice soft. Fleece-y. "I thought you were just appeasing Rio."

My breath hitches. "When was the last time you saw me appease anyone? Besides, you're the one who told me I was no coward that day in gym. Remember?"

"You're still so sassy even when you're losing." He sounds delighted.

"Losing?" I scoff.

"Don't be defensive. All I did was catch up after you caught me unaware with your cheating. You play dirty, girl."

"Are you blame-gaming me?" I put my hands on my hips. "Seriously, Ian. You don't wanna play with me. I've got a grudge list that goes back to first grade."

"Ah, the infamous grudge list. Do you know how many conversations you manage to work it into?" Then, without missing a beat, "Am I ever going to see it?"

I squint. "You wanna see my thing?"

"I wanna see your thing."

"Only if I get to see your thing."

"You're not ready for my thing, Joshi. My thing will blow your mind. It's digitized. Twenty-first century color-coded spreadsheet with macros you wouldn't believe."

"You lie, Jun."

We're both treading water. He swims a bit closer.

Our friends are laughing and talking, not seeming to pay us any attention at all, so he comes closer. My two-piece blue-and-white-striped high-waist bikini isn't any more revealing than my Mermaid Princess costume, but I feel exposed in a way I never have before. Goosebumps prickle over my chest and everything tightens. I swallow. Hard.

"I don't lie," Ian whispers ever so softly. His wet, clumpy eyelashes are strangely unblinking. He moves closer, but different from the way he moved before. This time it's a slow progression, like he's trying not to scare me off. Our chests almost brush.

I swallow. "So . . . if I ask you right now to tell me the name of the girl you like, would you do it? No lies. No games."

"If you ask me anything right now," he whispers. "I'll tell you."

I believe him. But I'm not sure I'm ready to hear the answer.

"Where did you learn to dance?"

His face flickers with surprise, then disappointment. Finally, he says, "My parents. When I was growing up, they'd always dance at the end of the night after closing the restaurant. Even if their feet hurt and they were tired as hell. Even if they'd sniped at each other during the day. Dad would clear the chairs away, then waltz Mom around the room to 'The Blue Danube.'"

"That's so romantic."

My muscles clench when Ian looks at me. My stomach is in a never-ending freefall, plummeting somewhere dark and cavernous that has no end. I want to wind back time and ask him what I should have asked him in the first place.

I can't ask him now.

So I give him something, instead, something I know he wants: how I see him.

I'm not great at the giving of things. But I can try because I owe him this, and because we've gone too far to back down now.

"I don't see you as the enemy," I say slowly. "I guess after we stopped being friends, I didn't really see you as anything until you started seeing me."

This sounds muddled and topsy-turvy; I'm not sure he'd understand even if I wrote him a twenty-page dissertation on the subject.

I take a breath. Exhale.

"There's always been someone better than me," I say. "I don't mean that in a self-pitying way or like I don't have self-esteem or something. It's just a fact. I'm not particularly the best at anything unless I work really hard at it. And sometimes not even then. I mean, I'm artistic, but it's not the kind of thing you can be the *best* at, you know? There are so many talented artists that you can never know where you fall. It's ambiguous. And sometimes I feel better when things are quantified. First place, second place. It wasn't until we started competing that I felt like someone else got me. Understood."

His eyebrows draw together. "I never wanted to be the best anything, Kavya. It was all I could do to keep up with you."

"Yeah, exactly. But you're perfect at literally everything. Even kayaking, somehow."

"I'm *not* perfect," he says, heatedly, but I cut him off.

"Our rivalry?" I gesture between us wildly. "Admit it. It makes both of us better. We're goal oriented, we're driven. There's no way anyone other than us is going to be valedictorian. We make each other level up. You're my measuring stick, Ian."

He gnaws on his lip. "I'm not sure any of that is as flattering as you're making it sound."

"I'm not trying to flatter you. Just giving you the honesty you asked for."

"How's this for honesty?" Ian floats close enough that I can feel his body heat, despite the cool water.

We're practically brushing against each other now. He

bends his neck just a tiny bit, just enough that our noses could touch if he wanted them to. "I like you, Kavya. I like you even if you strike out, or if you beat me, or hell, I like you better when you beat me."

My stomach bottoms out. There's no teasing glint in his eye, no arch coyness in his voice. Just a low, quiet statement that has me scrambling to keep up.

"W-what?" I almost want to back up, put some more distance between us, but the intensity in his face arrests me.

This is no game. Suddenly, I can't remember why I thought it was.

"I like you," he repeats, and I feel all twisted up inside when I hear the inflection of each word in a way I didn't hear it before.

I stutter, "But . . . but you can't."

He quirks an eyebrow.

"I-I-I mean you shouldn't. We're—"

"Don't say nemeses, please."

"We're not"—I flounder for a word—"whatever this is!"

"How will you even know what *this* is until you give it a chance?"

Damn him for sounding so reasonable.

His eyes implore me. "Just get to know me. Get to know me *again*," he amends. "You can always go back to hating my guts if we don't work out. But I have a feeling we will."

"Go back? I never stopped," I quip. But I'm hedging. I know it.

I can only hope *he* doesn't.

It's tough to read him. He's looking at me straight on, gaze unwavering, no hint of a challenge in his tone or body language, even though obviously it is one. Clever of him, masking his diabolical intentions in flirtation.

He's baiting me and we both know it, but the real question is . . . Does he know it's working?

His fingers graze my shoulder, electrifying a row of goosebumps on the back of my arm. He ghosts his hand down to my elbow, butterfly soft, and doesn't stop until he reaches my wrist, where he lingers.

My lips part at the sensation on my skin, light enough that if we weren't perfectly still, I wouldn't have been able to feel it at all. It's so different than the way anyone's touched me before. Certainly none of my ex-boyfriends.

And now that he's stopped, all I want is that feeling back.

Ian breaks the silence first. "Scared, Joshi?" he asks with a taunting edge.

"Of you? Dream on."

"Then take a chance. Get to know me." His grin is boyish and brave and lionhearted. Then, the three magic words he knows I won't be able to resist. He whispers, "I dare you."

When Ian and I come inside for pozole, my friends know something happened, but I shake my head in a silent *Not now*. Catey casts suspicious glances at Ian as Rio digs into the pozole, serving us up big, steaming, fragrant bowls.

When we finish eating, we thank Rio's dads, and the moon girls make their getaway.

On the way home, Val tries to talk about Rio, bringing up

something about how he spent more time on his phone than he did talking to her, but Catey cuts her off and demands to know what happened with me and Ian in the pool.

The badgering is relentless, and though it comes from a good place, I'm not ready to verbalize our new playing field, not even to my best friends. Instead of joining in our conversation, Val spends the drive home staring out the window.

Catey drops Val off first, then me, vaguely threatening that *We're having a group chat tonight and you better spill the tea.*

Mom and Dad look up from the movie they're watching as I kick off my shoes in the foyer. "You're back early," says Mom, not pressing pause. "Did you have a good time?"

I grunt.

"Is everything okay?"

She means did a boy try something, did a girl say something mean, were people doing drugs, the usual things. Things she can console me about, get righteously angry for. Ian liking me is on the opposite end of the spectrum, the kind of filmi love drama Mom would eat up.

I want to sequester this new knowledge away. Sharpen it like a sword and plunge it into a rock somewhere where no one will ever pull it out. Weigh it down and throw it to the bottom of the ocean. Anything but deal with it.

Ian and I are good as Sherlock and Moriarty; no need to complicate a rivalry that's in perfect working order with something infinitely more complicated. There's a reason Sherlock never made it work with Irene Adler.

"Yeah, Mom. I wanted an early night. I have all those

books from the library to finish before they're due."

Upstairs, I haul a stack of books to my bed, but don't crack any of them open. I can tell by the spines they're all contemporary romance. I groan. I don't want to read a kissing book right now—or possibly ever again.

Ian's mystery book is still on my desk, and it's probably not a romance, but I definitely don't feel like reaching for it right now. I'm far enough out of my comfort zone as it is. I stuff my face into my pillow and scream, but stop just in time because it's not anywhere as silent as it was supposed to be, and Simran's right next door.

So I take my phone and fire off a message to Ian, forgetting all about my earlier good intentions to give him a pleasant "hey."

Instead, I bang out WHY DID YOU HAVE TO GO AND SAY ALL THAT?, like my phone has personally offended me. I don't elaborate further.

Did you really not know?

> How am I supposed to know something
> like that? It's not like you've ever been
> remotely flirty with me.

Maybe you just weren't paying attention 😉

> Don't wink at me. I'm being serious.
> UR NOT CUTE!!! 😣

His reply flies back a second later. I mean . . . I'm a little cute.

I refuse to reply to that. I'm already slightly paranoid about how quickly he's been replying.

Ian doesn't let my nonresponse faze him. Joshi, I will woo your socks off.

Only he can make a sweet declaration sound so much like a threat.

> Just socks? You must not think very
> much of your flirtation skills . . .

Damn it. That sounded provocative.

His reply is instantaneous. By the time I'm done, you'll be giving me an A+.

> HA, HA I'd like to see you try.
> I don't give out A's easy.

It's only after I hit send that I realize how much that sounds like a challenge.

And when it comes to rivals, a challenge made is as good as a challenge accepted.

21.
Quelque Chose
de Magique

AS WE TRADE a humid June for a stickier, muggier July, Ian tries. He really does. I can't fault his effort, and his execution is admirable, but I'm made of way sterner stuff than he thinks. Sure, he knocks off calling me Sushi, but that's the least he can do for a nickname he started to begin with.

As our dance moves improve, so does our friendship. We start talking more, *actually* talking, not just zingers, although there's plenty of them, too. We swap fanfic recs that we swear are better than most books, keep one-upping each other on our summer reading, and count down the days until the Playhouse's away party.

The Grimaldi Castle Hotel is three hours north of Luna Cove, just shy of Michigan. The slate-gray stone is choked with trailing ivy, almost shrouded at the edge of a forest so lush that it almost swallows the castle whole. It's as if someone plucked it right out of a storybook. When we were bused in early this morning, the sun was peeking through the dense trees that surrounded the castle, crowning the towers with its glow.

We knew the birthday girl wanted a full-scale fairy-tale costume party, children and adults included, but we're all still a little taken aback with how into it they are. The first day's activities include a crash-course "charm school," welcome luncheon, and outdoor chess. We take a much-needed break when the kids go horseback riding, giving us just enough time to decompress before the feast and the ball.

The grapefruit-streaked July sunset casts the farthest reaches of the ballroom blush-pink, while a dripping crystal chandelier the size of a baby elephant bathes the center of the room in a Mikado yellow light.

I'm as exhausted as one of the twelve dancing princesses from keeping in character while waltzing. I've gotten a lot better, but Ian's sweeping and swinging and spinning me across the parquet floor with the kind of effortless, nimble grace that I know means it's not effortless at all. He's actually bringing moves that Poppy never even taught us. If I'm tired, I can't imagine how much more so he must be.

Our instructions are to dance with the guests who want to, which means every time a girl with stars in her eyes approaches Ian, he excuses himself with disarming charm to ask her for a turn around the ballroom.

As we fall back into the rhythm, I try my best to ignore the tingles on my body where he touches me, the power of his thighs as he leads us around the room.

I really don't want to think about his thighs.

He holds me in his arms, moving with practiced ease and completely oblivious to everyone other than me. Something tethers me to him, refusing to let me look away from his mesmerizing stare for even a second. God, he's so beautiful. He really is a prince.

I'm aware of nothing except him, and the way his dark eyes anchor me, unfurling a coil of heat in my stomach. My neck prickles hot. It doesn't just stop at my neck. Tingles run down my body like shooting stars, leaving light trails in their wake.

Even when the birthday girl—a pretty eleven-year-old white girl in a frothy pink ballgown who only stops her giggling long enough to ask him for a dance—cuts in, his eyes find me in the teeming sea of people.

His eyes zero in on me even when his body twists away, even when there's no possible way he isn't totally dizzy . . . and then, when I least expect it, he finds me again.

It's unconscionable how I never really saw him before, but Ian is *incredible*. Quelque chose de magique.

The music dwindles softer and softer, the string quartet fading out just as the grandfather clock strikes nine p.m. Ian comes to a stop, and the illusion is shattered. The guests, all teenage girls, begin talking at once, the sound grating and excitedly high-pitched.

The birthday girl sways on her feet, and Ian catches her against his chest in a heroic, manly way that sets my teeth on edge. He's been more gallant than any of the actual Prince Charmings, and it's hard not to envy his ease when it seems so effortless. He doesn't have to pretend to be someone else tonight like I do. He just has to be himself.

I still feel clenched and unsettled an hour later, when the party's disbanded for the night. We all head back to the castle's bunkhouse, which is normally used for guests who can't afford to stay in the castle itself, but tonight the dormitories are filled with the Playhouse cast.

I'm sharing with Amie in one of the nicer rooms, but it's still a squeeze with two full-size beds and cabin-y furniture. Some of the others are in bunk beds, four people to a room, but right now most of us are too wired to sleep, so everyone's snacking and hanging out in the common room since we have the whole place to ourselves.

Ian's probably there, too, unwinding after a long day.

Maybe that explains why I'm not.

The door opens behind me, letting in a burst of distant, raucous laughter. I turn away from the window to offer Amie a smile. She's wearing a fluffy pink bathrobe she brought with her and has her toiletry bag tucked under her arm.

"God, I hate shared bathrooms." She makes a face. "Good view?"

"It's breathtaking," I tell her, but even the pretty starlit night can't distract me from my thoughts.

She returns her toiletries to her suitcase before getting into bed and unplugging her phone.

"You don't want to shower and change?" she asks.

"I . . . no. I guess I just wanted to hold on to the magic a little longer."

While Amie's fresh-faced and scrubbed clean, my own

makeup has melted into my face, setting spray rendered useless after hours outside and then all the dancing.

"You and Ian looked good dancing together."

Even I knew that, despite the fact that my calves were tight, a headache pulsed between my eyebrows, and the soles of my feet ached with every forward half box, backward half box.

I throw her dartboard eyes, unsure of how much she'd seen. "Mm," I say, affecting a tone of disinterest.

"He's not out in the common room, by the way, if that's why you're in here. I ran into Samer in the hallway, and he said Ian went for a walk."

It's an odd thing to tell me, this assumption that I want to know, but I nod.

The truth is, no matter how much I want to cling to the familiar comfort of my rivalry with Ian, he's done a good job of dismantling my walls one crumbling brick at a time. And maybe it started with that kiss at Claudia's house, but I can admit something now that I couldn't have articulated back then: There's always been a flicker of something between us. Attraction, respect, annoyance, whatever heady cocktail it is, I feel like I've downed several glasses of it.

It was nice to not be us tonight. To be Mermaid Princess and Shipwrecked Prince. Me in my cloud of pink cotton candy gown, him in naval blue and crisp white. So easy to forget I wasn't supposed to like him, even though nobody told me I couldn't.

I was the only one who believed it. Who—always—stood in her own way.

Suddenly, the dorm room feels too small and all my thoughts too large.

"Do you think I could step outside for a while?" I ask Amie, waving at the window. "I could use some air after being in that ballroom for hours."

Both her eyebrows lift in surprise. "You don't need my permission. Just don't forget about that midnight curfew so we can be up bright and early to do it all over again tomorrow," she says, rolling her eyes. "I can't believe I was actually excited about an away party when it's two whole days of playing pretend with spoiled rich kids."

"They're not so bad. You saw how thrilled they were with the pomp and glamour of the whole day." Especially attending an actual ball with handsome princes in their finest regalia.

"Simran says goodnight, by the way," she adds as I head for the door.

I stop in surprise, staring at her phone. "You're talking to my sister?"

She blushes. "Yeah, it's a new thing, but . . . yeah."

I eye her. Amie's been a lesbian as long as I've known her, and other than the boys Simran dated in high school, I'm not completely sure where she falls.

"Well," I say. "You can tell her I said goodnight back."

"Be back before midnight!" Amie calls after me as I leave.

The sapphire satin sky is swept with brushstrokes of silver stars.

Luna Cove is hardly a big city, but even in my quiet, tree-shrouded cul-de-sac, you can't see the sky like this. Across the pond, the castle glitters like a ring in a black velvet box, and as I watch, the lights go out, as though the box has been snapped shut.

There's still enough light to walk by. The pathways, the courtyard, and the back patio twinkle with fairy lights strung on trees and arbors, and soft, buttery yellow light from the solar lights staked into the ground guide me to the stables.

My nose tickles with the scent of sweet hay and the muskiness of sweat. The stable hands are long gone, so it's just me and the horses. But as I walk past the tack room, I stumble.

I'm not the only one here.

Standing in front of me, hands shoved deep into his pockets, is Ian Jun. He's beautiful, bathed in a bolt of silvery moonlight streaking in from the entrance. I must have let a gasp slip, because he startles.

And just like that, after wandering the labyrinth for years, I find my center.

"Kavya? What are you doing out here?" His brow is creased in a way that makes me itch to smooth away all those worry lines.

"I was just taking a walk and . . ." I trail off. "Ended up here."

He nods, accepting my presence. "They're majestic, aren't they?"

I approach, standing next to him. Our shoulders brush.

Tilting my head to the side, I ask, "Do you ride?"

"Nah. Too expensive. Grace went to a one-week summer horse camp once."

He seems content to stand there and watch them, hands still in his pockets. I glance at the horses on either side of the chestnut Morgan mare he's so transfixed by.

Their nameplates read ARTAX and SHADOWFAX. I smirk. I'm about to lean over and ask him if he can recognize their literary namesakes when I catch the look on his face.

If I didn't know him as well as I do, I wouldn't have noticed that faint yearning in his eyes and the taut, stoic set of his mouth.

It's an expression I've become familiar with seeing on him lately.

"Her name is Astra," I say, quiet, even though no one's here to overhear and chase us out.

I see him glance at me from the corner of his eye. "Fitting on a night like this one," he says lightly. "All those stars out."

I think he expects me to ignore how badly he's trying to gear himself up into petting Astra. If he's waiting for his confidence to bolster, we'll be here all night. At the very least, past midnight. Which is probably any minute now.

"Can I?" I slide my palm against his, threading our fingers together. I nod with my chin at the horse. "We can do it together if you want." His hand jerks against mine, and the movement is so sudden that I instinctively tighten my grip.

"I can appreciate her without having to touch her," he all but stammers.

"Ian. C'mon. That's no fun, and it's not the same."

She seems to know we're discussing her and pokes her head

inquisitively toward us, tail swishing. Her soft whinny of encouragement has Ian taking a hurried half step back.

I glance between him and Astra, understanding dawning. "You're trying to do a scary thing again, aren't you?"

"Somewhat unsuccessfully," he says with a short huff.

"You're out here. Seems pretty successful to me."

"I don't know how to feel when you're acting this nice to me, Joshi," he drawls.

For a split second, I'm offended. Then he squeezes my hand and smiles down at me. Soft and starry. Wanting me to know he's just teasing.

It's an awful lot like something friends would do.

But my heart doesn't beat like this for my friends.

"If I ask you that question you wanted me to ask you that day in Rio's pool," I say. "Would you still tell me the truth?"

"I'll always tell you the truth."

His sincerity sends a jolt through me. Not *I don't lie* or *I always tell the truth*. He said he would always tell *me* the truth. As though I'm something precious to him.

"It's me, isn't it?" I whisper.

He doesn't pretend. We're past that now.

"It's always been you, Kavya," he says, voice low and tumbling and unguarded.

Since that day at Rio's, I knew Ian liked me. What I didn't realize was that *both* girls he liked were the same person.

I wonder why I didn't see it before: I am the girl who wouldn't have liked him back. I am also the girl who likes him now.

His smile is charmingly, infuriatingly self-satisfied. I want to wipe it off his face.

I pitch myself forward and up, straining to reach his height. I stop just shy of his lips, bringing my free hand up to cup the sharp slant of his cheek, trailing down his jaw and to the corner of his mouth.

He stays still, like he doesn't want to make any sudden moves to scare me off, or maybe because he needs a moment to adjust to this shift in our dynamic so *he* doesn't flee.

"You've never looked at me this way before," says Ian, voice as serious as his brow. "But tonight in the ballroom. And . . ."

The intensity of his stare is positively dehydrating.

"And?" I breathe.

"And now," he says. "There's something there that wasn't there before." He looks down at our hands, then closes his eyes to nuzzle his cheek into my palm before kissing the base of my wrist with reverence.

I squeak. His lips are as soft as I remember them, and I feel the warm press of his mouth. My nose tingles with the scent of cherry ChapStick, and I know if I kiss him now, I'll taste it, too. I pin myself against him, letting our hips meet.

The lean lines of his throat tighten as he swallows and stares at me with dark, unblinking eyes.

I don't go in for the kiss right away. I wiggle my hand free, then dance my fingertips across his forearms with tantalizing slowness. He tenses under me and his breath comes out in short pants.

I've wanted to shut him up so often in the past that it's hard not to shamelessly revel in the way he bites his lip, a little shiver going through him even on such a warm night.

"Well?" he asks, a touch of arrogance and insecurity and anticipation.

My lips twitch with the effort it takes not to smile. "Cold?"

"You've got rosebuds in your cheeks," he says, pulling me into his chest. His words are pitched low and intense, soulful and romantic like no one has ever been with me before.

It's what makes me close the gap between us without hesitation, pressing myself into him at the same moment our lips meet. The earthy smell of the barn is replaced with the clean scent of his usual Abercrombie & Fitch Fierce cologne and something unidentifiable that's just him.

Ian's hands dip to my waist, squeezing my hips. The possessive touch draws a gasp from me, then a sigh into his mouth. Though his lips are soft, the rest of him is hard and hungry. He pulls me achingly, impossibly closer. His hand runs up and down my back, strumming me until my body is ready to sing one name and one name only. His thighs press firmly against mine, and it's a good thing he's solid and he's *there*, otherwise my jelly legs would probably give in.

My eyes flutter shut. Pleasure scatters across my shoulders and spine; I'm somewhere between tense and relaxed, hyperaware of his closeness. I trail my hands up his chest, past his shoulders, and cup his face. I like soft and sweet, but this kiss is intense and all-consuming, full of everything that's been building between us for so, so long. It deepens the way our first one didn't have a chance to, until my only coherent thought is: *Rivalry is good, but kisses are better.*

"Maybe we should cut this short and head back to the bunk-house before you get me to show you my grudge list," I mur-mur, eyelids struggling to reopen when we part for breath.

"As if anyone could 'get' you to do anything you didn't want to, sweetheart."

I snap my eyes open at the whispered endearment, spoken so casually in his wry voice. Does he even know he's said it? Does he think of me like that? How *long* has he— I cut off my train of thought.

"Maybe you're playing the long game to get what you're after," I say.

Unoffended, he tilts his head and stares at me for a long mo-ment, as though trying to gauge how I'll respond to what he's thinking about. His features look sharper in the low lighting.

"I am. *Was*," he amends. "But you've got what I was *after* all wrong."

My heart sings with a giddy little strum. "Still not hearing a denial about the grudge list," I say, fingers twitching to dive into his hair, tousle it into oblivion. I settle for clutching at the fabric of the costume he's still wearing and try not to be mag-netized by his mouth.

He doesn't let me go, either, so his breathless laugh is hard enough to rock both of us. "You got me, Joshi. That must be why *I* was the one to saunter in here, reach for your hand, and seduce you." He brings one of my hands to his mouth and kisses my fingertips, cocking a devastating eyebrow. "Oh, wait."

"I hardly think this counts as seduction," I say, indignant and unrepentant. "And hey. We've kissed twice now. Why do you still call me Joshi sometimes?"

The arrogant roguishness fades from his face. In its place is boyish devotion that makes my whole body stutter. His eyes sweep over my face like he's making a memory while we're still right here in the present.

Ian sighs and drops my hand, but only to run the slightly calloused pad of his thumb across my lower lip, as if he's trying to stall. He twirls a loose curl of my hair around his finger before tucking it behind my ear. "Maybe I wanted something that was just mine."

22.
What Am I, a Monster?

EVERYTHING CHANGES AFTER that kiss.

Birds don't circle my head singing romantically, and woodland creatures definitely don't frolic with me in a field of daisies, but everything changes nonetheless.

Not all at once, but it slips up on me throughout the next week. First, when Ian messages me good morning exactly at eight a.m., almost as though he was up way earlier and was counting down the minutes until it reached a socially acceptable time. Next, when we run into Kaylee at her friend's party and her eyes light up when she sees us enter *together*.

And especially when he sends three blue hearts and a question mark along with a screenshot of this summer's drive-in movie theater schedule and upcoming Riverwalk concert series, including an open mic day.

I finally *get it.* The thing all those love songs are about. What Mom and Dad have, what Catey and Blaire have. After Parker, I never thought it would happen to me while I was still in high school, and definitely never thought it would be with Ian.

And I absolutely did not have "Ditch Khushi auntie's potluck dinner to voluntarily spend time with Ian Jun" on this year's bingo card.

I slip out the door just as the party starts singing "Kabhi Khushi Kabhie Gham." The music peters away as I escape across the cul-de-sac, heading back home to FaceTime Ian.

"We need to pick a movie for our first date," Ian says the second he picks up.

"Hello to you, too." I let myself in, flicking on the lights.

His smile freezes on the screen, and even though the rest of his face pixelates for a second, that smile is untouchable. "Hey, you," he says, Smile #9 still in place.

My abdomen tightens. "That's more like it."

"So what do you think? You, me? The drive-in this weekend?"

I kick my shoes off at the door, almost toppling over when Buster comes rushing at me, tail wagging and tongue out. "What's showing?"

He smirks like he relishes what he's about to say next. *"Pride and Prejudice."*

It's not lost on me that he clearly thinks I'm both those things. I roll my eyes.

He sets his phone down and fiddles with something on his desk. "Is that a yes?"

I scratch the top of Buster's head and pretend to think about it. "Depends. Firth or Macfadyen?"

"Macfadyen. What am I, a monster?"

Good, it's the newer one with Keira Knightley as Elizabeth. "Okay. But let's not call it a first date," I decide. "Not until the third contest is over. For now, it's a . . . reconnaissance mission."

"Recon? Is that what we're calling it now?" He exaggeratedly bats his eyes.

"While your guard is down, I'll exploit all your secrets and use them against you." I snap my fingers. "Now you know my master plan."

"I forgot your weird rules about fraternization." His lips twitch, holding back a smile. "So you're under no misapprehension that I won't be doing the same thing to you?"

"Oh, you can try." I hold his gaze so long that my eyes water.

He laughs like it's all in good fun—and it is—and holds Yeobo up to his cheek. "Meet Yeobo the fourth. At least, I think she's the fourth, unless Mom knows something I don't."

The golden-furred hamster peers inquisitively at me with beady black eyes, her little paws curled up to her chin.

"She's adorable. Buster, meet Yeobo."

"He loves her," pronounces Ian.

I raise my eyebrows as my dog steadfastly ignores the screen, whining for head rubs.

"Eh, not everyone's great at showing how they feel," says Ian. "Especially if those feelings scare them."

I shoot him a sharp look, but he's already got his back to

me, putting Yeobo back in her cage. It gives me the time to
school my features as if I didn't get his meaning.

There's a metallic sound as he latches the cage shut. "Oh,
by the way, did you get a chance to read the book I gave you
yet?" he asks.

Although I don't truly believe he'd try to sabotage my reading streak with a dud book anymore, I still haven't opened it.
Taste is subjective, as personal as the scent of a woman's go-to
perfume, and I kinda doubt he knows mine.

But I don't want to hurt his feelings, so I nod. "Yeah, it's
next on my TBR."

"I think you'll really like it. It's by my favorite author."

I grab a glass of water and head upstairs, Buster on my heels.
I'm surprised to find a sliver of light under Simran's bedroom
door. I didn't realize she left the Kapoors early, too.

"Hey," I say. "I know we said we were going to talk tonight,
but, um, there's something I need to talk to my sister about. Is
it okay if we—"

"Yeah, of course," says Ian before I can even ask. "Message
me later."

"Okay." Even though this is my cue to say bye, I find
myself strangely reluctant to end the video call. I want to
prolong our conversation because a part of me is afraid that
there won't be another time. That I'll do something that will
fuck all of this up.

Ian hesitates, too. "Kavya?"

My mouth opens to say bye, but what comes out is "It
was . . . nice talking to you. Thanks for making the time."

It's formal and stilted and oh my god, so awkward.

He grins, but before he can say a word, I end the call.

I can't believe I just said that. Thanks for making the time? He's a *boy*, not a job interviewer.

With a sigh, I knock on Simran's door.

"Come in!"

I twist the doorknob. "Why are you sitting in the dark?"

She's lying on her stomach, socked feet tucked under her pillow. Her laptop is open to an episode of *Schitt's Creek*, greenish screen glow catching all the shadows in her face. Her hand stills as she reaches for one of the many sweets on the plate in front of her.

"I wasn't in the dark. I was watching my show." Simran taps pause before asking, "What do you want?"

"Sheesh, sound happier to see me, why don't you?" I roll my eyes and slip into her room, flicking on the light switch. "Move over."

With a groan, she does, and I curl up next to her, snagging a perfectly round, golden boondi ladoo. When I break it in half, the ball is so fresh and tender that it crumbles into boondi balls right away. Cardamom and saffron fill the air.

"That's mine," says Simran, but she takes only half. She knows they're my favorite. "Why are you back so early?"

"The aunties were asking about you. Khushi auntie was dragging some finance bro around trying to introduce you," I say. "Mom told me she hadn't seen you since we arrived."

She jolts. "She sent you to find me?"

I give her a look. "No, nobody knows you're here. I told

them you were in the basement watching the kids."

She processes this. "Okay. Thanks."

I pick at my half of the ladoo until it's fallen apart in my palm, then squish it back together. Pinching it between two fingers, I drop it on my tongue.

Simran's watching me with a smile. "You always do that."

"And you always do this." I bump her with my shoulder. "Sneak away from gatherings and come back home with smuggled sweets. You think I don't know my own sister?"

She shakes her head, reaching for the plate. "You surprise me." She hovers for a second like she's not sure what to take, then selects a dark amber rectangle of chikki. The peanut brittle is her favorite, but she efficiently snaps it in half and holds one piece out to me without a word.

"Thanks." I let it crunch between my teeth. "So what happened?"

Because of course something did, I can see it on her face.

She hasn't dropped a single crumb, but she still goes through the performance of brushing the imaginary flecks off the sorbet-colored cotton kantha quilt our grandmother brought with her on her previous trip. "Nothing. I'm fine." Her hand moves to her laptop, about to tap play.

Simran had already finished the first season when I first heard about the show. I'd asked Simran if we could watch it together, but she said she didn't want to wait for me. So I watched it with the moon girls instead, and then on my own. Not once, not twice. Three times.

I glance at David and Alexis Rose on the screen. Siblings

who don't always understand each other, often can't stand each other, but who are always there for each other nonetheless.

"Simmy, wait."

Her hand freezes in mid-action. One black eyebrow quirks. "Yeah?"

"Tell me what happened," I say quietly.

My sister runs her tongue over her top teeth. Either she's working out the peanuts or she's nervous. "You wouldn't understand."

A challenge? She should know better. "Either you tell me or I use my authoritative auntie voice until you do."

This actually gets a smile from her until she tamps it down. "Fine. But if I tell you, I want you to hear me. Don't ask me if I'm sure or try to make me second-guess something that I've already been sure about for a long time. Deal?"

"Deal."

Simran brings her hands together, moving her thumbs back and forth in an agitated motion. "Do you remember Leela auntie's daughter Naina?"

"Sure. The neurobiologist who lives in Germany."

"Okay. Well, she's twenty-nine, right? Do you remember how she came over for her brother's wedding a few years ago?"

"Of course I do. They had a great buffet."

"Stop thinking with your tummy," says Simran, but she laughs. "I don't know how much she really enjoyed being back home. I caught her crying in the bathroom during the sangeet ceremony."

"I don't remember—"

"You were a kid. You wouldn't have noticed. All the aunties asking her when she was going to let her parents arrange her marriage, didn't she want children, how was she ever going to find a husband if she didn't stay out of the sun? I mean, for fuck's sake, she's a competitive cyclist. Surely they don't expect her to go everywhere with a parasol like a Victorian? Let her live. Some of us can be perfectly happy being not so fair and still every bit as lovely."

When she ran out of rickshaw money, Mom used to travel with a parasol to protect her skin from browning in the sun. She said her mother gave her a tube of the skin-lightening cream Fair & Lovely like a rite of passage when she turned eleven and made her stop playing cricket in the street with her brothers so she wouldn't brown. Mom made sure that was one particular tradition that ended with her.

"Leela auntie let them bully her like that?" It isn't surprising, but I'm still a little bit aghast. "She's always saying how proud she is of Naina for being at the top of her field, for relocating to a new country and learning the language and everything."

Simran shrugs. "Proud until it's time for her to start popping out babies."

"Ew. That's pretty backwards."

"It is what it is," she says, every word heavy and burdened.

I wet my lips, staring at a loose thread in her quilt. Childishly, I want to pull it. But I also don't want it to all come undone. "It's 'your turn now,' isn't it?"

Simran rolls onto her back and plays with the hem of her

shirt. "Yeah. Mom understands. She tells them I want to focus on my school and career, but without a solid publication and a nice check, none of the aunties think it's worth delaying marriage for. Khushi auntie even told me once writing isn't a real career. She said maybe I would finally make some 'real' money once I got married and got material to write romance novels."

She sighs. "I feel worse for Mom than I do for myself. She shields me so much, and I know how lucky I am to have that, but I hate that she's the one who has to deal with every nose-sticker-inner. And she has to do it all with a smile."

"Nose-sticker-inner? Clearly all that money spent on your education was—" I click my tongue, trying a stab at levity.

That gets a laugh. "I know I give you a lot of shit about not holding your tongue, but honestly? I'm proud that you don't. Envious, even. I don't know what it's like to be that free with your feelings. Sometimes I'm scared I never will."

"Oh, Simmy." I flop onto my back and wiggle my butt until I've sidled next to my sister, shoulder to shoulder.

I fight the instinct to put my arm around her because I can't remember the last time I did that, and part of me is afraid she wouldn't want me to.

"I don't know if I want kids, like, ever, but I do know that I'm not interested in being married off. And if I do get married, it probably won't be to a man. If there's one thing that dating in high school and college taught me, it's that I'm not into guys, at least not most guys. And it's hard to date when you feel the way I do."

"But you and Amie . . . ?" I ask. "Is there something there?"

Simran bites her lip. She eyes me like she's not sure whether to go on.

I keep my expression blank, holding still. Trying to prove I can be trusted.

"I like Amie. I always have, even when we were in high school. But I had a boyfriend back then, and didn't understand myself the way I do now. It wasn't until college that I—" She breaks off, bringing her hand to her chest, almost like she wishes she could stuff all the words back inside her. "I don't think I've ever said this aloud to another person before."

"You can tell me. You can *always* tell me."

I can tell she's not done, so I hold space for her until she's ready.

"I'm queer," says Simran. "I'm into boys, but definitely girls, too. I thought I was aromantic at first, but now that I've had time with it, I'm pretty sure I'm demiromantic. I fall in love, but only when the emotional connection is super intense."

She pauses. "I still like Disney and Bollywood as much as the next person, but . . . I don't get from it what you do."

I already knew that, but now it makes sense on another level.

She continues. "Romantic love feels more nebulous for me. It's hard to pin down what I feel into words a lot of times. But when I think of the future, someone who I could . . . I see Amie's face. The things I thought I didn't want, I think I could want them with her."

I'm moved that Simran, who has never found it easy to

confront a situation head-on, has shared something with me, the little sister who she isn't great at sharing anything else with.

And even if it stayed clenched tight behind her teeth forever, that would have been okay, too. It was nobody's business but hers. Not mine, not the aunties, not anyone's who she didn't want to know.

The only person you *ever* need to come out to is yourself.

"And it's hard, you know?" she says. "There's all these growing pains of feeling like you're a teenager again, struggling so hard to figure your shit out. Catey and Blaire were so confident in knowing they liked girls, and I just . . . I don't know, I thought it would be like that for me, too. It's scary being an adult and trying to figure out how you feel about someone when you're just starting to understand how you feel about yourself. When it's like, shouldn't I be past this by now? And sometimes it feels like coming in last even in my own life."

She looks me in the eye. "Mom already suspects, I think, and Dad would try to understand, but—I don't want to talk about it with them yet. This was just between you and me."

It's still registering that this is something she's been keeping a secret for so long. I don't know what reaction she expects. Shock? Confusion? She won't get either of those things, not from me.

Because Simran is, and always will be, above all else, my big sister.

"Thank you for telling me," I finally settle on because I don't think I know what the right way to respond is, and I don't want to embarrass or patronize her by continuing to talk about it, not if she doesn't want. "I promise I won't say anything. But for what it's worth, I don't think you're coming in last. You're not in a competition with yourself. We learn new things about ourselves all the time. You're right on time, Simmy. But if you *do* ever want to talk, um, I hope you feel like you can talk to me."

Simran smiles in a way that makes me feel like she already knows. She reaches above her head for the plate of sweets. "Share?"

I have a ladoo out of the plate before she's even finished asking the question.

She laughs. "Besharam."

I love you.

"Stuff your face or I'll stuff it for you," I threaten, pretending to drop the ladoo onto her face. Over her squeal, I know she hears me.

I love you, too.

I wake to the sound of my parents in the hallway. At some point, I must have drifted to sleep and crawled under Simran's covers. Her pillow smells like my shampoo and bodywash: ripe, cut strawberries and sweet gardenias and earthy, cracked coconut.

Drowsily, sleep still heavy in my eyes and fogging my brain, I wonder if Simmy's fallen asleep in my bed.

My parents are outside the door now, conspicuously trying not to make any noise. I make out Dad's deeper timbre, followed by Mom's sibilant whisper, and then Dad's footsteps heading to their bedroom.

There's a soft tap on the door before Mom pops her head in. "Kavya, is everything okay? What are you doing in here?" She runs her eyes over the empty plate of mithai on the nightstand, and sighs like this is going to be tomorrow's lecture. "You missed the singing and dancing."

"There was no way I was going to humiliate myself by singing in front of everyone," I say, pulling the blanket up to my chest. "I guess we both needed a quiet night in."

"And snacked on Khushi auntie's expensive mithai," she says knowingly.

My chest tightens with the faint flicker of indignation. "That was all Simmy!"

I leave out that I'm the one who ate most of the plate.

Mom laughs and comes into the room, budging me over on the bed until she can rest against the headboard. "I feel good that my two girls are getting along."

"Mom," I groan. "Don't say stuff like that. It's so cheesy."

"Oh, am I embarrassing you?" She pokes her finger lightly into my cheek. "And after all those sweets, did you brush your teeth?"

I pull the covers over my head and slide down the mattress, hoping she takes the hint. "*Mooooom.* You don't have to ask me every night."

I find a piece of nut wedged into my molar and work it out with my tongue. I have not, in fact, brushed my teeth tonight.

"Maybe not," she concedes, "but my little monster sometimes forgets."

I wriggle my head back out, static getting everywhere. "Why do you call me that?"

"What, little monster?" Mom gets up and pulls a library book from beneath my pillow with a perfectly arched threaded eyebrow. "Don't you remember?"

I shake my head.

"When you were little, you'd take off the couch cushions and pile them up as your tower. You'd tell Simran to be the princess and sit on the top, and then you'd shake the cushions until she cried."

She pauses, looks at me like I'm supposed to know where this is going. "At first, I didn't realize what was going on. All I knew was Simran was always the princess, so I told her to play nicely and let you be the princess once in a while. She got so huffy! Said she was the princess because *you* always wanted to be the dragon. When Dad and I asked you if you wanted to play the princess, you said no, the princess just sits there. The monster was the one who had all the fun."

Which, fair.

Mom's laugh tinkles. "The next time you were the ogre. You always wanted to be the little beastie, not the damsel in distress."

"I must have been a delight," I deadpan.

I get a kiss on the forehead. "You were," says Mom.

"Even in my terrible twos?"

"What do you mean, 'even in'? You never outgrew it." She grins and hands me the book she's still holding. "Goodnight, baby."

"Night, Mom. Love you."

23.
I'm Trying to Be with You

BETWEEN THE SATURDAY of the castle party and the approaching Saturday's drive-in—even though nothing can top the warm, hazy afterglow of my first kiss with Ian and the heart-to-heart with my sister—several things happen that make me feel like the main character in one of my YA novels:

1. Dad makes bhel for our Lord of the Rings marathon, and when we all pile into the living room to watch, Simran plops down next to me without leaving a seat between us. It makes my heart grow three sizes. Especially when she splits the puris with me, fifty-fifty. Well, sixty-forty. I *am* still me after all.

2. After a particularly hot, long day where we have

two back-to-back children's parties, Ian invites me to Holly Gogogi for strawberry-mango bingsu. With Mrs. Jun not-so-subtly grinning at us from behind the counter, we couldn't exchange more than glances over the sweet shaved ice, but when he walks me back to my car, we share our second kiss—third if you count the one from truth or dare. Even with my back pressed against my car's blistering metal door, I don't want to stop kissing him. "Is it like this every time?" I ask him, bewildered, touching my swollen lips and then running my thumb across his. Was Catey right that our chemistry is so great because of all the years of foreplay? "No," he answers, tucking an errant wave behind my ear, just as dazed as I am. "This is a first for me, too."

3. Every book I read, I envision me and Ian as the main characters. It doesn't matter if it's a sci-fi or a romance or a Gothic fantasy. When the love interest tenderly brushes hair away from the protagonist's face, I shiver, imagining the warmth of Ian's palm.

The feeling continues at Blaire and Catey's favorite thrift shop. Hollywood Regency–style OTT gilded mirrors line the walls, sparkling with the light reflected from the myriad of chandelier lighting. Tufted velvet settees and vanity tables piled with colorful glass perfume bottles and vintage costume jewelry are staged to look like a glamorous actress' dressing room. Everything about this moment makes me feel like a leading lady, especially the clothing try-on montage as they badger me for more juicy details about the moonlit kiss.

"Can we please talk about something—anything!—else?" Val complains, rifling through hangers with jerky, impatient movements.

"Sorry, V," I say. "I didn't mean to make you feel left out."

"Just because I'm single doesn't mean I'm left out," she says stiffly. "Do you realize that whether you hate Ian or love him, we constantly talk about him?"

It's a few hours before the drive-in movie, and what initially was meant to be just me and Ian has morphed into me, Ian, and all our friends. I guess that's what I get for insisting this isn't a first date.

While Catey brandishes a dress at Val, Blaire steals me away. "This is so you!" she crows, setting a stiff, wide-brimmed hat on my head.

I eye myself in the mirror. It looks like something Grace Kelly would have worn.

"It's a movie, not a garden party!" I take it off and hang it back up on the hat stand. It's the crown jewel at the top of a rather nice selection of straw hats, fedoras, and velvet cloches straight out of the 1920s. "Something from *this* century, please."

Blaire rifles through a rack of floral two-pieces. "One of these days I'm going to change your mind about style."

I groan. "Tell me again why you and the girls invited yourselves along?"

She laughs and slings an arm over my shoulder. "Are you kidding me? We wouldn't miss this for the world." With her other hand, she holds the two-piece set in front of me. "Try it on."

This is my own fault, I realize as she all but pushes me into a changing room. Telling my mother hen about tonight's date with Ian is a surefire way to make sure the hen's girlfriend finds out, too.

I slip into the dandelion-patterned blouse and skirt Blaire chose. The soft indigo fabric drapes loosely on my petite shoulders and hangs down to the elbows. "I look like someone's granny," I say, emerging from behind the fabric curtain. I pluck at the skirt and hold it away from my thigh, then let it fall back into place.

Blaire gets to work, twisting and knotting the ends into a crop top. The sleeves are rolled back to mid-bicep and held in place with two bobby pins she pulls from her hair. "Voilà. Who says grannies can't be chic?" She winks. "I'd totally wear this to a festival."

"That's because you're an upcycling thrifting queen and I'm—"

She cuts me off before I can insult myself. "Lucky to have me," she says dramatically.

We pay and leave, Blaire insisting I wear the dress out along with a purple felt hat she thinks I just *had* to have, even though it doesn't even match the outfit. She found vintage Levi's jeans for herself and picked out a blue-and-white gingham midi dress patterned with tiny red strawberries for Catey.

Meanwhile, Val has splurged on a red minidress with bow tie spaghetti straps, something her parents wouldn't let her walk out of the house wearing. She's happy and smiling—and just a tad rebellious—after having sold two of her original dresses to Catey's older sister earlier this week.

Swinging my bag of old clothes between us, I lead the way to our favorite boba tea shop along the Riverwalk. While Catey and Val wait for their drinks, Blaire and I sit outside, shaded under wide umbrellas, sipping our peach tea and people watching.

Cute hand-holding yuppie couples go in and out of antique shops, linger in front of the bookstore to browse the 50 percent off display, and try samples at the famous hand-poured chocolatier where Simran and I always buy Mother's Day truffles.

"Can I ask you something?" asks Blaire.

I chew on my straw. "Always."

"Has Val been acting weird lately?"

The breeze changes direction at just that moment, turning my forearms cool and goose-bumped. "Um, maybe a little," I say cautiously. I reach for my sunglasses and prop them on my nose. "Why?"

"The questions she asks. They're ones she knows the answers to, but she acts like . . . I don't know. Like maybe she's hoping the answers are going to be different?"

I don't know how to get into this without breaking Val's confidence. I bite my lip and ask, "How so?"

"Like 'Are Catey's parents still investing all that money?' Is my mom still going to let us pitch in on weekends and after school? I don't know, it makes us feel shitty and defensive." She sighs. "I've asked her a bunch of times if she was upset about something, but she swears she's fine. But I feel like every time she's getting madder about it, even though she fronts like 'I'm so proud of you! OMG so happy for your success, all the best!' in this weird voice that even Catey thinks is fake."

"You've already talked about it with Catey?"

On a rational level, I know I don't have a right to feel left out. They're girlfriends. Their families are going into business together. *Of course* they're going to talk things out with each other.

"Oh my god, it wasn't like that," Blaire says with a small, self-conscious laugh. "We could totally be misreading things here. We've been so busy and maybe we're just losing patience or whatever? Val can be—"

She doesn't have to finish the sentence. I know what she means.

She takes a long draw on her straw, sucking until the ice rattles. "We don't want to talk about Val behind her back, but we have to figure this out, right?"

Hoping she doesn't notice my hesitation, I murmur, "Right."

"She hasn't said anything to you, has she? I know things with her dad . . . She doesn't resent us, right? Because her parents want her to be a doctor?"

Fuck, how do I answer this?

There are some things you just won't get, not really, if you aren't Asian. The anvil weight of pressure and expectations that come from parents wanting to see their kids succeed. No, not just succeed. Excel. Leaving everyone else's kids in the dust. Even if Blaire and Catey think they get it, they don't *really* get it. Maybe I don't either.

Some kids are supported in chasing their dreams. I'm lucky; all my parents want is for me to be happy. They'll always support me as long as I work hard.

But so many kids are told to do what their parents want.

My stomach clenches like a fist. Maybe it would be better to let Blaire think she's misreading the situation. It's not my place to speak on Val's feelings. She'll talk about it herself when she's ready. I don't think she'd want me to betray her confidence.

"Kavs?" Blaire peers at me. She looks worried.

Shit, I've taken too long.

"No," I say, not sure what part of her question I'm answering. "We all know she's feeling the pressure from her parents. It isn't easy for her to fight for every little thing. It's probably just stress."

I don't know if Blaire believes me, or if she just wants to so desperately that she drops the subject. A few minutes later, Catey and Val are back, and while we chew the boba and listen to Val talk about Rio and whether he'll like her new dress, the moon girls are okay again.

The movie starts at nine, when the sky is draped in a beautiful blue-black velvet, silver stars peeking through. It's a busy night, the weedy gravel parking area packed. Luckily we're a little early, and thanks to Ian and Claudia we've snagged great spots. Claudia and Samer have both brought dates, and since Rio's sticking with Ian, Val stays with me.

The moment I get out of Catey's car, Ian appraises my look—complete with bright-yellow strappy sandals and matching toenails. "You look nice," he says. "I know this spiraled into a group outing, but you're still sitting with me, right?"

"Thank you. Um. You, too. And yes." I clear my throat. "Yes I am."

His periwinkle slim-fit Henley and tight jeans are doing things to me.

"Hey, Kavya," says Rio, sliding out of Ian's front passenger seat. "Take my seat. I'm gonna go grab some snacks."

"I'll go with you." Val's already grabbed her purse.

"V, can you grab me—" I start to ask, but Ian hands Rio a crumpled twenty.

"My treat," he tells me when I open my mouth to protest. "Rio, would you mind? Popcorn, sodas, and Sour Patch Kids, please. Anything else, Kavs?"

"You covered everything." My stomach flutters, but not unpleasantly. "I can't believe you remembered I like Sour Patch Kids."

"I think the fact you always ordered it at the movies might have clued me in," he says dryly. "You always liked things you could bite the head off first."

As our friends take off for the concession stand, Ian holds the car door open for me. "Might as well get comfy. The movie isn't starting for another fifteen minutes."

"Thanks." I glance through the windshield at the enormous blank screen.

He goes around the front and gets in the driver's seat. "So how much do your friends know?" He lowers his voice and reaches for my hand, eyes soft. "About *us*."

My stomach goes gooey. "I told them about the kiss."

He gets a knowing glint in his eye. "Kiss, singular? As in just the first one?"

"Both," I say under my breath, convinced he can hear my accelerating ninety-miles-an-hour heartbeat. "Believe me, they wanted a play-by-play in excruciating detail. I swear they think they deserve all the credit."

"They probably do. We wouldn't have spent as much time together if it wasn't for them." Ian squeezes my hand. "Scale of one to ten, how weird is this to talk about?"

I blow out a breath. "Part of me wants to say ten. The other part says not at all. Which makes it weird. Right?"

He shrugs, but doesn't loosen his grip. If anything, his fingers nestle against mine even more snugly. "You know, I didn't tell you the whole truth before."

My hand jolts and the whole moment becomes far more charged.

"But when I told you the reasons I got a job at the Playhouse, I sidestepped the biggest one. Yes, the money is good, but . . . it was you, Kavya. You were my biggest reason. You're why I wanted to do the scary thing."

I've been running through everything he's ever told me about why he wanted the job, but when he says that last sentence, I understand: *I'm* the scary thing.

He continues. "I don't want to fight you for the world. I want to share it with you. A rivalry requires a winner and a loser, but a relationship would only have winners."

Those siren-song words hold an allure. I'm not sure that even he knows how potent it is.

"There's something between us that I don't want to ignore anymore just because you think we're destined to be rivals. Every day since we kissed at Grimaldi Castle, I . . ." He swallows. "I've been waiting for you to pull away. That you'd get to know me and decide we were better off before. That everything between us would just turn into a footnote of summer. I don't want to lose you, but even if you don't want what I want . . . I hope we could at least be friends."

This is too much. This is A Lot.

Before I can stop myself, I pull my hand free and fist it against my thigh.

"I tried to tell you the day of Scrabble at the library," he says, face pained. "I threw my anxiety into the deep end by taking a job that required me to do something I'd never done before because I wanted to be around you. I wanted you to see me the way I've always seen you, even when you weren't looking."

Maybe a month ago, I would have rejoiced to have been Ian's scary thing. The bogeyman keeping him on his toes, cute but a threat. It hits different now. I don't want to be another dragon for him to slay, but I'm sure not the princess who needs to be saved, either.

"You wore jeggings for me," I realize. "You showed up to Kaylee's birthday party even though you had just come out of a panic attack."

I try to think about the things I've done for him. I tried to save him from truth or dare. I stepped in when Poppy asked him to waltz in front of everyone with Amie. I helped him take the first step in getting over his fear of horses. But those are things I would have done for anyone.

"It's not a competition, Kavya," he says gently, as if he knows exactly where my thoughts have gone. "You didn't challenge me to do any of those things. I chose to do them. Spending time with you this summer has been everything I ever wanted. *You* make me brave."

He reaches for my hand and I give it to him. If he notices my fingers don't curl into his the same way as they did before, he doesn't say anything.

Throughout our entire friendship and our entire rivalry, I've never felt as humbled as I do right now.

Because there's still the biggest thing he thinks he saved me from. The event in our past that I haven't allowed myself to think about until recently because that's the moment that everything changed. It's what cemented us as rivals, as two kids who went down a waterslide one day and averted eye contact the next.

I don't think he remembers it at all. But it's what set me on this course. I drew away from him because I didn't want anyone to ever think that I wasn't enough. That I wasn't strong and brave and number one. But most importantly, it reinforced that sharing first was as good as coming in second—as coming in last.

"I'm sorry I wasn't always a good friend," I say, voice small.

"You're a good friend now," says Ian. "You're a good . . . Can I say 'girlfriend?'"

I hope I'm not blushing. "I never thought of the chemistry between us as . . ." I let the words trail off, hoping he gets the idea, but his face is the picture of innocence.

Dick. He wants me to come out and say it, doesn't he?

"Romance," I finish reluctantly, not daring to look at him.

"Romance, huh?" There's a smile in his voice.

"Don't make it a thing," I groan. "I mean, it's not like I'm going to show you my grudge list or anything, if that's what you're thinking."

"Perish the thought." His eyes are sparkling. "Save that for marriage."

"Oh, this just got soooo icky."

He grins. "Does this mean you're giving me a chance? A real one?"

I bite my lip. "Ian, I don't know how to be—"

"Don't be anyone other than you. Undiluted, full-strength you. That's the girl I want."

More than anything I want to say yes, but what comes out is, "You're the bravest person I know. If this was a fairy tale, you've already slayed your dragons to win the princess's love."

I keep going because if I don't say this now, in this clunky, rambling way, I don't know if I ever will. "I always thought I was Belle. You know, bookish and brave? Willing to look past prickly, beastly exteriors to see the beating heart of someone good and kind? I prided myself so much on being like her, but the truth is, I'm Sleeping Beauty. I had my eyes closed the whole time you were trying to do all these things for me. I wasn't seeing you."

My breath catches and my eyes grow itchy with unshed tears. "You've given me so many chances to open my eyes. How can you still like me?"

"Because I like you," he says simply. Just like that. As if it really is just that obvious.

I stare at him.

"And that means," he continues, "I will always give you one more chance. And I'll never keep track of how many that is, because I'm not trying to be better than you. I'm trying to be *with* you."

Ian leans closer, and I find myself mimicking the motion as though our foreheads are magnetized. We stay like that for a moment—or maybe longer. At this distance, I can inhale him. He smells like summer and strong diner coffee.

When I peek at him, I can't quite meet his eyes, so I stare at the bridge of his nose instead. It was so much easier to look at him when I knew what I would see. The arrogant tip of his chin, his dancing, mischievous eyes, the knowing, bull's-eye smirk.

I still see all that, but now I see more, too. I see *him*.

Ian lets me take my time, waiting patiently until my stomach stops folding in on itself. The whole time I sense his brown eyes on my face, unwavering, as if he's saying he's not going anywhere. He's going to be there for me, no matter how competitive I get or how difficult it is to translate a rivalry into a romance.

He doesn't need to put it into words—I know.

I stare down at our still-held hands and my heartbeat calms.

"Thank you for giving me a moment," I say after the tide of emotion passes.

"You're welcome. But I did it for me a little bit, too. You tugged on my string."

I draw back in surprise to look at him.

The corner of his mouth twitches. "Not a literal string. It's how I describe my anxiety, like a sweater with loose threads all over. One of them could be pulled by something, and I never know which one until half a sleeve is unraveled."

I exhale. "I'm sorry I triggered that."

"It's okay. You needed to let it all out." He gives me an almost-smile, except his eyes are ringed with all kinds of worry.

"I'm a lot of drama," I say unnecessarily, because *hello*, that is painfully blatant by now.

This time he grins for real. "You're a Leo and you're Kavya," he cheekily reminds me.

My laugh comes out in a gust. *"God,"* I say, and that one word encompasses everything.

No sooner than the word is out of my mouth does the back door open. My instinct is to let go of Ian's hand, but as suddenly as the urge strikes, it vanishes.

Our friends know about us. There's no reason to spring apart.

"I'm back!" Val calls out, sliding in with four frosty, glass-bottle sodas and a few boxes of candy. "Sour Patch Kids for Ian, Junior Mints for me, and here's your change."

"Thanks. Where's Rio?" he asks, pocketing the bills.

"He ran into this guy from another school," says Val. "He said he just needed a couple of minutes and then he'd get the popcorn. I waited for him at concessions, but he'd disappeared. I thought he might have come back already."

"Did you catch the guy's name?" asks Ian.

"Um. Ethan, maybe? He was cute," she says as she tears into her candy and offers the box up front.

Ian's eyes flash with recognition.

I take a couple of mints and let the sweet chocolate melt on my tongue, remembering how Val tried to engineer ways to get closer to him this whole summer. I think about Rio grinning down at his phone the way Blaire does when Catey messages her.

"And he's still with him?" I ask, broaching it gently. I wait for the realization to slot.

Val licks her thumb and pointer finger where the melted chocolate has smudged a shade darker than her skin. "I guess. It seemed like they had a lot to catch up on."

Rio reappears when the movie starts, armed with popcorn and apologies, but I can barely pay attention. It has nothing to do with the movie and everything to do with the boy in the seat next to me. At some point, Ian and I both try to claim the armrest, and since neither of us backed down, our arms are flush against each other.

Every few minutes, Ian's fingers twitch as though he wants to reach for mine, but he never lets his hand cross his half of the armrest as though there's some kind of invisible barrier holding him back.

I can see now why Claudia thinks we're insufferable, me especially. Always making things a little harder for myself. Ian's different from Parker and all the other guys I've been with. We make each other better. We drive each other as much as we drive ourselves. I've seen it. I've *felt* it. I've got the test scores to prove it.

We're still the same rivals competing for the summer reading program, even though the last few days he's been a little cagey about his new totals. But I already know he's not the kind of guy to be threatened by me—Scrabble proved that.

A warm flush settles over my chest. He *admired* my win instead of resenting it.

Nothing has to be different between us. Except the kissing. That . . . that can stay.

A quick glance in the rearview reveals that Val's scooted to the middle seat, completely engrossed in the movie. Rio's curled into the window, the glow of his phone screen casting his face in a blue light. Val notices my half turn and offers a distracted smile, eyes sliding from my face to the screen, oblivious to both Rio's disinterest in the movie and my handhold with Ian.

Well, my almost handhold. His fingers are just shy of touching mine, and it's sweet, it's endearing, it's . . . taking entirely too long.

With a short huff, I hook my pinkie around his. Ian jerks, the sudden movement jostling the shared bucket of popcorn nestled between us.

His pinkie curls around mine, hesitant and achingly slow. He's careful not to look at me, and I think it's because his face is bright red, flaring even to his neck and cheeks.

The giddy thought enters my head: This is what power feels like. Bringing a boy to blush with just my pinkie finger. My insides fizz even more than the drink that's dripping condensation all over my lap. The thought that follows next is just as monumental: This feels phenomenal. Even better than winning.

A few minutes later, right after the famous Darcy hand-flex scene, Ian reaches over with his free hand. He gestures at our joined hands and I understand what he wants without having to be told.

I rotate my wrist to offer him my palm with a quizzical half smile.

He glances down, eyelashes sweeping his cheeks. Suddenly he looks shy, unsure. My heart thrums, waiting for him to make his next move. To take my hand, interlock our fingers together. He bites the corner of his lower lip and my stomach dives in a never-ending freefall like that day so long ago on the waterslide.

And then, like it's the most natural thing in the world, he drops all the red sour candies into my upturned palm. He's picked them all out for me. My favorite flavor: cherry.

I snap my eyes to his, a question on my face.

His mouth glimmers with a trace of a smile. "Whenever you have fruit snacks in class, you save the red ones for last," he whispers. "And that time you loaned me a pen, I saw all the cherry Jolly Ranchers in your pencil pouch. Sometimes you smell like them at the lockers, too."

"Okay, Edward Cullen," I whisper back, and this time, he can't hold back the grin.

He starts to shift, as if he's about to place the hand that was just kinda-sorta holding mine into his lap. And while I'm sure that's a wonderful place to be—not that I'd had the pleasure . . . yet—it's the last place I want him right now.

Lightning quick, I squeeze the cold, dripping bottle of soda between my thighs, transfer the Sour Patch Kids to my wet right palm, leaving my left free to snag Ian.

"Who said we were done?" I whisper, drawing him back to the armrest with an arched brow.

Something crosses his face that I can't quite translate, and he gives me a short nod, like I've done something he didn't expect.

The drink numbs my skin, my palm is sticky with wet sugar, and it's wholly uncomfortable. But as his fingers slip into the grooves of mine, twining us closer, I think, *I was wrong.*

This is even better than winning.

24.
Something There That Wasn't There Before

"ARE YOU *SURE* it's not done baking?" I groan, unable to resist putting my hand on the oven handle, ready to pull. "It *looks* done."

For the last hour, my kitchen has been simmering in the most delicious of smells, and it is unfair to the nth degree that the timer hasn't gone off yet on our pot pies. It's the afternoon after the movie and my throat is still scratchy with too many Sour Patch Kids, but in the best way. Because it's a reminder that last night with Ian was real.

"The crust isn't golden brown yet!" Catey swats my hand away. "I have no idea how we used to bake together when we were younger. Our moms must have had so much patience."

We used to do this all the time before she got busy with her farmer's market stall, and now, the bistro. As much as I love

Blaire and Val, I can't deny how special it is to get my first best friend all to myself. Even if it is just for an afternoon.

"Can I at least have an oatmeal cookie?" I snag one from the cooling rack before she can answer. The cookie is so soft it crumbles at my touch. Hot raisin juice squelches in my mouth. "Ah! Hot, hot, hot," I pant before taking another, more cautious, nibble.

Catey smirks like she thinks I totally deserved it. "I know how we can pass the time."

I know where she's going. "I already told the moon girl group chat everything!"

"I hope not," she teases. "A couple has to keep a few secrets."

I blink. We hadn't exactly talked about it, but is that what Ian and I are now?

I grab another still-hot cookie and shovel it in, chomping ferociously.

"You're impatient for everything in life except when it comes to him. It blows my mind how much of a slow burn you two are." She wipes down stray sprinkles of flour from the marble countertop and arches an eyebrow in her very best tell-me-I'm-wrong expression. "Worth it?"

We move to the kitchen table. She fusses with the flower arrangement, plucking out a few wilted blooms to tuck behind her ear. The wildflowers peep from her piece-y blonde waves just so. Her round, wire-rimmed aviator glasses dig a little into her cheeks, so she pushes them up. If she wasn't my best friend and dating my other best friend, I'd still have my middle school crush on her.

Speaking of crushes . . .

"I . . . yeah, I think he is," I admit. "He just . . . he gets under my skin. And not exactly the way he used to. You know? It's like there's something there that wasn't there before."

She smiles knowingly.

"I mean," I say quickly, "Who would have ever thought we'd get together?"

"Gee, I wonder who," she says laconically.

"How did you and Blaire do it?" I swallow an oatmeal lump. It's easier to be earnest when it's just her. "I remember the two of you circling each other like cats in eighth grade, but when we went to high school . . ."

"We grew up," Catey says simply, like this self-explanatory fact has been in front of me all along. "We were the only two girls who were proudly out and gay. Everyone began pairing off, and we were determined not to date each other by default. Like, what? Just because we're the only two gay girls we have to date each other?"

It's like when people ask me if I know the Kapoors. I always say no because I get so pissed off about being asked. It's not like all the brown people hang out at the same Indian store, right? I mean . . . in our case, we do. But only because South Asia Mart is the only one in town.

I squeeze her hand. "I remember. But then Rachel and—"

"Other girls came out, too," finishes Catey. "And you know what happened then?"

I've heard this story a million times, but she never tires of telling it, so I smile. It's like hearing my parents' Elco bhel story, the memory just as soft and bokeh-blurry and nostalgic as it had been that day in the kitchen.

Propping my elbows on the table, I lean my chin forward to rest in the weave of my hands. "Tell me."

"Rachel asked Blaire out. And Blaire says she only said yes because she didn't want to crush a new baby gay's feelings, but I'm pretty sure it's because Rachel is a total babe." Catey laughs, and I love how this doesn't bother her. "But right after that first date, Blaire texts me, 'Hey, wanna prove everyone right?' and I knew exactly what she meant."

"You and Blaire never hated each other. You weren't sworn nemeses."

"Of course we didn't hate each other. That's exactly my point." She looks at me so meaningfully that my chin almost falls out of my hands. "Kavs, it was so obvious to everyone who isn't you. This chemistry between you two?" She waves her hands. "What you *thought* was a feud was actually—"

"Don't you say it, don't you dare say it, Catey!"

"—foreplay."

The oven timer dings, followed by the sound of the garage door rolling open, signaling my parents' return. By unspoken agreement, Catey drops it when we hear conversation and the scuffling sounds of shoes being removed in the garage.

"Yash, I still feel badly about winning the match by such a huge margin," says Mom. "I mean, we crushed them in almost every game! I thought you said Dr. Cobb and her husband were good!"

"But you were better, Mona. I wasn't embarrassed."

There's a note of self-consciousness in Mom's voice when she asks, "Not even when I victory danced?"

Catey and I lock eyes. So *that's* where I get it from.

"Not even then," Dad says firmly. "They were grumpy ever since they lost the first set. They were clearly exaggerating their skill on the court. You know Shawn got so mad he wouldn't shake when I told him 'Good game'?"

"*Ass,*" says Mom, entering the kitchen. The black tennis racket case slung on her shoulder contrasts against the pristine white of her polo and skirt. "Hi, girls."

Dad's close behind. "Something smells wonderful."

"That would be KC's Pot Pie," Catey says with a grin as she takes both muffin trays out of the oven. "Thanks again for letting us use your kitchen."

"You're always welcome here whenever you want," Mom says affectionately.

Dad takes an enormous inhale and grins. "What does 'KC' stand for?"

"Kavya and Catey," I say. "This isn't your average chicken pot pie. It's Indian inspired, so it has masala spices and extra veggies. We're going to try a butter chicken filling next."

"Since Kavya was always my willing taste tester, I wanted to celebrate our friendship with a pie that was from both of us," Catey explains as she gently loosens the mini pot pies from the cups. "Kavya did the filling, and I used my grandmother's crust recipe."

"What a sweet idea," says Dad.

"Thanks." Her cheeks are tinged a faint pink. "I hope you like them. There are plenty."

"I'm sure we'll love them! If I can drag Kavya and Yash away, I might even have enough left over to share at tonight's book club," Mom says with a wink. "I've been talking up the Fork and Crumb to the other members, and they can't wait for your soft launch."

As my parents head upstairs to change, Catey slides the first pot pie over to me on a plate, along with a knife and fork. "Don't burn your tongue," she warns.

"I'm not a child," I huff, cutting the savory pie neatly in half. The crispy golden puff pastry top crackles and flakes. "You don't have to tell me twice."

We both lean in to look at the filling, sighing in rapture at the delicious smell of tender roasted chicken, cauliflower, and carrot, stewed in a creamy tomato tikka-masala-spiced sauce.

"Have you *met* you? You're pretty hardheaded, Kavs," says Catey, throwing an arm around my shoulder. "There's at least *one* thing I've been telling you on repeat that you were always too busy playing tug-of-war with Ian to hear."

"I *wasn't* ready to hear it before," I remind her. "It had been so long since Ian and I were friends that I wasn't ready to set aside my pride and see him as anything other than the rival he'd become. I was scared, but I'm ready now. I was even thinking of inviting him to the sunflower maze next weekend."

"Oh, Blaire and I are going, too—but wait, you do realize you're going to run into a bunch of people from school, right?"

Without an ounce of false confidence, I say, "I know. I'm ready."

Catey regards me thoughtfully. "You know, I think you are."

On the way home from a kid's party, Ian seemed pleasantly surprised that I took the initiative in asking him out. The punch of self-satisfaction in my chest when his face broke into Smile #9 was unparalleled. It's new and a bit alarming how much I enjoy being the reason he goes speechless, mouth twitching with a smile, eyes brimming with unbridled emotion.

It's definitely safe to say I'm not the same predictable girl I used to be.

"Thanks for letting me and Amie bum a ride," Simran says as she slips into the front passenger seat. "Before grad school starts, Dad said he's going to look into a car for me."

"No worries, I don't mind," I reply easily. "I'm picking Ian up, too. We're all going to the same place. Also, *wow*. You look incredible. Is that from our last India trip?"

Simmy's way more dressed up than I am. She's wearing loose white shorts and a sleeveless pink georgette crop top with multicolored embroidery and circular mirror work, showing off a toned midriff and a tiny blink-and-you'll-miss-it diamond belly button piercing.

"Nope, it's a Valika Mehra original," she says, buckling up. The stack of glass bangles on her wrist tinkles. "She always makes the cutest kurtis for herself, and while that's not really my style, I asked her if she'd design me a cute crop top. Amie got one, too."

"I'd love this in black." I flick the matching embroidery-floss tassels dangling from the shoulder, kind of regretting my combat boots and casual denim minidress with overall straps.

I wave to Mom and Dad with one hand while the other scrolls my phone for the perfect playlist. Olivia Rodrigo blasts from the speakers.

"How's everything going with Amie?" I ask, backing out of the driveway.

She grins. "Really good. I even told her that I'm demiromantic. I don't know why I was so scared she'd be freaked out wondering if that meant I'd never be in romantic love with her. It was very gentle and loving. I think it was easier after telling you."

"I'm happy you have her, Simmy. And that you felt so safe in telling her."

"I know it surprised her. I mean, I'd dated in high school. And it was . . . fine. I was starting to figure out I was somewhere on the aro spectrum, but I knew I definitely wasn't ace. I liked the, um, physical stuff. I just didn't realize that sensual and romantic needs can be different."

I make a left turn, exceedingly glad that paying attention to the road means I don't have to look her in the eyes while I respond. "Yeah. For me, the two go hand in hand. I don't think I could be kissing or more with Ian if I didn't also feel something romantically for him. Until my feelings started to change, I didn't notice him like that at all. Whether I was infuriated or into him, either way a *lot* of my passion was aimed in his direction. I mean, yes, he was objectively hot, but . . ." I make another turn. "All that to say . . . I'm not sure I'm a casual person."

Simran grins in my peripheral vision just as the playlist moves on to Lil Nas X. "Kavs, literally no one in the history of *ever* could accuse you of being casual. You throw yourself into everything with this, like, intense energy? I swear, your life is a spectator sport *only*, baby sis. I'm tired just watching you do *half* the things you do."

"I have youth and spite on my side," I say, rolling my eyes.

"Hey! You don't have to make me sound *quite* so decrepit."

I wave a hand. "Enough about me. You know I adore Amie, but you really never felt romantically attracted to any of those college boys?"

"I mean, sure, there were a couple of guys, but I could never be honest with them. But lately I've realized that not knowing how to talk about this with people—*the people I love*—wasn't a good enough reason not to even try."

I crank up the air conditioning. "What changed?"

"I was never that invested in the idea of a romantic relationship until Amie. I'd love to give her all the credit for inspiring me to be brave, but it's probably more that seeing who I am when I'm with her made me realize how much I wanted us. When you take a leap of faith, you just have to trust that if you have the right people in your life, they'll be there to catch you."

I feel like I know the answer, but I ask it anyway. "She makes you happy?"

I get my answer a few seconds later as we pull up to Poppy and Amie's house, a modern ranch with a very on-brand pink castle mailbox, and Amie comes flying out the front door, almost bowling over her mother, who's sitting on the porch with a book. She's wearing her commission from Val, a strappy marigold crop top with gold gota embroidery fit for a festival.

We pick up Ian next, and then continue on to Mightyoak Farm, an hour south of Luna Cove. We reach the end of my playlist right as we see the first sign for the farm.

"Growing up, my dad and I always came here to do whatever's in season," shares Amie. "It's my favorite dad-and-daughter tradition. I always miss him when he's traveling with the team." She squeezes Simran's hand. "I'm glad I can share it with you."

We pay for apple-picking bags and split up, Amie twisting back to slyly wink at me and Ian before linking arms with my sister and heading in the opposite direction.

"Thanks for inviting me," says Ian. He glances toward the sunflower maze that's already teeming with people. "Are you okay with kids from school seeing us together?"

"I am if you are," I counter. It's not meant to be a challenge, but also it is.

His eyes flash with surprising steel. "I'd never be embarrassed to be with you, Joshi."

"That's settled, then." I reach for his hand without even thinking about it. "Come on, that ten-year-old is getting all the best Golden Delicious."

The orchard is filled with couples and families with young children, but we still find an easy harmony as we pile our bags with enough Honeycrisp, Golden Delicious, and Jonamacs to make our moms panic about using them up before they go bad. Working in unison, I equally split the apples from the lower branches between our bags while he snags the apples higher up.

"We can get their fresh-pressed cider in autumn," says Ian, putting his bag on the grass so he can mop his brow with his forearm. "I'll make you apple cider donuts."

I struggle with the weight of my bag, praying the thin straps won't snap. "I've never seen those on the Holly Gogogi menu. New addition?"

"Well, no. I was thinking I'd make them just for you."

He makes it sound casual as an afterthought, even though it's anything but. It's impossible not to hear the honest gesture in his voice. My heartbeat pulses in every nerve ending until I can barely swallow. His hand touches my shoulder. His warm fingers are a lightning strike and I jolt, but into him, not away.

I strive for an airy, unaffected "Oh?"

Naturally, since I'm trying to be cool, it comes out as a hoarse croak.

Ian shoots me a smug look, like he's perfectly aware of the effect he has on me. Especially when he's wearing an untucked blue button-down that is absolutely wrong for this weather, a huge giveaway that no matter how cool he plays it, he's trying to look good for me.

Unfair tactics. I take a step closer, into his space, ready to wipe off his smirk. I let my bag rest on the grass, tilting my chin up like I'm a sunflower and he's the sun. My fingers dance across his nape, even under the camera strap looped around his neck. He huffs, throat tensing, and his arms wrap around me. His palms press against the curve of my back.

"You're trembling, Jun," I say, giving him a little nibble across his jawline.

"So are you." He slides one hand up to cup my cheek, eyes trained on my lips, but I pull back before he can claim a kiss.

"Should probably keep this PG," I say breathily.

With a rueful smile, he bends to grab both our bags.

"Ian, I can hold my own."

"Don't like it when I play the doting boyfriend?" he teases. "Bet you won't let me carry your books for you when school starts, either."

The blasé way he says *boyfriend* gives me a start, but either it just slipped out or he's got a better poker face than I do.

I roll my eyes, playing along. "Our school district is switching from textbooks to laptops, remember?"

"Then humor me and let me get away with the manly lifting this one time."

"*Fiiiiine.* Thank you."

After we drop the apples off in the car, the sunflower maze is our next stop. The stalks grow tall and proud, but provide pitiful shade with the noon sun directly overhead.

If I were here with anyone else, I might have been tempted to pull ahead and explore on my own, but I'm content to walk at Ian's side, our fingers brushing against each other. Once, his pinkie twines around mine. It's an *almost* that I can reach out and grab, and a second later, I do.

He looks down in surprise, like he didn't expect me to go for it. And his smile isn't an *almost* Smile #9, it's one so spectacularly full-blown that it overtakes his entire face.

Our pace is slow, content, leisurely. Every so often, he raises his Polaroid Go with his free hand and takes aim. I can't get a good look at the photos, and he tucks them all into the back pocket of his jeans like he doesn't want to make a big deal.

"I wish I could cut a bunch of blooms for you," he says, breaking the reverie.

"Didn't you see that huge sign at the entrance saying this field was strictly look, don't touch? Their U-pick field will open in autumn."

His voice is mischievous and amused as he asks, "Hinting something, Joshi?"

"Just trying to keep your decapitation urges to a minimum, *Jun.*"

His chuckle shoots straight through me.

We're both thinking about longer than this summer, but I have no idea if our newfound camaraderie will cave once we're back to being full-time rivals again.

More than a little embarrassed at what I inadvertently revealed, I march ahead. It takes his longer legs about two seconds to match me.

We hit plenty of dead ends in the maze, but we retrace our steps and try again. If anyone we see from school is surprised that we're not trying to outdo each other, they'd be even more taken aback if they'd seen him tug me into him during our latest dead end to finish what I started in the orchard. His camera presses into my sternum seconds before his lips fall over mine. The unexpected kiss is searing, ravenous but unhurried, Ian's fingers digging into my hips.

"Been waiting forever to do that," he murmurs against my lips.

"Impatient?" I ask, half coy, half snark.

"Kavs, you are very much mistaken if you think I've only been waiting since the orchard," he says. Each word is dripping in intensity and want.

Our surroundings fade into gray, leaving behind only Ian in full color. The low hum of the bees sticking close to the pollinators recedes, along with the gentle swish of the sunflower leaves in the wisp of a passing breeze.

"I found them!"

Ian's eyes dart over my shoulder. "Hi, girls."

Sorry, I mouth before turning around to see Catey and Blaire, their arms around each other. They both look dewy and happy, and I can't help but wonder how Ian and I look to them.

Blaire shoots me a sheepish smile. "Sorry for interrupting. We ran into Simran and Amie, and Simran said she saw you two take off into the maze. *I* said we should leave the lovebirds alone, but Catey"—she bumps hips with her girlfriend—"wanted to say hi."

"Oh, Ian, do you want a picture of the two of you together?" offers Catey.

"Thanks, that would be amazing." He slips the camera strap off his head and holds it out to her. "Can you take one for each of us? I have plenty of film."

I step closer to his side and grin up at him. "Decapitated sunflowers on three?"

"That's a bit of a mouthful," he says, eyes glued to my kiss-swollen lips.

"I have every faith in your lipular dexterity," I reply, straight-faced. "Keep it up and you *might* just earn yourself an A."

He guffaws just as Catey takes the first photo.

After finding our way to the center of the maze an hour later, we head back to the car. This time Ian's the first to take my hand, his thumb brushing over my knuckles. "I have a kinda maybe . . . weird ask for you. It's not a date exactly, like the Riverwalk concert series I asked you to attend with me, but I'd like you to be there. If it's not too heavy."

I don't need to think twice. "Name it."

"You know all that time Grace spent in the hospital or bed rest at home? She got bored with the games we had, so she started to make up her own. Not childish ones, either, but these really intricate boards with rules that actually made sense? She took it so seriously, and she wouldn't let us play until we understood the game. My dad always said she had a will of steel."

"Sounds like something she'd do," I say.

"Money was a little tighter back then," says Ian. He rubs

his nose fiercely, like this embarrasses him. "But there's this toy shop along the Riverwalk, do you know it? Cracked white paint, blue window trim? Teddy bears in the window?"

"Yeah, Simran and I got a jigsaw there for Dad's birthday once."

"They also manufacture custom games with all original art. It's really cool, but it costs a lot. That didn't matter to my parents, though. They wanted Grace to be able to hold her games, know that she created something amazing."

Ian pauses here, and I get it.

The games were the prom and the cap-and-gown and wedding pictures that she would never have. They immortalized everything Grace was and everything she could have been, would never be.

"Her last board game . . . I had to help her with it. She never let me before, insisted she could do it all herself." His smile is a little proud, a little sad. "She always had to be in charge."

I ache to do something more than nod, so I sweep my thumb across his knuckles the way he just did, back and forth until the tension seeps from his shoulders. He shoots me a tense smile, and I know it was the right move.

"We never picked up the last one. The day we were supposed to, Grace—" He breaks off to collect himself. "The owners said they'd hold it however long it took." He takes a deep, shuddering breath. "And I think I'm ready to do another scary thing. Maybe even get back into it. Will you come with me?"

My answer snags in my throat, but there's no way I'm letting him do this scary thing on his own. "Of course," I whisper.

25.
I Wouldn't Change a Thing

THIS SUMMER HAS been far from the relaxing respite between junior and senior year that I'd expected. I thought my days would be filled with entertaining at kids' parties, eclipsing the previous year's summer reading total, and meandering the Riverwalk with my friends.

Instead, I've worked in relative harmony alongside my rival, gotten sloppy at keeping up with my weekly reading quotas, and capsized into questionable green algae that I'm pretty sure has changed the composition of my hair forever.

I'm also pretty sure that I wouldn't change a thing.

It's the first week of August, the day of the third-and-final test, and I can't shake the bittersweet feeling that's clung to me ever since I woke up this morning.

Melancholy follows me like a cloak as I swallow my spicy

masala omelet for Joshi Saturday morning breakfast, as I walk an energetic Buster twice around the neighborhood, as I spend the rest of the morning jotting down all the books I've read on my summer reading program cards, making sure I haven't missed even one.

When I confirm to the moon girl group chat that we're still on for the third competition at my house this afternoon, that feeling of something about to happen doesn't vanish. It doesn't get swallowed down the drain when I shower, either, and though I take my time massaging shampoo into my thick, coarse curls and scrub every inch of my skin until it's pink, there's no sloughing away whatever melancholic heaviness this is.

The feeling lingers until the doorbell rings.

"Hey," says Ian as he enters, pie box from Holly Gogogi in hand. His friends are still getting out of Claudia's car parked on the curb. Or maybe they're hanging back on purpose so we can greet each other alone.

And that's the exact moment I figure it out, this feeling that's been haunting me all day: I don't want the summer to end. I don't want the challenges to end. I don't want *us* to—

Because it will, won't it, once senior year starts? We'll be back at each other's throats, and not in the good way.

"You have your overthinking face on," murmurs Ian as he kicks off his shoes.

I startle, fingers dropping from the door in shock at the way he's read whatever emotion crossed my face. I stand aside to let everyone in.

"Can you drop me off at Ethan's after this?" Rio asks Claudia.

"I cannot *believe* you seriously expect me to chauffeur you to your ex-boyfriend's house—" begins Claudia.

"Boyfriend, not ex," corrects Rio.

When I hear a sharp inhale behind me, my heart sinks. It can only be Val.

"When I only found out about it on the ride over here, *after* you told Ian and Samer." She practically grinds out the other two boys' names, then beams beatifically at me. "Hi, Kavya."

I hope Val scurried back up the stairs, but when I let the four of them in, lock the door, and turn around, she's still standing there with a look of frozen shock on her face.

"Hi, kids!" My mom bustles out from the kitchen. Her hair is set in barrel curls that bounce against the shoulders of the powder-blue silk shirt loosely tucked into straight-leg leather pants, and her warm brown skin is bronzed and highlighted with a summery glow.

Mom and Dad are leaving us the house and heading to Indianapolis for date night. Val got a little standoffish when she discovered my parents were fine leaving us alone. Especially because she had to lie to hers to get out of working at the store this Saturday.

Mom slings her purse onto her shoulder. "Ian, it's wonderful to see you. It's been so long."

Ian grins. "You too, Mrs. Joshi." He extends the box. "Mom sent this for you."

Mom takes an exaggerated inhale. "I smell her *delicious*

banoffee pie. Thank you, sweetheart. I'll text her from the road. Kavs, give me a hand?"

I take the box from her so she can walk to the door and slip into her skyscraper heels.

Then Dad comes down the stairs. While he claps Ian on the shoulder and shakes hands with the boys, Claudia compliments my mom on her outfit and asks where she bought everything, and Val scrambles upstairs to call Catey and Blaire down.

"I set out some snacks for you kids in the kitchen," Mom says, distractedly fixing Dad's collar. "Simran's out with Amie, but she said she'd pick up the pizza for your moon girl sleepover." Bringing me close for a squeeze, she adds under her breath, "Have fun tonight. I hope you'll have some juicy gossip about Ian to share with me."

"*Mom!*" I hiss, even though there's no way anyone else overheard. I refuse to dignify her fishing.

After waving my parents off and dropping the pie on the kitchen counter, I join everyone else in the living room. They've already helped themselves to the snacks Mom laid out: seven-layer dip with two kinds of tortilla chips; Catey's mouthwatering tarte tatin, grand-mère's recipe; homemade paneer-and-pea mini samosas that Blaire and Catey go wild for; orange swirls of sticky-sweet jalebi; and one of those giant bags of peanut M&M's she hides around the house from Dad's questing.

"The name of the game," Rio says, "is How Well Do You Know Your Rival?"

I notice Val isn't vying to sit next to him. She's sitting with the moon girls, squished up on the couch between the arm and Buster, who's determinedly claimed his spot for head scratches between her and Blaire. Val doesn't look in Rio's direction once.

"We're going to ask each of you five questions about the other person, and the one who gives the most correct answers wins. Now, these are meant to be hard," says Samer. "But we've vetted them so no one can ask something ridiculous that you'd never be able to guess in a million years."

"Behold, this might be the first time Ian actually flunks a test," Blaire says in a stage whisper. "Our questions for him are stumpers, Kavs. You've got this."

I summon a smile of bravado, but it flags at the end. Ian's friends are going to ask me questions about *him*, too. The thought makes my guts clamp, so I can't do more than nibble at the syrupy jalebi pinched between two fingers.

I mean, if they ask about his pet's name, his GPA for the last three years, or the number of smiles he has, I've got this in the bag. But that's not very likely, is it?

Ian and I sit on opposite sofas, but I don't really feel like we're at odds when he's giving me that dimpled smile that sets off a fluttery cascade of butterflies.

"Who wants to go first?" asks Catey, looking between us.

Everyone casts expectant glances at me to claim first dibs, so I shrug halfheartedly. "Guess I will."

Claudia looks at her phone. "Kavya, what is Ian's favorite color?"

Oh good, an easy one.

But then I realize that I actually *don't* know his favorite color. My mind races through his outfits this summer. I can't recall what he wore under the Adidas track jacket the night of Claudia's party, but I do remember the coral button-down cruise shirt on the day of our Scrabble bet in the library. The baby-blue restaurant shirt when we kayaked. The softness of his periwinkle Henley when his arm was pressed against mine at the drive-in. The smart blue button-down that matched the clear skies on our date at the sunflower maze.

The odds are in blue's favor, but should I even be considering his clothing? I mean, I love bright colors, so unless you knew me, you'd never guess that a party princess's favorite shade is black, right?

"Kavya?" Claudia prompts.

Even Ian looks a little perplexed.

"Blue," I decide, forcing myself not to cross my fingers for luck.

Relief blooms over Ian's face, and I'm rewarded with another smile that I definitely don't deserve, not at all.

"Okay, Ian," says Catey. "Your turn."

He doesn't look worried at all. I bet he knows *my* favorite color.

Catey grins like she knows she has him. "Kavya's favorite thing to eat at Holly Gogogi?"

What? My stomach lurches. That's such an easy one. Fuck. My friends don't know that Ian helps out in the kitchen sometimes and knows my family's order. Ian's friends, on the other hand, look victorious.

"Bulgogi burger," says Ian. Then, showing off, he smugly adds, "With extra pickled carrot and daikon."

Rio grins. "One point, Kavya. One point, Ian. Niiiiice."

The questions volley back and forth, until we're tied 4–4.

Ian's got all his questions about me right so far:

Q2: What form of dance did Kavya receive professional training for as a child?

A2: Bharatanatyam.

Q3: What's her favorite candy flavor?

A3: That's an easy one. Cherry.

Q4: Who is Kavya's favorite princess?

A4: She's a bit like all of them, but she sees herself as Belle.

Each question makes me feel worse. He's answered everything confidently, whereas I've only known two answers for sure, and taken two stabs in the dark and miraculously come out lucky. Khushi auntie and some of the other older relatives might call me besharam, but I'm not without shame. I feel it right now, pooling in my stomach and stress-ball-squeezing my heart every time it's my turn again.

Like a mantra, I fervently tell myself *Just one more and you're done. One more and you're home free. One more and you won't get caught.*

I'm not Belle after all. I told him I saw him, but have I really been looking?

When I'm ashamed, I get defensive, and when I'm defensive, I prickle. Who cares if I got lucky with his favorite color? Who cares if I don't know these small, superficial things? It doesn't compare to the other things he's shared with me that I have remembered: "The Blue Danube," horses at midnight, Yeobo.

I mentally shake myself out of self-pity. I know things about him, damn it. I know the *important* things.

"Okay, we're on the last question," says Claudia. She takes a deep breath as if to mark the momentousness of the occasion. "Kavya, who is Ian's favorite author?"

My mind goes as blank as a blinking cursor on a new Word document.

Ian's smile is encouraging, eyes bright with anticipation.

Am I supposed to know this? I rack my brain, going over all our conversations in two-times speed, but my living room slow-mos, time crawling by at the pace of an astronaut walk.

I think back to all the times I'd run into him at our school library during a free period. By unspoken accord, no matter how we'd argued in other classes, in there we always called a cease-fire. Sometimes we talked about a book one of us had just read and loved, which guaranteed the other would be the next to check it out. But right now, none of the titles come to mind.

Maybe . . . yes, this has to be it. He loved the Artemis Fowl series.

"Eoin Colfer?" There's a wobble to my voice like unset Jell-O.

Ian's smile dwindles. His eyes dim.

Claudia's face falls. "Um. No. It's Rick Riordan."

My breath catches. "Percy Jackson."

Of course. Fuck. My brain screams at me to avoid Ian's intense, disappointed gaze, but I'm drawn to him despite my sense of self-preservation. His eyes hold me hostage, bleeding emotion, but the rest of his face is shuttered.

I could read his emotions so readily before, but now he's blanking me the way he's *never* blanked me before. I tear my eyes away, and it's like a tether has snapped.

"Ian's turn," says Catey, announcing it extra loud like it'll make up for the silence. "What is the one thing that Kavya's most embarrassed about?"

I jerk. Seriously?

She angles toward me with a steadying smile as if to say *We've got him now, Kavs.*

A beat passes. Ian meets my eyes, a current of disappointment traveling the width of the coffee table. There's none of the anticipatory fear that he knows about my aversion to singing in front of an audience. It's nothing like that night of truth or dare at all.

And suddenly I don't even care anymore if he does know. If he's known ever since Claudia took Rio's dare. Let it all come out. I deserve it.

"Kav—*she*," he corrects himself, jaw rigid. His voice is hollow. "She hates singing in public because she thinks she's bad at it. If she isn't good through hard work or talent, she doesn't want to do it at all. Appearances matter too much to her."

Val and Blaire gape at the bull's-eye they'd never anticipated he knew.

Catey gives a long, owlish blink. "He's right."

"Ian got five! He wins!" Rio erupts, leaping up to fist pump the air. Samer's reaction is less effusive as he gives Ian's back a hearty clap, but Claudia's eyes glitter at me like she *knows* that I barely scraped by this whole game.

Neither Rio nor Samer seem aware of the undercurrent in the room. The stunned disbelief of my friends, Claudia's animosity, and Ian's halfhearted smile summoned up, I suspect, only for his friends' benefit. Ian gets up, returns Samer's one-armed hug, and meets my eyes.

"You didn't read the book," he says.

I don't pretend not to know what he's talking about. "I meant to," I say in a small voice, but the truth is that I didn't. It hadn't even crossed my mind to rip the paper.

"Don't worry about it," he says. "It's fine. I just thought you would have—but it's fine."

He said that twice. I press my lips together until I can feel my teeth.

Too late, I remember seeing his summer reading cards with Riordan titles and the phone call where he *asked* me if I'd read the book by his favorite author yet. I'd shrugged it off as unimportant. I'd had no idea back then just how important it would turn out to be.

"So, Claud . . ." Rio awkwardly mimes steering. "How about that ride to Ethan's?"

Claudia stands up so abruptly that Samer stumbles.

"Wait, you don't have to go," I say. "Stay and hang out." The invitation is for all of them, but my eyes are imploring Ian.

"Claudia's our ride," he says shortly. "I think this is over, anyway, don't you?"

Rio and Samer are quiet now, catching up to the tension crackling between us. Claudia takes out her keys in a wordless command, and all four of them move toward the door.

"Am I still coming over for dinner on Monday night?" I blurt out.

It's the wrong thing to say and it's not the right time, not with everyone here hanging on our every word, but I had to ask. There's a horrible taste of desperation on my tongue, filling my mouth with the aftertaste of medicine.

Ian freezes halfway to the door, put on the spot. He looks as if he's swallowing past thorns as he looks at me. "Yeah. Why wouldn't you be?"

Claudia opens her mouth as if to answer, then snaps it shut, aiming a pissy look at me.

"If I say something, I stick to it," says Ian.

I stiffen. That was unmistakably a dig.

It's only when they all file out the door without any of the happy chatter that they had on their way in that I realize I was so afraid of losing Ian that I'd forgotten all about his win. And I don't care, but also I do. We're 2–2 now. Tied.

Catey comes to the same realization. "We're going to need another contest."

Blaire bites her lip. "Let's leave it for a few days. Jeez, Kavya, he gave you a book and you didn't even open it? You devour every single book you can get your hands on, but just because this one came from him, you didn't even want to—"

"Blaire," Catey says in a warning tone.

I look at my friends, but all my wet, shimmering eyes see are the shattered shards of a once spectacular summer.

26.
Episode One
Crybaby Sailor Moon

"SO," VAL SAYS around a mouthful of jalebi. "Are we just not going to talk about it?"

I shoot her a not-on-your-life death glower.

"Do you want to talk about it, Kavya?" asks Blaire, who's just raided the kitchen for her favorite masala plantain chips. She sits on the floor with Catey, leaning against the sofa.

Val starts tapping her socked foot—something she only ever does when she's agitated. I eye her, but before I can ask what's up, she speaks.

"I wasn't talking about Ian," she says sharply. "I meant Rio."

"Oh. Sure." Catey smiles as she sidles close to Blaire. "Why don't you ask him to come to the Fork and Crumb? Everything's almost ready for our soft launch."

"That wasn't what I meant." Val's tapping gets faster, more

vigorous. "Anyway, I'm sure you have enough people."

"Yeah, but everything's 50 percent off to get people in on the first day, so if you wanted to have a date or something, we'd love the extra butts in seats," says Blaire.

"Yeah, I'm not sure *Ethan* would love the idea of me asking his *boyfriend* out." Val's foot abruptly stops moving. "Wait. You'd charge me for something I helped you set up?"

Val looks agitated, Blaire looks stunned, and Catey's wearing a confused expression. Like recollecting a dream that's already faded out of memory, Rio's and Claudia's words come back to me: He's back with his ex.

"Catey cooked everyone dinner as a thank-you," says Blaire, voice tight. "And FYI, we wouldn't have charged you."

"*Babe*," whispers Catey. To Val, she says, "We really appreciate everyone turning out to help us, and you did a really nice job on the painting—"

"Stop," says Blaire, combative now. "We've talked about this."

This is the incendiary spark that shoots Val upright. "You've been talking about me?"

"Only about how bitchy you've been lately," snaps Blaire. "God, we were just trying to suggest something nice, and you act like we're trying to take advantage of you or something."

Val moves closer to me. "So you and Catey think I'm a bitch?"

Catey stands up, too. "Val, no—"

"About this, yes!" Blaire shouts, cutting Catey off. "Babe, stop. We have to tell her. We're done ignoring your snide little comments and passive-aggressive questions. Seriously, Val, chill. We're sorry that you're jealous of us, but—"

"Me? Jealous of you?" Val's laugh is sharp, brittle, and everywhere. "That's a laugh. You actually think you two have anything that I need to be jeal—"

"All of you shut up!" I exclaim.

Everyone looks at me.

"What is the matter with you three? What happened to moon power and supporting each other and having each other's backs? We're fucking best friends!" The words scrape against my throat, rubbing it raw.

"Of course we're best friends," says Blaire. She circles her finger around the room, landing on me, Catey, and then herself. "I didn't start it."

Val snorts. She takes a step closer to me, so we're shoulder to shoulder. "Kavya's the only one of you all who actually gives a shit about how I feel. The only one I can even talk to."

Catey and Blaire swing their faces to me.

"You two talked about us?" Catey's eyes are wet. "We didn't even do anything."

Val laughs, but it's like dark chocolate—a little bitter at the end. "You've got that right. You two *don't* do anything unless it's for your stupid restaurant."

Catey's mouth falls open but nothing comes out. She looks like she's just been run through.

Blaire's eyes are like drawn daggers. "Excuse you," she snaps.

"It's true," Val fires back. "Whenever we're together, it's

the Fork and Crumb this, 'Oh no, I hate Ian again!' that. It's always about you three. Always. When is it my turn? Maybe if one of you was a better friend to me, you would have realized that Rio doesn't like me back. He got back together with his *ex* right in front of me at the drive-in, and I didn't even realize it until today." Her laugh is bitter. "I've been making a fool of myself all summer."

Blaire's face softens. "V, I'm sorry. I—we—didn't even notice."

It's the wrong thing to say. Val's face twitches. "Yeah, that much was obvious."

Catey tries. "I'm sorry, too. I didn't realize you liked him so much. We would have tried to figure out if he felt the same way if we'd known, right, B? Kavs?"

I give a short, shamefaced nod. I'd suspected at the drive-in when I'd heard about Ethan for the first time, but it was only confirmed when Rio said he'd gotten back together with his ex.

"We didn't realize your crush was that serious. I mean, you never said," says Blaire.

Val's face is aghast. "You're supposed to be my best friends! I shouldn't have to tell you everything for you to know it. Maybe if the three of you could get over yourselves and your boy drama and your perfect lives long enough to notice *me* for once—"

"We have included you in everything!" Catey says shrilly. "What the actual *fuck*. Why are you being like this?"

Catey never curses. The word shocks us all into shutting up.

There's a horrible silence, and my heart stops *boom, boom, booming* long enough to think that maybe the fight is over, but then Val goes in for the kill. Her face tightens and all her jealousy and anger comes out as she says, "Not all of us have parents who support our pipe dream of running a restaurant even though they're know-nothing seventeen-year-olds."

Pipe dream? Know-nothing? Where is this coming from? I stare at her.

Catey's been in hospitality for *years*. She's privileged, but she also works really hard and knows her stuff. Sure, the Hills have helped all their kids start their careers, but it's not like our friends are going to be single-handedly running a restaurant while we're seniors, and Val knows that.

"You're the one who doesn't know anything." Blaire's voice trembles and her eyes glaze. "And definitely not about friendship." Her gaze slices to me, unforgiving.

I know she's at least partly including me in that. But I can't seem to move. Can't unstick myself from Val, from this nebulous *we* that we've become.

"Forget about being a moon girl," says Catey. "You've gone full-on Negaverse."

"Being moon girls was always the dumbest thing I'd ever heard of," Val shoots back, earning gasps from the rest of us. "I wanted to laugh my head off when you came up with it."

But it didn't stop her from wanting to be part of it all the same.

We all freeze, like we're waiting for her to take it back. I still can't believe she Went There and Said That. There's a ringing in my ears that won't go away, and I'm hot all over.

"Forget Negaverse. You're episode one crybaby Sailor Moon," says Catey. She looks stricken. "No, you're worse. At least Serena was a good friend. You can't even be supportive without being resentful." Her breath catches. "I feel so sorry for you."

That's it.

This is the line that's just been crossed.

I think Val realizes it, too, because disbelief catches on her face for a second. She looks at each of us, eyes wide and lips quivering, like that time in third grade when a boy jeered at her for wearing a kurti to class—he didn't say it again, because I decked him, and Blaire sat on him while Catey fed him a fresh, made-to-order playground mud pie.

We didn't really know Val then, but that had been the first spark that sent us all to detention, setting in motion whatever cosmic forces would make us best friends years later.

That was the first time the four of us were an *us*.

But now, whatever girl-squad thread was holding us together has been snipped. Whatever power we had, multiplied by four, is decimated. Because if Val doesn't believe in being a moon girl anymore—maybe she never did—then what was the point of it all?

We all seem to realize it at the same time, because Catey and Blaire find each other's hands, while Val marches straight for the front door.

"V, don't," I say. "Stay, we can talk this out."

Ignoring me, she scoops up her sleeping bag and backpack.

She thrusts her feet into her shoes, phone already in hand. "I'm going to wait outside for my parents to pick me up."

She punctuates her exit with a door slam.

"We should go after her," I say. No one moves.

I half wonder whether the others will take off, too, and Blaire must see it on my face. "She was messy, and she needs to clean up after herself. She'll come back when she's ready." More gently, she adds, "We're not going anywhere. Moon girls until the end, right?"

For once, Catey doesn't try to mediate. Instead, she rounds on me. "You know, when Blaire asked you if something was up with her when we got boba, you didn't have to lie and act like you didn't know, Kavs."

I throw a quick look to Blaire, but she bites her lip and looks away.

Regret surges in my chest. Right. I should have known it wasn't just between us.

Catey shakes her head in disappointment. "You're always willing to fight everybody, to speak up! And god knows I love you for it—but you just sat by and let this play out. Your favorite character might be Belle, but you can't even see that you're the *perfect* Ariel, losing your voice right when you should have used it the most."

27.
Once a Villain, Always a Villain

LAST NIGHT'S SLEEPOVER was arguably the worst we've ever had. Val's parents were shorthanded at the store, so it took them almost an hour to show up. I went out and tried to get her to come back, but she refused my overture. She hovered on the driveway and wouldn't talk to any of us. Even after she got picked up and Simran brought back pizza, the sleepover was ruined. I had to give my sister the CliffsNotes version of why we were one moon girl short. And while Catey, Blaire, and I worked our shit out, we couldn't escape the pall in the air of Val's departure.

We went to sleep early, and when Catey's soft, snuffling snores started and Blaire's relentless shifting ceased, I'd known they were fast asleep. I sneaked back up to my room, ripped into Ian's book, and read the whole thing through the night.

Since he'd messaged me at exactly eight a.m. the first time he wished me a good morning, I set my alarm for seven-fifty-five so I could wake up to message him at seven-fifty-nine.

After three hours of sleep, I did just that.

> I read the whole book. You're right, I loved it. Maybe I should give Rick's other books a go? There's so many, it'll probably tip me into the lead. And it'll be all your fault.
>
> Also good morning. Sorry about yesterday.

He didn't reply right away, but I knew he'd read my messages and so I went back to sleep.

When I wake up, it's hard not sending off a message to Val, but last night we decided to give her space. Before we went to sleep last night, Catey sent the group chat a single message that went unanswered: We're here whenever you're ready to talk.

Nothing from Val or Ian all day, so I have nothing else to do except attack my TBR. After spending the whole day reading, I get a reply as I turn in for the night.

> Goodnight, Kavya.

I think he's still mad, until he sends a blue heart all by itself.

On Sunday morning, I send him a photo of almost the library's entire collection of Rick Riordan Presents imprint

titles and my new total: 45! How about you? Oh, and don't
forget the last day of the summer reading program is Monday!

I don't have to wait a whole day this time. I've been busy.
Forgot to keep track.

My forehead scrunches. I know it's hard to gauge tone, but
he seems a little cool with me.

Ian's friends have no idea what happened in the wake of
their departure, so when Samer suggests the summer reading
program for a fourth contest to break our tie, we agree.

On Monday I shave off five minutes on the way home from
a Snow White and Prince Charming party with Samer, because for once I don't hit a single red light. I even shower and
re-shave in record time, detangle my hair, and redo my makeup for my dinner date with Ian at Holly Gogogi with his parents.

But then I make the mistake of bemoaning I don't have
anything to wear within earshot of my parents. Which of
course then means I have to listen to Dad's lecture about how
I have too much stuff, which derails into Mom pointing out I
also have too many books, and it wouldn't surprise her if we
get a bug infestation from all the paper lying around.

Then Simran gets in on it by pointing out the tops in my
closet that still have the tags on, which sets my parents off
again, and *my god* do I wish I were an only child. But just for
a second.

I wear my pj's until I settle on a high-waisted white
Madewell denim skirt, and then try to decide between three
different tops.

"Spending an awful lot of time deliberating on a shirt for a boy you very recently *claimed* you didn't even like," Simran snarks from the doorway.

"Get thee away, traitor!" I ball up my damp towel and chuck it at her.

She catches it with a grin. "Kavya and Ian, sitting in a—" she starts.

"Don't you dare finish that sentence!"

"My, don't we sound shrill and very, very defensive." She makes bold eye contact.

I wag my finger. "Don't you do it."

Simran opens her mouth.

I widen my eyes the way Mom does when I'm about to be in trouble.

She flashes a wicked grin. "Tree."

I lunge for her.

She shrieks midway through singing K-I-S-S-I-N-G as we spill into the hallway.

We laugh as we run down the stairs and into the living room, dodging Buster, who runs back and forth between us like he's not sure who to root for, but definitely wants to be part of it.

Simran turns around, grinning. "First comes rivals, then comes romance . . ."

Buster's tail wags and his tongue lolls as he looks up at me goofily.

I'm about to leap over him when Mom shouts, "Kavya!"

"Why's it gotta be my name?" I call back. "Simmy's here, too!"

Buster takes our yelling as his cue to bark nonstop.

"You shall not"—Simran extends her arms like wings—*"pass!"*

Oh, she's done it now. I pterodactyl screech and frog jump over the dog. "If you're not a fan, don't quote from it!" I chase into the kitchen after my sister.

Smack. I barrel into her.

Simran stumbles forward.

"Uh," she says. "H-hi, Khushi auntie."

Mom is sitting at the table with Khushi auntie, who raises her eyebrows at me in my ratty oversize sleep shirt and short shorts.

Why oh why did I change into my pj's after my shower?

"Fu—" I start to hiss.

Mom's eyes flare.

"Fudge," I finish weakly.

"Not fudge," says Khushi auntie. "Mithai."

She peels the plastic lid off a large container to reveal blocks of sweet chocolate mithai studded with crushed pistachios and edible gold foil.

Khushi auntie pushes the container toward me. "Going somewhere?" She gestures to my golden-hour makeup: metallic gold eyeshadow, a sweep of bronzer and highlight, raspberry blush and matching matte lips.

"Just out," I say. If I say it's with a boy, it'll shoot straight to the auntie grapevine.

Khushi auntie opens her mouth.

"Why don't you finish getting ready?" Mom says quickly.

"Stay, stay," says Khushi auntie. "We're just discussing the kitty party. You always make the same halwa, Mona. I brought the mithai over so we can have a little variety."

Or you just couldn't butt out for two seconds. It's not even your turn!!!!

Mom already has something in the fridge that she'd spent this morning making.

Let it go, Mom's eyes convey.

Simran stays quiet, her usual tactic so it'll all be over quicker.

Well, that doesn't work for me.

Once a villain, always a villain.

I open my mouth. "I think"—I know—"Mom already made gajar halwa. It's delicious."

It could seriously rival the best of carrot cakes. The main ingredient is gajar, the humble carrot, grated and stewed down into a super sweet, rich, thick pudding flavored with cardamom, golden raisins, honey, and slivered almonds. And it's no secret that Khushi auntie has always coveted the recipe, even though Mom would just give it to her if she asked.

"Kavya," Mom prompts, tilting her head toward the door. "You'll be late."

I waver between doing what she wants me to do and doing what I want to do.

"Simran, sit down," says Khushi auntie. "Let me tell you about my friend's son. He's just got his green card."

My sister's face is white and tight-lipped.

"Oh, no," Mom demurs with a laugh I recognize as fake.

"She's only twenty-two. She's going to grad school. When the time is right, *Simran* will decide what she wants."

"Career can come after marriage," Khushi auntie insists. She's not taking any of our cues, not reading the room. "Or not at all. Once the first child comes—"

I see red. My sister is not an incubator. "First child?" The words are out of my mouth faster than I can think them.

Maybe Mom is trying to be polite, but I'm done. D-O-N-E, done.

"So," I say, chest heaving. "Basically we're expected to make straight A's from first to twelfth grade so we can get into a good college, but not because you actually care about education. Oh no, it's so we look more marriageable, do I have that right?"

I'm on a roll now. "Good grades are for landing us a rich, educated husband, and college is just the stepping-stone to nabbing him! Who cares about that degree you worked hard for and the countless hours spent studying? Let it gather dust!" I throw up my hands. "Fulfill your destiny! It's time to be a baby factory!"

Mom looks torn between amusement and horror.

Khushi auntie has her hand pressed to her chest.

Nobody says a word.

"My sister is an amazing poet. I'm proud of her. And," I add even louder, "I'm going on a *date!*"

"Arey baap re, Mona! How besh—a—ram," Khushi auntie manages to gasp.

I am shameless, what of it? But I know better than to push

it further, so I stomp out of the room. The last thing I need is to get grounded before my date.

Footsteps patter behind me.

Not Buster, because he's scrambling off the couch with a guilty look.

"Kavya." A hand closes around my wrist.

"Simran." I don't need another lecture from her about how I'm not a good Indian girl. "I know, I know, I shouldn't have gone off like—"

"Thank you," she says emphatically. She lets go of me with a chagrined smile. "I wish I could have said even half of what you just did."

Huh. Not the response I expected. I rub at my wrist. "Yeah, well."

We start to head up the stairs side by side this time when Mom's icy voice carries through. "Khushi, you aren't taking the hint. Simran is not interested, and I'm proud of Kavya for standing up for her sister. You say *besharam* like an insult, but we should all encourage boldness in our daughters. If my mother had, I would have said this to you long before today."

Simran and I stare at each other in shock.

"I think she's actually rendered Khushi auntie speechless," says Simran.

I sigh. "I've just made it harder for Mom, haven't I? *Oh, god.* The kitty party. 'Poor Mona with her unmarried older daughter and the mouthy younger one who talks back to her elders,'" I say in an auntie accent.

Once we're in my room, Simran sits cross-legged on my

bed. "Self-pity doesn't suit you. Mom's more like you than you think. She knows there are ways to get a point across without yelling."

"Sure, but my way is more effective," I mumble.

Her mouth twitches like she wants to laugh. "Maybe," she allows, "but speaking up for yourself doesn't always mean raising your voice. People hear you when you speak, Kavya. You don't need to obliterate their eardrums."

I give her a small, tentative smile. "I'll try to remember that."

"My beastie little sister," says Simran. "Not such a villain, after all."

She glances over the clothing on my bed before picking up the white denim skirt and the band tee. Throws them at me. "You know, all these years, we've been wondering how long it was going to take you and Ian to get together. Even when you bitched about him besting you at things, I knew you had a thing for him."

I roll my eyes. "Not you, too. Catey's convinced all our competition and banter was a masquerade for our torrid love affair."

Simran boops me on the nose. "You always did have a cute little rapport with him."

"If by that you mean open hostility . . ." I mutter.

She gives me an arch look. "And when you get back, maybe we can . . . I don't know, catch up on our love lives?"

Like sisters hangs in the air between us, unspoken.

"I'd like that, Simmy. I'd like that a lot."

28.
I'm Ready
If You Are

"FAIR WARNING, I'M in a bit of a fighty mood," is the first thing I say to Ian when I walk into Holly Gogogi. Five minutes late, because I swung by the library to return due books and my last batch of reading program cards.

To his credit, he doesn't respond with *When are you not?*

He holds up his phone. "Just about to message you. Thought you weren't going to show."

"And miss this date that you've promised will astound and amaze me?" I deadpan.

"It's a date, not a magic show," he says with a grin.

"You mean I *don't* get to saw you in half?" I snap my fingers. "Rats."

"Ha, ha. How about we make that attitude disappear?"

I slow clap. "Oooo, punny."

He actually takes a bow and I blush ferociously. My god, this boy . . .

Holly Gogogi is closed on Mondays, so the place is empty except for Ian's parents in a corner booth, a neat stack of receipts between them. Ian's dad punches numbers into a calculator while his mom writes the figures in a ledger.

I've seen Val's parents do it at the Indian store after closing time, too.

A pang. Val.

"Hi," I greet the Juns, a little embarrassed it took me this long to notice them.

"Hi, Kavya," says his mom. She gives me a big smile.

"Hello." His dad is a little more reserved, but still friendly. "It's nice to see you again."

"You kids go on back," Mrs. Jun says. "Ian, you shout if you need us, okay?"

"C'mon, Kavs." Ian beckons me to follow him.

He leads me into the spotless kitchen and hands me an apron and a knife.

"Oh," I say in mock delight, "so I *do* get to cut you in half?"

He covers his heart with his palm. "Careful, Joshi. One of these days I'll actually believe you mean all your flippant murder-y comments."

We grin at each other.

Ian's the first to break the moment, clearing his throat a little nervously. "How do you feel about cooking together?"

The word *apprehensive* comes to mind. "Cautiously excited?"

He grabs a second knife. "Why cautiously?"

I eye him warily. "Um. Your chef's knives are huge, and I happen to be rather attached to my fingers."

"Oh, you mean there's something you *can't* do?" He stares at his gleaming reflection in the steel. With a wicked smile, he opens the fridge and grabs a bunch of green onions. He rinses them in the sink while I look on. "Watch and learn," he tosses over his shoulder.

He whips back around and before I know what's happening, he's chopping the long green stems like he's Gordon fucking Ramsay.

"That was some serious wrist action," I say faintly.

"Yeah, I've had a lot of practice," he says, sounding smug, and then he goes bright pink.

A second later, I get it. Laughter bubbles up my throat like fizzy soda.

Pretending to be shocked, I glance at the closed kitchen door. "Dude, your parents are, like, *right there.*"

Even his ears are aflame. "That's not what I meant. That's not how I . . . developed that muscle."

Even though I know that, it's cute watching him dangle.

He clears his throat. "You're actually supposed to wear this—" Leaving his knife on the chopping board, he slips behind me to loop an already knotted apron over my head.

"It's a little loose," he says, untying the knot. His warm fingertips dance against my neck.

I twitch.

"Sorry," he says, blushing even harder. "Are my hands too cold?"

"I—erm—no. They're fine. Perfect." Oh, crap. "I mean fine!"

Ian laughs softly. His hands drift to my shoulders, applying gentle pressure to turn me around to face him.

"Kill me now," I mutter under my breath.

He smiles impishly. "You want me to kiss you now?"

That's *not* what I said. His face is innocent. Maybe too innocent.

I make intense, unblinking eye contact.

Ian starts to smile, then tamps it down, but it breaks free again.

"Nice try," I say with a smirk. "Are we cooking or are we flir—"

Ian shoots one hand in the air. "Flirting! The second thing. Definitely. I prefer that one."

I successfully school my features before my grin gives away how much I'm enjoying this. I snatch the knife I'd set aside. "Maybe *you* prefer flirting, but I'm hungry. And the best way to this girl's heart is through her stomach." A pause. "Um, do you think you could show me how to do that knife thing?"

He takes a step closer. "Can I?" he asks, pointing to my hand.

At my nod, he comes up behind me. His right hand covers mine, and considering I'm holding a knife, it's a really good thing I don't jump out of my skin. His left hand lands on the counter on the other side of me. His thumb grazes my pinkie, then settles comfortably against it.

This shouldn't feel so good, and yet . . .

Ian's torso brushes against my back, but he's careful not to let anything else touch. He's respectful in a way Parker never was. The gentlemanly side of Ian is something I caught a glimpse of the night of the castle party, and once I noticed its presence, it was shocking I'd never seen it before—or, I ruefully admit, maybe I just wasn't ready to.

Am I ready now?

"Are you ready?" Ian asks. His breath ghosts the curve of my ear. Another ticklish spot.

I snap out of my thoughts. "What?"

"For the chopping," he says.

I feel like I'm in one of those rom-coms, about to be taught how to play golf or pool by my ridiculously competent love interest. It's so cheesy, so clichéd, and yet so . . .

"Right?"

This time I yelp, "How are you *doing* that?"

"I said," he says patiently, "You're ready, right?"

Great, I'm losing my mind *and* my heart. This isn't a two-for-one special, damn it.

"I'm ready if you are," I say, deciding to be ready even if I'm not sure I'm there yet.

He pauses. His dark-brown eyes are somber and inscrutable. So different from when he's out on the tennis court, lion eyes blazing topaz. I'm truly a goner if I'm starting to notice how his eyes look in different light. Gold flecks aren't a real thing outside of YA books, I'm pretty sure.

The quiet moment between us lingers for so long that we both know we're talking about more than just cooking. My neck prickles when he exhales, goosebumps skittering over my skin.

He grins, his hip nudging mine. "It's nice being on the same side for once, huh? Though I will miss the contests, weirdly. I mean, it got us spending time together outside of work. Almost like we were friends."

A coil of guilt springs in my stomach. "Ian, we *are* friends."

"Yeah, *now*."

It's the perfect opening to tell him about the fight with Val. About the uncertainty of not knowing where we stood, of having the group chat go unanswered, of suddenly feeling alone even with Catey and Blaire, because now *I* was the third wheel.

But this is the first time since the castle that we've been alone, like really alone. It's just us. And I think, after having so many people around as our buffers for so long, tonight should stay just us.

"You're staring at the chopping board like it's a quadratic equation you need to solve," he says, but it's not a criticism. More like he's drawing me back to him.

And I want to be drawn back, so I let him.

"I still can't believe I didn't realize that I was the girl you like sooner," I bemoan. "It was right there! A girl whose name starts with K. I never thought for a second it could be me."

"Why would you?" he says reasonably. His fingers brush against my wrist.

"I felt so shitty for you, forced to kiss me when you liked someone else at the party," I confess. "I tried to get you out of it until it backfired."

Ian's laugh is low and gravelly. It makes me squirmy all over, but in a good way.

"I can't say I was happy about how it all went down. My friends were a little fed up that I hadn't made a move. I kept telling them I was waiting for the right time, the perfect moment . . . Samer kept quoting 'Faint heart never won fair lady' at me like a bitch, so Rio thought he should create the right time *for* me before it's 'too late and you've graduated and you never speak to each other again.'"

I take all of this in. "I know you must have been anxious, but um, I just wanted you to know that even though it was in front of basically our entire grade, it was, um, pretty nice. You're a really good kisser."

He seems surprised but pleased. "So are you."

My stomach gives a little *zap* of electricity. "Thanks."

"Yeah." He laughs. "Um, so let's get back to it? I promised my parents dinner, and I could really use your help with that."

Part of me wants to slide out of his arms and put some much-needed distance between us because the urge to wind my fingers through his hair and kiss him again is overpowering. The other part wants to stay there more than anything else in the world. It's surreal to think that just a few weeks ago, my inner Evil Queen would have assumed I'm playing right into his hands, that he's got me right where he wants me.

But this isn't a game anymore.

"You're blushing," Ian murmurs.

"Yeah, well, so's your face," I grumble.

"Good one," he deadpans. I hear the grin his voice as he

says, "Now, get ready for the best salmon tacos and kimchi slaw of your life."

This face-saving victory he hands me, but I'll take it. After all, I've given him something, too. I press a hand to my chest, right over my heart.

But something tells me I won't miss it.

29.
To Be Continued

DINNER WITH HIS parents is just like dinner with mine.

Mr. Jun tells at least three dad jokes, Mrs. Jun starts a story off with "Back in Korea," and nobody bats an eye when I reach for seconds.

When Mr. Jun stumbles over Grace's name, Ian's mom covers his hand with hers.

She pivots the conversation to college plans. "What are you going to major in, Kavya? Ian reads so many books, we keep telling him he should be a writer! Are you thinking about schools? Practicing for the SAT?"

"Please stop grilling her. I like a little mystery," Ian mumbles.

"Um, we took the Pre-SAT at the beginning of junior year," I say, gesturing at Ian. "But most of the art programs I'm considering have waived that requirement."

Mrs. Jun gives her husband a beady look, like she's prompting him: *Your turn.*

"Ian said you liked to draw," says Mr. Jun. He looks pleased to know this.

"I'd like to study and eventually work in animation. Pixar, DreamWorks, that kind of thing," I say. "Video games would be really cool, too."

They both look impressed.

"Ian loves *Over the Garden Wall*," says Mrs. Jun, beaming at us both.

"Do you want to see my room?" Ian asks when we finish eating.

He tries to take the plates, but his mom gets them first.

"You kids go; we'll do the washing up," she says, snatching my plate before I can offer to take it to the kitchen. "Thank you for helping Ian with such a wonderful dinner, Kavya."

Flushing, I say, "It was mostly Ian. He's really good in the kitchen."

Her eyes twinkle. "He says such nice things about you, too."

I flash back to the day of my first kids' party with Ian and coming here after for burgers:

"He talks about you a lot."

"We do enjoy a very healthy rivalry."

"We'll let you kids go," says Mr. Jun. "Door open, Ian."

Ian tugs at my hand and we head for the stairs. The moment his bedroom door closes behind us, Ian heaves a visibly relieved sigh.

"I like your parents," I comment. "Also, weren't we supposed to leave the door open?"

"Dad only said that because he thinks he's supposed to." Ian nudges it ajar, anyway, just wide enough for a shoe to fit. "You're still the only girl I've had up here."

It's not like he has a reputation for hooking up or anything, but it's nice to know that I'm the first girl and only girl he's had in his bedroom.

"Oh," I say, swallowing hard.

I take a moment to look around. I've been in Parker's room a few times, but the stark-white walls, king-size bed, and giant wall-mounted flat-screen were as impersonal and unwelcoming as the withering "Charmed, I'm sure" his mother had once greeted me with.

Ian's room, on the other hand, is cozy and inviting. His favorite color is everywhere, from the Yale-blue walls to the fluffy slippers in front of his electric-blue metal nightstand. Above the nightstand is a corkboard pinned with dozens of Polaroids of him and his friends.

There are so many familiar faces, but the one that jumps out last is the one that should have been most visible of all. It's the picture Catey took, but it's not the same as mine.

In this one, I'm looking at him, not the camera. The sun bronzes us both, the sunflowers behind looming a foot taller than both of us. Their yawn toward the sun is as expressive as the joy blooming on both our faces. My smile is spectacular, head tilted back just a little bit so I can look at him. There's a lightness in the lift of my mouth and the crinkles of my eyes.

I can't remember what he'd said to make me look like that. Maybe he didn't do anything. Maybe I just wanted to look at him and how happy he was, even though he was flushed and sweaty and threatening to decapitate flowers for me seconds before the photo was taken.

I almost want to reach out and trace the expression on my face, verify its authenticity somehow. With scary, vivid recall, I remember exactly how I felt in that moment, and it surges across time to jumpstart my heart. I love who I am when I'm with him, whether we're rivals or whether we're . . . more.

This is how it feels to be with someone who accepts me for everything that I am. I'd always thought love was about who the other person was to me, not who *I* was when I was with them. This is me being myself, a little audaciously ambitious and a little bit besharam but a whole lot of other things, too.

And one of those things, unbelievably enough, is Ian Jun's girlfriend.

"We'll have to add more to your collection in autumn," I say, surprised at how steady and light my voice comes out. "Hot cider on a hayride and winding our way around a corn maze."

"We'll go back before then," he says. "I did promise you apple cider donuts."

"And you always keep your promises, don't you?"

He gives me a cheeky grin. "I never joke about food, Kavs."

I like the way he says it.

"You don't call me Joshi as much anymore," I point out.

He tilts his head. "Do you want me to?"

"No, I don't mind it sometimes. It can be kind of hot and combative when we banter. I just wondered because you said you wanted something that was yours, and I—*Oh.*"

We stare at each other. Suddenly, I can't remember why I ever thought he was hard to read.

"I don't think of you as mine in a weird way," says Ian, sounding just a tiny bit defensive. "I'm yours just as much."

"Well, I should hope so," I say faintly. "I'm going to continue the room tour now."

"Right," he says in a strangled voice. "Okay. Yes. You should. Do that."

His bed is pushed into the corner, neatly made, with blue plaid bedding. Hanging on the wall above his pillows are two old-fashioned tennis rackets crossed at the grip with the signature W in the netting.

His ocean-toned bookshelves are the coolest thing I've ever seen; they look like they're made out of old skateboards, and they've been mounted next to a lumpy, squashed orange beanbag big enough for two, and three gaming consoles on a small entertainment unit.

But what catches my attention the most is the brushed steel, blue apothecary cabinet on top of his wooden desk, next to Yeobo's cage and a towering stack of library books. The compartments are open, large enough to fit three or four books upright, but there are also other trinkets and oddments. But before I can get a good look, Ian distracts me.

"I'm glad you like my parents. But you should know, that was my mother when she's restraining herself," he says, breaking the silence. He smirks. "Better be prepared next time."

"*Next time*, is it?" I ask, air-quoting. "Someone's confident."

He playfully bumps my arm. "Maybe someone has a reason to be."

"Aw, man, you think you're super cute or something, don't you?" I groan.

His mouth quirks upward. "You tell me."

I roll my eyes. "You . . . are . . ." His eyes light up. "A solid . . . B plus."

It's probably the worst academic insult for goal-getters like us.

"What? That's basically a C. And from there, it's a slippery slope to an F."

That gets a laugh out of me. "It's the gateway grade."

"Not worried, though," he says, looking as unflappable as ever. "We both know how easy it is for me to get A's. What did you call me freshman year? A point piranha?"

"Well, you were! You did *all* the extra credit."

"No one stopped you from doing it!"

"I wasn't expecting to be that one point short of an A, obviously," I grind out.

Ian gives me a not-my-problem shrug and a leisurely, toe-tingling smile. He's loving this.

I can't decide if I want to kiss him or clap back. I'm loving this, too.

"So are there any art schools in Indiana you want to attend? Or would you be looking out of state?" he asks.

There's something in his tone I can't decipher. But maybe it's only because he asks it so softly.

"A lot of the best schools are on the East and West Coasts. But it would save a lot of money to stay in state, and it'd be nice to be close to home." I take a seat at the foot of his bed. "What about you? I mean, what do you want to do?"

"I haven't really given it much thought," he says.

I give him a dubious look. How is that even possible?

Ian squeezes my hand. "I mean, I guess I'm good at a lot of things."

"I'm familiar with your skills and humbleness," I say dryly. I wait for a swift and witty repartee, but it doesn't come.

"You know how when you're really good at something, people always say, 'Oh, you should, like, do that for a living'?" At my nod, he continues, "There's so many jobs I could technically do, but . . . they're not my passion. Which would make more sense if I knew what I *did* want to do, but I don't."

"Couldn't that mean you'd be happy doing whatever you're good at? Which, like you said, is pretty much everything." I give him a teasing eye roll.

He shrugs and sits down next to me, our thighs touching. "Maybe. But I'd feel better if I had a clue what would make *me* happy because I actually want it. Not because I'm good at it. That's why I hate when people think I'm perfect. I know I don't work as hard as others do to make the same grades or win games. I shouldn't get compliments for things where I don't even need to try. People mean well, but I wish it wasn't the first thing they associate me with."

"No offense, but that doesn't seem like such a terrible problem to have." I think about Val and her stifling responsibilities. "Everything is open to you. You're capable of pursuing so many career paths *and* your parents support you. Do you know what a gift that is?"

His lips twist in acknowledgment. "I'm grateful that my parents would be happy if I studied English or did literally anything I wanted, but like . . . I never know if I enjoy something because I actually enjoy it or because I enjoy the feeling of being good at it. I don't want to just be 'capable.' I want to feel passionate. You know?"

Before I can respond, he continues.

"But then I feel guilty, too." He purses his lips. "Grace wanted to be a doctor. My parents were so proud. But she'll never get to *be* anything, other than—"

I understand the word he doesn't want to say.

"Is that what you want?" I ask gently. "To be a doctor?"

Ian shrugs, turning to face me. "How can I rule it out? I can't say it's what I *don't* want."

"Yeah, you can." I hold his gaze. "If you don't want to do something, you say it."

"Like you, you mean?"

I send him a half smile. "Nah. You say it like you."

"I'd miss you if we went to different schools," he says.

"You jest, but you'd totally miss me. I keep you on your toes."

There's an earnestness on his face that takes us far beyond just kidding around.

"I'm not jesting," he murmurs. "I really would miss you."

"Ian?" I wait until he's looking at me before I say, "I have no doubt that you are going to achieve everything you ever want in life, and be so beyond successful, and wildly happy. Just because you haven't found your thing yet—whatever it is that sets your soul on fire—that doesn't mean you won't find it. I know you're going to get whatever you set out to, and I know this because you are the smartest guy I know, and if you ever repeat this to anyone, I *will* deny it."

I shoot him a small smile. "And if by some chance you don't figure out what your passion is, you're good at everything, so just go to the same place I go and keep me on *my* toes. Point piranha all you want, and we'll both graduate summa cum laude."

"That is both sweet . . ." Ian stifles a laugh. "And incredibly, shamelessly self-serving."

"Beauty and the besharam," I quip.

"What does that word mean?"

"It means I give great advice. So you should believe me. I'm always right."

"Sure, besharam." He presses a soft kiss to my cheek. "Whatever you say."

"Hey! I could have been the beauty, you know?"

"Kavya, you're both."

This beautiful boy has no idea how right he is.

"I like how you walked that one back," I say, unable to keep from smiling. "Smooth."

He grins. "So what I'm hearing is," he drawls, completely unrepentant, "you're inviting me to attend the same college as you."

Incredulous, I say, "*That's* what you got from my pep talk?"

His hum is noncommittal.

"Ian Jun, you just made me regret being super nice to you," I huff.

He flashes a smile. "I'll make it up to you."

His eyes are a dark promise of exactly how he plans to do so, and we both lean in at the same time. His wavy, brushed-back hair falls over his forehead, and he makes a soft sound of impatience. Without thinking about it, I push my hand into his hair, fingernails dragging over his scalp, and his breath hitches. I make up my mind to do it again at the earliest opportunity.

His hair is silky soft, but I can tell he's used some product. A thrill shoots down my spine as I imagine him trying to impress me. You could never call Ian of all people sloppy, but he's never looked this roguish before. It's a good look on him, hair longer than it was on the last day of school, and the sides all grown out. I love the piece-y way it falls now, like my fingers have just dived through. Which they have. It's intimate and possessive, and I'm still reeling that it's with him.

His hands cup my face, and the pad of his thumb traces my lower lip, all shivery and soft. Our lips are just a whisper away from meeting when the moment is interrupted.

"Ian! Fruit's ready!" Mrs. Jun calls.

He winces. "Sorry about the cliffhang. I'll go grab it," he says, close enough that I can feel his breath ghost across my lips. At my silent nod, he pulls back with a rueful smile, getting up with effort, as though he can't quite bring himself to leave.

He hovers in the doorway, eyes searching mine. "To be continued?"

It strikes me then: Ian and I are both main characters in the same book—once upon a time I had considered him to be my obvious nemesis and therefore the antagonist of my story— but now he's rewritten everything I thought was true.

Ever since our first kiss, I've had to reconcile my rival with this swoony, sweet boy. It had been like reading book three and not figuring out you've missed the first two.

Now I'm a girl who knows the trilogy inside and out, and is obsessed enough to make an incorrect quotes account on Twitter.

I want book four and five and six, and I want to fill them up with memories like Mom and Dad, like Catey and Blaire, like every romance novel couple I've ever shipped.

"To be continued," I agree, and he slips out of the room.

Ordinarily I would never even think about snooping amongst his personal possessions, but the secrets in each little cubby of the apothecary cabinet are too tempting to resist. Yeobo peeks at me with her beady black eyes, and a bit nonsensically, I press a finger to my lips.

The first thing I notice is the collection of small geodes, sliced in half to reveal shimmery pink and purple crystals. There are a few weathered paperbacks that didn't fit on his skateboard shelves, their spines soft and cracked like they're old favorites he returns to often, and the cute Polaroid Go that captured all those photos.

In another compartment are open envelopes and bits of

junk mail. His desk is scattered with loose paper, but the one with a Monopoly-style rectangle draws my eye because of Ian's signature blue ballpoint scribbled all over the edges, too cramped to read. It's not at all like the usual neat writing on the assignments he hands in. In fact, the desk is the only part of his room that isn't fundamentally tidy.

And then I see something that quite literally takes my breath away.

In the top right compartment are all four of the bookmarks I'd designed for the library this year. And the ones from last year, too, crisp from unuse. He saved them as mementos. For a *year*. Because they were mine.

Along with the note I'd left in his Pocket Full of Sunshine. *He kept it.* I hadn't even bothered to look through mine after seeing the first few sour notes.

I don't need to pick it up to know what it says. I'd only thought about it a million times before writing it and then another million times before giving it to him.

My stare snags on something else, too. Tucked next to the bookmarks is a small bundle of white cards. My heartbeat roars in my ears as I hesitantly reach out to pull them closer.

Maybe Ian wouldn't have minded that I knew all the little memories he'd saved, but this . . . this I'm sure was meant to be kept hidden.

I forget to blink. There are six cards here, with three book titles written on each.

It's the last day of the summer reading program.

It rattles me, seeing these bone-white cards still in his room.

They were *due* today and it's not like Ian to miss a due date. There's no way he could have forgotten. I'd even reminded him!

Those eighteen books are the difference between giving me his best and giving me a win I didn't earn. Where's his sense of competition gone?

And then it dawns on me. He doesn't have one anymore.

My insides spark. Even when we were enemies, he respected me enough to give me a fair fight. But now that we're dating, suddenly everything changes?

What I liked best about him was that he could give as good as he got. He didn't back down. He was unapologetic about competing with me. He didn't expect me to make myself smaller just so he could feel like a big man. And that's what makes this worse.

I swallow hard. This was why he stopped updating me on his book totals? It hurts. It hurts that I actually believed he wouldn't change. It hurts that I let him close enough to hurt me.

I can't believe I let him.

The roaring intensifies. I was wrong. I should have stuck with rivalry, not romance.

I don't want to win because someone thinks he has to let me. And the only way to prove that is to take these cards straight to the library, drop them off myself. I have to leave now if I'm going to make it there before it closes.

I barrel past Ian on the stairs. The plate of sliced oranges, pears, and peeled lychee teeters precariously in his hands, but I keep going without looking back.

There's undisguised panic in his voice as he calls "Kavya?" after me.

Downstairs, Mr. and Mrs. Jun are sharing their own plate of fruit. I smooth my expression and smile as I thank them for having me over and ignore their bewildered faces, clearly wondering why I'm fleeing and Ian isn't seeing me to the door. My thin smile is tighter than my voice, and it hurts my cheeks.

But it's still not as fake as whatever *this* was.

30.
You Know, Fun?

THE MOON GIRLS would know what to do. If all of us were talking, that is. Or, to be more accurate, if Val was talking to us. I hunger to talk to my friends—all of them—but I don't want it to be because I need their advice or their help. I want it to be because we're an *us* again.

Because if we get back to normal, then maybe Ian and I have a chance, too.

We're like strangers orbiting each other at Tuesday's birthday party. The kids may not notice, but I sure do. At the start of the party, Ian tries desperately to make eye contact, but I can't meet his laser eyes.

Later, from the way he folds his arms across his chest and looks everywhere but at me when I start the sing-along, I can tell he wants to be anywhere but here. Annoyance spikes under my skin. It's not like *he* has a reason to be awkward. He's not the one who was betrayed.

I deserve the dignity of him giving me his best, even if it means thoroughly trouncing me, if that's what it takes. How dare he take it easy on me because he likes me?

Over the music the kids know by heart, he lets his voice fade until he can hiss in a jagged voice, "Kavya, what's going on? Why did you run out of Holly Gogogi like that? You didn't even say goodbye to me."

"We're working," I say from the corner of my mouth, still pasting on a smile for the kids' benefit.

"I don't understand what happened. Were we moving too fast? Going in my bedroom? I didn't expect—I mean—" He gestures between us. "I don't want you to think that I brought you up there to hook up." There's a hint of vulnerability in his voice as he asks, "Did I do something wrong?"

"I never thought that." My wooden smile falters but doesn't slip. "It's that you wanted me to win so badly that you were willing to cheat to make sure I did."

"I did *what*?" he shoots back in a heated whisper. "For fu— fin's sake, Joshi."

Too late, I realize the music has stopped.

The children are all staring at us in open-mouthed horror, and the parents peer out from behind the glass-enclosed sunroom. "Everything all right?" the mom calls, opening the back door. "I'm so sorry; I lost track of time. Who's for cake?"

"That was so unprofessional," I say once the kids race past us. For a second, the embarrassment makes me forget I'm mad at him for something else. "I can't believe you did that."

"*You* can't believe," he starts to say, then stops. "You've been ignoring all my messages and I didn't know how else to get your attention."

I'm more convinced now than ever—I want someone to take me head-on instead of waving the white flag and side-stepping out of my way.

He should have known that.

My eyes sting with unshed tears.

He was *supposed* to have known that.

"I don't understand you. I thought we were giving this a real chance," he says.

The buildup of desperation lumps in my throat. I'd thought things about him, too.

Things like *You're different from other guys,* and *I thought you saw me, too,* and *You let me think this was something real.*

"You really can't see why I'm upset that you threw the reading competition?" I ask.

He stares. "Competition? I was doing it for fun. And I never 'threw' anything."

"Fun?" I repeat.

"Yes, fun," he says impatiently. "You know, *fun?*"

"This is just like when we were kids and you were so sure you had to save me on the waterslide! I didn't need your help then, and I don't need it now," I snap. "I've never hidden who I was. You knew from day one that winning, being the best . . . All of that is important to me."

"And I want that for you!" He's not even trying to keep his

voice down now. "I will *always* root for you to win. How do you not see that? I want you to be the best because it's *who you are,* and I will never not admire the hell out of that."

"How is rigging my victory 'admiring me'?" I scoff. "If you beat me, then you beat me. How could you think for a second that I wouldn't want you to give me your best? *Letting* me win is more humiliating than losing to you fair and square."

Patches of color explode in his cheeks like rouge. "I wouldn't do that! Why won't you belie—"

His defensiveness makes this worse.

"I saw them, Ian. Okay? I found the cards in your room and dropped them off at the library so neither of us would have any reason to question the results."

"You can't pin your paranoia on me because I'm a convenient target, Kavya. If I forgot to turn them in, it's because I forgot. I did tell you I wasn't really keeping track because I was busy," he says stiffly. "But I guess I see now where I stand. At arm's length, where you've always kept me. Winning still means more to you than anything." He scoffs. "Than *every-thing.*"

Tears pricking at my eyes, I start to turn away, to pack up, but he's not done yet.

"You know what gets me? I always thought this thing be-tween us"—he gestures—"was just how we were. I thought it was our thing. That we both got off on the banter. But that underneath it all, maybe there could be something real. But you're so convinced it can only be one or the other, romance or rivalry. It's so fucking binary and it's *small.*"

My lips won't unstick. My stomach is in freefall, trying hard to grab on to anything to soften the landing. It hurts. Everything feels twisted and bent and broken.

I've always been good with my words, with a swift parting shot, with a snappy repartee. But now, when I need my voice the most, it's stolen from me. Not by a sea witch, but by my own actions. Catey was right: I *am* an Ariel.

It's what I knew all along: I'm the evil queen, the sea witch, the sly trickster who has just gotten their comeuppance for believing they could win. Every way I look at it, I'm the antagonist. This isn't the beginning of a love story, it's the end of one.

I am the beast.

Ian shakes his head, looking resigned. "I just wanted things to be different between us. But I don't want to convince you of who I am anymore. I can't open your eyes for you. You're the only one who can do that. You are my happy beginning, Kavya. I'm not walking away, but I can't spend forever wondering if you're going to cut and run again."

There's an awful finality in his rigid posture. His breath catches as if thorny vines are climbing in his throat. It's gratifying that I'm not the only one losing my composure. The silence lingers between us like the last desperate petal of a rose, trying to hold on past its time.

My heart *thump, thump, thump*s.

Somewhere along the line, Ian became someone I didn't want to disappoint, and even if I'm pissed at him right now, I loathe the feeling of it going both ways.

"This is the part where you decide what you want to do

next," says Ian, face carefully blank, like it's taking everything he has to say this without a wobble. His stoicism is betrayed only by the slight tremble of his hands, fisting the hem of his costume. "You either see me or you don't. I hope to god you do, but I'm really scared that you aren't brave enough to."

31.
So Not a
Morning Person

IAN JUN HAD some nerve telling me that I'm not brave.

From the moment those words left his lips a few days ago, they've been simmering under my skin, stewing inside my brain. Thinking about him is more dangerous than it's ever been before—because he's right.

And that's the most confusing part of all. He's *right*, and while I resent it as much as all the other times, all I want to do is tell him so. But I'm still me, so I can't.

It's a given that until I tell him whether I'm truly brave enough to take that chance on us, radio silence is all there can be between us. I miss the good-morning and good-night messages, always accompanied by the blue heart emoji he's not embarrassed to overuse. I miss the cheeky GIF wars and our *really* good banter. I miss the way he's superimposed on every YA book boyfriend I've ever read.

And the thing is, once I start cataloging everything like they're more smiles I have to puzzle out, I can't stop. I miss the way he holds me when we dance, touch tentative at first, then emboldened and sure of his welcome. I miss the intensity of his smolder and smirk, but not as much as the way his whole face changes when I do something that surprises him.

More than anything, I miss *him*.

I can't believe I ever thought he was playing games . . . Ian Jun wears his heart on his sleeve more than anyone else I know. And if this summer has taught me anything, it's that I do know him, and somehow, defying possibility, he knows me. He sees me. He *gets* me.

Not knowing the words is a new one, I think huffily. I never thought I'd be the one speechless. But there is one thing I can do. A decision that I don't have to think twice about because it's one I already agreed to. I won't let him down—again.

With every day that passes, Ian's ultimatum corroding me from the inside out, we get closer to the date marked in my phone calendar as simply "Toy Store."

But even though all three of my reminder alarms have gone off, I can't bring myself to get out of bed, frozen as a child wary of monsters grabbing them if so much as a toe peeps out from the blanket.

"Tell me what's wrong," Simran whispers, tracing her fingers down my hair. "Your alarms have woken up everyone else in the house but you."

She shifts on the edge of my bed and tries to get me to take the consoling cup of black tea she's brought with her. When I make no move to take it, she sighs and sets it on the nightstand.

"Go away," I say sullenly, knowing there is exactly zero likelihood of it happening. I bury my head under my pillow. "It's summer and I don't have work today; just let me sleep."

"But you *do* have somewhere to be."

Even though she has no clue that I still plan to go with Ian to collect Grace's game after all these years, the reminder rankles. I'm sure she suspects my funk is Ian related.

Buster's woof announces his arrival, and he takes his chance before Simran can admonish him not to jump on the bed. His tail gets me in the face as he circles the bed a couple of times before burrowing into my side, one paw draped over my hip.

If his weight wasn't pinning the blanket down, I'm pretty sure she would have tried whisking it off me by now. When we were younger, it was her job to make sure I woke up to get ready for school, so she knows how crabby it makes me.

Simran *tsks*. "Kavya, you're one of the most expressive people I know. Every year, like clockwork, you start celebrating your birthday a whole week early, but this year you haven't even picked out the largest, most obnoxious cake from the bakery. When you've lost your joie de vivre for food coloring and sprinkles, something's up."

"Maybe I'm growing up," I say, voice muffled.

She laughs. "You're getting older, but I don't know if you're 'growing up.'"

I try not to take it personally, but taking things personally just so happens to be a skill I excel at. "Do you really think that, Simmy?"

Maybe it's the vulnerability in the way I say her name that

makes her hand pause the comforting strokes down my hair and back. *"Well,"* she says, stretching it into two syllables. "No, I guess not. You've been different this summer. Like you've found equilibrium."

I roll the word *equilibrium* around in my mind, feeling it out. There's a rightness to that word. A heft that's nearly tangible.

After a long moment of contemplative silence, I say, "I think I've lost it."

Whatever else Simran wants to ask, she doesn't pry. "Do you remember when you told me I would never be late for my own life? You were right. We're always exploring and evolving, and we're bound to make some mistakes along the way. Some colossal fuckups, too. It's inevitable, even when we think we've got our shit figured out. What matters is how we pick ourselves up after. How we put ourselves back together, along with anything we broke along the way."

My shoulders shake with the force of my scoff. "It can't be that easy."

I can imagine her shrugging as she says, rather cryptically, "It can if it's worth it."

"I hate it when you're all wise and shit."

Her laugh is a balm more soothing than tea could ever be. "You haven't lost anything. You've just had a little wobble. Pick yourself up, little sis."

"How did you do it?"

"I took a chance with Amie," she says simply. "I didn't want to say anything until you and the moon girls made up. But.

Um. I invited Amie to come to the lake with us."

For this I stick my head out from under the pillow, staring incredulously. "You told Mom and Dad you wanted to bring your girlfriend to my birthday weekend? Simmy, that's huge!"

"I told Mom and Dad we're together, yes. I'm sorry, I should have asked. I just got so excited," she says, words quick and flustered. "It was inconsiderate. I can tell her not to—"

I hold up a hand. "Don't be ridiculous, I love Amie. I'm happy for you both even if I feel shitty for me."

"So will you get your butt out of bed?"

A few weeks ago I would have flouted her big-sister authority. But today I listen to her.

Simran's right. Ian thinks I'm brave and brainy and beautiful, but when it comes to my relationships, I give up without even trying. I don't want to be a girl so afraid of striking out that she doesn't even step up to the plate. Where would Belle be if she hadn't pursued and protected the father she loved? If she hadn't opened her heart to the Beast?

Okay, granted, she wouldn't have been temporarily imprisoned in a castle full of talking antiques, but she also wouldn't have had adventure or wonder or a love worth fighting a whole damn village for.

"Yes," I tell Simran. "I'm getting up. I do have somewhere to be."

I've been the Beast. Now maybe it's time to take a page out of Belle's book.

....

I'm so not a morning person, but I show up at the toy store ten minutes before it opens wearing black for bravery, snagging the last available parking spot a few storefronts away. The banners strung between lampposts advertise the schedule of Luna Cove summer activities, including the Riverwalk concert series starting tomorrow.

I smooth my palms over nonexistent wrinkles in the black floral minidress, the flowy peasant sleeves grazing prickly just-shaved calves that I forgot to lotion. All that mattered was racing through showering so I could be here at the time we'd agreed on during our walk back from the sunflower maze.

It's weird not knowing how to work out my feelings. If this were a math problem, I would attack it over and over again until I had the right answer. But solving for X is impossible when it comes to matters of the heart.

There's a right answer here, a way to get everything I want. The happy beginning Ian promised. But I don't know how to get there. So instead I'm here, because being here makes sense and everything else is tangled.

I don't have to wait for long. I'm so attuned to finding him in a crowd that my gaze is almost preternaturally drawn to him making his way down the Riverwalk.

But he's not alone.

I fight every instinct to duck, even though there's no way he can see me.

Ian and Rio are walking so close that their shoulders brush, like they're seeking comfort. Rio wears none of his irrepressible cheerfulness, and Ian's face is a little closed off.

I'm too consumed with reading Ian's undefinable expression to realize where they're going. It's only when Rio pulls the door open for Ian that I clock their destination—the toy store.

He said he wanted to pick up Grace's board game with *me*.

Rationally I know I have no right to the knee-jerk wringing of my heart.

Irrationally, my knuckles whiten against the gray steering wheel, and I lean as far forward as I can without headbutting the windshield, pretending that I have telescopic x-ray vision that can see through the toy store windows. I haven't switched off the ignition, so I know exactly how many minutes pass before he and Rio come out. They both look a bit lighter.

There's a bag swinging from Ian's fingers.

I have zero business feeling betrayed. I know this. This is Ian's summer of scary things, and now that it's coming to an end, it makes sense he'd want to end it strong. I'm proud of him, more than I've ever been of anyone *ever*.

He might have wanted it to be me there with him, but he didn't need me there to be strong. It's so clear that ever since the waterslide, *he's* always been the brave one between us.

I don't pull out of my parking spot right away, watching as both boys head back in the direction of Holly Gogogi. I can't be mad that Ian had someone he loved with him.

It's just that I had hoped that person would be me.

But if it isn't, then at least it's his best friend.

Their togetherness almost makes up for the people who aren't here in person but who I always carry with me, my moon girls. I miss Blaire's humor, slightly biting, just like mine. I miss the way Catey always tries so hard to take care of us. I miss Val and her earnestness, watching her test her wings and go after what—who—she wanted.

Maybe coming here didn't work out quite like I'd hoped, but Kavya Joshi isn't a quitter. I grab my phone from the passenger seat and open up the moon girl group chat.

Moon girls, I type out.

> I should have reached out earlier instead of letting things stay weird. I'm just realizing how much I tend to do that, with Simran, with Ian, with us.

> I hate that we're fractured. I hate that we're hurting. Most of all, I hate that I could have spoken up before it got to this.

> I'm sorry I didn't protect us the way I should have.

> But I have to believe that no matter what, we're still moon girls until the end. Sure, we fight like all sisters do, but we also find our way back to each other like all sisters do. Across time, space, galaxies.

We're Usagi/Serena and Rei/Raye.
And that means even when we're angry,
we relentlessly love each other and
we definitely don't walk away.

I know you're all working today, but can
you swing by when you get off?

We're the moon girls. I miss us.

I hit send before I can second-guess myself.

32.
We're the Moon Girls

BRRRRRNNNNNGGGGG!

I fly from the couch to the front door, flinging it open before the doorbell stops.

They're all here. With sleeping bags under their arms for some reason. In response to my quizzical eyebrow, Val shoots me a hopeful little smile, but doesn't hold my gaze for long, like maybe she's still feeling a little raw and apprehensive. Blaire looks embarrassed, pressing her lips together the way she does on those super rare times she's nervous.

Catey takes charge, grabbing Blaire's hand. "Moon girl rendezvous upstairs, stat."

We all traipse up to my room, Buster at our heels. We're assured of privacy since my parents already left for date night, and Simran and Amie are at a poetry reading at the library, followed by—actually, I have no idea. But I'm sure she'll fill me in tomorrow. So weird—*so great*—that this is our relationship now.

"You know my parents won't care if you all spend the night, but are we going to talk about the sleeping bags?" I ask, flicking my eyes towards Val's. "Wait. No. Starting over. Before we talk about anything else, I have to say this. I'm sorry. This summer has been, well, it's been a lot. And I took it for granted that we were okay, because we're always okay when we're together. I didn't know how to talk about what was happening with us. I'm . . . better at destroying than healing," I admit, breaking my gaze to swipe at my eyes. "I thought I was a beast for so long that I didn't even try. I'm so, so sorry that I let us all down."

"Kavs, no." Val's laugh is a little weepy. "It's not just on you. I bottled things up. I was jealous about the restaurant. Angry that Catey's and Blaire's parents believe in them so much that they'll do everything it takes to make their dreams come true. Frustrated that my dad can only see two possible options for my future. Either I inherit his dreams or inherit his store."

She takes a breath and cuddles Buster to her. "It wasn't just that, though. This thing with Ian . . . I could tell that you were changing your mind about him. We all saw it coming, even when you couldn't see it yourself. This summer changed everything, and I didn't want to be the only one left out. But I wasn't being fair to any of you."

Blaire's up next. "And that's on us. We *never* wanted you to feel left out. All those times we talked about the restaurant, we weren't trying to flaunt it. We wanted to share it with you. But we didn't see that it came across insensitive. With the restaurant about to open next week, we've been tackling everything this summer like a to-do list, but we will never treat our friendship like a box that needs to be ticked *ever again*."

"Never," Catey promises, throwing her arms around Val and Buster both. "I'm sorry we didn't recognize our privilege. I'm sorry we didn't see you were hurting. We'll do better."

"Thank you," Val whispers into Catey's hair, but her words are for all of us. "It's hard for me to be open about what I'm feeling because it's always felt like I want too much, at least according to Papa. Sometimes even with you three, I don't know how to ask for what I want because I'm scared someone will tell me I can't have it."

Tears are openly running down all our faces now.

"But one good thing did come from all this," says Val, pulling away from Catey. "When we weren't hanging out . . . Well, you know how Papa is whenever he sees me being idle. He put me to work in the store. It focused my anger like you wouldn't believe."

I gasp. "Did you finally tell him how you feel?"

"I wanted to ever since they picked me up from your house that day," she says. "But it took all those extra hours at the store to really light a fire under my ass. I wouldn't know if I never tried, right? So I told them. And they're not happy about it, but Papa finally agreed that some things could change. Starting with the sleepovers." She nods to the sleeping bag.

"Oh my god, Val!" Blaire pumps her fist in the air. "You rock star!"

I grin big. "Did you tell him you didn't want to be a doctor?"

"Uh, the whole 'You have to be a doctor' thing is probably part of a longer argument," Val says with a wince.

"Baby steps," Catey says encouragingly. "We're so proud of you for having the courage to do this super hard thing."

"It was pretty scary. It felt like I was killing their dream," says Val. "But maybe by the time I start applying to colleges I can whip up a PowerPoint good enough to convince him to let me major in business with a minor in fashion merchandising. You know I've started selling a few of my designs recently? I was thinking maybe I could make a website or even just an Etsy to reach more customers. It was actually Simran who suggested it. I wish Papa supported me on his own, but maybe if he sees that other people do, he'll believe in me, too."

"We'll help you with that," Blaire promises, slinging her arm around Val's shoulder.

"Absolutely," says Catey. "We just did the website for the Fork and Crumb; it was so easy using Squarespace and it looks amazi— Shoot. Sorry. I was doing it again."

"It's fine!" Val laughs. "I don't want you to *not* mention the bistro. Doing better goes both ways. And I would love the help from friends who know more than I do."

"Moon girls again?" I ask hesitantly.

"I'm so sorry I mocked it," says Val. "Being a moon girl is the best thing that ever happened to me. I'm an only child, so this is the closest I'll ever have to sisters."

"And we always will be," I say, squeezing her hand. "We're the moon girls."

Val's eyes say it all. "Tell me everything I missed with Ian?"

"Are you sure? We don't have to talk about boys."

Val fixes me with a no-nonsense look. "Ian has never been just 'boys,' and you know it."

About a hundred gasps from the moon girls later, I've filled them in on everything that happened. Not the sanitized, stripped-down version, but the unabridged one that acknowledges how much of a troll I was. From finding the reading program cards to his challenging me to make a decision, and finally, to seeing him with someone else at the toy store when it was supposed to be *our* thing.

"I should have believed in him," I say, wrapping up the entire saga. "I just couldn't get over the fact that Ian Jun of all people just *forgot* he had eighteen books unaccounted for."

"The summer reading wasn't even one of our original contests," Val points out. "Samer only suggested it last minute because you and Ian were tied two-to-two."

Blaire sighs. "Remember what I said about you making it easy to get your goat?"

"He said he would always give me another chance. But it looks like maybe it wasn't as open-ended as I thought," I admit. "Like, I'm happy he got closure. I could never be mad about that. But when I saw him with a shopping bag, I just . . ."

"Kavs, you can't lose hope," says Val. "If you do, you lose everything. If you want to be with him, he's worth fighting for."

"I *know* he is, and I *want* to tell him that I see him, but it's too late," I say miserably. "I don't even know if he wants to hear it anymore."

"You're jumping to another conclusion," says Catey. "Yes, I know it looks like Ian didn't wait for you. But isn't it possible that he was at the toy store for another reason? He said he would always give you another chance. If you don't even try, then *you're* the one walking away, not him."

"The love of my life is correct, as always," says Blaire. "Ian never stopped rooting for you, and I bet he's still hoping you'll come through. I remember watching him that day you played Scrabble in the library. He cared about the moves you were making as much as his own. And not just because he was trying to win. He was *proud* of you, Kavs. His feelings for you didn't stop him from trying his best."

Catey nods along. "And I have to believe that in the same way Ian didn't want you to change yourself into being the kind of girl Parker wanted, he wouldn't give you anything other than himself, too. Changing what makes you *you* is not a good way to find your person."

My voice is small as I ask, "But what if I tell him how I feel and it's too late? And I pour out my feelings for nothing? It'll be so embarrassing."

Cate gives me a gentle smile. "What's the one thing you've always wanted?"

A yearning steals over me so strong and so vivid that it grips and yanks me backward through time: Prem, amore, ishq. Being with someone who wouldn't want me to hold back. Sharing the world instead of fighting for it.

The conversation idles when I don't say anything, and eventually turns to other things. It's gratifying that we fall back into our friendship without any awkwardness, but I feel a little detached from it. It's not that this isn't enough . . .

It's that I know that just a few days ago, I had more. And I miss it. I miss him.

"Hey, Kavs," says Val. There's a crinkle of paper as she grabs my Pocket Full of Sunshine from my desk. She gives it a little shake, then stares at me in surprise when there's a soft flutter of movement inside. "Why do you still have this?"

"I liked my design! Don't tell me you threw out yours. Your dress sketches were gorgeous, V." I try to take it back, but she dumps everything out on the floor.

"Of course I kept *my* artwork," she says. "But I threw out all the shitty affirmations."

"Thinking that would been a smart move," says Blaire, crumpling up a handful. "Get your grudge list ready, Kavs. I recognize some of these assholes' handwriting."

"Babe!" Catey laughs and leans in to kiss her. "I thought we talked about how we don't use our observational skills for evil?"

I scrape the carpet with my palms, gathering up every little barb. "I love you all, but it's not like I don't already know how everyone else sees me."

"Can we check out what's in the fridge?" asks Catey. "I can whip us up some dinner."

"Yes, please!" Val is enthusiastic, dinner plates in her eyes. "My stomach was in knots all day, and I'm ravenous. Maybe some of those delicious pot pies you two were working on?"

"Um, actually . . ." I bite my lip. "How would you feel about Korean fusion?"

It's still a little early for the dinner rush, so we find street parking in front of Holly Gogogi without a problem. I have our order memorized, but all the moon girls know what we're really here for, and it's not the seafood scallion pancakes and kimchi fries.

"You've got this, Kavs!" Blaire calls from her rolled-down front window.

In the back seat and driver's seat, respectively, Val and Catey both flash me two thumbs-up and their widest this-is-your-moment smiles that bolster my courage like a gulp of something strong. My blood scorches with adrenaline, skin buzzing with the knowledge that in a minute I'll be inside, telling Ian exactly how I see him.

The last guy I ever thought I'd fall for, but the one who had always been there. Like a stats assignment, Ian always shows his work. Showing me who he was not just with pretty words, but with his actions.

He's the Prince Charming it took me a lot longer than chapter three to find.

And he's also the Prince Call-Me-on-My-Shit and Prince Could-Wake-a-Princess-from-Her-Enchanted-Sleep-with-His-Kiss and Prince Sunshine-Too-Good-for-This-World-Cinnamon-Roll I can't walk away from.

I push open the door to Holly Gogogi, already seeing how this will play out. I'll stroll up to the counter and ask for Ian. He'll come out and see me perched on a bar stool. I'll apologize for not believing him and not seeing him. I'll grovel, I'll plead. Show him it's not just about appearances for me. It's about him and me. What's real.

But when I enter, it's like I've taken a wrong turn somewhere and wandered off the path in the middle of a forest dark and deep. I've walked into the wrong fairy tale.

Ian's standing next to an occupied table, serving bulgogi burgers to Khloe-from-kayaking and her parents. Khloe faces me, but she's only got eyes for Ian, saying something that makes him laugh as he sets her plate down. Weeds of jealousy sprout tall as beanstalks.

There's nothing romantic about them, but I can't help but watch Ian's face, trying to read his expression. Seeking out any hint of the smile he reserved for me. The words I'd rehearsed in my head on the way here shriveling in my throat. This isn't my happy beginning after all.

"Kavya?" Mrs. Jun's waiting at the counter. "Hi, sweetie. Ready to order?"

I was right, after all. I don't walk away from him.

As if every ravenous wolf in the forest is after me, I run.

33.
I Will Always Give You One More Chance

THE MOON GIRL reunion sleepover had the same funereal pall hanging over it as our last one. It sucks, and while no one said it, I knew it was my mood bringing us all down. I also knew there was probably nothing between Ian and Khloe, who he said was just a family friend, but I can't chase the image of them together out of my mind.

If I'd waited there a moment longer, would I have seen him flash her one of *my* smiles?

Even the idea is devastating.

Maybe if I'd been brave and gone over to ask him if he had a minute to talk . . .

Instead, I'd fled the second his mom noticed me. Again. I can't even *begin* to imagine what she must have made of me beelining for the exit like the clock was about to strike midnight.

"Girls, breakfast!" Mom calls from downstairs.

"I smell your mom's chocolate chip pancakes and crispy bacon," Catey says with a grin as she finishes rolling up her sleeping bag. "Kavs, need some help making your bed?"

Blaire bounds into the bedroom with her toiletry bag. "Val's almost done brushing her teeth if you need to use the bathroom, babe."

"You go ahead," I tell Catey. "This'll just take a second. You should head down. Simran's as territorial about bacon as she is about puris."

The small stab at levity makes Blaire look relieved I'm almost back on form.

I remember zoning out while we were watching *Outer Banks*, barely touching the olive-and-pepperoni pizza and spicy wings we wound up bringing home instead of Holly Gogogi's, but I wasn't that much of a killjoy last night, was I?

"Seriously, I'm fine," I insist. "If anything, I could use a moment alone."

The back of my nose still tingles and smarts, but before I can have the good cry of frustration I'd been hoping for, my eye snags on a little piece of paper on my carpet.

Another mean-spirited affirmation, no doubt. I narrow my eyes as though that's enough to set it on fire. "Guess I missed one," I mutter, crouching to pick it up.

You're the best part of class. Wish I'd been there to see you show up Mr. G in stats! I would never have the guts to argue with a teacher over a grade, even if I knew I was right. You're a badass, Kavya. Never stop.

Wow. Stunned, I reread the words. One of my classmates didn't think I was Too Much?

On autopilot, I grab the brown bag and dump it over my still rumpled bed. One note lands faceup.

I've never told anyone this, but my boyfriend broke up with me because I "had too much confidence." WTF? How insecure do you have to be to NOT want that for your partner? All this to say, Parker's no prize. You deserve the best. You inspire me. Whenever I doubt myself, I ask WWKD (What Would Kavya Do), and I've never regretted it. Thank you! xxx

The nasty notes are still there too, but there's also this. In neat blue ballpoint.

No one makes me feel as myself as I do when I'm with you. You always have. You have this charm somehow, to make people be their most honest, authentic selves. It's like you expect nothing less from the rest of us, so we strive to give as good as we get.

I wish I could tell you everything that's inside my heart, but I always swore I would never be one of those weirdos who wrote unsigned love letters. When I tell you, I want to be looking at your face. And I hope when that happens, you see me.

I know you sometimes see me as the little kid who tried so hard to help you that one time. And I get it. OF COURSE I know you can look after yourself, but how can I care about you and not want to protect you always? That's when it started for me, but it's when it ended for you. I hope that day won't always be The End. I hope one day you'll see what I see.

Guess this isn't so anonymous anymore.

I stare down at Ian's handwriting, head buzzing. I hadn't looked at my notes all summer. Had he even asked me if I saw his confession? A memory flashes in front of my eyes—surrounded by our friends at our lockers and the question he'd started to ask—and my heart sinks. He *had* tried to ask. How could he stand it all these weeks not knowing? If I'd seen his note, I would *never* have left him hanging.

If he'd felt anything like how sucker punched I'd felt wondering whether Khloe had seen Smile #9 . . .

I'm moving before I even have a plan formed. Flying into the kitchen, I throw myself into the only available seat and grab the maple syrup. Without a word, I start cutting my entire stack of pancakes, shoveling in a thick, soggy mouthful.

"Kavya?" Dad's fork halts midway to his lips. "Are you . . . okay?"

The entire table is gaping at the rushed way I'm eating, so different to my usual slow appreciation.

"I'm good, Dad." I take a long glug of orange juice before wiping my mouth with the back of my hand. "Girls, I know what I have to do."

. . . .

I know exactly where he'll be. Today's the first day of the summer concert series along the Riverwalk. And it's open mic between sets. We get there with just minutes to spare thanks to Catey refusing to go even one mile over the speed limit.

The stage is being set up by faded rock-star-looking middle-aged men in band tees and leather vests.

"You want to sing?" asks the guy in charge who introduced himself as Perry. He pushes his sunglasses down his nose to look at me. "Honey, we had sign-ups for a reason. You're too late."

I wring my hands. "Please. I really need to do this."

Perry gives a long-suffering sigh. "Got something to prove, do you? You and your . . . back-up singers?" He raises a bushy salt-and-pepper eyebrow at my friends. "Sorry. It's impossible." He shakes his head and walks away.

"Claudia tweeted a car selfie in her driveway a little bit ago," Blaire informs me as we walk off the stage. "They should be here any second now."

I nod, already scanning the growing crowd for Ian. The stage has been erected on a small square of grass along the Riverwalk. All the restaurants are at full capacity, outdoor seating claimed by customers who've already ordered lunch.

"What was your plan, anyway?" asks Val. "A public apology?"

I give her a distracted smile. "Something like that."

"HELLO, LUNA COVE! ARE WE READY TO ROCK?" Perry shouts into the mic, his voice hailing over everyone in the immediate vicinity. Claps and whoops erupt.

"There!" Catey points. "They're coming."

I see them. Ian and his friends are walking over from Holly Gogogi, drinks in hand. Claudia's saying something, but while Rio and Samer are hanging on to her every word, Ian's smiles seem a little halfhearted.

Words like *too late* and *impossible* remind me of the girl who jumped over a desk to the horror of her teacher and the rest of the class.

"Fuck the sign-ups," I say.

Fuck being terrified to sing. Fuck doing it in front of all these people, my best friends, and my once-upon-a-time rival.

"Kavya, what are you doing?" Val calls after me as I dash away, making my way to the stage.

I don't have time to be timid. Not that anyone could call me that and live to tell the tale, but I especially can't second-guess myself now. I must be bold. I must be the girl Ian sees when he looks at me.

I must be besharam.

I clamber up, trying not to think about how ungainly or ridiculous I must look. My black miniskirt is way too short to be climbing, and my hair's falling in my face, and my moon pendant has gotten caught in the sweaty cleavage heaving from my white tank top, but I'm not stopping.

Perry scowls down at me. "Hey, what do you think you're—"

"Hi, everyone. I'm so sorry to do this," I say breathlessly. My gasp catches on the mic as I snatch it from his grasp, sidestepping him as he tries to swipe it back. "Some of you know me. I'm a Leo and I'm Kavya. I made a huge mistake and I'm actually really nervous about singing in front of all you folks right now, but the person I'm dedicating this to is worth it. I don't think he'd like to be identified, but if you let me, I'd really like to sing this one for him."

Perry stomps after me. "You are *way* out of line, young la—"

"Let her!" someone screams from the crowd. Like wildfire, the crowd roars their agreement, all bellowing to give me a chance.

Ian's eyes are wide and shocked as we lock eyes across a sea of people.

"This is the last fucking year I run this," Perry mutters before throwing up his hands and walking off the stage.

"Um, thank you," I speak into the mic as soon as the cheering tapers off.

I don't have any music to accompany me like all those times singing "Part of Your World." It's just me and my creaky, slightly off-tune voice attempting to do justice to both Ian and *Schitt's Creek's* rendition of "Simply the Best."

But the truth is, I'm no butter-voiced beau, and it doesn't take more than a handful of lyrics for the crowd to realize it. I keep going, feet planted firmly on the wooden floor even when the audience turns on me and and starts to boo.

Ian covers his face with one hand like he's mortified, and my heart shrivels, but then I catch the smile. This one is new and brilliant. The *Oh my god, you are terrible, and you're doing this anyway with absolutely zero shame* smile. One day, science will credit me for having discovered Smile #10.

I see the song through and make an awkward bow when no one claps except my friends and a few scattered people in the crowd.

"Girl, after that performance, I *really* hope he forgives you!" someone shouts as I skedaddle from the stage.

My jaw aches from smiling. Exhilaration sweeps through me. I did it. I fucking did it.

I swing my gaze around our friend groups, trying to find him.

"He went that way!" says Claudia, pointing. "He wanted to talk to you alone."

The million knots in my stomach unclench when I see Ian waiting for me near one of the less-crowded pubs, and he's fighting a grin.

"Well, that was embarrassing," I say lightly when I reach him.

The laugh is startled out of him. He claps his hand over his mouth immediately.

"It's okay to laugh. It *was* embarrassing," I point out.

"It was," he agrees. He meets my eyes with a chagrined smile. "It was also pretty fucking epic. You *hate* singing."

"Every romance has to have a grand gesture, right?"

"Girl wins back boy after a third-act breakup," says Ian with a knowing smile.

I swallow. "Did she?"

"Did she what?"

"Win him back."

He blows out a long, exasperated, but completely fond breath. "You never lost me."

A warm flush steals over my chest, and it has nothing to do with the heat.

"I'm sorry I messed up. Again," I say. "You've never given me a reason to think you'd throw any of the contests. You actually went out of your way to tell me about Scrabble so we'd have the same advantage. You were right. I should have seen who you were instead of seeing the rival I'd built you up in my head to be."

He dips his head in acknowledgement and tosses his empty cup into a trash receptacle. "Can we take a walk?"

At my nod, we make our way down the Riverwalk, past all the cafés and art galleries and pubs. Far from the crowds. In the distance, strums of a guitar pluck the air, tingling my lobes.

Pink and orange coneflowers line the sun-dappled path. I step out of the way of a bumblebee and graze Ian's arm. My spine shivers.

His pinkie almost curls around mine, and *I want him to, I want him to, I want him to—*

And then he slides his fingers into the between-places of mine.

My breath hitches. I steal a glance at him and catch him looking at me. I give his hand a little squeeze so I don't float away. He squeezes back. The pads of his fingertips tickle my knuckles, spike my heartbeat.

Discordant twangs of a guitar peal out. A few loud boos from the crowd.

The moment shatters.

Ian catches the look on my face. "Someone's mother didn't force them to practice."

"Sounds like it," I say with a wry smile.

When we come to a bench overlooking the river, he gestures at me to sit. "There's something I want to give you. But I have to run home to get it. Would you mind waiting here? Five minutes, that's it."

"I—okay. Sure."

While I wait, a family of ducks swims by in a line, water rippling behind them. The noise from the concert dulls to a low throb. I watch the ducks until they swim downriver, gliding past a father and son fishing on the banks.

Ian comes back within the promised five minutes, a little out of breath. He has a flat rectangular box in his hands, sheathed in pretty silver wrapping paper.

"My birthday isn't for another week," I say, a little bemused.

He makes a small huffing sound and sits down next to me. "Just open it."

I want more than anything to rip into it like a beast, but I force my finger to slide carefully under the folds to peel the tape off.

"It's a game," I say in surprise.

Not just any game, but a custom Monopoly game. The packaging is retro, and when I lift the lid, I see the theme has carried into all the items inside. There's a folded playing board and a handful of tokens in a black velvet pouch. I empty it out into my palm: there's a hamster, a standing sunflower, a mermaid, a stack of books, and a kayak.

Each square on the board has something to do with us and Luna Cove. Instead of houses and hotels, we're buying up local businesses. I can see the pink castle for Poppy's Playhouse, the bulgogi burger for Holly Gogogi, and the fork for the Fork & Crumb. It's all so intricate and creative that he must have been working on this for *weeks*.

Suddenly, it makes sense.

Being too busy to update me on his book totals.

The sketch on his desk, all the proportions and notes that I barely glanced at because contrary to what actually happened, I hadn't *intended* to snoop.

My heart spasms painfully. He thought making my birthday present was a better use of his time than squeezing in a few more books.

"I'm so sorry, Ian," I say after what feels like an eternity. "I love my present. It's amazing. *You're* amazing. I should have believed you and you were right to call me on it. I ran scared and I pushed my paranoia on you when you didn't deserve it. I'm so sorry I couldn't be as brave as you. *Of course* I see you. How could I not? Sometimes my vision just fills up with you and only you, that's how much I care about you. It's always been you. That day on the waterslide . . . that chapter wasn't The End. We're the whole damn trilogy."

"You finally read my note," he breathes out.

"Somehow I'm always late, but I get there eventually."

Ian's arm stretches over the back of the bench, hand creeping up my neck to play with a few loose tendrils of baby hair at my nape. "Yeah," he says, voice rough. "Yeah, you do. What made you go for it and sing?"

"Do you remember I told you once that it's not worth the effort to do something unless the payoff is worth it? *You* are worth it. You've always backed up your words with your actions, and you deserved that from me, too. I never want to look bad, but for you, I will embarrass myself on stage in front of the entire town a million times."

His eyes are soft. "I never expected you to do that for me. But when I saw you up there, bedheaded and determined and ready to wrestle the mic away from anyone who dared take it from you, you've never looked more beautiful."

"I know better than to call you a liar," I say, "but you've got to be kidding. Me rushing through getting ready for you is starting to become a habit. I didn't even put on lipstick."

He cups my chin, thumb stroking my full lower lip. "I wouldn't say that's a downside for me." He pauses. "What do you mean 'rushing'? When else did you rush?"

"Uh . . . I may have been talking myself into and out of coming to the toy store yesterday. I saw you and Rio."

"You mean you came?" He seems stunned. "To pick up Grace's game with me?"

"Yeah. I'm sorry I was too late."

"What?"

I gesture at the box on my lap. "I guess you picked hers up at the same time?"

"Kavya, no. I can't say I didn't think about it, but you're the one who I wanted by my side. I only picked up the game I designed for you. I told you that I will always give you one more chance. I wouldn't go back on my promise."

That's all I need to hear. I start to lean in, eyelids fluttering a second away from closing, but Ian pulls back. Hurt fists hard around my heart. "What's wrong?"

"Kavs, there's just one more thing we need to talk about."

34.
I Owe You, I Dare You, I Love You

"I WANNA SHOW you something," says Ian, pulling his phone out of his pocket.

"Oh god, please don't tell me you filmed me," I groan.

He chuckles. "It's an email," he says, and I glance at his phone screen.

Congratulations Library Patron,

You are a summer reading prize winner!

Please collect your winnings at the information desk within two weeks.

"Big 5" Participants are as follows:

Kavya Joshi—64 (Grand Prize ARC winner!)

Sarah Dietrich—55

Ian Jun—45

Jayme Kennedy—39

Blaire Tyler—35

Diana Carnegie
Information Specialist
Luna Cove Public Library

I stare at our names for so long that Ian has to clear his throat.

"Even with those extra eighteen cards I turned in, I still beat you," I say, stunned.

"Yup," he says cheerfully, pocketing his phone. "That means you won the tiebreak. Congrats, Kavya."

I search his face for sarcasm and bite my lip when I find none. Old habits die hard. "Thank you. I suddenly can't remember why it was so important to win these bragging rights," I admit with a rueful shake of my head.

One corner of his mouth crooks upward. "You know, I'm not sure I'm ready for this to end. Maybe I should demand a rematch."

"You're kidding."

"I never kid about anything as serious as *bragging rights*," he says severely.

"What's on the line this time?" I ask, only half teasing.

"Hmm. Let's see." Ian taps his chin. "Well, there is something on the table that I've wanted for quite a while. And you have been teasing me with it, so . . ." He leans down, his nose brushing mine. "I want . . ."

I push myself closer into him in anticipation.

". . . to see your . . ."

I flick my tongue over my lips.

". . . grudge list."

Wait. What. I hover near his lips, blinking furiously.

Did I hear him right?

"Just kidding," whispers Ian, and then he's kissing me. Soft and sweet and just right. My eyelashes flutter closed, and I wrap my arms around his neck, deepening the kiss.

This is the kind of smooch that could wake Snow White up from her glass coffin.

Oh, he's good. He's very, very good.

And if he plays his cards right, I might just cross his name off my grudge list.

We break apart just long enough to breathe, and then I'm kissing him again. My fingers claw up his neck, grip his hair, and the shuddering noise he makes in the back of his throat shoots bolts of electric pleasure down my spine. When I swoop my tongue across the seam of his lips, his hands tighten around my waist.

"I've never seen you this relaxed," Ian murmurs against my lips.

"It's all you," I say, giving credit where it's due.

He shakes his head. "Nothing to do with me." When I try to object, he places a finger over my lips. "You were just standing in your own way."

Did! He! Just! Shush! Me?!

But then I hear him. Really hear him. And he's right.

Sometimes I can be my own worst enemy.

So even though I don't love his finger over my mouth, I don't get mad.

I get even.

"Why are you looking at me like that?" he asks, dropping his finger. He squints at me with suspicion and just the tiniest bit of fear.

I let the silence linger but keep right on smiling.

"You're, uh, shark-smiling kind of like Bruce from *Finding Nemo* right now," he says with a little laugh.

"Am I?" I keep my voice sweet.

"Kavya, you're weirding me out."

"Don't feel uneasy. I'm just plotting, scheming, strategizing . . ." I reach for his hands and slide my fingers through his. "The usual."

It takes him a second to catch on. "This is about the shushing, isn't it?"

"Oh, this is definitely about the shushing. And, for the record, there was a much nicer way to get me to keep quiet." I look meaningfully at his lips. "I just need to be, um, incentivized properly."

His eyes sparkle and he leans in, but—

I pull out of reach just a second before his lips can make contact.

He holds his pucker for a moment, eyebrows scrunching in confusion. Then his eyes fly open.

I try not to smirk.

A slow, sensual smile spreads over his face. "You're evil," says Ian.

"Yes, but you knew this," I say cheerfully.

"Oh, I almost forgot to give you—" He lets me go so he can slide his hand into his pocket. He emerges with a folded napkin from Holly Gogogi's. "For you, my Evil Queen," he says with an exaggerated bow and flourish.

It's cheesy, but I love it. I dip into a curtsy. "My hero," I say in return, matching his posh, princely accent. "Thank you for this . . . trash?"

He rolls his eyes. "Just read it."

"Fine, fine." I open the napkin, feigning slowness when he starts to look impatient. His familiar handwriting covers it in ballpoint scrawl.

"It's not as cool as your grudge list, maybe . . ." Ian bites the corner of his lower lip, jutting his chin toward me. "Even if I'm still on your list, I thought you should know you'll always be on mine."

But this isn't Ian's grudge list.

Across the top of the napkin is:

The Girls I Like List

It's underlined so it looks official.

The only name under it is mine.

Kavya Joshi

I almost use the napkin to swipe at my eyes, but catch my-self just in time and use the back of my hand instead. This boy is a goddamn cheeseball, and no, I'm not crying, you're crying.

"Just in case there's any doubt as to who I'm into," he says lightly. "Doesn't matter how many contests we have, Kavya," he says, "I will always be on your side."

"I thought we weren't competing anymore?"

We both lean in; our noses touch.

"Old habits die hard," says Ian. "I'm okay with you coming out on top."

"And maybe," I add, "a little competition is healthy."

He hums in agreement.

We look at each other for a long moment before I make up my mind. "Or," I suggest, "we could clear the scoreboard completely?"

"How would we do that?"

I flip my hair over my shoulder and throw him an arch look. "Oh, I am so glad you asked."

And then I tilt my face up and show him exactly how we can both come out as winners. His mouth curves into a smile right before our lips graze. I press my apology into him, hands mussing up his hair, and he reciprocates with a message of his own, something I feel in my bones even though he hasn't verbalized it yet: *I owe you, I dare you, I love you.*

His voice is hoarse when we pull away. "Kavya, one; Ian, one?"

"If you kiss me again, you'll be in the lead." I'm a little breathless, too.

"You're handing me a win?" he jokes. "I dunno, Kavs . . . do I really want such an easy victory?"

While he pretends to think, I decide.

I'm not perfect. Tomorrow, when I wake up, I'll still be competitive. Maybe I'll even be impossible at times. I'm not changing myself for him, or for any boy, and here's the thing: The right boy wouldn't want me to. Ian doesn't want me to. He wants me, warts and all.

And so I carefully fold the napkin and tuck it into my bra. "Keeping score is for weenies."

"And we are most definitely not weenies," he says gravely.

I place my hands on either side of his face. "We're winners. And that means we don't fight each other for the world; we share it."

I feel his cheeks warm. "You remembered," he says, looking oddly touched.

Now it's my turn to blush. "It might have taken this Evil Queen a little while, but eventually Prince Charming's wise words sank in."

"Charming? Wise? All these compliments, I might swoon," he teases.

"Yeah, yeah, don't get a big ego about it or anything," I grumble good-naturedly.

"I'm too wise for that, remember?"

"Ian!"

"And charming!" he hoots.

"Don't forget infuriating!"

••••••••••••••••••••••••••••••••

The next time we kiss, nobody keeps score.

Or any of the many, many times after that.

After all, ruining Ian Jun's hair with my kiss is the favorite part of my day.

Acknowledgments

I NEVER SKIP the acknowledgments. Sometimes, in my rush to flip to the back of the book, I inadvertently glimpse the ending. Thankfully, I'm one of those weirdos who doesn't care about seeing spoilers! But I can't deny how utterly fascinated I am following the trails of bread crumbs that authors put in their thanks, because those acknowledgments are just another story. One of adventures and stumbles and camaraderie and all those things that give the journey meaning.

And oh my gosh??? At times, this book has felt like vanquishing my own formidable dragon, losing my way in a dark forest, and holding on to an enormous amount of hope on the journey to publication. In short, a Sisyphean endeavor. But *this* is one of my favorite parts—the Happily Ever After, when my part in this story is complete, and the characters live on without any further interference from the writer, the benevolent (ha!) ruler who makes them suffer until The End.

Much like love, writing is *work*, and there's no magic spell to make any of it easier or faster. The closest thing to magic might be the way a story is transfigured from words on a doc to a gorgeous, gorgeous book. Publishing involves a lot of people working together to overcome obstacles, though not necessarily those of the fairy-tale variety involving evil queens and enchanted sleeps!

So to that end, I'd like to thank everyone at Penguin Random House/Viking Children's, because whether we're talking about falling in love or fairy tales, it's impossible not to begin at the start, at the Once Upon a Time of it all . . . Thank you to my editor, Dana Leydig, for believing in the magic of *Beauty and the Besharam*, and my agent, Jessica Watterson, who saw the first glimpse. Dana, I lucked out to have your guidance and insight into the psychology of character. Thank you for helping me get unstuck!

My deepest gratitude also goes to the rest of the PRH team: copyeditors Abigail Powers, Aliza Amlani, and Rebecca Blevins; managing editor Gaby Corzo; production editor Krista Ahlberg; jacket designers Kaitlin Yang and Theresa Evangelista; interior designer Jim Hoover; publicist Tessa Meischeid; and everyone on the marketing and social media side—including Felicity Vallence, James Akinaka, Shannon Spann, Bezawit Yohannes—who help bring this book to readers all around the world.

Jenn Bennett, Adiba Jaigirdar, Kara McDowell, Aiden Thomas, Emily Wibberley and Austin Siegemund-Broka, Jennifer Dugan, Nina Moreno, Kristina Forest, and Sona Charaipotra—thank you for your support and kindness. Sonia Hartl, you were right. Gabby Romero, you brought my characters to life in a way I could never have imagined, and I am so honored to have the gift of your art.

To all my friends, readers, booksellers, and librarians who

have hyped me up, cheered me on, and bolstered my spirits after *gestures animatedly* *everything* over the last few years, you have been invaluable. Always especially Kate the most.

Mom, thank you for reading every single draft of this book. You loved Kavya first and best, let me ramble at you about the wonders and frustrations of writing, and always found the "labyrinth."

This book was first written in a pre-COVID world, and since then, much has changed both within these pages and outside of them. I hope that Kavya, Ian, their friends—and all their summer shenanigans—provide you with fun, laughter, and distraction when you need it most. If this book makes you feel seen or just gives you happy feels in general, I always welcome hearing from you! The young people in this book make *me* feel seen every day, and imagining this story in the hands of readers who need it is its own incandescent form of magic. Like writing, like love, like fairy tales, summer has always felt full of hope and possibility, and I hope *Beauty and the Besharam* encapsulates all those big emotions in book form.

And while I'm no fairy godmother and I definitely don't wave a magic wand, this is what I wish for you, if you want it:

Prem. Amore. Ishq. (Romantic or platonic, you all deserve Smile #10.)

Courage to fight for your fairy tale, whatever that looks like.

A fierce besharam heart. (I said this book was for the besharams, and I meant it.)

So now we've come to the end of the story, but it's in no way the end. I see Kavya and Ian good-naturedly squabbling on the first day of senior year, running against each other for student government president (this was the stakes of the very first draft!) but championing each other even as they campaign. Ian's definitely going to figure out what his own dreams are, and he's going to have the courage to go boldly after them. They're definitely playing a *lot* of competitive Wordle.

One day, Ian's family will be ready to mourn the final Yeobo. Simran will be exactly who and where she needs to be. Val will get everything she's ever wanted, with her family's love and support. Kavya will marginally improve her singing, but only by exponentially annoying everyone else in her vicinity; she wants you to know she's unrepentant. Buster will—to no one's surprise—continue to be the best of boys.

And last but not least, Ian is still picking out all the cherry Jolly Ranchers for Kavya. (They are *clearly* the superior flavor, although Kavya grudgingly concedes that Ian's fave, green apple, comes a close second when she tastes it on his kiss.)

Oh, yeah. And she still has her grudge list. Ian's not on it anymore. 😉